Norman Russell was born in Whiston, Lancashire, but has lived most of his life in Liverpool. After graduating from Jesus College, Oxford, where he studied English, he served in the army in the Bahamas and Jamaica. He returned to Oxford to study for a Diploma in Education and later was awarded the degree of Doctor of Philosophy from the University of London. He now writes full time.

THE HANSA PROTOCOL

In January 1893, the German peace crusader Dr Otto Seligmann is blown to pieces in the Belvedere, his garden library at Chelsea. Detective Inspector Box and Sergeant Knollys interview Seligmann's associate, Count Czerny, who reveals that Britain is infested by agents of the German war party. In the fog-shrouded garden of Seligmann's house, Box encounters Colonel Kershaw, the sinister head of secret intelligence, who enlists his aid to search for Seligmann's killer. Box finally discovers the true purpose of the Belvedere explosion, but his mission ends in a desperate confrontation on which the nation's future will depend.

Books by Norman Russell
Published by The House of Ulverscroft:

THE DRIED-UP MAN
THE DARK KINGDOM

NORMAN RUSSELL

THE HANSA PROTOCOL

Complete and Unabridged

ULVERSCROFT
Leicester

First published in Great Britain in 2003 by
Robert Hale Limited
London

First Large Print Edition
published 2005
by arrangement with
Robert Hale Limited
London

British Library CIP Data

Russell, Norman
    The Hansa Protocol.—Large print ed.—
    Ulverscroft large print series: non-ficton
    1. Assassination—Investigation—England—
    London—History—19th century 2. Detective
    and mystery stories 3. Large type books
    I. Title
    823.9′14 [F]

    ISBN 1–84395–552–0

Published by   F
F. A. Thorpe (Publishing)
Anstey, Leicestershire

Set by Words & Graphics Ltd.
Anstey, Leicestershire
Printed and bound in Great Britain by
T. J. International Ltd., Padstow, Cornwall

This book is printed on acid-free paper

Contents

Contents

1

Returned to Sender

Detective Inspector Arnold Box stood in an obscure rear corner of St Swithin's Hall, and cast a professional eye over the motley audience who were listening intently to a lecture on Anglo-German Friendship. A rough poll-count had shown him that there were over fifty men occupying the rows of pine chairs. So far, nothing untoward had happened. A venerable and respectably dressed old man had passed a collection box for the Dockside Mission along the rows, and there had been a decent clinking of copper. Then the lecture had begun.

The lecturer, a scholarly man of seventy or so, with an abundant shock of white hair, spoke perfect English, with just the trace of a foreign accent. At a table behind him on the platform, sat a distinguished gentleman in evening dress. Box recognized him as Sir Charles Napier, the Under-Secretary of State for Foreign Affairs.

Most of the men in the audience looked harmless enough. There was the usual crop of

1

elderly eccentrics who turned up for these political discussions, men with untidy hair and pince-nez, men clutching baggy umbrellas, and parcels of tracts. There were a few roughs there, too, one or two tramps sheltering from the cold, and a number of cocksure young men in loud suits, who had come there presumably for a laugh, or a row. For the moment, though, they were all listening intently to the lecturer's exposition of the theory of just and unjust wars.

St Swithin's Hall, a huge wooden tabernacle of a place, had been designed specifically for public meetings and concerts. It rose gauntly at the top of some steps in an alley sandwiched between Walbrook and St Swithin's Lane. A good deal of the London fog seemed to have seeped into the hall, merging with a cloud of thick pipe smoke to create a blue haze. Gas mantles flared on their brackets between the windows, their rising heat causing the festoons of British and German flags strung along the walls to nod and tremble.

Superintendent Mackharness had summoned Box to his first-floor office at King James's Rents in mid-afternoon, and told him to 'look in' on this particular meeting, which was to begin with a lecture delivered by the eminent German scholar and retired diplomat Dr Otto Seligmann, President of the Anglo-German League of Friendship.

'I want you to look in, Box,' Mackharness had said, 'and see that all's well. You know what kind of people can turn up at these political affairs, so stay for an hour or so, and see how things shape. It's the last day of the old year — well, I don't need to tell you that — and there may be some imprudent revellers loose on the streets. But the City Police will be there in sufficient numbers, so if anything unpleasant happens, leave them to deal with it. You'd better take Sergeant Knollys with you.'

'This Dr Seligmann, sir — '

'Dr Otto Seligmann, Box,' the superintendent had volunteered, 'is very well esteemed in high political circles — a well-known enthusiast for peace, and so on. He's the president of this Anglo-German League. And Sir Charles Napier, the Under-Secretary of State at the Foreign Office — you've heard of him, I suppose? — well, he's the vice-president, and he'll be there too, as chairman of the meeting. He and this Dr Seligmann are old political friends and allies. So do as I say, Box, and get down there this evening. The lecture starts at eight o'clock.'

Inspector Box did not pay much attention to Dr Otto Seligmann. Of greater interest to him was a little knot of men who had congregated near one of the rear exits. There were plenty of vacant seats, but they had curtly refused to sit down. They were well-dressed and prosperous-looking men, but there was potential danger in the way they carried themselves, with a sort of half crouch, as though contemplating a lunge at some potential adversary. As they listened intently to the speaker, Box could see the mounting anger convulsing their faces.

It had always seemed extraordinary to Arnold Box that men could work themselves up to fever pitch over political niceties. What was so special about Anglo-German friendship, that it could bring this lot out of their warm houses on such a bitterly cold night? Did they really understand what the speaker was saying? Did they really care? Had they no wives, no mothers and fathers, no children, to occupy their leisure time in the evenings?

Next Tuesday, his aged and ailing father would be placed under the surgeon's knife at the Royal Free Hospital in Gray's Inn Road. When the decision had been made, last October, to sever his leg, January had seemed a long way off. Since Christmas, he had started to feel a mild panic, which he refused to recognize as fear. It was Saturday today. What might have happened to Pa by next

Saturday? They could do wonderful things, nowadays. But they couldn't provide an antidote for fear.

Dr Otto Seligmann was still talking. Sir Charles Napier, Box noticed, had shifted his position behind the table, and was making renewed efforts to fix his attention on the speaker. Even professional diplomats could experience boredom. If he and Seligmann were old friends, then he had probably heard it all before.

A sudden marked change in the speaker's tone suggested that he was going to stop.

'So that, gentlemen,' said Dr Seligmann, 'is my plea. Trust in the good sense of the various and varying peoples of Germany. Do not allow yourselves to be swept up by your British fear of foreigners. There must be no war in our time. Let that be the slogan, the watchword, of the Anglo-German Friendship League. No war in our time!'

Was that it, then? Had he really finished? Dr Otto Seligmann had been talking for over an hour. Really, it had been more than flesh and blood could stand! Box saw his sergeant, Jack Knollys, suddenly open his eyes, and sway slightly, as though he had been asleep on his feet. A giant of a man, he had taken up his station next to the knot of angry men. There were another six police officers in the hall, an inspector, a sergeant, and four constables. They were all City Police, there to see fair play, and keep the peace.

Dr Seligmann sat down, to a half-hearted barrage of clapping, a few cheers, and a bit of foot-stamping. Sir Charles Napier stood up, and thanked the speaker for all his time and effort. He was sure that the audience had been fascinated by the many insights that they had been given into the complexities of the issue under debate, and that they would take his words to heart. Dr Seligmann, he said, would now be happy to answer any questions.

One man had already stood up from amid the serried ranks of chairs, and had waved his hand in the air to attract the chairman's attention. Hello, thought Box, what's this? It was one of the cocksure young men, a fellow of about thirty, with a shock of yellow hair.

'If what you say about Germany is true, Dr Seligmann,' said the young man, in a loud and belligerent voice, 'what about the French in 1870? That wasn't very peaceful of Germany, was it?'

Strewth! A troublemaker. Some kind of nark with a mouth too big for his mind. Why couldn't they just sing the National Anthem and go home?

Dr Otto Seligmann sprang to his feet.

'My friend!' he cried. 'I am only too well aware of the shadow cast by the events of 1870. I myself was present at Versailles in that year, when the German Empire was promulgated with great triumph from the old palace of Louis XIV, the Sun King! I witnessed Prince Bismarck proclaiming our Prussian King, William I, as Emperor of Germany — '

The knot of well-dressed men near the exit suddenly gave a rousing cheer, and waved their hats in the air. Some members of the main audience turned round to look at them, and one or two joined in their cheering. Box was suddenly alert. He moved closer to Sergeant Knollys. The elderly German scholar on the platform held his ground.

'But don't you see, my friend, that there was no need for the rise of faction and dissent? To people like me, the establishment of that new empire meant that Europe could look forward to a new era of stability and prosperity! Already, in the sixties, we had averted war by the subjugation of Denmark and Austria — '

'Very pacific, I must say!' shouted the man in the audience. 'Very peaceful for the good folk of Denmark, and the Frenchies you butchered in Alsace — '

Another man sprang to his feet, overturning his chair as he did so. He began to jabber in a shrill, angry voice. No one could hear what he said, but a murmur began to weave its way through the audience. It was turning into a crowd, thought Box, and a crowd will soon turn into a mob.

One of the knot of men standing near Sergeant Knollys began to shout something in what Box took to be German. It sounded like an accusation: '*Verräter! Verräter!*' The man's face was convulsed with hatred, and a vein pulsed and throbbed in his temple. He shook his fist at Seligmann, and at the same time his companions picked up the word as a furious rallying-cry, and howled it as a special imprecation in the general direction of the platform.

Somebody unseen began to winch the heavy velvet curtains closed across the stage.

'Right, Officers,' Box shouted. 'Get *him* out, and shut *him* up!' He had jabbed an urgent finger first at the raging German, and then at the young man with the yellow hair.

Sergeant Knollys had evidently been waiting for the word. He put two massive arms round the shouting German, lifted him bodily off his feet, and virtually ran out of the hall with him through the door leading to the vestibule. At the same time, one of the uniformed City Police hauled the original troublemaker out of his seat, and dragged

8

him away into a side-room.

As though by magic, the atmosphere in the hall returned to normal. The German's companions suddenly became very meek and embarrassed, and left the hall, though not before darting venomous glances at the now inscrutably curtained platform. They were followed by the venerable old man, who was still clutching his collection box. The inspector gently restrained him, and propelled him out of the hall and into the front vestibule overlooking St Swithin's Lane. Sergeant Knollys was just coming through the entrance. He was smiling rather grimly to himself.

'All's well, sir,' he said. 'Our German friend assures me that he meant no harm. He's very sorry for any trouble he may have caused. I've taken his name and address. He's a pork-butcher by trade, so he tells me.'

Box permitted himself a rueful laugh.

'What a waste of police time, Sergeant Knollys! It'll be in the papers, tomorrow. 'Scuffles broke out'. That's what they'll write. You don't know our venerable friend here, do you? This is Birdy Sanders. He goes round shaking an imitation charity box, and collecting coppers for himself. It won't do, Birdy! You're a wicked old man, and you won't get to Heaven at this rate. See to him, will you, Sergeant?'

Inspector Box handed the collecting-box to Knollys, and re-entered the hall. It was cold in the vestibule, where a chill wind managed to blow the outer doors open and closed with a dull thudding sound. The bare boards were wet and stained with recent deposits of mud. A single tear began to roll down the old man's cheek.

Through the flapping doors, Knollys glimpsed a dark figure slowly mounting the steps up from the street. Presently a tall, round-shouldered man of fifty came into the vestibule. He wore the instantly recognizable peaked cap and long double-breasted overcoat of a constable in the River Police. He was a hollow-cheeked man with a drooping moustache and bright, irreverent eyes.

'I'm told Inspector Box is here tonight,' he said. 'We've something down at Waterman's Pier that he'd like to see. It's only a few minutes' walk from here. This side of London Bridge. Are you one of his posse, or has he just took you up for assault and battery?'

'I'm Detective Sergeant Knollys, Constable. I'll tell Mr Box you're here.'

The constable nodded towards the wretched old man who was standing in absorbed misery beside Knollys.

'This your old dad, then? Or shouldn't I have asked?'

Knollys laughed. He looked out at the bleak, cold alley, where a few winking lights could be seen at the corner of St Swithin's Lane. The last day of December, 1892, had chosen to furnish the inevitable crowds of revellers with a bleak prospect for the New Year. He thrust the collecting box into the old man's hands.

'Hop it,' he said. 'Don't let me see you round here again.'

Uttering shrill cries of thanks and blessing, the old man stumbled away down the steps, clutching the box of coppers to his chest.

'Have you got a name, Constable?' asked Knollys. 'Or do you prefer to go around incognito?'

'Joseph Peabody, 406, Lower Station, Blackwall Hulks. You go in there, Sergeant, and tell your gaffer Joe Peabody's here. We've something waiting for him down at Waterman's Pier. Something that's on the turn, and won't keep.'

★ ★ ★

It was dark in the narrow lanes beyond Walbrook, but Joe Peabody moved surely and swiftly, bearing steadily downhill towards

11

the river. After about ten minutes or so, the three men emerged on to a wide pier, where the darkness of the alleys was banished by the blaze of light from gas standards along the quay. They could see that the river was alive with ships of every description, and winking mast lights seemed to cross and re-cross each other in the gloom.

Two men were waiting on the pier. They stood beneath an iron arch, flanked by two lanterns, stamping their feet, and blowing on their hands. It was becoming bitterly cold.

'Good evening, Inspector Cross,' said Box, 'you've something for me, I'm told?'

Sergeant Knollys knew about the River Police, but he had never encountered one of them at close quarters until Joseph Peabody had treated him to a bit of mild impertinence back at St Swithin's Hall. Inspector Cross looked no different from his constable, or from the shivering sergeant accompanying him. In their long thick coats and peaked caps, they all looked the same.

''Good evening' be damned, Arnold! There's nothing good about it. And what's all this 'Inspector Cross' business? I'll not waste words, as we'll all be dead of the cold if we stay out here jawing much longer. Just on an hour ago, we tied up the galley at this pier, having come up on shore patrol from

Blackfriars. We'd just stepped up on the boards when we saw a little steam launch down there, hugging the shore. It sounded its whistle, as though to attract our attention, and then — well, you tell him, Jimmy.'

The shivering sergeant took up the tale.

'Somebody on the launch chucked a dead body over the side. Before any of us could move, Inspector, the launch was off and away. There's a little skiff down there, and we used that to bring the body in — '

'We've laid it out on a table in the pier-master's office over there. As soon as ever Dr Kelly comes, we'll go in and take a proper look.'

At that moment, a rowing-boat approached the pier, propelled by yet another huddled member of the river force. Sitting upright in the boat, was a stout man wearing a fur-collared coat and a dark wide-awake hat. He seemed to be complaining angrily in a strong Irish brogue about being disturbed from his dinner at such an inopportune time.

'You're just a gang of galley-slaves! What do you mean by disturbing a respectable doctor with your dead bodies? Pirates, most of them. Why don't you leave them to float out to sea? Come on, man — help me up the ladder.'

Inspector Cross surveyed the newcomer from head to foot with a detached interest, as

13

though the big, bluff Irishman was a specimen in an anatomical museum.

'You're very civil, as always, Dr Kelly,' he said. 'Now, here's a little thought for you to ponder, before we look at the latest pirate to be fished out of the river. We're policemen, Doctor, so we have to account to higher authority for every corpse that we find. But you — you can bury *your* mistakes.'

Dr Kelly bellowed with laughter, in which the River Police joined. They moved swiftly across the quay towards the pier-master's office.

★　★　★

The dead man taken from the river lay on a trestle table, which had been dragged under a flaring gas burner suspended from the ceiling. Box looked at him, noting his heavy features, and the stubble on his chin. His black hair was plastered close to his skull by the river water, and his rough seaman's suit of dark serge was heavy with moisture.

Inspector Cross pulled open the man's jacket to reveal his blood-stained shirt and waistcoat. He pointed to a torn inside pocket, and turned to Box.

'There was something in that pocket, Arnold, that decided us to send for you. We knew you were up there at St Swithin's with Sir Charles Napier. We'll talk about that later. Come on, Doctor, take a look at this man, and tell us what he died of. Jimmy, you give him a hand.'

Dr Kelly seemed to be no respecter of persons, living or dead. With the help of the River Police sergeant he closely examined the man's chest, where a gaping wound had been revealed beneath the shirt, and then turned him over on to his front with a sickeningly wet thud. For five minutes or so he poked and pummelled the body, then stood back, wiping his hands on his overcoat.

'Well, now,' he said, 'I can't do anything much till you've brought him up to Horseferry Road mortuary tomorrow. As you can see, he's a man in his early forties, a trifle overweight, but nothing that would have mattered much. He's been shot in the back from close up with some kind of medium calibre pistol, and the bullet's passed right through him. Shot in the back, so perhaps he was running away from somebody. That's all. Give me a hand again, Jimmy.'

Dr Kelly and the sergeant hauled the heavy body on to its back again, and then they left the pier-master's office, accompanied by the man who had rowed the doctor to the pier. They could all hear a fresh outbreak of banter, accompanied by the doctor's full-throated laugh, which turned into a fit of luxurious coughing as he descended the iron ladder to the rowing-boat. Inspector Box broke the silence.

'Why did you send for me, Bob?' he asked Inspector Cross. 'This is divisional work. Nothing to do with me.'

Cross jerked his head towards Constable Peabody, who had said nothing at all since Box, Knollys and he had arrived at the pier.

'Joe there will tell you what it's all about. I'm going back to the galley. I'll wish you good night. And you, Sergeant.'

Inspector Cross strode out on to the quay, closing the door firmly behind him.

Joe Peabody glanced uncertainly at Knollys, seemed to make up his mind about something, and then spoke.

'You know what I am, don't you, Mr Box? Mentioning no names, of course.'

'Yes, Joe. I know what you are. So what do you want to tell me?'

PC Joseph Peabody glanced at the dead man. He shook his head slightly, and then gave his attention once more to Box.

'This man, Inspector, is Stefan Oliver. He was a Foreign Office courier, one of Sir Charles Napier's people. You'll understand, sir, that I know something about him

— being what I am. When Bob Cross opened his jacket to search for a wound, he found something thrust in the inside pocket.'

Joe Peabody produced a stout linen-backed envelope, to which a number of wax seals had been attached. It was only lightly stained, and Box could read a series of letters and numbers written in bold Indian ink on the front of the packet. It had been roughly torn open, but the contents were still intact. Box carefully drew out two folded sheets of notepaper, and opened them by the light of the flaring gas burner. They proved to be two sheets of blank paper.

'I wanted you to see that, Mr Box. I know that in the nature of things you can't be one of us, but you've worked with us before. That's a Foreign Office cipher written there, on the cover, and this packet was to be delivered to Sir Charles Napier himself. You'll understand, Mr Box, that I know what this is in general terms, because I can read the cipher, but I don't know anything at all about the particular nature of this packet. It's nothing to do with us — our crowd, you know. But I think it was what they term a 'dummy run'. A rehearsal, if you get my meaning. But somebody thought it was the real thing, and shot Stefan Oliver in the back in order to get that letter.'

'But whoever it was, Joe, put the letter back in his pocket. Why should he do that?'

Joe Peabody carefully closed the envelope, and concealed it in his coat. He turned away towards the door.

'I don't know, Inspector. Not for certain, anyway. I'll see that this packet gets to Sir Charles Napier. But I'm thinking of how that fellow in the steam launch tooted his whistle to attract our attention, and then dumped poor Stefan there into the river. He wanted us to see him! Sir Charles was only a quarter of a mile away from here — I expect he's still up there, at that meeting, or whatever it is.'

'So you think — '

'I don't think anything special, Mr Box. But it did just occur to me that Stefan Oliver was being sent back to his master by an assassin with a sense of humour. You know, sir: like you can do with a letter. 'Not at this address. Return to Sender'.'

★   ★   ★

In St Swithin's Hall, the audience were dispersing, and the lights were being turned low. The heavy velvet curtains had once again been winched closed. Dr Otto Seligmann and Sir Charles Napier sat at the table on the stage, talking together in low voices.

18

'What did you make of that row, Seligmann? Louts? Or something else?'

Dr Seligmann did not reply for a moment. He poured himself a glass of water from a carafe that had been provided for the lecture, and Napier saw how his hand trembled. Seligmann thought of his opponents, and their growing belligerence. Years ago, he had engaged in courteous arguments with men of differing minds, men whose interpretation of German history had differed from his. They had usually agreed to differ, but always with a strong measure of courtesy.

It was different, now. His opponents were turning into deadly enemies. He had seen their impotent reflection in the enraged knot of German so-called 'patriots' earlier in the evening. Frustrated exiles, they longed to see their native land develop into the colossus of Europe. He recalled the ringleader of that knot of men, the puce-faced lunatic who had shouted 'Traitor! Traitor!' — a vile slander, which his brainless friends had taken up as a battle-cry. Their obvious hatred of him, and of his mission, had unnerved him.

'They were not louts, Napier. They were part of the great and growing army of the prosperous ignorant. You and I have known each other — what? — twenty years, and for most of that time we have watched together

19

the gradual degeneration of peace in Europe. What you saw tonight will tell you that things are coming to a head. The war party's out for blood, and soon, violent words will be replaced by violent deeds.'

Sir Charles said nothing for a while. He was thinking of the deep trust that had grown up between him and the elderly German former diplomat turned scholar. When those men had called him a traitor, Sir Charles Napier had felt personally affronted.

'Do you think that those men were part of an organization?' he asked at last. 'We've a lot of Germans in London, and the vast majority of them are quiet, decent citizens. But there are societies — clubs, debating groups — where various forms of mild subversion are practised. I wondered whether our friends tonight came from that quarter.'

'They may well have done so, Napier. But the real danger to peace lies in Berlin. There are new ideas abroad there that have taken hold of the heady imagination of the young, and the calculating opportunism of the older cynics. You have heard of Friedrich Wilhelm Nietzsche? He exhorts us all to reject what he calls the 'slave morality' of Christianity, and replace it with a stern new ethic, leading to the development of the superman . . . You don't have many ideas in England, Napier, so

20

you don't understand their danger — '

'Oh, yes I do, Seligmann! That's why I agreed to go along with your plan to warn these people off — these dreamers in Berlin.'

Dr Seligmann looked very grave. To the English diplomat watching him, he seemed the very picture of despair.

'The dreamers are bad enough, Napier, but behind them is a cold and orchestrating intelligence, the Baron Luitpold von Dessau. That man is the prime exponent of the new pan-German militarism. He's currently the darling of the Reichstag. He's a friend of that madman Nietzsche. But von Dessau is something more than merely a fanatical nationalist. He's innately prudent, a quality that he inherits from his father, a careful diplomat whom I knew long ago at Jena. Von Dessau would only ever match his words with deeds if he knew that the way was clear to do so — '

'Which brings us,' Sir Charles Napier concluded, 'to the day of destiny — Friday, 13 January, when von Dessau addresses a mass rally in Berlin of the Pan-German Congress. That, my dear Seligmann, will be a tinder-box waiting to be ignited, and if the orators there get their own way, Europe will be plunged into war.'

Seligmann sighed, and began to gather up

his papers. How painful it was to talk about Germany to this British minister as though his native land was an enemy country! But they were living in dangerous times, and Napier was an old and trusted friend.

'They'll all be there on Friday, the thirteenth, Napier. That date! It sounds as though it was a deliberately perverse choice, perhaps a device of that madman Nietzsche! All the half-crazed brotherhoods will be there, encouraging each other to condone and commit excesses. The *Eidgenossenschaft*, the Prussian Banner, the Junkers of the First Hour — all the deadly demons who want to push the borders of the Reich east to Moscow, and west to the English Channel — '

Sir Charles Napier laughed.

'They'd better not try, Seligmann! If they ever do, we'll be ready for them!'

'Ah, but will you?' asked the old German scholar softly. 'You cannot be sure. And that is why I have written a secret memorandum to von Dessau, which one of your couriers will place in his hands on the very eve of his accursed rally. I cannot in honour tell you what I have written in that memorandum, my dear Napier, but I can promise you that it will strike von Dessau like a thunderclap! Once he reads it, he will use all his great influence to stifle at once the danger of German aggression in our time.'

'And you won't tell me what that memorandum contains?'

'I cannot, Napier! I have almost compromised my own integrity as a German in revealing certain things to von Dessau that should have remained a close and fast secret.'

'Very well. You can, of course, trust me to see that your memorandum is delivered sealed and intact. I will undertake to see it delivered at the time of our choosing by one of my special couriers. Until that time, Seligmann, it will repose in the Foreign Office strongroom.'

'Excellent! Your man came as planned to Chelsea earlier this evening, to conduct the rehearsal. I expect all will be well.'

'I trust so. We have fourteen days before von Dessau attempts to unleash the dogs of war. Have your memorandum ready and sealed in the packet that I gave you by next Tuesday, 3 January. It will be collected by a man called Fenlake. Lieutenant Arthur Fenlake.'

★ ★ ★

Inspector Box and Sergeant Knollys walked back up from Waterman's Pier. They said nothing until they had emerged from the gloomy alleys to the south of Walbrook, and were within sight of the vast meeting-hall in St Swithin's Lane. Its windows were now dark, and the collection of ostlers and coachmen who had been there earlier, had disappeared from the street.

'Let's walk up to the Mansion House, Sergeant Knollys, and take a cab from there back to the Rents. This is the coldest New Year's Eve I've ever known. There's no need for us to go back into that hall. It's nearly ten now, and they'll be done by half past.'

Knollys did not seem to hear what Box was saying. He stopped in the lane, and glanced back towards the dimly lit alleys that led down to the Thames.

'Sir,' asked Sergeant Knollys, 'what was that constable talking about? PC Peabody? For a rough-and-ready riverside character he seemed to know far more than was good for him.'

'Joe Peabody is a constable in the River Police. He's been a galley-man since he was a lad. He joined the force when they still had the old floating station near Somerset House. But he's also a recruit into a special body of men who assist the security services. I don't know much about them, but I once found myself on the fringes of some business that

24

involved them, and the man who runs them. That's when I met Joe Peabody.'

'So he's got special powers — '

'No, Sergeant. He's just a police constable. But over and above his daily work, he'll do little portions of a job for someone, without necessarily knowing why he's doing it. This time, he recognized the man in the river for what he was, and told his inspector. Bob Cross knows about Joe, and asks no questions. And it might be a good idea, Sergeant, if you did likewise.'

At the Mansion House they hailed a cab to Whitehall. Quite a throng of New Year's Eve revellers were making themselves heard on the crowded pavements as they rattled towards the Strand.

'You're on duty all day tomorrow, aren't you, sir? A bit of a tall order, is that.'

'I don't mind, Sergeant. Somebody's got to step into the breach on a Sunday. It's not as though it's a bank holiday, like in Scotland. Mahogany, they call it.'

Knollys hid a smile behind his hand.

'Do they, sir? Mahogany? Well, I never knew that!'

'Oh, yes. And in any case, I'm off duty all day Monday, in lieu. I arranged that months ago with Old Growler. So on Monday afternoon, Sergeant, I shall accompany my friend Miss Whittaker to the theatre, followed by a slap-up dinner at Simpson's.'

'I'm sorry I won't be able to come with you, sir. But duty calls, I'm afraid.'

Box was silent for a moment. He glanced out of the window at the crowds congregating at the brightly lit doors of public houses and taverns. Each of those men and women had a right to call upon his services. Knollys had meant his remark as a tease, but it held its own truth.

'You're right, Sergeant. Duty always calls. I'm thinking of that poor murdered man, Stefan Oliver. Shot in the back — for what? It's none of our business, and in the nature of things it won't be made public. But I wonder . . . How did Joe Peabody know that I'd be up there, listening to old Dr Seligmann? And why *me*, Sergeant? Maybe it's a hint from higher up. Maybe I'm going to be drawn into this business of Stefan Oliver whether I like it or not.'

His mind conjured up once more the bleak environs of Waterman's Pier, and the lifeless body of the Foreign Office courier. Duty had called for him, too, and had led him to his death. What had that cynical old constable said about him? Someone had delivered Stefan Oliver like a badly addressed parcel: Returned to Sender.

2

Calls of Duty

Laughing and chattering, the matinée audience erupted on to the pavement in front of the Savoy Theatre. The busy Strand was thronged with people, most of them warmly wrapped against the bright, frosty weather of the second day of the New Year. Steady streams of horse traffic poured along the wide carriageway on their way to and from the City and the West End.

Detective Inspector Box stole a glance at the beautiful, raven-haired young woman who was linking his right arm. Miss Louise Whittaker seemed unusually quiet. No doubt she'd rally in a minute, and say something provocative to catch him out. She was very clever — a scholar, no less, which he would have thought an occupation more fit for a man. But there, the world was changing.

The young lady linking his *left* arm suddenly made a comment. He hadn't met young Miss Vanessa Drake before. She looked no more than twenty or so, very fair and slim, but with a kind of controlled jauntiness that suggested hidden reserves of strength.

'Mr Box,' she said, 'you must enjoy working in that beautiful new building on the Embankment. New Scotland Yard it's called, isn't it?'

Louise Whittaker burst into laughter, but said nothing. Her friend Vanessa looked at her anxiously.

'Oh, dear,' she whispered, 'have I said something wrong? I'm so sorry!'

'Nothing to be sorry about, Miss Drake!' Box assured her. 'It's just that Scotland Yard's a sore point at the moment, and a bone of contention. I'll tell you all about it at dinner.'

How young and vulnerable she looked! Her youth seemed to be emphasized by the dark-blue, high-collared coat that she wore, and by the designedly frivolous hat adorned with dyed feathers. There was something else, too. This girl was troubled. It showed in the sudden shadows that fell across her bright blue eyes when she thought that no one was observing her. Perhaps she'd be more forthcoming once they had availed themselves of the delights of Simpson's, Mr Crathie's splendid eating-house in the Strand.

★ ★ ★

Box spent quite a long time admiring the overpowering luxury of Simpson's Tavern and Divan, especially the awesome shrine to food and drink occupying the centre of the big dining-room. It was a sort of altar, piled up with offerings of decanters and glasses, flowers, and frothy confections, with four great silver-plated wine coolers for company, one at each of its four corners. When the efficient, dedicated waiters were not gliding around serving the crowd of hungry customers, they appeared to pause near the great altar, as though to offer brief prayers for support and sustenance.

'Aren't you going to tell Vanessa about the delights of Scotland Yard? You promised, you know.' Louise Whittaker glanced at Box mockingly, treated him to a rather unnerving smile, and then continued her task of eating breaded whitebait.

Inspector Box put down his knife and fork on his plate, and turned to Vanessa.

'You see, Miss Drake,' he explained, 'when the main body of the force moved to that fairy palace on the Embankment in '91, a goodly number of us were left behind to hold the fort in what remained of Scotland Yard. The *real* Scotland Yard, you know. So I work in a dilapidated old heap of bricks called King James's Rents, which you'll find just a few yards on across the cobbles from Whitehall Place. I'd invite you to visit, but you'd probably catch pneumonia, or plague, or whatever else has soaked into the walls along with the mildew — '

'So you don't like it there?'

'What? Yes, of course I like it,' Box replied, defensively. 'They left the best men behind there when they made tracks for the fairy palace. Yes, Miss Drake, I like it very much!'

'And so you should, Mr Box,' said Vanessa. 'Your days are filled with excitement, whereas mine — well, I seem to spend my time envying other people whose lives aren't as humdrum as mine! So, hurrah for — what did you call it? — hurrah for King James's Rents.'

They turned their attention to the serious business of eating lunch. The two young women began a desultory conversation, leaving Box to his own thoughts for a while. What a fibber he was! If word ever came down from above, he'd be off like a shot to Norman Shaw's brand-new building, with its acres of windows, and bright electric lighting. Until then, he'd continue to soldier on in a soot-stained old office where the spluttering gas mantle stayed lit all day, and people stumbled on the dark narrow staircases linking the warren of rooms and landings.

It had been a marvellous afternoon, and very pleasant to have two girls in tow. Vanessa Drake's young man, apparently, had been forced to cry off at the last moment, but had urged her to go with her friend Miss Whittaker. Vanessa's beau was a soldier, and had to do what he was told without demur. Well, Box could understand that. He was a man under orders himself.

★　★　★

Louise Whittaker and Arnold Box walked Vanessa Drake home to her lodgings near Dean's Yard, Westminster, and then made their way to Baker Street, where they climbed into one of the Light Green Atlas buses that ran out to Finchley. They journeyed through Lisson Grove and St John's Wood until the Finchley omnibus reached its terminus at Church End, and the two steaming horses were uncoupled from the heavy vehicle. Arnold Box hurried down the curving rear stair in time to hand Miss Louise Whittaker down the steps from the interior saloon.

They walked decorously side by side along one or two pleasant roads of new, redbrick houses, skirted a playing field, and then came to the wide avenue of modern villas where Miss Whittaker lived.

Louise Whittaker opened her smart black-painted front door with a latch-key, and after they had attended to the business of hanging up their coats and hats on the hall stand, she preceded him into the front room. Miss Whittaker indicated a chair near the fireplace, and Box sat down.

Arnold Box was no stranger to Miss Whittaker's study. He had met her more than two years previously, when she had appeared as an expert witness in a fraud case. He had visited her a number of times since then — purely in a professional capacity, of course — and had taken tea with her several times, once in an ABC tea-shop in a quiet road near the British Museum, when he had been spotted by a beat constable. He hadn't heard the last of it at King James's Rents for weeks.

'Repose yourself, Mr Box,' she said, 'while I make us both a cup of tea. Coffee's all very well, but it doesn't quench the thirst.'

Louise Whittaker left the room, and presently Box could hear the vigorous rattle of the sink pump as his hostess filled a kettle in the kitchen. It was followed by the chink of cups on saucers. Box glanced across the room at the large desk in the window bay. Many books and papers were spread out on it, and there seemed to be a positive barrage of ink wells and pens. This quiet room was a kind of sanctuary, a temporary refuge from the hectic life of the Metropolitan Police, the irascible Superintendent Mackharness, and all the inconveniences of King James's Rents.

But today, it was not quite the same. He had tried not to think of his old father during the afternoon. 'Don't go worrying about me, boy,' he'd said. 'Enjoy yourself with your lady friend. I'm only lying in there, on Monday, while they do some tests, you see, and make everything ready. Mr Howard Paul will do the job on Tuesday. About midday, so he says.'

Louise Whittaker returned, carrying a tray of tea things, which she placed carefully on a small round table near the fire. As she poured the tea from a patterned china teapot, she talked to him in a low voice. He watched her spoon sugar into his cup, and noted how carefully she poured the milk. She had real silver spoons . . .

Twelve o'clock, at the Royal Free Hospital in Gray's Inn Road, on Tuesday, 3 January, 1893. Tuesday was tomorrow.

'So what did you think?'

Arnold Box started guiltily out of his reverie.

'Think? Think about what?'

Miss Whittaker sighed with amused impatience.

'There! I knew you hadn't been listening. I

33

was asking you, What did you think of Vanessa Drake? Not her pretty face, you know, or her cornflower-blue eyes, or her corn-yellow hair — but *her*. What did you think?'

'There's something worrying Miss Drake,' Box replied. 'I noticed it almost at once, and evidently you did, too. Perhaps Miss Drake has confided in you?'

He left the question hanging in the air. It was a stilted way of putting it, but then, he was never entirely at ease with Miss Whittaker. She was gazing into the fire, and he saw her bite her lip with evident vexation. He waited for her to make up her mind.

'Mr Box,' she said at last, 'I've known Vanessa since she was a very young girl of sixteen, with her own way to make in the world. She earns her living as a skilled needle woman — she is, in fact, a vestment maker with Watts and Company in Westminster. Well, she has fallen for a young man, a soldier. Or he has fallen for her. He was supposed to have come with us today, but cried off at the last moment.'

Louise sipped her tea for a while without speaking. Box saw how she was eyeing him with some kind of speculative concern. Did he, perhaps, look as worried as he felt?

'According to Vanessa,' Louise continued,

'this young man — Arthur, she calls him — is a steady, decent fellow, but she thinks he's being led astray by an older man, who's introducing him to gambling of a dangerous nature. That's why she looks worried.'

Whenever she speaks of men, thought Box, she describes them as though they were a quite distinct species. A young man. A steady, decent fellow. Arthur, she calls him. Well, why not? That was his name, no doubt.

'This young man, Miss Whittaker, this Arthur — you say he's a soldier. Do you happen to know what kind of soldier? It makes a difference, you know.'

'Well, he's an officer. And the man who's leading him astray is an officer, too.'

Miss Whittaker suddenly blushed. It was an unusual reaction, thought Box.

'You must wonder why I'm telling you all this, Mr Box. We've had such a splendid outing, a genuine holiday for a single afternoon, and now I must spoil it by seeming to ask you favours. But is there anything that you could do? In an official capacity, I mean. For Vanessa's sake, at least.'

'Well, Miss Whittaker, gambling's curbed and reined in by statute law, but it's very difficult to police it. It's a moral delinquency, but not a crime in itself — '

'So nothing can be done!' He saw his

friend's face flush with anger. He held up a restraining hand.

'There's plenty that can be done when gambling leads to folk flouting the law. And there are some legally prohibited games — ace of hearts is one of them, basset, dice (unless you're playing backgammon), faro, roulette — but of course you can't have a policeman standing behind every gambler when he's behind locked doors with his friends. Still, Blackstone says that gambling 'promotes public idleness, theft and debauchery', so if you can give me a few more details, I'll ask around, as they say. See a few people I know.'

Box was understandably pleased to see the look of respect that came to Miss Whittaker's eyes as he spoke. It wasn't often that he was able to parade his own specialist knowledge in front of her. She was the clever one, not he.

'Vanessa told me that her Arthur had become very friendly with this senior man . . . He's in the Artillery, and his name's Lankester. Major Lankester.'

'Major Lankester. And do you know where he and this Arthur are supposed to do their gambling?'

'I don't know exactly where it is, Mr Box. But it's a sort of club or society, run by a man called Gordon. Mr Gordon.'

Box smiled, and sat up in his chair. Gordon! This was more like it!

'Well, now, Miss Whittaker, I'll be delighted to look into this little matter for you. Mr Gordon is not entirely unknown to us at Scotland Yard. I'd be very happy to pay him a call. And I'll ask him about this Major Lankester, and what he's doing to Miss Vanessa Drake's Arthur. I expect Arthur's got another name?'

'His name's Fenlake. Lieutenant Arthur Fenlake.'

'Fenlake. Bear with me a while, Miss Whittaker, while I make a note in this little book of mine.'

He scribbled a few lines in his notebook with a stub of pencil that he carried in his pocket. When he had finished, he saw that his hostess's eyes were fixed on him, and he realized that she was no longer thinking about Vanessa Drake's problems.

'What's the matter, Mr Box? There's something worrying you. Why don't you tell me what it is? Drink some tea, and then tell me.'

Box sipped his tea obediently, and began to order his thoughts. He was unwilling to intrude his own private concerns into this calm and ordered sanctuary. He brought professional problems here, conundrums that his clever friend would help him to solve, or at least to clarify. Personal worries — well, that was a different matter.

'It's my old pa, Miss Whittaker. I don't know whether I've mentioned him to you before? He's a retired police sergeant — a uniformed man, he was — and he keeps a cigar divan and hair-cutting rooms in Oxford Street. He wasn't a detective officer.'

'And what happened to him? How old is he?'

'He's seventy-three. Well, way back in '75 he was shot by a villain called Spargo. Joseph Edward Spargo. Shot in the leg. This Spargo went on to commit a murder, and he was hanged at Newgate in 1880. Pa has suffered with that leg for eighteen years, and the upshot of it is, that he's to have it cut off before it kills him. Amputated, that's what they call it.'

'Why didn't you tell me?' Louise Whittaker's voice held a tinge of reproach, as well as sympathy. 'I thought there was something troubling you this afternoon. Why didn't you tell me?'

'Well, Miss Whittaker, it's not the kind of thing a lady wants to hear — '

'*This* lady does! To think of all the times we've had tea together — it's become a kind of ritual — and yet you never told me about your father and his predicament. When — when is the operation to take place?'

'Tomorrow, miss — '

Miss Whittaker sprang to her feet. She shook her head in evident exasperation, but Box was startled to see the tears standing in her eyes.

'*Tomorrow*? And yet you entertained Vanessa and me, and put up with my begging for favours when all the time — tomorrow?'

'Yes, miss. Mr Howard Paul's going to do it, at the Royal Free Hospital. Pa went in there today. This morning. So, I've been a bit anxious, as you can understand. But don't you worry about it, Miss Whittaker. I'll go now, and have a word straight away with our gambling friend, Mr Gordon. Whatever's going on there with this Arthur Fenlake and Major Lankester, I'll make sure I know all about it.'

Arnold Box got to his feet. How beautiful she was! And she'd been sorry for Pa!

As he approached the door, Louise Whittaker suddenly put her arms round his neck and gave him a kiss on the cheek.

'You great silly boy,' she said.

Arnold Box blushed, and blundered out of the room.

Discretion, as Arnold Box well knew, was the hallmark of Mr Gordon's establishment in Eagle Street, Holborn. It looked sober enough from the outside, a genteel four-storey residence clad in immaculate stucco, one of a row of town houses built in the 1860s. Behind the respectable façade, though, all was luxury. Mr Gordon's gaming-house boasted crimson flock wall-paper, crystal chandeliers, and sumptuous Persian carpets. A suite of rooms on the first floor contained the gilded gaming salon, and an elegantly appointed supper-room for the use of the clients. There was an excellent cellar, and the kitchen, too, was above reproach.

Mr Gordon, a supple, olive-skinned man with curly black hair and expensive garments, was rumoured to hail originally from Italy. Some of his associates addressed him as Mr Giordano, which always brought a slight frown of annoyance to the olive brow. Mr Gordon liked to think of himself as one of the Bulldog Breed. He operated strictly within the law, so he said, and it was very difficult to prove otherwise.

'It is my practice, always, Inspector Box,' said Mr Gordon, 'to assist the police.'

'I know it is, Mr Gordon.'

Inspector Box looked round the gilded and ornate room.

'Have you taken the precaution of insuring these premises, Mr Gordon?' he asked.

'Indeed I have, Inspector. These crystals, these antiques — priceless! But tell me, Mr Box, have you come about something specific? Or do you wish to recommend an insurer?'

'I've come to ask you what you can tell me about a young man called Lieutenant Fenlake, an Artillery officer. I'm told that he frequents this place of yours.'

Mr Gordon paused for a moment, evidently to gather his wits.

'I have a high-class clientele of ladies and gentlemen here, Mr Box. Among them was Lieutenant Fenlake. He made a few desultory visits at first — about six months ago, it would be — but then he came more and more frequently. I could see he was fatally attracted to the gaming tables — '

'Would I be right, Mr Gordon,' Box interrupted, 'in thinking that Lieutenant Fenlake was lured into this place by a fellow officer? Someone who, perhaps, wished to corrupt him by letting him amass impossible debts? This is all in confidence, of course. I'm referring to a man called Major Lankester.'

41

Box saw immediately from the bewildered expression on Gordon's face that he was completely wrong in his assumption. Mr Gordon was suddenly in the mood to tell all.

'What you have said, Inspector, could not be further from the truth! Mr Fenlake and Major Lankester are officers in the same unit — the 107th Field Battery of the Royal Artillery. Major Lankester has been a member of this club for many years. He is a seasoned gambler, who plays for high stakes, and who usually gets up from the table richer than when he sat down. At least — ' Mr Gordon stopped abruptly. Evidently he wished to change the subject.

'Young Fenlake, though — well, he was not so fortunate in his choice of recreation. There came a time when he incurred a debt to me that he was unable to repay. I began to insist that he fulfilled his obligation. These are debts of honour, you understand. I told him that I would be obliged to inform his commanding officer if he did not pay me.'

Box watched Mr Gordon as he moistened his drying lips. He's beginning to skate on thin ice, now, he thought. There were unpleasant ways of making a man pay his 'debts of honour'.

'The upshot of the business was that Major

Lankester came here, bringing the unfortunate Fenlake with him. Major Lankester informed me that he would pay young Fenlake's debt himself from his own future winnings, which I considered a very handsome thing for him to do. Then, in my presence, he said: 'Fenlake, you must cease immediately your visits to this house. You are too young to be embroiled with villains like Gordon here, and your work is too valuable to be jeopardized by such foolishness'.'

'So Lieutenant Fenlake never came here again?'

'He didn't, Inspector. Major Lankester was as good as his word, and very quickly paid off Mr Fenlake's debt. I don't know why, but his doing so impressed me very deeply.'

Inspector Box rose to his feet and glanced once more around the ornate room.

'You know, Mr Gordon,' he said, 'all this finery, these crystal chandeliers and sham antiques — they look very tawdry and sordid in the light of day. I expect they appear better in candlelight. Watch out for naked lights! Good afternoon.'

As Box stepped out into Eagle Street, he felt a chill north wind blowing. It seemed like an ominous signal of bitter squalls ahead. He turned up the collar of his coat, and made his way towards Farringdon Street.

Mr Howard Paul, visiting surgeon to the Royal Free Hospital, removed his frock coat and turned back his shirt cuffs. One of the three theatre nurses handed him his rubber apron, and when he had lifted it gingerly over his head in such as way as not to disturb his well-brushed but sparse hair, she tied the linen tapes behind him at the waist.

He nodded briefly to the three young doctors who were present, and glanced swiftly around the room to see that all was in order. Sister, as always, stood guard over the tray of instruments as though she feared that somebody would steal them. Dr Avebury, the anaesthetist, was ready with his bottle. A young male nurse attendant was adjusting the carbolic spray apparatus on its little round table near the door. Mr Howard Paul addressed the elderly, white-haired man lying on the operating-table.

'How are you, Mr Box?'

'I'm very well, thank you, sir.'

Mr Howard Paul could hear the tremor of fear in the man's voice, which a recent injection of morphine and atropine had done little to mitigate. He was securely strapped to the table, and the tourniquets were in place, though not yet screwed tight. The waiting was as much an ordeal as the operation itself. He wouldn't keep him waiting too long.

'Ladies and gentlemen,' said Howard Paul, 'this patient is Mr Toby Box, a retired police sergeant, aged 73. He was referred to me in October last by Dr Hooper, of Bryanston Street, and has very sensibly agreed to the amputation of his infected leg. He has been severely crippled for many years as the result of a criminal attack, and both Dr Hooper and myself fear gangrenous complications, and resultant necrosis.'

He gave a slight signal to the theatre sister, and at the same time the doctors and nurses moved close to the table. An attendant turned up the twin glass-shaded gas lamps positioned over the patient to their brightest glow. Howard Paul heard Toby Box draw in his breath sharply.

'Now, Mr Box,' said Howard Paul, 'a nurse is going to place some cotton wool, and a pad of gauze over your nose and mouth — that's right, there you are! There's nothing to fear, and you will feel no pain. None at all. Just breathe as normally as possible. That's right.'

Dr Avebury, the anaesthetist, moved close up behind the patient, and began to pour ether on to the thick pad of gauze. The patient flinched, and a nurse placed the fingertips of one hand briefly on his forehead. It would take from ten minutes to a quarter of an hour to render the patient unconscious. It was essential to allow the vapours to be thoroughly diluted with air, otherwise the patient could go into fatal convulsions.

'Miss Maynard,' said Howard Paul in a low voice to one of the young doctors, 'what would you say was the chief danger attending this operation?'

'The chief danger, sir, is haemorrhage from the severed arteries.'

'Good.' He noted that the female student doctor's voice was calm and sufficiently detached. The anaesthetist continued his measured pouring of ether on to the gauze. The patient was nearly unconscious. Another two or three minutes would do it.

'Mr Hobbes,' said Howard Paul to a smart young man in a light grey suit, 'what must we fear when the cutting is over and done with?'

'Sir, there is the immediate fear of shock, then secondary haemorrhage, and the onset of sepsis.'

'Very good. Are we ready, Dr Avebury?'

'We are, sir.'

'Good. Then let's get on with it.'

The attendant screwed the tourniquets tight. The sister placed a scalpel into Howard

Paul's outstretched hand. The young attendant stationed at the door turned on the carbolic spray.

* * *

Arnold Box stood at the narrow side window of a room on the fourth floor of the hospital building in Gray's Inn Road, looking out on to an array of roofs and tall, gently smoking chimney stacks. The small room was some kind of office, with a closed roll-top desk and a few chairs arranged against the walls. There was a cloying smell of something peculiar to hospitals — carbolic? Chloroform?

Who was this? He turned from the window as he heard footsteps on the stairs. Two figures passed the open door, two ladies talking quietly to each other, and with a calm authority that showed them to be doctors. This hospital specialized in training women in medicine. The two ladies pushed open the doors to the ward on the right of the landing, and disappeared from Box's line of view.

His mind seemed to be filled with images of violence and vulnerability. He saw again the old German scholar on the platform at St Swithin's Hall, valiantly arguing what seemed a very flimsy case with the yellow-haired young man in the audience. Then he saw the face of the German pork-butcher, twisted with passion and hatred, an ordinary tradesman with the potential for killing as part of his nature. And Stefan Oliver, shot in the back and flung contemptuously into the river, only to be thrown about on a trestle table by Dr Kelly, as though he was a carcass in an abattoir . . .

Here they were! Mr Howard Paul was a tall, handsome man with a healthy farmer's face and kindly grey eyes. He paused for a few moments on the landing, talking in low tones to two other gentlemen. Then he came into the small office, and shut the door. He sat in an upright chair near the roll-top desk.

'Well, Mr Box,' he said, 'I think that all's going to be well. The surgery was a little tricky here and there, because whoever extracted the bullet all those years ago made rather a mess of the procedure — but we did well.'

The door opened, and a nurse slipped into the room. She deposited a small glass of amber liquid on the desk beside Howard Paul, and quietly withdrew.

'There'll be a protracted period of convalescence,' Howard Paul continued, 'because I've taken the leg off above the knee, and it will be a very long time before we can consider fitting a prosthetic — a false leg, you know. But believe me, Mr Box, removing that leg will have prolonged your father's life.'

Mr Howard Paul picked up the small glass, and began to sip its contents. Box realized that it was brandy.

'I'm keeping him here at the Royal Free for several weeks, so that I can keep an eye on him. I'm here virtually every day, you see. The great danger now, Mr Box, is sepsis. Alien infection, you know. He's in the recovery-room at the moment, but in an hour's time he'll be moved to the surgical ward.'

Mr Howard Paul drained his glass, and took a notebook from his pocket. He scribbled something on a sheet of paper, tore it out, and handed it to Box.

'There are fixed visiting times here, Mr Box, but because of the shifting nature of your duties, I've written a special pass that will get you in here at any reasonable time of day — or night.'

'That's very kind of you, sir.'

'Not at all. It's only right and proper, considering the work you do. You can come and have a little look at your father now, Mr Box, while he's still in the recovery-room. After that . . . well, he'd be better left alone with us here for the next forty-eight hours.'

Toby Box lay quite still, his eyes closed, his

chest rising and falling with encouraging regularity. The scanty white hair that fringed his bald head lay neatly around the pillow, as though the attendant nurse, a young woman in starched white apron and cap, had arranged it like that. Maybe she had. His face was as white as marble.

Arnold Box looked at his father for a while without speaking. He could smell the ghastly hospital scents more strongly in the small room — ether? Chloroform? — and behind them, the reek of congealing blood.

'Pa,' said Arnold Box aloud, 'you're not going to die on me, are you?'

The eyelids flickered for a moment, and the eyes partly opened. They looked in Arnold Box's direction, but did not focus.

'Not yet awhile, boy,' Box's father whispered.

Mr Howard Paul smiled, nodded to the attendant nurse, and deftly guided Inspector Box out of the room.

3

A Sacrifice to Bellona

The man from Quaritch's bookshop stepped over the threshold of Dr Otto Seligmann's warm and welcoming house in Lavender Walk, a quiet enclave of ancient dwellings not far from the Chelsea Physic Garden. The butler closed the door, shutting out the bitter, searching wind of the January night.

The visitor found himself in a long, oak-panelled hall, with a staircase rising to the right. Small gaslights winked and blinked in their round glass shades, and a fiercely cheerful coal fire burned in the hall grate. There was a strong smell of brass-polish and beeswax.

'Mr Colin McColl? Dr Seligmann will be here presently to take you out across the garden to the Belvedere. He's engaged with his secretary at the moment, but he'll be here in a trice. It's a raw night, if I may say so, sir!'

The butler's voice was cheerful and welcoming, and suited his patriarchal appearance. He had a round, pleasant face, adorned with a very fine set of old-fashioned white whiskers.

As the butler finished speaking, a petite, slender girl, seemingly in her twenties, appeared at the top of the stairs. She wore a very becoming evening dress of dark-green velvet. Her arms were bare, and she wore no jewellery. Her blonde hair was arranged loosely as a frame for her small face.

'Who is it, Lodge?' Her voice was musical enough, but held an edge of imperiousness.

'It's the gentleman from Quaritch's book-shop in Piccadilly, Miss Ottilie.'

'Ah, that, yes. It was for that reason, no doubt, that we dined at six o'clock today, and must starve for the rest of the evening. It's of no moment to me. Old books, and musty papers. Scholars and their playthings!'

The girl's eyes met McColl's for what seemed an uncomfortably long moment. He returned her gaze steadily, with the suspicion of a smile playing around his lips. She dropped her eyes, turned abruptly on the stairs, and was lost from sight. The butler turned an anxious face to the visitor. Really, it was a bit of a strain working for these excitable German folk!

A door to the right of the hall opened, and a tall, striking, elderly man emerged from a book-lined room.

'Mr McColl,' said Lodge, 'here is Dr Seligmann now.'

Colin McColl had spent a long time researching the life and opinions of this man. In earlier years he had attracted attention as a scholar in the field of English and Germanic philology. Then he had been drawn into the diplomatic service of the Kingdom of Brandenburg-Prussia. Now, in 1893, he was seen as a theoretician of European governance, and one of the luminaries of the German Empire. To some, he was a great patriot. To others, he was something else.

McColl watched Dr Otto Seligmann as he swept back a shock of white hair with both hands. For a man nearing seventy, he had reason to be proud of his abundant locks, which just touched the shoulders of his sober evening dress coat.

'Mr McColl! We've not met before, so let me bid you welcome. How kind of you to call at this late hour! Thank you, Lodge. That will be all.'

Otto Seligmann adjusted his gold pince-nez, and looked at his visitor. He saw a fresh-looking, clean-shaven young man of thirty or so, who was standing close to the hall fire, and clutching a stout leather briefcase to his chest.

'So you are the gentleman from Quaritch's.

53

You said in your note that Mr Bernard Quaritch would value my opinion of some pages of a recently unearthed Anglo-Saxon manuscript. I must say that I was flattered that your distinguished employer should still think of me as an expert in such matters. Are you personally acquainted with my work in that field?'

'Indeed, yes, Doctor. Who has not heard of Seligmann's Law of Unaccented Syllables? And, of course, your *Specimens of Anglo-Saxon Verse* is still consulted and honoured.'

The young man spoke with an eager forcefulness tinged with what seemed to be nervousness. It was an odd combination. Seligmann was attracted by the man's pronounced but educated Scots accent. He himself spoke perfect English, but still retained traces of his Prussian intonation.

'You flatter me, Mr McColl, and make me forget that I have spent the greater part of my life embroiled in politics — politics! That was not through choice, but in response to the call of duty — duty to Germany, my native land, but duty also to all the peoples of Europe. But come, Mr McColl, you don't want to hear all this! Bring your briefcase with you out to the Belvedere, where I keep my academic library.'

Seligmann took the young man's arm,

guided him through a stone-flagged passage, and threw open the rear door of the house. The bitter cold of the January night immediately enveloped them both. They emerged into a wild, narrow garden, surrounded by high walls, where some ruinous brick sheds shared the cramped space with a few blighted oaks. The sky was clear, with one or two brilliant stars shining, though heavy black cloud was spreading rapidly from the north.

'If only it would snow! This cold is unendurable!'

They were words uttered in a way that did not invite any kind of response. McColl silently agreed with them. It was wretchedly cold, even for January.

In one corner of the garden, a great stone hemispherical building loomed up in the pallid light shed from the various windows of the old Tudor house. The two buildings seemed to be jockeying for position in the narrow confines of the garden. The stone structure was a kind of two-storeyed classical temple, crowned with a leaden dome. Its grey walls were mellowed and blotched with lichen.

'The Belvedere, Mr McColl — that's what they call it. It's my special retreat, where I can busy myself with my books and papers without too much fear of interruption! At one time, I suppose, the Belvedere stood in some secluded grove of a nobleman's park, but that must have been in the Chelsea of long ago! Come inside, out of this infernal cold.'

★   ★   ★

Dr Seligmann observed his visitor's reaction to the interior of his retreat with kindly amusement. He had warmed to the young man as soon as he had seen him standing in the old panelled hall of the main house. A fine, strong young fellow, with the litheness of an athlete. He could sense the physical force of Colin McColl, an innate power that he seemed to hold in deliberate restraint beneath a smart and rather prim exterior.

Like all visitors, McColl had expressed surprise at the luxurious comfort of the Belvedere. He had glanced appreciatively at the cheerful fire blazing in the stone fireplace built into part of the curved wall. He had placed the fingers of one gloved hand lightly for a moment on the heavy iron door.

'This old house of mine, Mr McColl,' said Seligmann, 'dates back to the time of Sir Thomas More, who is reputed to have written part of his *Utopia* here. I read it, once: it seemed only right to do so, as I was living in that great humanist's house!'

Seligmann watched his visitor's keen blue eyes ranging around the interior of the building, where tier upon tier of shelves, all seemingly filled with leather-bound books, rose up as far as the ornamental plaster ceiling. The young man appeared fascinated by the books, and was only half-listening to what he was saying about More. Was this eager young man more interested in the books than in their elderly owner?

Dr Seligmann sat down at a massive desk placed centrally to the chamber beneath a many-branched gas chandelier, which lit up the book-lined chamber as though it were day. Colin McColl unfastened the straps of his heavy briefcase and carefully removed an envelope, which he handed to Seligmann.

'As you'll see, sir, these ancient pages seem to be part of a meditation on mutability, and we're inclined to think it dates from about AD 940, which would make it contemporary with the Exeter Book, and perhaps written by the same scribe.'

Dr Seligmann examined the pages carefully for a minute or two, and then slid them back into their envelope.

'Yes, yes; you could well be right. They're certainly genuine. But Anglo-Saxon texts are dubious things, Mr McColl, as you know, and

I'll need to verify the morphology and syntax of these passages before I can date them with any certainty. I take it that I can keep these pages for a while?'

'Indeed, yes, sir. Let me pack them away again in the briefcase. I'll leave it here with you.'

Without waiting to be asked, the Scotsman picked up the envelope, and returned it to the briefcase, threading its leather thongs securely into their buckles. Then he stood up, and looked around the Belvedere once again with a kind of naïve interest that Seligmann found amusing. He watched as McColl put the briefcase down on top of a large crate covered in sacking, and fastened with iron hoops, which stood in the space beneath an iron staircase, curving upward to an unused upper chamber.

Seligmann recalled an old Anglo-Saxon saying: *Wyrd bith ful araed*. You could translate that, roughly, as *Fate plays strange tricks*. That crate, like this young man's visit, was another unexpected reminder of his early career as a specialist in Germanic philology. It had arrived that very afternoon from Chaplin's, the carriers at Victoria, and it contained a gift of books from his old university of Bonn. They had written to him some weeks earlier, advising him that the gift was on its way. He and Schneider would open it tomorrow.

'I was musing, McColl, on the old aphorism, *Wyrd bith ful araed.*'

'"Fate does odd things to a man"? Well, sir, that's very true. And this is your academic library? A curious and very interesting place, isn't it? All those tiers and tiers of leather-bound books . . . '

'Yes, Mr McColl, the Belvedere's a curious and interesting place. But come, I have another visitor arriving any minute, so I must turn you out into the cold! Come back in a day or two, and I will have a written report ready for you. You can make an appointment with my secretary.'

When Seligmann opened the door of the Belvedere, both men winced at the penetrating cold still clinging to the grass and blighted trees of the dank garden.

'It continues bitterly cold, Mr McColl. Still, it's only the third of January. It's bound to change soon, and then we shall have snow. Lots of snow!'

He bade the young man good evening, and returned to the snug warmth of the Belvedere, where he resumed his seat behind the desk.

Had he been successful in hiding his anxious foreboding from his visitor? For some months now, he had experienced what he could best describe as an evaporation of trust in those around him. London, and Chelsea in particular, had been his sanctuary for nearly twenty years, but perhaps he had always misjudged his opponents. There was a new sense of menace gathering round him, which the arrival of his young and pretty niece from Germany six months earlier had done nothing to dissipate.

There had been an estrangement between the two branches of the family, and he had last seen Ottilie when she was a little girl of ten, lively enough, he recalled, but ailing from some kind of affliction of the lungs. She had grown to be a very striking, lively and energetic girl, with a mind of her own, and a determination to get her own way in all things.

Dr Seligmann looked apprehensively round the Belvedere. Was it still safe? He had taken to spending the bulk of his days and some of his nights in the old building, but nothing, he knew, could ever be safe. There was an unused floor above the study, and at times he imagined that he heard noises there. Only his fancy, of course, but even now, he felt that the building had subtly shifted its identity, and was hiding some undefined anomaly. The stout iron door, installed for some long-forgotten reason in the past century, could withstand any physical attack, but all doors yielded to treachery.

So engrossed was he in his thoughts that he started in surprise when the door of the Belvedere opened to admit Schneider, his private secretary. As always, he was correctly dressed in a tightly buttoned frock coat and pinstripe trousers. He held himself stiffly, but gave his employer a sharp bow. What a proud Saxon he looks! thought Seligmann. But when he spoke, his voice held an unconditional deference.

'Lieutenant Fenlake has arrived, Herr Doktor,' he said.

Dr Seligmann looked at the young man who had followed his secretary into the Belvedere. Lieutenant Fenlake wore civilian clothing, topped by a heavy serge overcoat against the bitter January weather. Seligmann judged him to be about thirty years of age, or perhaps younger, a slim, well-made young man. He might have been mistaken for a young toff, but his stance was that of a professional soldier.

'Thank you, Schneider. You may leave us now. I shall not need you for the rest of the evening.'

As soon as the secretary had closed the

door, Lieutenant Fenlake spoke.

'Dr Otto Seligmann? I am Lieutenant Arthur Fenlake. I have the honour of waiting for your instructions.'

The young man produced a square of card from his pocket, and held it up for Seligmann to read. The German scholar peered at the close, rather spiky handwriting, which he recognized as that of Sir Charles Napier. He nodded in satisfaction, and Fenlake returned the card to his pocket.

'Lieutenant Fenlake,' said Seligmann, 'at half-past six yesterday evening, one of your fellow couriers, a man called Stefan Oliver, came here to the Belvedere secretly, gaining entrance to the premises through the rear garden gate. I gave him a decoy package, which I assume he has delivered by now to Sir Charles Napier — '

'I beg your pardon, sir, for interrupting. Stefan Oliver's attempt to deliver that decoy package was unsuccessful. For that reason, Sir Charles instructed me to come openly to the house, with no attempt at subterfuge. I sent a note to that effect early this morning, which I assume was seen by your secretary.'

'It was. And has Sir Charles given you any specific instructions for this evening?'

'He has, sir. I am instructed to receive from you the sealed memorandum that you have written to Baron von Dessau in Berlin. The packet will consist of a linen envelope, marked on the outside with a Foreign Office cipher known to me, and closed along the flap with three red wax seals. I am instructed to leave immediately if the package is not made up exactly as I have described.'

Seligmann listened to the young man's purposeful delivery, and thought to himself: this smart Foreign Office courier is too enamoured of carrying out orders to the letter, too addicted to formulas and formalities. It is the curse of a man without imagination . . . He stands there stiffly, and rather impatiently, as though he's simply called in for a moment on the way to somewhere else. Perhaps he has.

Dr Seligmann unlocked a drawer in his desk, and removed a stout linen envelope, to which three red wax seals had been attached. He handed it to Fenlake.

'I cannot over-emphasize, Lieutenant Fenlake,' he said, 'the necessity of this memorandum being placed into the hands of Baron von Dessau before the thirteenth of this month — '

'With respect, sir,' Fenlake interrupted, 'I am not authorized to talk about the document, only to verify and receive it.'

The courier glanced at the packet, nodded

in satisfaction, and then placed it in an inside pocket of his greatcoat. He brought himself quietly to attention for a moment, and then moved towards the door.

'I will take my leave of you immediately, sir,' he said, 'as my mission here is accomplished. This memorandum will be with my superiors within the hour.'

Dr Seligmann smiled, and opened the heavy iron door of the Belvedere, wincing yet again at the deep cold of the January night.

'Thank you, Mr Fenlake,' he said. 'You have relieved me of a crushing burden. I bid you good night!'

Seligmann resumed his place at the desk. He was hugely relieved to know that the sealed memorandum was finally safe out of his house. He wondered in what way Stefan Oliver had been unsuccessful, and what had happened to him. For some reason he had shied away from asking Fenlake directly. Perhaps it was just as well not to know.

Whom did he suspect, and of what? Ottilie was a dear girl, clearly bored with life in Chelsea, and longing for the glittering salons of Berlin. She seemed to spend a dispropor-tionately large part of her days locked in combat with Mrs Poniatowski, who was a good housekeeper, but a sour, forbidding woman, impatient of young people and their desire for novelty.

Count Czerny, his Austrian associate, was involved so intrinsically in his work for harmony among the nations of Europe that it was simply foolish to suspect him of . . . of what? His fears were ill-formed, intangible. Czerny had lived in his house for over five years. In political terms they thought as one man. If anything were to happen to him, Czerny would carry on his mission to frustrate the ambitions of the war party in Berlin.

The war party . . . Three years earlier, the old Iron Chancellor of Germany, Prince von Bismarck, had been dismissed. 'Dropping the pilot' they'd called it here in England. There were people in Berlin, in the very heart of the German Reich, who were bent on a trial of strength with Great Britain. Baron von Dessau was such a man. A member of the Reichstag, he held minor office in the German Foreign Service, but his strength lay with the brotherhoods and their fevered dreams of expansion. It mattered nothing to von Dessau that the Emperor William II was Queen Victoria's grandson. Well, he, Otto Seligmann, was doing all in his power to avert the possibility of such a war.

Seligmann listened to the settling of coals

in the grate, and the loud ticking of the clock. That young fellow Colin McColl was clearly a trained philologist. Odd, that an expert firm like Quaritch's should seek out an obscure German scholar to verify those pages, when there were infinitely better informed people at London University to do it for them!

Friday, the thirteenth . . . A wicked, perverse choice of date. They would all meet in Berlin, to encourage each other in rash adventures. There was no language like German for stirring the emotions of the mob. But von Dessau was essentially prudent, and would be first stunned, then sobered, by the information contained in that memorandum. Pray God it reached him before the thirteenth!

Seligmann looked round the serried rows of shelves rising above him, and smiled. Then he became aware again of the small agate clock on the mantelpiece. Surely that clock had never ticked as loudly before? He glanced across the room to the iron staircase, where McColl's stout briefcase still reposed on top of the unopened crate of books from Bonn. That had been an unexpected present. Odd, that it had arrived on the very day that —

Too late, he saw the meaning of the sealed crate, the closed briefcase, and the loud ticking. Otto Seligmann sprang up frantically from his chair.

★   ★   ★

When the door of the Belvedere closed behind him, Lieutenant Fenlake passed through the chill garden and into the rear quarter of the ancient house. The prim little man in the tight coat — he had heard Dr Seligmann address him as Schneider — was waiting to conduct him to the front door, which gave immediately on to Lavender Walk. Fenlake hurried through the warm, panelled hall with its glowing lamps and stepped out purposefully on to the pavement.

He had taken only a few steps when the air was rent asunder by a tremendous explosion. A shock wave crashed through the street and flung him to the ground.

The young officer took only seconds to regain his feet. People were gathering from all sides to jam the narrow street, and to gaze in dumb awe at the scene. The door of the house opened, and Schneider, his clothing singed and smoking, staggered out and down the steps, crying aloud frantically in some foreign tongue. Fenlake plunged back into the smoking interior of the house.

The door to the garden had been blown off

its hinges, and lay shattered on the floor. Fenlake clambered over it, and emerged into the garden. It was a terrifying scene. The Belvedere was burning like a monstrous firework. Sinuous arms of flame had burst through the windows, and reached as high as the tops of the stunted trees, though the stout iron door still held. The back of the main house was lit up as though it was day. Most of the windows had been shattered by the force of the explosion. The earlier bitter cold had yielded to a dangerous and stifling heat.

Lieutenant Fenlake was conscious of the presence of others in the garden, and of voices chattering excitedly. It was immediately clear to him that there was nothing that anyone could do: the heat was now so fierce that it was virtually impossible to approach the blazing building. The trees were beginning to catch fire.

Suddenly, Fenlake heard a strong Scots voice calling from the direction of the house.

'Is Dr Seligmann still in there?'

There was a muttered reply, which Fenlake did not catch, and then a man emerged into the burning garden. The man looked swiftly around him, and then picked up what appeared to be a heavy plank that had been lying on a grass verge close to the house. He began to run across the grass, and as he came into the lurid circle of light, Fenlake saw that he was crouched low, his arms crooked around the heavy plank. His pace increased as he neared the Belvedere, and, suddenly realizing what he intended to do, the young officer cried out:

'Stop it, man! It's certain death!'

The man paid no attention, and continued his relentless charge straight at the still-closed iron door of the Belvedere. There was a mighty clang as he hit the door squarely with the plank. It crashed open, still on its hinges, and instantly an inferno of fire leapt out at him, and he staggered back, falling to the ground. At the same time, the flames from the doorway seemed to be sucked backward and upward, and then the stone ribs of the roof tore away from their supports, and fell inwards with a screaming roar. A colossal fountain of sparks and fragments of glowing timber shot upwards into the night sky.

With an impatient oath, Lieutenant Fenlake dragged the man by main force away from the blaze, and beat out the deadly little flames that had started to singe his clothing.

'You're a brave man, but a foolish one, sir,' he said. 'Were you contemplating a rescue? No one could have survived that explosion, or that fire.'

The other young man turned a soot-stained face to his rescuer, and smiled.

'I did what I felt was necessary under the circumstances. I had just concluded some business with Dr Seligmann before this accident occurred, and was still in the area. A frightful business, this. Gas, I expect.'

The Scotsman's face seemed to hold some kind of mocking challenge, exaggerated by the flickering light from the Belvedere. He was staring fixedly at Fenlake, as though memorizing his features. Or perhaps — yes, surely they had met somewhere before?

'I, too, had business with Dr Seligmann this evening,' said Fenlake. 'Your face is familiar to me. I believe we've met before, somewhere.'

'Very likely, sir. Where three and a half million people are cooped up together in one city, their paths may cross and re-cross. You evidently choose not to tell me your name, but I'll tell you mine. It's Colin McColl, and I work for Mr Quaritch, the antiquarian bookseller in Piccadilly. One day, perhaps — '

Colin McColl broke off as the thunder of horses' hoofs heralded the arrival of the fire engines. The throng of people in the road began to disperse, and the damaged and bereaved house was tacitly returned to its legitimate occupiers. Fenlake saw a young woman in a green evening dress standing in the shattered rear entrance of the house. An older, rather forbidding woman came and stood beside her. Neither said a word. They looked like marble statues, or waxworks posed in a tableau.

It was time for Fenlake to go, before anyone asked him awkward questions. There was work still to be done. He could feel the weight of Seligmann's memorandum in his inside pocket.

That man, McColl . . . He had seen him somewhere before, not in the daily criss-crossing of London's teeming millions, but somewhere connected with his own line of business. He'd remember one of these days. Soon, the police would be there. It was time for him to fade discreetly from the scene. He looked around him to see if Mr McColl was still in the garden, but he had disappeared.

★   ★   ★

Sir Charles Napier drew his heavy astrakhan coat around his shoulders. It was bitterly cold in the untenanted garden lodge where he had been obliged to meet Lieutenant Fenlake. A single-storey building, covered in flaking stucco, and all but overgrown with thickets of bramble, it stood in an obscure corner of the grounds surrounding the Chelsea Royal Hospital. It was, he mused drily, a far cry from the Italianate splendours and embracing comfort of the Foreign Office.

From where he stood at the grimy rear window, he could see the flames rising high into the air a quarter of a mile away in the direction of the Chelsea Physic Garden. An accident? If one were naïve enough, he thought, one could believe it to have been an accident. No doubt it would provoke an international incident. Dr Otto Seligmann, worker for peace, sacrificed as a burnt-offering to Bellona, the Goddess of War.

Only the previous evening they had shared a platform at a meeting of the Anglo-German Friendship League, both of them unaware that Stefan Oliver had been done to death, and that his murdered body had been thrown down, as it were, at his feet, in a supreme gesture of contempt. One of Kershaw's shadowy people, a blunt, graceless fellow from the River Police, had placed the water-sodden dummy memorandum into his hands, and mumbled some inelegant words of commiseration.

Poor Seligmann! They must have hated him very much to prepare such a death for him. Immolation . . . A pagan sacrifice. What was the name of that fellow Seligmann had mentioned? Nietzsche. Germany seemed to thrive on half-crazed fanatics who fancied themselves as geniuses.

He had known Otto Seligmann intimately for twenty years. Their views on the future condition of Europe were ultimately formed by the same humane political ethic. They had toiled together to build the Anglo-German League of Friendship. Seligmann had spent many a weekend at Napier's country place down in Wiltshire. And to what purpose? It had all been a chimaera. Germany would go wherever Fate was leading her.

Sir Charles Napier turned away from the window, and looked at the young man standing stiffly and patiently near the door of the lodge. He had a photographic memory where his couriers were concerned, and he recalled this young man's dossier now.

Arthur Ernest Henry Fenlake. Born 8 October, 1862. Lieutenant, 107th Field Battery, Royal Artillery. Seconded to the Foreign Office, January, 1889.

Sir Charles sat down at a dusty table.

'Good evening, Lieutenant Fenlake,' he said. 'So your mission was successful!'

'It was, sir.'

Lieutenant Fenlake took Dr Seligmann's memorandum from his pocket and handed it to Sir Charles. Sir Charles ran a hand through his hair, which was still dark, though greying at the temples. He gave a little sigh, and then a short laugh.

'I don't relish all this cloak-and-dagger business, Fenlake,' he said. 'But it would have been foolish not to have used a secure house for the purpose of this little transaction. As for what has happened in Lavender Walk — well, whatever our private feelings, it's none of our business. The police will be there by now.'

Sir Charles placed the sealed memorandum carefully in an inside pocket of his greatcoat. He looked with genuine appreciation at the young courier, who had proved a staunch, and refreshingly unimaginative agent for the Foreign Office's special services. He never questioned his instructions, and carried them out to the letter. Perhaps he would employ him to take the memorandum to von Dessau in Berlin when the right moment came to do so. He would wait a little while before making up his mind.

'Lieutenant Fenlake,' he said, 'you never knew your fellow-courier, Stefan Oliver. I feel it's only right to recall him here at this moment, with that hellish bonfire blazing away in Lavender Walk. He was half Polish, half French, brought to England in early childhood. His parents had fled from one or other of Europe's vile revolutions. His is a long and complex history. Suffice it to say, that I was proud to know him. May he rest in peace.'

'Yes, sir.'

Sir Charles Napier smiled to himself. Fenlake was a gem. Nothing ever distracted him from his duty. The only words he seemed to understand were words of command.

'Fenlake,' he said, in formal tones, 'your day's mission is now accomplished. Folio 6, of the 3rd January, 1893, is turned and sealed.' Lieutenant Fenlake drew himself briefly to attention, then left the lodge, slamming the front door behind him. Sir Charles listened to the ring of his emissary's boots as he walked quickly away into the bitter night.

Friday, the thirteenth . . . Poor Seligmann knew more than most about the seething undercurrents of German politics, and he expected the great rally of pan-Germanists called for the thirteenth to give the signal to set Europe ablaze. Whatever he had written in this sealed memorandum, it would be sensational enough, apparently, to stay von Dessau's hand. He was a mob orator of the first water, but a shrewd politician for all that.

Sir Charles Napier took the package out of his pocket. He examined it, looked at its official seals and signatures, and for one disquieting moment he felt the temptation to open it. After all, poor Seligmann was dead. Surely it would be prudent to ascertain the nature of his secret hold over Baron von Dessau?

No. That was not the way. To open the memorandum would be to dishonour himself, and betray Otto Seligmann's memory. He put the memorandum carefully back into his pocket, and left the secluded lodge.

4

The Smell of Evil

Detective Inspector Box hurried out of Whitehall Place and across the frosty cobbles fronting the complex of old buildings known as King James's Rents. He noted that a heavy four-wheeler had drawn up in Aberdeen Lane, near the stables, and that a heavily muffled constable up on the box had seen him, but not saluted. As he mounted the steps to the front vestibule, a neighbouring clock chimed eight.

Ahead of him, across the sanded floorboards, the glazed swing doors of his office beckoned him invitingly. He could see the fire blazing merrily in the fireplace at the far end of the room, and Jack Knollys doing some vigorous morning exercise with the poker, while talking to a man in the uniform of an inspector. The man had his back to the door, so Box couldn't see his face. No doubt he had something to do with the conveyance in Aberdeen Lane. He'd find out, in a moment.

Box had just returned the greeting of the constable on duty in the reception-room at the entrance, when he was stopped in his tracks by a voice from the landing at the top of the stone stairs that rose steeply from the vestibule to the floor above.

'Is that you, Box? Come up here, if you please. I'll not detain you more than five minutes.'

Superintendent Mackharness had evidently stationed himself on the upper landing to await Box's coming. Box mounted the stairs, and joined the superintendent in his dark front office on the first floor of King James's Rents. As always, the room smelt strongly of mildew and stale gas.

'Good morning, sir,' said Box. 'I believe you wanted to see me?'

'What? Well, obviously; otherwise I wouldn't have asked you to come up here.'

Box looked appraisingly at his superior officer, as he sat down behind his massive old desk, upon which he had neatly arrayed a collection of books and papers. Neatness was his watchword, as Box knew. His yellowish face was adorned with neatly trimmed mutton chop whiskers. His thin hair was neatly brushed and combed. His civilian frock coat was well brushed and smart. His voice, precisely tuned to the pitch of irascibility that he reserved for Box, was well enunciated, and surprisingly powerful for a man who was well over sixty, and beginning to feel his age.

'Just sit down there, will you, Box. I wanted to catch you as soon as you came in. You'll find Inspector Lewis from Chelsea downstairs. He's with Sergeant Knollys at the moment. He wants a detective down there, and I think you'd better be the one to go. I don't suppose you know yet what happened out there last night?'

Box recalled his breakfast that morning, in his cheerful set of bachelor rooms in Cardinal Court, a secluded enclave of old houses behind Fleet Street. Mrs Peach, his landlady, had treated him to a dramatic story of an explosion in Chelsea, which she had heard from a neighbour, a stableman, who had just returned from his night-shift at Chelsea Barracks. 'The night was turned to day, Mr Box,' she'd told him, as she deposited a plate of poached egg and haddock in front of him. 'They say it was a gas-leak what done it, but it sounds like foreigners to me. Russians. Or Prussians. And the master of the house blown to pieces. It doesn't bear thinking of.'

Box felt the presence of a kind of imp of the perverse, which came to him whenever Mackharness asked him a question that was designed to show off his imagined superior knowledge.

'No, sir,' said Box, 'I've heard nothing at all. What happened at Chelsea?'

Superintendent Mackharness eyed Box with a kind of defensive wariness.

'Heard nothing, hey? You should keep your ears to the ground, Box! Well, you'd better listen carefully while I tell you. No doubt you'll recall looking in on Dr Otto Seligmann's lecture last Saturday? Well, last night, Box, Dr Seligmann was blown to pieces in an explosion at his house in Chelsea.'

'Strewth!'

'As you say, Box, though I wish you could develop a wider range of epithets and expletives, especially when talking to me. What is right for the costermonger is not necessarily fitting for a police inspector. But the point is, Box — the point is . . . Where was I? Your constant interruptions interfere with my train of thought.'

'Dr Seligmann had been blown up in Chelsea — '

'Yes, that's it. And the interesting point is, Box, that Inspector Lewis requested us to take PC Kenwright with us out there. To Chelsea, I mean. Now, Kenwright's a uniformed man, and he's here at the Rents ostensibly to recuperate from fever; but perhaps you'll remember — '

'Yes, sir. Last year, when we investigated

80

the explosion in Euston Road. The Home Office moved in, and sent Mr Mack from Explosions to look at the pieces. Mr Mack was very impressed with the kind of help that PC Kenwright gave him. So maybe in this case — '

Mackharness waved his hand impatiently, as though to dismiss the whole topic. 'Yes, yes, Box, your logical deductions do you credit, but if you'd waited for me to finish, instead of interrupting — as you constantly do — I'd have said the same thing.'

'I'm sorry, sir. I would never knowingly — '

'Yes, yes, well never mind all that. Get out there, will you? Lewis came with a four-wheeler, so you can take Sergeant Knollys and PC Kenwright with you. Seligmann lived in a kind of square in Chelsea, somewhere behind the Physic Garden — Lavender Walk, it's called. The Chelsea Police are there, of course, but I want you to show the people in the house that Scotland Yard is interested in the case.'

'Perhaps it was a gas explosion, sir. We've had some corkers in that line, recently.'

'Yes, Box, perhaps it was.' Mackharness's voice held a mixture of irascibility and sarcastic humour. 'Or perhaps this building — the Belvedere, they called it — was struck by lightning. Or earthquake. Or it may have

81

been the Fenians. One way of finding out would be to go there, and investigate! Find out what Mr Mack's up to. The Home Office doesn't involve the Explosions Inspectorate for a domestic gas explosion. Go, now, Box, and talk to Inspector Lewis. Then get out there to Chelsea.'

★ ★ ★

Inspector Lewis stretched his hands out gratefully to the blazing fire. At last, he was beginning to feel warm. He wore a long serge uniform overcoat and regulation hat, but it had been keenly cold in the ruins of that garden tower place at Dr Seligmann's — cold, and soulless. Gas, everyone had whispered, but it hadn't been gas. He'd felt the evil in the dank air. You couldn't say that to fellow officers, or put it into a report. He straightened up and turned from the fire as the doors of the office swung open.

'Inspector Lewis? Box. Arnold Box. We've not met before. How are you?'

Lewis looked at the slim, smart man who had just erupted into the office. He was wearing a tightly buttoned fawn greatcoat, and carried a brown bowler hat. He looked more like a civilian than a policeman — but then, that's what a detective ought to look like. This Mr Box had a dashing sort of military look to him. What was he? Thirty-five? That carefully trimmed moustache made him look a bit older.

'I'm very well, thank you, Inspector Box. I've got a four-wheeler waiting to convey you out to Chelsea. I thought it best to see you here first, on your own ground.'

Box's visitor was a man nearing fifty, with a narrow, weatherbeaten face, and hunched shoulders. He was the kind of police officer who had spent many years on duties that kept him out of doors. There was a thin, hollow quality to his voice, suggestive of weakened lungs.

'Well, Mr Lewis, it's not much of a place, as you can see! The ceiling's black with soot from that old-fashioned gas mantle. It's a bad burner, but they won't replace it. And we've being trying to get them to paint the walls for years.'

'But these walls of yours, Mr Box, don't have ears. I'm not so sure about the kind of walls they have down our way, in Chelsea. So let me give you the gist of what happened last night.'

Inspector Lewis sat down on the edge of a chair near the fire. He had removed his braided uniform cap, and placed it on the crowded office table.

'Mr Box, there was a monstrous explosion last night, at half past eight, at Dr Otto Seligmann's house in Lavender Walk, Chelsea. The explosion occurred in a kind of fancy stone tower or summer house standing in the rear garden of the house. This tower was known as the Belvedere.'

Box sat on the opposite side of the table, writing in a notebook. He had donned small round gold spectacles, which made him look older than his years.

'And what was this Belvedere? What was special about it?'

'It was a library, Mr Box, where this German gentleman studied. There's another library in the house. My men are out there, you'll understand, keeping a watch over things. It's a terrible business. We all heard the explosion in Chelsea Police Station, and didn't wait for any one to call us in. We went round there as soon as we could, and arrived just after the fire engines — '

Lewis broke off as a gigantic uniformed police constable emerged from a tunnel-like passageway to the right of the fireplace. An impressive man by any standards, he had a flowing spade beard, which added to a natural gravity of manner. He was carrying a wooden tray, containing two steaming mugs of tea. Lewis watched as he placed his burden

84

carefully on the table. He was unaccountably pleased when the constable briefly stood to attention and saluted him.

'PC Kenwright, sir,' the big constable said. 'This here tea is sent with Sergeant Knollys' compliments. It's rare cold outside. This should warm you up a bit.'

Kenwright left the room the way he had come, and Inspector Lewis continued his story.

'Well, Mr Box, the fire was too strong for anyone to go in, though everyone in the garden was talking about a gentleman visitor who'd managed to burst the door down before we came — '

'A gentleman visitor? Tell me about him, Mr Lewis.'

'Well, he was a gentleman called Colin McColl, and he'd called to see Dr Seligmann by appointment. We got all this information out of the secretary, later, you understand, a German chap called Schneider; and from Mr Lodge, the butler. This Mr McColl managed to burst the door in — a heavy, iron door. Trying to rescue poor Dr Seligmann, you see. There was another visitor, who came just as this Mr McColl left. A young man called Fenlake — '

'Fenlake?' asked Box, sharply. 'Lieutenant Fenlake?'

'Yes, Mr Box, that's right! Do you know him?'

'I know of him. I know a young lady friend of his.'

'Well, this Lieutenant Fenlake, according to Mr Lodge, was the last person to see poor Dr Seligmann alive.'

'An interesting point. And what did you do next, Mr Lewis?'

'We stayed all night — us, and the fire brigade, I mean — and by first light this morning the fire had all but burnt itself out. We'd brought gas flares in, and worked by the light of them to find out what we could. We located what was left of Dr Seligmann just before dawn. A terrible affair, as I said. The ruins of a man . . . '

Inspector Lewis sipped his tea. His eyes, Box saw, held a renewed awareness of the sadness of things. There was no need for him to commiserate. Each knew that the other had witnessed terrible sights in the course of their often thankless duties.

'Oddly enough, Mr Lewis, I helped to police a meeting addressed by this Dr Seligmann only last Saturday. Shocking. Shocking altogether. And so you thought of us? Scotland Yard, I mean.'

'I did. There was the smell of evil all around, Mr Box, though you might think me foolish for talking like that. Then, just after six, Dr Janner, the Home Office forensic pathologist, arrived in a cab. That told me that something funny was in the wind. He'd brought another Home Office man with him, an old chap who said he was Mr Mack, from the Home Office Explosions Inspectorate.'

'Mr Mack's an old friend of ours here at the Yard. I know Dr Janner, too. What did he do?'

'He — well, he gathered the remains together. He and his assistants put them in a deal coffin, and conveyed them to the Chelsea Union mortuary. But it's time we set off, Mr Box. I want you to see the site of this atrocity with your own eyes.'

★   ★   ★

As they turned the corner into Aberdeen Lane, they were assailed by a sudden squall of hailstones. They hurried over the setts to the waiting four-wheeler, and by the time they had clambered in to the heavy vehicle, the hailstones had turned to tentative sleet. The constable on the box released the brake, and turned the horses' heads in the direction of Whitehall.

For a man on the small side, thought Inspector Lewis, Mr Box chose giants for his companions. PC Kenwright, sitting opposite him, was imposing enough, but the sergeant sitting beside him was massive, to put it mildly. An ugly customer, too, by the look of him. He had close-cropped yellow hair, and a livid scar running across his face from below the right eye to the left corner of his mouth.

Lewis caught the amused gleam in the sergeant's piercing blue eyes, and realized that he had been reading his thoughts. He felt himself blushing, but was spared the indignity by Box, who suddenly broke what he thought was becoming an embarrassed silence.

'Inspector Lewis, I didn't have time to introduce you properly back there at the Rents. This is my sergeant, Jack Knollys. He's from Croydon, originally.'

'Oh, Croydon? Really. Pleased to meet you, Sergeant.'

The heavy cab had reached Parliament Street, and Box glanced at the magnificent Italianate palace built by Sir Gilbert Scott to house the Home Office. It made him think for the moment of old Mr Mack, who had a little room somewhere in that impressive pile.

'And you reckon it wasn't a gas explosion, Mr Lewis? A gas leak?' Lewis shook his head decidedly.

'It wasn't gas, Mr Box. Two men from the Gas, Light and Coke Company came out within the hour, turned the gas off, and hammered the broken pipe flat. But it wasn't gas. It was as though a shell had exploded, or a magazine gone up. There's devilry behind it, and for my money it's not the Fenians this time. Still, that's for you to decide, Mr Box, when you've seen the place. The Belvedere, I mean.'

The cab turned into Broad Sanctuary, and proceeded at a good pace down Victoria Street. Evidently, the driver was following a well-known route of his own out to Chelsea. He'd turn into Buckingham Palace Road just opposite Grosvenor Gardens, then into Pimlico Road, and go round the long boundary wall of the Chelsea Royal Hospital.

'I must confess, Mr Lewis,' Box said, 'that I'm not well versed in these high-class German political thinkers, and how they live. What should I know about this house in Lavender Walk, and the folk who live there?'

Inspector Lewis coughed, and drew a sleeve across his mouth. This infernal cold! The old cab smelt of stale tobacco and damp straw. He'd be glad when they got to Chelsea.

'Well, Mr Box, Dr Seligmann's house has always been a popular sort of place. We've a lot of thinkers and artists and so forth living in Chelsea. There's always been a lot of coming and going at Dr Seligmann's. Poor old Mr Carlyle used to visit there, years ago, and he'd gabble away in German with Dr Seligmann and the other Germans in the house.'

Sergeant Knollys suddenly spoke, causing Lewis to start in surprise.

'Any Englishmen, sir? Coming and going, I mean?'

Sergeant Knollys' voice was well enunciated and slightly mocking. The man looked like a thug, but was evidently something else. He dressed well, too. There was more to Mr Box's sergeant than mere bulk and brawn.

'Yes, Sergeant, there were some Englishmen from time to time. Learned men from the universities, and more than one Member of Parliament. Sir Charles Napier, the Under-Secretary, has called there more than once. He and Dr Seligmann were old friends. But usually there'd be a lot of foreigners turning up, some of them with huge pointed moustaches and what I'd call hectoring voices. Germans, most of them, I'd say.'

'And who's inside the house at present?' asked Box.

'Well, there's Mr Schneider, who was Dr Seligmann's personal secretary. Very stiff and foreign — all heel-clicking, and so forth — but a very decent, honest kind of man, I think. I've passed the time of day with him

90

more than once. I told Mr Schneider that I was going to Scotland Yard. Everybody else seems to have been prostrated with grief. So Mr Schneider said.

'Then there's Count Czerny — C-Z-E-R-N-Y. They say he's an Hungarian, and that may well be so, but he speaks better English than most English people. I don't know exactly what he was supposed to do in the house, Mr Box, but he lives there, and was very close to Dr Seligmann.'

The clumsy four-wheeler rumbled its way out of Pimlico Road, and proceeded along Royal Hospital Road, which at that point was flanked by spacious, tree-lined gardens. They were passing the gracious buildings that housed the Chelsea Pensioners, and for a fleeting moment Box imagined that they were in the countryside.

'And then,' Inspector Lewis continued, 'there's Miss Seligmann — Miss Ottilie, as she's called. She's Dr Seligmann's niece. She's little more than a girl, very pretty, and very nice to the English staff. I don't know what she's like with the Germans, as I don't speak German. I think she just lives in the house because she's no parents. Came here six months ago, she did.'

'What about the staff?'

'There's Mr Lodge, the butler, who I

mentioned to you before. A very nice man, he is, fond of a glass or two of stout when the fancy takes him. I know a niece of his in the Borough. There's a full house of English servants, and Mr Lodge is in charge of them. They're all local folk. And there's Mrs Poniatowski, who's the housekeeper. All starch and vinegar, she is. I rather think — '

Lewis broke off as a clutch of lively men in raincoats and bowler hats suddenly appeared at the corner of a narrow lane, waving their arms excitedly. Some of them were carrying notebooks. Inspector Box smiled.

'The gentlemen of the Press, unless I'm very much mistaken,' he said. 'So the flies are already buzzing round the jampot. I take it we've arrived at Lavender Walk?'

'We have, Mr Box. It's just along that little lane. I don't know why it's called Lavender Walk. It's more like a little square. We'll leave the cab here, and walk down beside the hospital wall. Look at those men! What do they expect me to say?'

'Would you like me to vouchsafe them a few words, Mr Lewis? I'm used to them, you know.'

'I'd be very grateful if you would, Mr Box. Flies around the jampot? Vultures, more like!'

As soon as the four police officers alighted from the cab, they were surrounded by the reporters. Each represented a different newspaper, but they also had a team spirit of their own, a communal identity. Box leapt on to a low wall at the side of the road, and immediately the gaggle of men congregated eagerly in front of him.

'Now, gents,' said Box, in a loud, clear voice, 'you all know me, and I won't let you down. This is a very sinister business, and there are implications that, at the moment, it would not be prudent to make public. So if you come along at noon today, to the Clarence Vaults in Victoria Street, I'll make a statement, and answer any questions. For the moment, though, I'll ask you to disperse. Good day.'

The reporters seemed very satisfied with Box's words. They moved away slowly in the general direction of Ormond Gate, chattering among themselves, and glancing back occasionally at the cab, which had been halted at the side of the road. The driver had come down from the box gratefully and shut himself up snug inside.

There had been a sickly sun shining for most of the journey, but now the fog began to descend with greater determination. The four policemen made their way into Lavender Walk, which proved to be a number of very ancient houses of modest size arranged around a patch of green. A few people were standing around, apparently heedless of the cold rain. They were talking quietly together, and looking up at one of the houses, an old Tudor dwelling with mullioned windows and carved beams. The front door stood wide open, despite the bitter cold. The onlookers parted to make way for the policemen. Box was conscious of their curious glances as they stepped over the threshold of the stricken house.

★   ★   ★

'Behold, Herr Schneider, the majesty of the British Law!'

Ottilie Seligmann was looking down at the neglected garden from one of the few rear windows of Dr Seligmann's house to have escaped the destruction of the previous night. The secretary, stiff and respectful, stood on the landing behind her. He had heard the Scotland Yard men being admitted to the house a few minutes earlier. Lodge would have conducted them through the hall passage, and out into the garden.

Ottilie turned to face the secretary. He looked pale and drawn, though she could see that he was making a monumental effort to preserve his Saxon formality.

'Come here, Fritz, and stand beside me. What are you afraid of? God in Heaven, do you think I will bite you? Look, here are the men from Scotland Yard. The dapper little man in the smart fawn coat — he, without doubt, will be the inspector. The other one, the hulking brute with the scarred face — that will be the sergeant.'

Ottilie watched as the cold winter rain turned suddenly to thick sleet, which began to freeze instantly on the grass and leaves. Towering up from the twisted and charred trees, the burnt-out Belvedere, she thought, looked like a sightless skull.

'See, the constable on guard in the grounds has saluted, and the little inspector has raised his hat. So has the hulking brute. How formal — the ballet of the British Law! But there will be no dancing, my good Fritz! Not yet, at least.'

Ottilie moved further along the landing where she could look out of a round window almost opposite the ruined Belvedere.

'Look, the brute sergeant has clambered up on to the ruins in that wretched building. He turns, and offers his hand to the little inspector. Soon no doubt, they will seek out the sad old man who crawled over the debris earlier, by the light of the flares. He came in the dark hours, that old one. He looks like a walrus. Bah! It does not interest me.'

Ottilie looked at Fritz Schneider with a sudden stab of guilt. He had listened patiently to her chatter, but it was clear that his mind was elsewhere. How could it be otherwise? He would be shocked by her callousness, but would be too in awe of her to ask the reason for her attitude. It would not, perhaps, be prudent to make a confidant of him.

Schneider, she knew, had entered Seligmann's service when he was still renowned as a scholar, and Schneider himself was well versed in the mysteries of old Germanic tongues. Like many Saxons, he had been schooled in the virtue of dumb loyalty. He had never expressed the slightest interest in the politics of his own or any other country.

'You, see, don't you, Fritz, that all is over here? You should go back to Germany, to Leipzig, your native city. You have a sister there, no? You will not lack for money. Go back! You see the ruin here. There may also be danger. So make plans soon to return to Leipzig.'

'And you, *Fräulein*? What will you do?'

'Me? I have my plans, good Fritz. Meanwhile, there will be much to do here, repairing the damaged house, and putting things to rights. The police, also, they will demand attention. But for you, do as I say. *So, sehr geerhte gnädiger* Herr Schneider: return to Leipzig!'

★ ★ ★

Detective Inspector Box blinked upwards through the sleet at the shattered rear windows of the house. He was in time to see two pale faces regarding him from an unbroken circular casement, which looked as though it was designed to throw light on to a staircase.

'So, Sergeant Knollys,' he said, 'our arrival has not gone unnoticed! The good folk in the house will be shocked and stunned, no doubt. But they can spare time for a little peep at us from the upper storey. That's human nature, Sergeant. There's something to be learned there, I've no doubt. And this, I take it, is the Belvedere.'

The devastated building loomed up at them out of the mist. The ruined entrance framed a virtual hillock of shattered stone and timber, which was being delicately covered with the gossamer touch of unmelting sleet. A buckled iron door hung inward from its hinges, and on the grass nearby lay what they both took to be the plank with which Colin McColl had made his assault.

Knollys all but leapt across the threshold, and gave a hand to Box, who clambered up after him.

They were standing on a tumulus of debris. Pieces of charred beam and twisted metal protruded from the ruin like broken teeth. They could see the remains of a chimney breast, and a great, gaunt gas chandelier, twisted and crushed, lay straddled across the hillock like a dead giant spider. Knollys stooped, and pulled a fragment of leather from the ruin.

'Looks like the spine of a book,' he said, half to himself. He threw the fragment down again, and pulled up his collar against the rapidly thickening snow.

Box touched one of the walls. He fancied that the brickwork was still warm.

'Look at these walls, Sergeant! Eighteen inches of stone, then lined with brick. A sledgehammer to crack a nut! You can smell foul gas trapped in the foundations. And something else . . . What was it Mr Lewis said? 'The smell of evil'. Maybe he was right. There's nothing useful that we can do here at the moment. Let's go and find Mr Mack. He and his searchers will have been through this place with a fine-toothed comb. He'll tell us for certain what happened here.'

They found Mr Mack sitting in a small brick shed that seemed to be growing out of the old garden wall beyond a clump of stunted trees. They had to stoop through the low door of what Box assumed to have been at one time the hub of a gardener's empire. From the state of the grounds it was evident that horticulture had not been among the late Dr Seligmann's interests.

Mr Mack was sitting hunched over a small cast-iron stove, which was burning rather smokily. His watery eyes were half closed, and his prominent nose was very red. It was impossible to read his expression fully, as most of his face was concealed by a straggling yellow moustache. He was puffing away at an old briar pipe, and not for the first time Box thought that he looked for all the world like a cocky-watchman. PC Kenwright was standing impassively beside him.

The iron stove spluttered away. A sound of hammering came to their ears, and Box saw that the paved yard behind the house had been commandeered by a number of glaziers and joiners. He closed the shed door, and sat down. Mr Mack opened his eyes, and began to speak.

'This explosion, Mr Box, was caused by a

device concealed in a stout leather valise of some kind — a device that you, I suppose, would call a detonator. I'll not teach you your job, but find out who brought a leather valise into that Belvedere and left it there. The device in the valise was controlled by a timing mechanism, set to operate at eight-thirty, which it did.'

Mr Mack stopped speaking, and emitted a sound that could have been a sigh, or a suppressed chuckle.

'Now here's the interesting bit, Mr Box. There was already a massive cache of high explosive in the building. I rather fancy it was concealed in a crate of some sort — a box of books, to judge from what we've found in the ruins. Whatever it was, it must have been brought into the Belvedere on an earlier occasion. When the valise exploded, what we call a 'brisant' effect occurred — a kind of explosive sympathy, if you see what I mean, which sent the whole thing up sky high. Beautiful. A beautiful job.'

Mr Mack gazed morosely at the stove for a while, drawing at his old pipe. Box remained quiet. It was best not to interrupt the expert when his thoughts were running on the task in hand.

'It wasn't the Fenians, Mr Box. And it wasn't Murder Malthus and his gang. I can't tell you much yet until I've done some tests, but from the smell in there I know that we're dealing with dynamite. Nothing fancy, you know: just the ordinary stuff you'll find in mines or quarries. I can't be very specific, but I reckon it's come from the Feissen Werke armaments concern in Bohemia.'

'"Can't be specific'? You fill me with awe, Mr Mack. It's like magic. You're a shining ornament, if I may say so.'

A strangled noise from Mr Mack suggested that he was laughing. He was never unpleased if someone chose to praise his efforts.

'It's like wines, Mr Box. Some folk can tell a claret from the smell of the cork, or identify a brandy blindfold. Well, I can often sniff out explosives by the smell. Nitro-glycerine. Porous silica . . . The bouquet, Mr Box.'

Mr Mack laughed again, and then began to cough, as there was a lot of pungent smoke in the shed. He stooped down, and with a poker opened the small iron door at the stove's base. The air rushed in and presently there was a cheerful blaze, and a little shower of sparks shot out from the rim of the lid on top of the stove.

'Oh, Lord, Mr Mack,' said Box, 'you must be inspired! Did you see those sparks? That stove. It's like a little Belvedere. Open the door at the bottom and the fire rushes out at

101

the top. Didn't this McColl realize that? Or maybe — '

Inspector Box was silent for a moment. His mind was on the edge of a discovery, but its exact nature eluded him. If only he could think more clearly!

Mr Mack lumbered to his feet.

'Well, Mr Box,' he said, 'I'll leave all that to you, as is right and proper. Now, I'm not given to offering advice where it's not my business to do so, but I've already had a quiet word with PC Kenwright here, and he agrees with what I've suggested. He and I have worked together before, as you know, which is why I took the liberty of speaking to him.'

'And what have you suggested, Mr Mack?'

'I suggest that you sift through every piece of dust and debris left in that Belvedere, and in these gardens, until you've found everything that might be of relevance to this crime — this murder, for murder it is. There's bits of all sorts in there — fragments of paper, and leather, bits of china and clockwork. All kinds of shattered things. Let PC Kenwright here sift through the lot, and take his finds back to that drill hall of yours at King James's Rents — if you're agreeable, that is, Mr Box.'

'I am, Mr Mack. PC Kenwright's a giant of a man, but he's got sensitive hands.'

'Good. I'll send a Home Office van down

here late this afternoon, and you can beg some empty ammunition boxes from Chelsea Barracks, or the Duke of York's. I'll leave three of my men here to help. I'll have to go now: I'm wanted back in Whitehall. Goodbye, Mr Box. I'll send you a written report later today. Meanwhile, take my advice. Sift.'

5

A House of Cards

Dr Seligmann's study was at the front of the house, and had thus been largely unaffected by the previous night's destruction. The long room, with an ancient window looking out on to Lavender Walk, seemed agreeably comfortable. An ample mahogany desk stood to the left of the fireplace, and near it was a small, baize-covered card-table, upon which a deck of playing-cards had been carelessly thrown down.

'Mr Lodge,' said Box to the elderly butler, 'my sergeant and I will need to talk to those members of the family and household who were here last night. We need to see them now, you understand. The secretary — Mr Schneider, isn't it? — can you send him along to see us straight away?'

'I will ask Mr Schneider to come along at once, sir. Count Czerny has just expressed a desire to speak to you. He returned just over half an hour ago — '

'Returned?'

'Yes, sir. Count Czerny was not here last

night. He fulfilled a dinner engagement at his club, and stayed the night there.'

'Did he, now? Well, we'll be happy to see Count Czerny when we've finished talking to Mr Schneider, and to the lady of the house. I take it that she's still on the premises?'

'Miss Ottilie is upstairs in her private sitting-room. I will inform her that you wish to see her.'

While Lodge was speaking, Inspector Box's eyes had been drawn to a painted heraldic shield hanging above the fireplace. The shield depicted a black eagle on a white ground, edged with red. The eagle's head bore a royal crown, its wings were spread wide, and its talons grasped an orb and sceptre.

'The arms of the old Kingdom of Prussia,' said Box. 'Presumably it reminded Dr Seligmann of happier days. I must confess, Sergeant Knollys, that I don't much care for that particular bird, or for its offspring. And over there, in that alcove, there's a framed photograph of the German emperor, William II — the Kaiser, as he calls himself. There's not much to choose between the two of them, in my book. That eagle's on the lookout for prey, and so is that mad fellow on the wall.'

Box withdrew his glance from the offending heraldry and examined the mantelpiece, which held an array of well-thumbed books kept upright between two ebony book-ends. The titles seemed to be in German, though some of them, Box saw, were in English. He was suddenly overwhelmed with the same conviction that had come to him earlier in the frozen garden — a feeling that he had overlooked some obvious anomaly, and that, ever since his arrival at Chelsea, he had been fed with misleading morsels of information by a source which he could not identify.

Voices in the passage announced the arrival of the secretary. Box sat down behind Dr Seligmann's desk, and motioned to Sergeant Knollys to station himself in an armchair near the window. The door of the study opened rather cautiously, and Dr Seligmann's secretary came into the room.

Inspector Box looked at the elderly man who stood stiffly in front of the desk. He was very formally dressed, in tightly buttoned black frock coat and pin-striped trousers, but behind the man's formal mask of respectful attention Box could discern a suggestion of unquenchable defiance. Schneider's bearing reminded him strongly of his own attitude when confronted by Superintendent Mackharness.

'You are Mr Schneider?' asked Box.

'Fritz Schneider, sir. I had the honour to be Dr Seligmann's personal secretary.'

106

Box watched as the German secretary glanced briefly at Knollys, and then sat down unbidden in a chair placed in front of the desk. He fixed his eyes not on Box, but on the leather blotter, the wooden calendar with its little knobs for changing the date, the crystal ink wells, the ivory pen and the little brass clock arranged on the desk. They were familiar, everyday things which had suddenly become memorials of his vanished master.

'I've only a couple of things to ask you, Mr Schneider. It would seem that the last person to see Dr Seligmann alive was a man called Fenlake. Lieutenant Fenlake. I'd like you to tell me about him, if you will.'

When Schneider spoke, it was clear that his mind was only partly on what Box had asked him.

'Fenlake . . . yes, that was his name. But he was not the assassin of my poor master. This room, Herr Box, was Dr Seligmann's study — his bureau for public affairs. He was a great philologist, but his academic library was housed in the Belvedere, and so perished with him. This study, secure at the front of the house, was where he wrote and strove and struggled for peace. Here are the year-books, the political commentaries, the minutes of meetings — all the desiderata of a political crusade — '

'And a man called Lieutenant Fenlake was the last person to see Dr Seligmann alive. You say he was not the assassin — '

Herr Schneider sat upright in his chair and looked haughtily at Box.

'And you disagree? Then I am wrong. I apologize. Evidently you think differently. The police, of course, are very clever. So, yes, he was the last person to see Dr Seligmann alive, and I will tell you about him. The Herr Doktor apprised me earlier in the day that a young gentleman called Lieutenant Arthur Fenlake would be visiting him. He instructed me to conduct Mr Fenlake to the Belvedere as soon as he arrived.'

For a fleeting moment, Arnold Box recalled the blonde girl with the cornflower-blue eyes who had accompanied Miss Whittaker and himself to the Savoy Theatre on New Year's Eve. Her absent beau and Dr Seligmann's visitor were surely one and the same person — the young officer in the 107th Field Battery of the Royal Artillery who had been warned off from Mr Gordon's gaming hell in Eagle Street, Holborn. Or perhaps not. A man bent on mischief could call himself any name he liked . . .

'What was he like? This Lieutenant Fenlake, I mean.'

'Well, Herr Inspector, he was much like the

usual run of young gentlemen of that sort — well dressed for his generation, smart, of soldierly bearing. I am surprised to hear that he was an assassin. He said nothing to me, either at that time, or later, when I conducted him to the front door. What is the English expression? A man of few words.'

'I don't suppose you know why he came to see Dr Seligmann?'

'No, sir, I do not. The Herr Doktor received many people of all ranks and stations. He was renowned throughout the world — he conferred with the legislatures of the nations. Though he has perished at the assassin's hand, his name will endure for ever!'

Box sighed. He looked at the secretary, and experienced a curious sensation of affinity with the man mingled with a rapidly growing impatience with his flowery sentiments. He thought: he's doing it on purpose, to annoy me. He was a lively enough man, despite his prim exterior, but he was in imminent danger of turning himself into a bore on the subject of his late master's virtues.

'Are you in charge of the daily arrangements in this study, Mr Schneider?' asked Box. 'Looking after the blotters, trimming the pens, and so forth?'

'What? Yes, so I am. To you, no doubt,

these things are trivial: the labours of a servant. But the Herr Doktor was a man of great affairs. It was not for him to busy himself with the minutiae of study and office — '

'Oh, quite, Mr Schneider,' said Box. 'So why doesn't the calendar show today's date? Today is the 4th January. This calendar reckons it's Wednesday, the 25th.'

He turned the wooden calendar round for the secretary to read.

'But there's no need to answer that question, Mr Schneider. Instead, you can tell me about the other visitor. The man who came into the house carrying a briefcase. Was he, too, expected?'

Schneider seemed not to hear. He was looking in puzzlement at the calendar.

'That calendar — I have not been in here since yesterday ... Someone has been tampering with it. I will speak to Mrs Poniatowski. Everything in this room is sacred ... The man with the briefcase, you ask? Yes, he was expected. There was no secret about Mr Colin McColl. He came from Mr Quaritch's bookshop in Piccadilly with some rare pages of manuscript for Dr Seligmann to examine. Those pages — ah! They, too, will have been incinerated. But I digress. Our butler, Lodge, admitted Mr

McColl to the house, and I heard him talking to the Herr Doctor in the hall passage.'

'Can you recall any of their conversation?'

'Dr Seligmann told him how much he regretted having to be involved in politics. He spoke of his duty to Germany.'

'And what did Mr Colin McColl say?'

'He made some technical remarks about philology.'

'About philology. And did you understand, Mr Schneider, what those technical remarks meant?'

'I did, sir.'

The German secretary closed his lips in a sort of tight smirk. Box glanced across at Sergeant Knollys, who smiled and shook his head. Inspector Box leaned forward across Dr Seligmann's desk, joined his fingers together in a delicate cradle, and treated Schneider to a rather wolfish smile.

'Your English is excellent, Mr Schneider,' he said. 'So maybe you know the English expression 'like getting blood out of a stone'. I'd be unwilling to think of you as a stone. So will you please tell me exactly, or as well as you can remember, what Mr Colin McColl actually said? Perhaps you think I'm too dense to understand clever matters, but in fact that isn't the point.'

'Sir, I stand corrected,' said Schneider,

blushing, either through embarrassment or vexation. 'My apologies. I was not aware that you were a specialist in languages. Dr Seligmann asked the young man whether he was acquainted with his scholarly work.'

'Did he, now? And what did Mr McColl have to say to that?'

'Mr McColl replied: 'Yes, indeed. We have all heard of Seligmann's Law of Unaccented Syllables. And who does not still consult your honoured *Specimens of Anglo-Saxon Verse?*' As far as I can recollect, those were his very words.'

'So you think he was a genuine scholar?'

'But yes, of course. And then, later — what heroism! Such men as he are rare. At the height of the hideous blaze he rushed into the garden, seized a plank, and ran full tilt at the Belvedere door. He burst the door off its hinges — too late, alas! to save the Herr Doktor from the flames. What selflessness! What — '

'At last!' cried Box. 'A little light's showing through the gloom. A few straightforward words have emerged from the jungle of verbiage! He seized a plank, did he?'

Box stood up, and looked down on the startled German. His voice was stern, and almost comically menacing.

'Why should he seize a plank?'

'Why shouldn't he?' quavered Herr Schneider.

'Because, Mr Schneider, in the best regulated households, one doesn't have planks to seize. Planks — planks are thick, brutal lengths of wood, invariably caked with dried cement. They don't form part of the decoration of a gentleman's establishment. Why was this heroic Mr McColl able to find a plank so easily?'

The little self-satisfied smirk returned to the secretary's face. He sat upright in his chair. He was determined that this chirpy Cockney policeman was not going to get the upper hand.

'Mr McColl was able to find a plank, Herr Inspector, because yesterday morning two workmen arrived to point an area of brickwork over the rear dining-room window. They left the plank, and a few other implements of their trade, on the grass.'

'Well, thank you, Mr Schneider, you've been a great help — a fund of information, so to speak. In a few minutes' time I hope to have a word with Count Czerny. Perhaps you'd tell me what kind of count he is? We don't have counts in England, you know, though I believe France is snowed under with them. He's not a Frenchman, is he?'

'No, sir. And he's not a Prussian count,

113

either. He's an Austrian nobleman, sir — what in our language we call a count of the Roman-German Empire. I expect you are looking forward to having the honour of conversing with His Excellency.'

The secretary bowed, but could not resist giving the ghost of a smirk as he left the room. Box glanced at the playing-cards thrown down on the little baize-covered table, and smiled, almost in spite of himself. Was Mr Schneider the joker in this particular pack? Perhaps. For all his German formality, there had been an irreverent air about the secretary that Box had found appealing. The joker . . .

Box picked up the wooden calendar, and turned the knobs until the correct day and date showed in the windows: Wednesday, 4 January 1893.

'Sergeant Knollys,' said Box, 'when we've finished in here, we'll go outside, and get one of those men working on the repairs to look at that wall. The one that Schneider says needed to be pointed. I don't believe it. It's a plant. It's the same trick that Smiler Carmichael used in the Hartwell sweet-shop murder in '86. That plank was left there for this McColl to use. He knew it was there. And so he was able to burst the door in. It's a plant — '

The butler, Lodge, appeared at the door.

'Sir,' he said, 'Miss Seligmann is here to speak to you.'

Arnold Box banished all thoughts of secretaries and planks as Miss Seligmann came into the room, and stood hesitating by the chair near the desk. How charming she looked! Surely she was no more than twenty, or perhaps twenty-two? She was wearing a very becoming black silk dress relieved by white lace at the neck and cuffs — not quite mourning attire, but certainly the next best thing.

'Pray sit down, Miss Seligmann,' said Box, gently. 'There's nothing to be afraid of.'

'I'm sure there isn't, Inspector. And I can assure you that I'm not afraid of *you*!'

Her voice was clear and firm, very pleasant in tone, and with a slight foreign intonation. Before Box could frame a reply, the German girl launched into speech.

'My name is Ottilie Seligmann. I am the daughter of the late Ernst Seligmann of Mecklenburg — from Rostock, which is a city there. You have heard of it, no? And so I am the niece of the late Dr Otto Seligmann. I have lived with my uncle since my father died six months ago. I am twenty-two years old.'

Knollys stirred in his chair near the window. Glancing in his direction, Box was disconcerted to see the look of frozen hostility on his sergeant's face. Perhaps he was one of those men who were easily offended by pertness of Miss Ottilie's kind.

'Thank you, Miss Seligmann. My purpose today is really to see the various members of the household. I have seen your late uncle's secretary, Mr Schneider, and in a few moments I hope to speak to the Austrian gentleman, Count Czerny — '

'Czerny? Bah! He is one piece of my late uncle's baggage that can go. Out he goes! He is a mountebank, a professional diner at other men's tables. Do you know how he speaks? Like the English milord. He was brought up in England, at a school called Stowe, and then at Cambridge. And yet this Austro-Englishman claimed to have a vast web of confidants throughout Europe, and Uncle Otto believed it all. For years and years he has had his feet under poor uncle's dining-table. He will go. I have told him so, this very morning. And that Polish woman. She sneers at us all, and bullies the English staff. This house is mine, now. She, too, will go.'

Ottilie looked quizzically and rather tauntingly at Box. A fascinating young lady, he thought, but she can't be allowed to have the last word.

116

'Very interesting, miss, to hear your arrangements for the future. And I take it that you have been devastated by your uncle's murder?'

It was a shrewd thrust, and it went home. The black lashes dropped to veil the bright blue eyes, and there was a little silence. Ottilie drummed the fingers of her right hand impatiently on the desk in front of her. Finally she sat up straight in her chair and fixed her glance on the inspector once again.

'My uncle was kind and good. You must catch the men who killed him and hang them high on the gallows. They are wicked. But no; I am not devastated. Fritz is devastated — Herr Schneider, you know. He was devoted to Uncle Otto, though he is a Saxon ox, and doesn't care to parade his sorrow. Me, I will go back to Germany. I have no part in all this *politik*. When my uncle's money comes to me, I will dance, and wear fine clothes, and go to Court in Berlin. I will look for a noble youth and beckon him to me, and we will marry. There will be fine children — noble boys and beautiful girls. That, then, is Ottilie. You have seen her and you have heard her.'

'Thank you, miss. You're very frank, a point which I very much appreciate. We'll talk further, perhaps.'

Ottilie suddenly smiled at him. It was a captivating smile.

'You are not angry with me? You will shake hands, yes?'

'Certainly, miss. And of course I'm not angry with you. Not at all!' Inspector Box gravely shook hands with Ottilie Seligmann. She half bowed to him, and glided out of the room. Box sat down again.

'Phew!' he said. 'There's a charmer, if you like, Sergeant Knollys. A very enchanting young lady, quite frank and fearless — '

'Tickled your fancy, did she, sir?' There was genuine amusement in Sergeant Knollys' voice, though Box could hear the exasperation lurking behind it.

' "Tickled my fancy'? Really, Sergeant, I don't know where you get these coarse expressions from. I thought she was a charming and brave young lady. I'm sorry you've taken a dislike to her.'

'And what card would you pick for her, sir? The Queen of Hearts? 'I am twenty-two years old'! Thirty-two, more like it — '

There came a stir and bustle at the door, and a tall, ramrod-stiff giant of a man, blond and blue-eyed, all but erupted into the room. The somnolent air of the study seemed to be agitated, as though the man had been accompanied by a blast of wintry air. And yet,

Box realized, there was a stillness about this man, an air of calm command underlying a natural volatility.

'Detective Inspector Box? I am Count Czerny. I flatter myself that I was the late Dr Seligmann's closest confidant. I place myself at your disposal.'

Box was startled by Count Czerny's faultless English. It held not the slightest trace of a foreign accent. True, he sported a short, trimmed beard, and wore a rimless monocle screwed into his right eye, but unless you knew the man's name and nationality, you'd swear he was an English gentleman. Box was surprised to see that Czerny was no more than forty years old. He had assumed that old Dr Seligmann's confidant would have been nearer to him in age.

'Good day, Count Czerny,' said Box. 'Sit down, if you will. First, sir, I'd like to get clear in my mind your standing in Dr Seligmann's entourage.'

Count Czerny thought for a moment before replying. He removed the monocle from his eye and slipped it into his waistcoat pocket. The absence of the monocle made him look even more English.

'I was Otto Seligmann's secret eye on the centre of Europe, Mr Box. As an Austrian subject, I was well placed to advise him on the close machinations of the dangerous war-parties in the lands of the Austrian Empire — in Hungary, in Bosnia, and in Serbia. All these things I know about through a network of contacts in the capitals of Central Europe.'

Count Czerny glanced across towards the window, where Sergeant Knollys was busy writing in his notebook. He frowned slightly, and then continued.

'I am the successor to Dr Seligmann in his struggle for peace, and for a lasting coincidence of interests between the German and British Empires. That work will go on. But I am faced with tiresome difficulties. You have just seen Ottilie — Miss Seligmann — I think?'

'I have, sir. A most attractive and personable young lady.'

'Yes, yes. Maybe so.'

Count Czerny suddenly flushed, and banged a fist on the table.

'But she is stubborn, and a vixen, and a selfish little baggage! She thinks of nothing but fashion, and parties, and how she will spend her uncle's hard-earned money. I have been back from Town only half an hour, and already things have happened. Yes, they have happened.'

Count Czerny scowled, and bit his lip.

'What kind of things have happened, sir?' asked Box.

'This morning — minutes ago, you understand? — I attempted to convey my horror of last night's atrocity to Miss Seligmann. And what does she do? She quells me with a glance. If looks could kill, I, too, would be a dead man, now. 'Czerny', she says, 'you are a fool. It is all in the past. This crusade, this politicking, it was my uncle's hobby. It interested him. But now it is done. Go back to Germany'.

'I was astonished, stunned. 'But what of all the books and records in the library? Surely',' I said, 'you will not abandon those?' 'You may take them with you', she said, 'as long as you go!' Then she stamped her foot and stormed off. So I will do as she commands, and return to Germany. The work can go forward from there.'

Count Czerny clasped his strong hands together, and glanced at both men briefly. He seemed to be making up his mind to reveal some intimate secret.

'Sergeant,' he said, 'will you please close that notebook for a moment? I am going to tell you gentlemen some sensitive information, which is best left unwritten — for all our sakes. Our household here at Chelsea is breaking up, and I must share this knowledge with you before I go.'

Count Czerny paused for a moment. He glanced at a heavy gold signet ring that he wore, and unconsciously traced with his finger the image of an imperial eagle embossed on it.

'There is in Germany today, gentlemen,' he continued, 'a growing network of brother-hoods and societies which see war as the ultimate endorsement of the validity of the German Empire. The members of these parties know — or think they know — that war with Britain will set Europe aflame, and that from that conflagration a new, cleansed Europe will be born.'

Box's view of Count Czerny was undergo-ing revision. Surely Miss Ottilie had been gravely mistaken in dismissing him as a mountebank? Perhaps she was too immature — or too frivolous — to realize that he had important things to say.

'Among those fanatics,' Czerny continued, 'the most dangerous organization is called *Die Eidgenossenschaft*. You will find its members in Germany, in Austria, in the Balkans, in France, and — yes! — here in England. I take it that you don't understand German? No, well, that's understandable. But a good rendering of those German words would be 'The Linked Ring'. There are some folk in England who already employ that translation.'

'The Linked Ring . . . '

'Yes, Mr Box. I believe it was members of the Linked Ring who wrote to Otto — to Dr Seligmann — from Bonn, pretending to be from the university there, and telling him of a present of books that they were sending him. I cannot prove that, but it is so. They appealed to his vanity as a scholar, you see, and he rose to their bait. As for the rest — the terrible assassination — well, it was *my* fault! It was as though I had done the deed myself . . . '

Count Czerny held his head between his hands and groaned.

'That accursed crate, Mr Box, was delivered to the house only yesterday afternoon. It was at my suggestion that Otto had it taken out to the Belvedere. 'Let it alone until tomorrow,' I said. 'You've visitors coming tonight. You and Schneider can open it in the morning'.

'Late in the afternoon I set off for my club. Schneider tells me that one of Otto's two visitors last night brought a device with him that detonated the explosives concealed in that crate. By advising him to take it out to the Belvedere, Mr Box, I unwittingly sentenced my old friend to death!'

6

The Man in the Mist

'Begging your pardon, sir,' said the bashful young man in overalls, 'but there's nothing wrong with this wall. It don't need pointing, and if you was to try, you'd make a right mess of it. A plank? No, you don't need a plank for work like that. A ladder's all you need, and there's no ladder there, as you can see.'

Box smiled encouragingly at the young workman, who stood twisting his cap in his hands.

'What's your name, my boy?' he asked.

'George French, sir.'

'Well done, George French, you're a credit to your trade, and you've helped the police. I'll write your name down in my report, and there you'll stand, when the history of this case comes to be written.'

The lad looked mightily pleased with Box's words. He smiled, shuffled a bit, and then returned to the group of men who were busy repairing the ravages of the previous night's outrage. Box turned to Knollys.

'What did you think of Count Czerny?' he

asked. 'I'm thinking of those playing-cards . . . He seemed a worthwhile kind of man to me — sharp, and shrewd. I see him at the moment as the King of Diamonds.'

'You might be right, sir. But he wasn't here last night, and there might have been a reason for that. And he told us a lot of interesting things, but that might have been to disarm us. So maybe Count Czerny's the Knave, after all.'

Box made no reply. He was watching a procession of dim figures, shepherded by Constable Kenwright, who were carrying boxes and buckets. They disappeared into some obscure area of the grounds behind the Belvedere. It was still bitterly cold. Box glanced briefly up at the house, and then turned to Sergeant Knollys.

'I don't like this, Sergeant,' he said. 'I suspect that there are peculiar things going on in that house. You wouldn't think an intimate member of that family had just been foully murdered. Maybe Dr Seligmann's murder was a political assassination. Or maybe it was a well-laid plot to do away with a man for some dark private motive, cleverly presented as an assassination. I don't trust any of them. Not even the Queen of Hearts.'

Box looked across the misty white garden towards the stunted grove of trees, where a thin column of wood-smoke still rose from the chimney of the brick garden shed.

'Sergeant,' he said, 'go back into the house, and try to get Mr Lodge, the butler, into a quiet corner somewhere. See if you can get him to tell you about these peculiar people from his point of view. When you've finished here, I want you to go back to town, and call on Chaplin's, the carriers at Victoria Station. Find out about that crate, and how it got through Customs filled with dynamite. Then call on Mr Bernard Quaritch, the bookseller, in Piccadilly. Maybe he'll tell you that there's no such person as Colin McColl. Or maybe not. We'll see.'

'What will you do, sir?'

'I'll stay here for a while, and see how PC Kenwright's getting on. Then I'll hare it back to Victoria Street, to spin a decent yarn to those reporters in the Clarence Vaults. After that, I'll come back to the Rents.'

Knollys went back into the house through the now-repaired kitchen door. Box walked thoughtfully across the scanty grass, his boots crunching the rapidly freezing snow. Suddenly, he saw something that made him draw in his breath sharply, A cloaked figure was standing motionless just far away enough not to be seen clearly. For a moment he felt a little shudder as though faced with the

126

uncanny. Then the figure moved into focus, as it trod soberly and warily across the frozen flags.

'Oh,' Box muttered, 'so it's you, is it? I was right. It's going to be one of those sort of cases.'

Box opened the door of the shed, and stepped into the grateful warmth. The stranger followed him, stooping below the lintel of the door, and sitting down beside the still glowing stove. He smiled almost apologetically at Inspector Box, deposited his tall silk hat on the floor beside him, and pulled the skirts of his cloak around his knees.

'Good morning, Detective Inspector Box,' he said.

'Good morning, Colonel Kershaw. So it's like that, is it?'

'Yes, Box, it's like that.'

Inspector Box had worked with Colonel Kershaw before. This slight, sandy-haired man with the mild face and the weary, sardonic voice, was one of the powers behind the Throne. He was feared by his enemies; but it was perhaps more significant that he was feared, too, by his friends.

'Will you smoke a cigar with me, Mr Box?'

'I will, sir.'

Colonel Kershaw withdrew a stout cigar

case from an inside pocket, opened it, and offered it to Box. Three slim cigars reposed in the case, and beside them a rolled-up spill of paper secured with twine. Colonel Kershaw's pale-blue eyes looked speculatively at Box for a moment. Box took a cigar, and also the spill of paper, which he placed without comment in the pocket of his overcoat. The two men lit their cigars and smoked in silence for a minute or two. Then Colonel Kershaw spoke.

'Listen carefully, Inspector Box. I came in here through the gate in the garden wall leading to an alley. That's why nobody saw me, and that's why nobody will see me leave. There are deep waters here, and you are not dealing with a private murder, so I'm going to help you by telling you some things of interest.

'First, Lieutenant Fenlake, the young man who came here last night, is a bona fide Foreign Office courier. I expect you were going to check whether that was so? I thought so. Question him by all means. He has already reported to Sir Charles Napier, the Under-Secretary. It might be a good idea to mention at this point, Mr Box, that I am keeping a benevolent eye on Sir Charles Napier and his couriers. They don't know that, of course. I'm very interested, you see, in what they're doing at the moment.'

So that was it. Sir Charles Napier ran the Foreign Office's semi-secret courier service, and was accountable to the Prime Minister. Colonel Kershaw was the head of Secret Intelligence. It was generally thought that he was accountable to no one.

'I have a kind of indirect connection with Lieutenant Fenlake, sir,' said Box. 'I know a young lady friend of his.'

'Do you indeed? What's her name? What kind of young lady is she?'

Box raised his eyebrows, but made no comment. When talking to Colonel Kershaw, it was well to answer his questions without demur.

'Her name's Vanessa Drake, and she's an embroideress with Watts & Company of Westminster. She and this Fenlake are supposed to be sweet on each other.'

Kershaw absorbed this information without comment, though Box saw a speculative gleam briefly light up his eyes. He asked Kershaw a question.

'Is it in order for me to ask why Lieutenant Fenlake came here? Why did he want to see Dr Seligmann?'

'He came to collect a memorandum that Seligmann had written. It was to be delivered to a man in Berlin, a man called Baron von Dessau. A rehearsal of that collection had

129

been attempted on the previous day, but had met with no success. Well, you know that, of course. And you've seen the body of the Foreign Office courier who made that unsuccessful attempt.'

'I have, sir. And I've been told his name.'

'Yes, I know you have. A villainous-looking fellow calling himself Stefan Oliver. He was one of Sir Charles Napier's more picturesque couriers. He was half Polish, you know.' Kershaw added cryptically, 'It's a dangerous thing to be Polish in this particular part of the world.'

Box briefly conjured up the image of the overweight, unshaven man lying dead on the trestle table in the pier-master's office, his body probed and manhandled by a police doctor who had become inured to violent death. Stefan Oliver, one of England's unsung and unrewarded heroes.

'Where is that memorandum now, sir?'

'It was successfully collected by Lieutenant Fenlake last night. By now, it will be locked safely in the strongroom at the Foreign Office, where it will stay, presumably, until it sets out on its journey to Berlin.

'But now, Box, I'll tell you about Colin McColl, the other man who called upon Dr Seligmann last night. Colin McColl is a dangerous social and political pirate, who attaches himself to the disaffected, and offers them his services. He deals only with the disaffected of high rank. He expects — and receives — rich rewards. He traffics in secrets on his own account, and has been known to slaughter other rivals in the same field of activity.'

'Not a very nice person, then?'

'No, Box. He's not a very nice person. He's been active now for just over two years. Or perhaps I should say that he has come to my notice during the course of the last two years. He's extremely dangerous, because he always carries conviction. No doubt you'll check at Quaritch's bookshop? Yes, well, you'll find that McColl was, indeed, a part-time consultant to them. He's carried out a number of minor but successful assignments for them. But Quaritch's won't see him again. And between you and me, I don't think you'll catch him, Box. He's a decidedly slippery customer, with a positive genius for hiding himself away from prying eyes like mine.

'Now, I think, you can see why I have interested myself in this business of Seligmann's memorandum. Colin McColl is a dangerous man to spar with. In the nature of things, Sir Charles Napier at the Foreign Office will not even have heard of him.'

'I've just been talking to Dr Seligmann's friend Count Czerny,' said Box. 'He told me about a dangerous conspiracy of war-mongers called The Linked Ring — '

'Did he? Did he really? The *Eidgenossenschaft*. Yes, they're on the loose again.'

Colonel Kershaw drew thoughtfully on his cigar before adding, 'They could well be the people behind this assassination. Sir Charles Napier thinks so. He said that Seligmann told him as much at that meeting of his last Saturday. They're shrewd enough, you see, to realize that Colin McColl is the obvious choice of assassin. He's a very intelligent man. He has a degree in English from one of the northern universities. He's a pleasant enough young man to speak to, so I've been told, but he enjoys the anonymity of ordinariness. Sometimes people remember him, but for the most part they do not.'

'And Colin McColl is working for this Linked Ring?'

'Oh, no, Box; not he! Oh, dear me, no! Colin McColl is . . . how can I put it, without sounding melodramatic? McColl attaches himself to causes, and to subversive groups like the *Eidgenossenschaft*, and lets them think that he is their paid servant. But all the time, Box, he is using *them*, for his own dark ends.'

'What are those ends?'

'To my way of thinking, Box, McColl is something more than a mere man. He's the vehicle for a dark, manipulative force — a terrific force of evil. You ask me what are his ends. There's somebody in *Macbeth* whose ambition it was to 'pour the sweet milk of concord into hell'. That's what McColl wants to do. And the danger at the moment, Box, is that his sentiments accord with those of the German war groups. Each sustains the other. They follow fanatics and cranks, who crave for a new world, founded on all the old cliches about freedom, fraternity, and all the rest of it.'

Colonel Kershaw drew thoughtfully on his cigar for a moment, and then continued.

'On the 13th of this month, Box, which is a Friday, there is to be a grand meeting in Berlin of the Pan-German League, to be addressed by Baron von Dessau. I have people there, and in Jena, who tell me that new resentments against French policy in Alsace could lead to rogue units of the German Army violating the borders. I need hardly remind you what the consequences of that would be! What happens will depend on what Baron von Dessau does. And this is where the memorandum comes in. Sir Charles Napier tells me that its contents will make Baron von Dessau persuade the hotheads to rein in their ardour — at least, for a time.'

'Sir Charles has read the memorandum?'

'No — at least, he says he hasn't. Seligmann told him what the result would be, but not what the memorandum contained. So we must ensure that the fiery Baron von Dessau receives the memorandum. There are quite a few parties on both sides of the Channel who'd like to get their hands on that document. It's part of our task to see that they don't succeed. The thirteenth is the day of destiny.'

'Then we've only ten days left, sir! Sir Charles and his folk will have to guard that memorandum well. I wonder what would happen if it was never delivered?'

'Well, Box, I think that von Dessau would unleash the dogs of war. That, I know, is his intention. Without the secret constraint contained in Seligmann's memorandum, I think that certain elements of the German Army will violate the French borders. There'll be war of some kind, and we shall be dragged right into it.'

The two men were silent for a while, listening to the coal settling in the stove, and to the distant murmur of voices in the ruined garden. Then Box spoke.

'Did this Colin McColl murder Stefan Oliver?'

'I'm almost certain of it. McColl has a vindictive, vicious streak in his nature, which is why he had the temerity to dump poor Oliver's body practically at Sir Charles Napier's feet. Not a nice person, Box, as you say.'

'Why didn't he try to murder Lieutenant Fenlake? If he was after this memorandum — '

'Ah, but was he? Or was he bent purely upon the political assassination? I can't answer these questions, Mr Box, because my mind is trained to consider the broader canvas. I need to stand back from the minutiae. McColl's concocting some grand scheme, I'm sure of that. But I've no idea what it is.'

'Mr Fenlake's not one of your people, is he, sir?'

'No. Like me, he's an Artillery officer, but he's not one of my secret intelligence crowd. Fenlake's the wrong type of character to be one of my people. He's a Foreign Office courier — quite a different kind of animal, Mr Box.'

Box drew thoughtfully on his cigar for a while, silently eyeing the quiet and imperturbable man sitting by the stove. Joe

Peabody was one of Kershaw's crowd — the 'nobodies', as he liked to call them. Joe had known that he would be at the St Swithin's Hall last Saturday night. He had come up specifically from the river to find him. Whatever was going on, Colonel Kershaw was pulling the strings.

'You're drawing me into something, aren't you, Colonel Kershaw? You're poaching on the Commissioner's preserves.'

Colonel Kershaw suddenly looked grave. When he spoke, he made no attempt to respond in kind to Box's reserved banter.

'So far, Mr Box, I've simply told you things. I've told you the name of a double murderer, and all your policeman's instincts will impel you to go after him. I've told you about the memorandum, and the approach of a dangerous European crisis. There's a conflict of duties for you there, Mr Box, and if you throw in your lot with me over this business, it's a conflict that you'll have to resolve without my help. So what do you say? You've got a mind that works differently from mine, and it's your special qualities of mind that I want near me during this business. Will you consent to work with me?'

'I will, sir.'

Colonel Kershaw smiled, retrieved his silk hat, and stood up. He dropped the butt of his cigar into the stove.

'It's a pity that you are so well known, Mr Box,' he said. 'If you were reasonably obscure, I'd try to recruit you permanently into my crowd. But to be one of my nobodies, you've got to be rather in the shade. Like Joe Peabody. You were an excellent help to me last time, when we unmasked the murderous Dorset subalterns, and I'd like to feel you were around me when this business blows up. I'll go now.'

Colonel Kershaw opened the door of the shed and walked quietly out into the thickening mist.

7

The Fragments Assembled

Sergeant Knollys surveyed himself critically in the big, fly-blown mirror rising above the office fireplace. At one time, he thought ruefully, he'd been considered a handsome kind of man, but since the Philpotts Gang had rearranged his features with a sharpened length of iron railing, he felt that any little child who saw him in the street would run away screaming with fright.

Inspector Box, in his chirpy fashion, had assured him that he was too sensitive.

'We can't all be beautiful in this life, Sergeant Knollys,' he'd said, 'and from some angles you look quite presentable. Just keep away from strong gaslight.'

Knollys smiled, and let his image go out of focus. He read some of the cards and scraps of paper pasted round the edges of the mirror, many of them stained and faded. 'Mr Shale did not call on Wednesday', 'Tell Mr Box that there's nobody of that name in Harpenden'. What name? One of these days he'd clear away all these remains of long-dead cases, and give the mirror a polish. If he didn't do it, nobody else would.

The swing doors of the office flew open, and Inspector Box bustled in. Knollys' reverie faded. Whenever the guvnor burst in like that, eager for the fray, the present began to move back firmly to centre stage.

'Sergeant Knollys! I'm back at last. How did you get on at Victoria? I just made it to the Clarence Vaults. They were all there, in the cellar bar, the gentlemen of the Press — but never mind them. How did you get on?'

Inspector Box pulled off his leather gloves, and struggled out of his overcoat. He sat down at the cluttered table, and looked gratefully at the blazing fire.

'I went down to Chaplin's office at Victoria, sir,' Knollys replied, 'and spoke to a Mr Lloyd. Sure enough, he remembered the crate and had the original manifests. It came ostensibly from Bonn, and was despatched to England through Hamburg. It didn't come into the Port of London — '

'Which is decidedly odd, Sergeant, when you consider that its destination was Chelsea.'

'Yes, sir. It was sent on a German cargo steamer to Dover. It was opened by the customs there, and found to contain books. They resealed it, marked it 'Contents without value', and let it go on by rail to Victoria.'

''Contents without value' — evidently they're not great readers in the Customs, Sergeant. But you can see what must have happened. Someone engineered a substitution between Dover and here. It could be done. Or they switched labels on two different consignments. They packed their dynamite into the crate, and sent it on the final leg of its journey. Very interesting, Sergeant. And very sinister.'

'Yes, sir. I've also been to Quaritch's bookshop, in Piccadilly. They knew all about this Colin McColl. He'd carried out a number of tasks for them — things to do with old books and the like. They'd no doubt that he was a genuine scholar. They said it would be quite impossible to pose as such a man. But they'd never commissioned him to show manuscripts to Dr Seligmann. They don't deal in manuscripts.'

Box said nothing. Knollys watched him as he lit a thin cigar, and sat smoking in silence, gazing at the office fire.

'Sir,' said Knollys, 'While I remember it, I must tell you something I noticed about Miss Ottilie. I've already mentioned that I think she's older than she lets on. But I also noticed a pale indentation around the finger where you'd expect to see a German woman's wedding ring. I think she's married, sir.'

Box stirred in his chair, looked at Knollys, and smiled.

'Yes, Sergeant,' he said, 'I saw that little pale band of skin on the ring finger myself, and came to the same conclusion. As for Miss Ottilie's true age — well, she can't be much more than thirty-five, if that. So she's not trying to look younger out of vanity, Sergeant. I think she's doing it for disguise. She's passing herself off as a certain young woman of twenty-two.'

'Strewth! Do you mean she's not Dr Seligmann's niece?'

'It's just a thought, Sergeant Knollys. Something to ponder in a quiet moment. And I wish you'd try to acquire a choicer range of exclamations. 'Strewth' is all very well for a Billingsgate porter, but hardly suitable for a detective sergeant.'

'An impostor, sir? That could explain why she wasn't entirely overcome with grief. It could explain — '

'Save it for a quiet moment, Sergeant. And don't even hint it to anybody outside this room. Now, I'm going to tell you something else that you're to keep under your hat. I can't see how I can possibly continue with this investigation without telling you the whole story.

'After you left the house in Chelsea this morning, I found a phantom lurking in the fog, waiting to confront me. This phantom, Sergeant Knollys, is the man who controls Joe Peabody, and a hundred others like him, and his name's Colonel Kershaw. We sat by the stove in that brick garden shed, and he told me all about Colin McColl.'

As Box recounted his meeting with Kershaw, he contrived to convey the sense of menace and danger that seemed to be attached to the person of Colin McColl.

'And then, Sergeant,' he concluded, 'Colonel Kershaw made a reference to one of Shakespeare's plays. Something about 'the sweet milk of concord'. I'm a perky sort of fellow, as you know, but I felt intimidated by his words.'

Sergeant Knollys closed his eyes for a moment, as though recalling something. Then he quoted the chilling lines from *Macbeth* to which Kershaw had referred.

''Nay, had I power, I should
Pour the sweet milk of concord into hell,
Uproar the universal peace, confound
All unity of earth'.

'We learnt that at school, sir. They're the words of an anarchist with a lust for power — '

142

The sound of voices came from the drill hall beyond the office. Box held up his hand in a warning gesture.

'What's all that commotion back there? It's PC Kenwright. He'll be bringing some of his 'siftings' back from Chelsea. Better not say anything more now, Sergeant. We'll talk about this business later. An anarchist with a lust for power . . . Not a pleasant thought. But then, this Colin McColl's not a pleasant man.'

Sergeant Knollys produced a notebook, and turned over a few pages. It was time, he knew, to change the subject.

'I talked to Mr Lodge, the butler, sir. We snatched half an hour together in his pantry. There wasn't much that he could tell me that we didn't know already. Miss Seligmann's a bit of a handful, but very well regarded below-stairs. Mrs Poniatowski is a morose sort of woman, with her own ideas of service, which, needless to say, are not Mr Lodge's. There's a bit of a mystery, there, sir. Mrs P. says she's a Pole, but one of the Seligmann's neighbours has a Polish maid, who claims that Mrs Poniatowski can't speak Polish, only German, and some other language — Czech, she called it.'

'Well, well, Sergeant,' said Box, 'fancy that! Czech. That's the language spoken in Bohemia — '

'How do you know that, sir?'

'I don't know how I know, Sergeant. I just know it, that's all. Like you know *Macbeth*, and I don't. The important point is, that Mr Mack said that the dynamite used to blow up Dr Seligmann in the Belvedere came from Bohemia. An interesting point. Anything else?'

'Count Czerny and Miss Ottilie had another blazing row after we'd gone out into the garden. Apparently, it was a continuation of the unpleasantness that Czerny told us about. Mr Lodge didn't approve. 'You'd think they could have behaved with a bit more respect, Sergeant', he said to me, 'with the house being in mourning, and all. There should be crepe on the door, and a myrtle garland, but they've no time for the decencies'.'

'A blazing row . . . I wonder what that was about?'

'Mr Lodge doesn't know, because it was all in German. But apparently there was an awful lot of shrieking from Miss Ottilie, and Count Czerny was like a raging lion. It only lasted a few minutes, but what it lacked in time, it made up for in ferocity. Your friend Mr Schneider has promised to tell Mr Lodge what it was all about. Lodge could hear the two of them going at it hammer and tongs all round the house while it lasted.'

'Not very nice for Mr Lodge. He seemed a first-rate servant to me. Properly trained from boyhood, as like as not. He's too good for that madhouse, Sergeant Knollys.'

'I think he'd agree with you about that, sir. He'd already arranged terms of notice with Miss Ottilie, and had been offered a very attractive post with Sir Marcus Braintree at Henley. The household at Chelsea's breaking up. I think it was only poor Dr Seligmann who held it together.'

Box got to his feet. He peered into the mirror, and unconsciously smoothed his moustache with his right forefinger.

'There's something peculiar about that house in Chelsea, Sergeant Knollys. There's more to Miss Ottilie than meets the eye, and now you tell me this Mrs Poniatowski's a Czech — what we usually call a Bohemian. And these rows . . . People don't behave like that, Sergeant, after outrage and violent death on their premises. We'll have them all watched, and see what they do.'

'Sir, about Lieutenant Fenlake — '

'Yes, I know what you're going to say, Sergeant. We need to talk to him, if we can run him to ground. He was the last man to see Dr Seligmann alive. I'd very much like to hear what he said to Seligmann in that

Belvedere, and what Seligmann said to him. I'll do my best to track Mr Fenlake down — tomorrow, if possible. Unless, of course, the Foreign Office try to hide him away. Meanwhile, there's something else I want to do.'

'What's that, sir?'

'Mr Schneider, who evidently thinks I'm an ignoramus, told us that the library in the house was the political library, and that the one in the Belvedere was the academic library. Now, I don't think Schneider would tell any fibs, and I don't think others in that house would trust him to do so. But I think he's had it drilled in to him to make that point about the two libraries. It may mean nothing — or it may mean everything. So I'm going off now, to consult my own personal expert in philology.'

★ ★ ★

Louise Whittaker sat down in her chair at the fireside, and looked at her visitor. How would he want her to behave? He had come on business, to think aloud about a case, and invite her to exercise her judgement. She remembered the keen pleasure that she had felt in the previous autumn, when he had come to discuss with her the awful fate of

Amelia Garbutt, cruelly murdered and thrown into a canal. Mr Box regarded her home as a sanctuary, a place where he could be quiet, and indulge in speculation. She must be careful not to spoil that ordered tranquillity that so obviously attracted him.

'What do you want to know, Mr Box?' she asked.

'I want to know about the late Dr Otto Seligmann, miss. More than one person has told me that he was an eminent philologist. He appears to have produced an edition of old English poems — Anglo-Saxon verse, I think they call it. And then he propounded a rule or notion about syllables. I don't think anyone's trying to confuse me deliberately, but all this kind of thing is beyond me. Now you, miss, are a philologist, so I was wondering if you knew anything about this Dr Seligmann from that point of view.'

Louise joined her fingertips together, and looked thoughtfully at Box. She saw beyond his question to what he was actually thinking.

'Well, Mr Box, you've really answered your own question, haven't you? Dr Seligmann's *Specimens of Anglo-Saxon Verse* appeared in 1878. There has not been a second edition. If you want to embark upon the study of Anglo-Saxon, you would turn to other primers. And Seligmann's Law, you know, is just a grand name for a very simple observation, something rather obvious to anyone who has made a study of the vowels in unaccented syllables. Do you know what I am talking about?'

'No, miss.'

'No; in one way, I suppose, you don't, but in another way you do. What I am saying is that Dr Seligmann was a gifted and enthusiastic amateur. He turned his mind to editing texts and to the laws of phonology with equal enthusiasm, but I suspect that his true vocation lay in politics. Part of him, I'm sure, thought it more satisfying to be known as Dr Seligmann the distinguished scholar than Dr Seligmann the mere politician!'

'Dr Seligmann had a very unusual library called the Belvedere — '

'Yes, I know it. Just over a year ago Dr Seligmann invited me to see a very rare page of an old medieval chronicle that he had acquired.' She added softly, 'You see what I mean? Phonology, manuscripts . . . Dr Seligmann was a good, sound, dabbler.'

Miss Whittaker frowned, and gave a little shiver of disgust.

'Oh, dear! I sound so mean and ungenerous — that last comment of mine had all the pettiness of a jealous rival! The poor man has just died by violent means — I suppose it was murder?'

'It was a political assassination, Miss Whittaker.'

'Frightful! But what I've told you about poor Dr Seligmann is true. He liked to play the role of the scholar forced by circumstances to be a politician. But in his heart he knew that what scholarly work he had done in the past had long been superseded.'

'There were two libraries in that house at Chelsea,' said Box. 'The Belvedere library was the doctor's academic library, and the one in the house was his political library. That's what they told me at the house.'

Louise Whittaker was quick to detect the doubting tone behind Box's words. 'And you have your doubts, I take it? I suppose nothing remains of the Belvedere library?'

'No, miss. It's just rubble and ashes. The library that I saw was the one in the house. There was plenty of political stuff there, but all around the fireplace was a collection of well-thumbed books which I could see were all about language, and poetry, and suchlike. I had an image in my mind, Miss Whittaker, of a man sitting beside that fireplace, reading those books as though they were old friends. They weren't novels, and there were no pictures in them, but that's what I think they

149

were — old friends.'

Miss Whittaker sat quietly for a while, gazing thoughtfully at the fire. Box was content to wait.

'Mr Box,' said Louise Whittaker, 'I wondered about that library, too! The one in the house, I mean. Dr Seligmann showed me around it. It was just a courtesy on his part. He wanted me to admire the very fine carved Tudor panelling.'

'And did you, miss? I must confess that I never noticed it.'

'I was content to listen to him talking about it, while I looked all round the room. Like you, Mr Box, I realized that it was there that he kept the books he actually read! I was waiting to see whether you, too, had seen the truth of the matter. Oh, I know it was filled with interminable reference material to do with Germany and German politics, but those books around the mantelpiece — well-thumbed volumes, some with the spines sprung loose from constant opening — they conjured up for me the younger Dr Seligmann, the man who, perhaps, would have liked to become a scholar of international repute. But in his later years, you know, I think his enthusiasm was largely nostalgic: he had become a politician — perhaps a statesman in the making — and philology had become something of a romantic regret.'

Box watched Louise Whittaker as she smiled, and shook her head.

'But that library in the Belvedere, Mr Box — well, I thought it was a very peculiar place. It was there that Dr Seligmann showed me the medieval manuscript that he'd bought. While I was there you may be sure I cast my eyes around very thoroughly! As I remember, there were three shelves containing a wide range of modern German books on European history — three great shelves, completing the circle of the Belvedere. But above those shelves, Mr Box, rose tier after tier of leather-bound dummies! I wasn't fooled — I've seen that kind of thing before, and they make a good show.'

'Dummies?'

'Dummies. Very much like filing-boxes, but with a leather-covered false spine. People keep sets of magazines in them, or use them to tidy away items that look untidy when left lying about. Sometimes they have amusing names printed on them. I remember feeling slightly shocked when I saw them. They suggested a kind of deceit, which I'd never have associated with a man of Dr Seligmann's reputation.'

'Dummies . . . And why did Dr Seligmann send for you in particular, Miss Whittaker? To look at this old manuscript, I mean.'

'Well, you see, Mr Box, about eighteen months ago I went with some other scholars to a symposium on Germanic Philology at the university of Jena, in Prussia. It was a very learned affair, with lectures and discussions for most of the day, but some opportunities for sight-seeing as well. I was invited to dinner one evening by Professor Adolf Metternich and his wife, and among their guests was Miss Ottilie Seligmann, who is Dr Seligmann's niece — '

'Miss Ottilie? She has been living at the house in Chelsea for the last six months, Miss Whittaker. I don't know whether you realized that?'

Box saw the bewilderment in Louise's face.

'Ottilie? Here in England? I had no idea, Mr Box. I gather that there was an estrangement between Ottilie's father and Dr Seligmann — some wretched family quarrel. Perhaps that's why she never thought to make contact with me.'

'Miss Ottilie's father died six months ago, so I've been told. She was an orphan, and came to England in order to live with her uncle. She's been here ever since.'

'We were very friendly at Jena,' said Louise. 'She was a vivacious girl, you know, disconcertingly frank, but with an engaging personality. She was very pretty, too, rather like Vanessa Drake, with yellow hair and bright blue eyes, but not as healthy as Vanessa — consumptive, I think. But you asked me a question. I think Dr Seligmann invited me because he knew that I had seen his niece, though when I went to Chelsea he never asked after her.'

Louise Whittaker suddenly made up her mind to visit Ottilie Seligmann at Chelsea. Whatever quarrels had kept her father and uncle apart, they were irrelevant now. It would seem both rude and heartless not to call with her condolences.

Box picked up his curly-brimmed bowler and drew on his gloves. He would have to digest what Miss Whittaker had told him, or rather sift through her account of the libraries at Chelsea. At one stage in her account he had almost had a revelation of the truth. She had unwittingly revealed to him something about Seligmann's death that so far had been hidden from him. Whatever it was, it had retreated to the shadows.

'Thank you very much, Miss Whittaker,' he said. 'You've been a beacon of light today, if I may put it like that. Without being too dramatic, I think I can say that you have helped your Queen and country in a moment of acute crisis.'

It had seemed a noble sentiment when he conceived it. After he'd actually said it, it sounded faintly ridiculous. As he turned to open the door, the lady scholar's mocking voice rang out.

'One day, Mr Box, there may even be a woman detective at Scotland Yard to help you. And the Queen and country, too!'

Inspector Box smiled, and thought for a moment before replying to what Louise had meant to be a friendly taunt.

'Very well, Miss Whittaker,' he said, 'although I don't imagine there'll ever be any official lady policemen, I herewith enrol you as the first and only member of my unofficial female posse. There — does that satisfy you?'

Miss Whittaker laughed, and turned her attention once more to her books and papers.

'Away with you, Mr Box,' she cried. 'Go and solve your mysteries!'

Detective Inspector Box chuckled to himself, and left the room.

★ ★ ★

Box walked through the low passage that led from his office to the long, lime-washed room at the back of King James's Rents. It was a forlorn place, used partly as a storeroom, and partly as a venue for meetings.

154

Superintendent Mackharness always referred to it as 'the drill hall', which was the kind of description that came easily to an old Crimea veteran's mind.

PC Kenwright was sitting at one of a number of trestle tables, writing in a large foolscap ledger. The tables were covered with what Box estimated to be hundreds of shattered fragments, each carefully reposing in a chalked circle. The huge bearded constable glanced up from his work, and lumbered to his feet.

'Good morning, sir,' he said. 'I didn't hear you coming in.'

'Carry on with what you're doing, Constable,' said Box. 'I've just come in to see how you're getting on. I heard you yesterday, shifting all this stuff in here from the lane. These tables — and all these pieces that you've ringed in chalk — excellent, PC Kenwright! Have you drawn any conclusions yet from all these fragments?'

'Yes, sir. Do you see all those pieces of brown leather that I've collected at the end of this table? They're parts of the valise that was used to bring the detonator into the Belvedere. I was given a great deal of help by Mr Mack's men yesterday at the site, sir. I reckon we've collected just about everything of significance.'

Box examined the pieces of the valise. Kenwright had drawn a rough impression of a briefcase on the wooden surface of the table, and had positioned the fragments over it. They included both a buckle and a strap, and a discoloured brass lock.

'Excellent,' Box murmured. PC Kenwright continued to exercise his careful penmanship, his great frame bent over the ledger. Box watched him as he glanced at specific objects that he had salvaged, before turning once more to the ledger. He realized that PC Kenwright was compiling an inventory.

He looked at the second table, and saw that Kenwright had ringed a further collection, this time of what looked like strips of green leather, charred and soaked with moisture. Box suddenly recollected Sergeant Knollys in the Belvedere, stooping down pulling a fragment of leather from the ruin. 'Looks like the spine of a book,' he'd said . . .

'Constable, what are these green fragments here, do you think?'

'Those, sir? Well, they look like parts of books until you examine them closely. They look like bits of the covers of books, but when you turn them over there's no white or marbled paper gummed on them, which is what you'd expect to see — like on this ledger that I'm writing in. I don't rightly know about those bits. They look like parts of books, sir, but they may have been something else.'

Yes, thought Box. They looked like something else. Dummies . . .

PC Kenwright left his task, and joined the inspector at the second table.

'We salvaged hundreds of things from that wreckage, sir. You see all those little things glinting in that jar? Little cogs and wheels. They'll be from the timing-clock in the detonator, I expect. Or perhaps Dr Seligmann had a clock in there, and they're part of the clock. Or maybe it's a mixture of both.'

He pointed to some further items arranged in a wooden tray.

'Those tiny wheels and bits of metal are what's left of the poor doctor's watch. There's all sorts coming out here, sir.'

Box picked up a small picture frame, which Kenwright had used to hold a thick piece of paper on which was printed the letters EISS. Mounted beneath it was a brief note, written in what Box recognized as the sprawling and spiky handwriting of Mr Mack:

'FEISSEN WERKE. This is part of one of the labels attached to sticks of dynamite and other explosives made by the Feissen armaments and explosive factories in Bohemia.'

Box placed the little frame carefully back on the table.

'We uncovered that little scrap of paper, sir, while Mr Mack was still at the site. I showed it to him just before he left, and he kindly scribbled that note. And on this big board here, sir, I've pasted a whole pile of little fragments of paper — thirty-six pieces I've found so far — all with printed words on. I don't know what they mean. They're all in that fancy German type you see at the top of newspapers, so I expect they're German words.'

'It's quite remarkable, Constable. I've not seen anything quite like this before. I know you've a light touch for a giant of a man, but all this fine, detailed work — smoothing out the bits of paper, flattening them out, mounting them behind glass — it's excellent. You're a shining ornament.'

PC Kenwright smiled appreciatively into his beard.

'Well, sir, I suppose this kind of task comes naturally to me. When I was a little boy, I used to help my father to make his models. He made models of Nelson's ships from the days of the war against Napoleon. We used to make little sally-ports and little spars from pieces of wood he brought home from Covent Garden. He was a porter there for nigh on fifty years.'

Kenwright returned to his ledger, and Box went back through the passage to his office. The fire was burning brightly, and the rackety old gas mantle trembled and spluttered, as though gasping for air. Box pulled one of the chains, and the light burned brighter. He sat down at the table, and gave himself up to thought.

Pieces of leather that looked like the spines of books, but weren't. Dummies, Miss Whittaker had called them. A collection of fragments of paper, with German printing on them. Where did that lead him? Maybe the dummies were like boxes, filled with papers printed in German . . .

The Belvedere was supposed to have been Dr Seligmann's academic library, but that had not been the truth. The people in that house at Chelsea were adept at dropping subtle hints about things. A pack of playing cards thrown carelessly down . . . Perhaps they were good at playing tricks.

The Belvedere . . . It hadn't fitted in with the house. It was too big, too menacing, for its modest surroundings. And it had thick walls, lined with brick. And an iron door, which Colin McColl had seemingly risked his life to breach. The Belvedere.

Of course! It was the Belvedere, not Seligmann, that had been the subject of Colin McColl's fiendish attention! Seligmann could have been disposed of less expensively by pushing him under a cab, or chucking him in the river at Chelsea Reach. There was no need to blow him into atoms.

No; they'd needed that massive charge of explosive in order to destroy the Belvedere — and its contents. Something to do with PC Kenwright's carefully garnered scraps of paper. That had been the object of the whole diabolical exercise. Killing Seligmann in the process was by way of being a bonus.

Box felt inside his coat and removed the spill of paper that Colonel Kershaw had passed to him on the previous day in the garden shed at Chelsea. He had already glanced at it, and realized what it signified. It was inscribed in small, neat letters with a name and address.

★　★　★

Mrs Prout, Bagot's Hotel, Carlisle Place, Archbishop's Park.

Whoever Mrs Prout was, she would be able to grant him access to Colonel Kershaw. It was time for Box to take himself to Carlisle

Place. He committed the name and address to memory, and then burnt the spill in the office fire. He watched the slip of paper curl rapidly and fly up the chimney in a shower of sparks.

8

The Hansa Protocol

'Dull!'

Louise Whittaker paused in the act of stirring her coffee, and looked at her young friend Vanessa Drake. A moment before, she had asked the girl how she found life at the moment. Vanessa had uttered the single word so vehemently that several of the other ladies taking lunch in the restaurant of the Acanthus Club had looked up disapprovingly. Vanessa blushed, and lowered her voice.

'I never felt like that until I met Arthur,' she continued. 'I had my way to make in life, and a gift for needlework and embroidery. And the people at Watts & Co are all that one could desire. But it's all so deadly dull, Louise! I envy you, because you meet so many different people, you know detectives at Scotland Yard, you travel abroad to romantic countries, you're a member of this marvellous club for professional women — '

'I'm thirty-five, Vanessa,' said Louise. 'You're a mere chit of a girl of twenty. You've plenty of time to expand your horizons in life. And why has knowing Lieutenant Fenlake unsettled you? Inspector Box was able to set your mind at rest about your Arthur's gambling propensities, and the good intentions of Major Lankester — '

'Yes, it was very good of him to do that. But it's something about Arthur's work that's making me chafe at the bit. He's something more than just a soldier, Louise. Why is he always at the Admiralty? Why is he never in barracks? He disappears, sometimes for days, on mysterious errands, and shies away if I try to ask any questions . . . He's having adventures while I'm languishing among the silks and damasks in Tufton Street!'

Vanessa Drake laughed in spite of herself, and a lady sitting at a table nearby looked up from her newspaper, caught Vanessa's eye, and smiled. She was an affable-looking woman of fifty or so, wearing a businesslike black dress. Vanessa had noticed her earlier, because her auburn hair was enlivened by a single tress of natural silver. She had been peering at her copy of The Times through gold pince-nez, but now she put the paper down on the table.

'I couldn't help but hear what you said just now, my dear,' she said. 'I hope you'll forgive me speaking to you like this, but I know just how you feel. My name is Mrs Prout. I'm an hotelier.'

'I'm Vanessa Drake,' said Vanessa, in some confusion. Mrs Prout seemed to be a kindly, comfortable kind of woman, but there was something very shrewd in her expression that was slightly unnerving. 'And this is my friend Miss Whittaker. I'm only a guest here today. Miss Whittaker is a member.'

'Well, now, isn't that nice? How do you do, Miss Whittaker? I don't think we've met before. I don't come here very often, these days.'

'Perhaps you'd care to join us for coffee?' said Louise Whittaker. She wondered about this Mrs Prout. It was not usual for a lady of her generation to be so informal about introductions. She watched as Mrs Prout pulled her chair across to their table, and sat down.

'You see, Miss Drake, when I was your age — twenty? — I worked in my father's little printing-house, binding up parcels of tracts for the Chinese Mission. Day after day I'd turn the handle of the special machine that bound the sheets together, and then I'd pack them in dozens in shallow wooden boxes. I couldn't read them, of course, because they were printed in Chinese! Day after day . . . I'd done that for three years, and I began

164

to think that I'd carry on doing it for another thirty.'

'And what happened?'

'Well, Miss Drake, the mission decided to establish a printing-house at Canton, and Father agreed to go out there and set it up. And so we went. As soon as we got there, the war broke out — well, one of several wars. Canton was occupied by rebels, people who didn't care much for foreigners. Our little mission house was surrounded by a fearful mob, and the upshot of it was that they set fire to the place. Then they set fire to the neighbouring houses. There was a lot of shouting, and shooting, and we were all quite convinced that we were going to be slaughtered.'

Louise Whittaker had made two efforts to pour Mrs Prout a cup of coffee, but on both occasions she had been stopped by the dizzying speed of the older woman's narrative. She glanced at Vanessa, and saw her blue eyes shining with excitement. Her young friend seemed to have lost sight of the quiet, elegantly appointed restaurant of the Acanthus Club, and she herself, for all her cool, academic detachment, was beginning to be enthralled by the friendly woman's tale.

'What happened next?' asked Vanessa.

'We were rescued by the provincial

governor and his loyal troops, but then we had to make our way alone and unseen down to Hong Kong. Eventually, of course, we got back to England, and a few years afterwards the Viceroy of China and General Gordon restored what passes out there for law and order.'

'And did you resume your work for the mission?' asked Louise. Mrs Prout treated her to a good-humoured smile, and shook her head.

'Oh, no, Miss Whittaker. I'd had my fill of adventure! I married into the hotel business soon afterwards, and have been there — very contentedly! — ever since. So there, my dear Miss Drake. Life doesn't have to be all stitching and sewing. The most amazing things can happen — if you're willing to take the risk.'

Mrs Prout declined to take any coffee, and after a few pleasantries, she gathered up her paper, and left the room.

'I wonder who she was?' asked Louise Whittaker.

'Why, she told us who she was — '

'I don't mean that, Vanessa. That was a true story she was telling, something unbelievable that once happened to someone who is now a comfortable, commonplace woman. But she was telling it for a purpose, and I have a

166

feeling that she was watching *you*, seeing how you'd react to her story. It's just a little odd, that's all. Perhaps I'll ask Inspector Box about this Mrs Prout.'

'You like him, don't you? Really like him, I mean.'

Louise Whittaker blushed, more with vexation than embarrassment. It was mortifying to like a man who seemed constantly overawed by one's academic abilities. They'd never once addressed each other by their Christian names. Like him? Of course she liked him. She liked his defensive boastfulness, which masked some kind of sensitive vulnerability. And he'd lightheartedly made her the one and only member of his female posse.

Suddenly Louise Whittaker realized that she, too, was envious, just as Vanessa was envious of Arthur Fenlake. Arnold Box was part of the official establishment of the country. He had powers of arrest, privileged access to all kinds of influential people denied to her. But he came to her when a case began to puzzle him, content to avail himself of her scholar's trained mind, and female insights. Why shouldn't women have their share of such privileged authority? She would make as good a detective as Arnold Box, given the opportunity.

'Well, do you?'

'What? Yes, I really like him. I'm hoping that one day he'll stop treating me as a kind of idol or oracle of wisdom, and treat me like a woman! Come on, Vanessa, let's leave the Acanthus, and return to the big, wide world of Arnold Box and Arthur Fenlake! That Mrs Prout's tale of derring-do has made me determine to beat these proud and secretive men at their own game, if ever I have the chance!'

★ ★ ★

Box had never heard of Bagot's Hotel, but the cabbie whom he hailed at the corner of Whitehall Place made no comment when he asked to be taken there. He turned the head of his rather unwilling horse, and the cab rattled off on its journey to Westminster Bridge.

Bagot's Hotel proved to be a small but high-class establishment, tucked discreetly into a cul-de-sac behind the rear garden wall of Lambeth Palace. Box paid off the cabbie, and walked up three steps into the dimly lit foyer of the hotel. An affable lady in a businesslike black dress occupied a little glazed office near the door. Her well-tended auburn hair was enlivened by a single silver streak, that somehow added distinction to her appearance.

The lady marked Box's arrival by darting a quick and unexpectedly shrewd glance at him over pince-nez, and then continued talking to a gentleman who had evidently arrived only moments before Box.

'It's so nice to have you back with us, Major Lankester,' said the lady, 'even though it's only for a few days. Just passing through, are we?'

This, then, thought Box, is the officer who saved young Fenlake from ruin. A handsome, fine-looking man in his mid-forties. That sleek black hair owed nothing to artifice. His clipped and waxed moustache told of a man with pride in himself. His tailored black overcoat with its warm astrakhan collar, suggested that Major Lankester was a man of means, and a smart dresser by inclination. Another military man ... Perhaps Bagot's was an establishment for military and naval officers. Or perhaps it was something else.

'Just passing through? Yes, Mrs Prout, that's what I'm doing. Any chance of dinner, soon? I know it's confoundedly early, but it's dashed cold out there.'

'Dinner's whenever you like, Major Lankester. Down here, or upstairs. Just as you like. Mr Gordon was in, earlier. He said he hoped they'd see you soon at Eagle Street.'

'Did he, by George? Well, we'll see. I suppose he looked as prosperous as ever?'

'Oh, yes, Major. Very spruce he looked — very dapper, if you understand me.'

Box watched Mrs Prout as she smiled rather archly at Major Lankester. That woman, he thought, can speak two languages at the same time. If you were sharp enough, you could divine what she meant by delving beneath her spoken words to what lay behind them.

'I know what you mean, ma'am.' Lankester replied. 'Always very well turned out, is Mr Gordon.' He lowered his tone a little. 'You see men like him at the Italian opera. Tenors, mostly.'

Mrs Prout crowed with delight, and Box saw Lankester smile. It was a good-humoured smile, he thought, from a man without malice. Major Lankester turned away from the little glass office towards the staircase.

'I'll have dinner upstairs, Mrs Prout. In half-an-hour's time, if that's convenient.'

Box had taken the opportunity of glancing into the cosy, panelled lounge beyond the vestibule, where a good fire was burning, and a number of middle-aged men were sitting around, talking to each other in loud, commanding voices. They seemed to know one another, and Box judged that they were all military and naval men, some still on active service, and others obviously retired. There was a pervasive aroma of tobacco and brandy about the place.

'Can I help you, sir?'

Box saw that Mrs Prout was regarding him with half-concealed amusement. He watched her glance briefly at a document on her desk, and then back at him again. Once more he saw the shrewd expression behind the rather arch, flirtatious exterior.

'Would you care to go up the stairs to the first floor, sir? Knock on the door of room six. You are expected.' She had not asked his name.

A deeply carpeted staircase led up to the bedrooms. The carpet was unworn, and spotlessly clean, with gleaming brass stair-rods. There was, Box mused, a decidedly military air about the buffed and polished surroundings of Bagot's Hotel. He reached the first-floor landing, and knocked at the door of Number 6.

The door was opened by Colonel Kershaw, who had evidently just left an armchair placed in front of the fire. He was clutching a copy of *The Morning Post* in one hand, as though he had been reading it when Box had summoned him to the door.

Box took in the large, well-furnished room in a single glance. He saw the regimental shields and crossed swords above the fireplace, the shelves of books, and the wealth of framed photographs. This room in Bagot's Hotel bore all the marks of being personal to the man who occupied it.

'You live here!' he exclaimed.

Colonel Kershaw laughed, and motioned to a chair facing his by the fire. He looked much the same as he had done in the brick shed at Chelsea. Slightly built, with thinning sandy hair, and a cast of countenance that was habitually apologetic, he looked more like a senior clerk approaching retirement than a professional soldier. Box wondered whether he cultivated different identities, and tried them out for consistency on people like himself.

'Well, living here's not a crime, Mr Box. One has to live somewhere, you know! In any case, I have other places where you'll find me — always supposing that you're looking for me. But you sent a note by special messenger, saying you had something to tell me.'

'Yes, sir. I'm going to outline a theory, if I may. It's based on the premise that the massive charge of explosive concealed in that crate at Chelsea was intended not to kill Dr Seligmann, but to destroy the Belvedere.

Killing Dr Seligmann in the process, sir, was just a bonus, so to speak.'

'Why should they want to destroy the Belvedere?'

'Because of what it contained. Some kind of documents, sir, concealed in filing boxes disguised as large books. Shelf after shelf of dummy books. I've a constable back at King James's Rents who's salvaged over thirty fragments of these documents, so far. They appear to be printed in the German language. Do you want to hear how I arrived at these conclusions, sir?'

'No. What I want to do, Box, is send a man — one of my crowd — to look at those fragments, and read what they say. Printed, you say? I wonder . . . If I allow myself to become immersed in the detail, Box, I'll lose sight of the overall picture. So, no, I don't want to hear how you found this out, but I'm sure that you're right. Well done! I knew I'd made the right decision when I ran you to earth in that foggy garden at Chelsea. You'll definitely be around me, now, when this business blows up.'

'You're very kind, sir.'

'Not at all. I trust that your friend Miss Whittaker is well? And Miss Vanessa Drake — is she still plying her busy needle?'

'The answer's 'yes' to both your questions,

Colonel Kershaw. I suppose it would be idle if I were to ask you why you want to know?'

'Totally idle, Box. I just like to know things, that's all. I'll send a man down to see these fragments of yours. Can you see him later this afternoon? About five o'clock? Excellent. His name is Veidt. Monsieur Veidt. I already have an inkling of what he's going to find. It opens up interesting possibilities ... We'll talk further, Box, and sooner rather than later. Meanwhile, any message delivered here at Bagot's will always find me.'

'The lady in the office, sir — Mrs Prout — is she the owner?'

Colonel Kershaw smiled. He looked secretly amused at Box's question.

'The lady in the office is quite content to let people assume that she's the owner of Bagot's. But the ultimate owner, Mr Box, is a widowed lady, who lives in a castle at Windsor. This place belongs to her. And so, of course, do I.'

★   ★   ★

'Well, Monsieur Veidt, are you making any progress? Is there any way in which I can be of assistance?'

Box had received Colonel Kershaw's emissary at the door of King James's Rents, and had conducted him immediately to the drill hall. He had wondered what to make of the very tall, thin and bearded man who had glared at him rather balefully through blue-tinted spectacles. He looked more like an enemy than an ally.

'All I need, *monsieur*,' said Veidt, 'is a little space, and a little quiet. Remember your story of the tortoise and the snail. The tortoise ran fast, but it was the snail who won the race.'

An interesting man, thought Box. Very few men had such black beards as his, or such a black hat, or such a very black suit. What was that word? Funereal, that was it. Give him a glass-sided hearse and a few plumes, and he'd be in business.

The tortoise and the snail . . . Surely it had been a hare? These foreigners could never get anything right.

Monsieur Veidt suddenly sighed with satisfaction, and thrust a magnifying glass that he had been using into one of the capacious pockets of his flapping black coat. He turned round from the table where he had been working, and treated Box to an unnervingly brilliant smile.

'There was very little to go upon, *monsieur*. So many of these fragments are too small for any of the characters printed on them to suggest anything of much significance. Nevertheless, I have solved the riddle.'

Monsieur Veidt pointed to one of the fragments with the little finger of his right hand. The gesture had all the delicacy of a connoisseur examining a rare painting.

'This piece, for instance, contains the letters '*übec*', and this one '*eifswal*'. This third piece had a complete word: '*Wismar*.' I suggest that '*übec*' is 'Lübeck', and '*eifswal*' is 'Greifswald'. Both those places were members of the Hanseatic League. The other principal cities were Visby, Reval and Danzig.'

Monsieur Veidt walked over to the second table, where most of the fragments collected together by PC Kershaw had been laid out for inspection.

'There are nearly forty fragments of paper here, *monsieur*, and I have noted seven different typefaces in use. They may look the same to you, because they are all variants of the German script, what many English people call Gothic. Twelve fragments are in the same typeface as the piece of paper containing the word 'Greifswald'. Nine belong to 'Lübeck', and fourteen to 'Wismar'. Does that suggest anything to you?'

'It does, Mr Veidt. It suggests a system of classification — '

'Precisely. And perhaps the most important fragment, M. Box, is this piece, here, which you have placed in a little frame of its own. It is the most fully preserved, and, as you may see, it is in the Roman typeface used in England, and elsewhere on the Continent. This, then, belongs to a further document, all of which has been lost. It reads, translated into English: 'The Hansa Protocol: Greifswald. Codes of the Imperial . . . ' And there it ends.'

'What do you make of it, Mr Veidt?'

'I suggest that there once existed in the Belvedere a volume entitled *The Hansa Protocol: Greifswald. Codes of the Imperial German Navy*. I suggest that for two reasons. First, I know that such a volume exists. It is a closely guarded secret in Berlin. Secondly, a number of these fragments confirm my suggestion. For instance, these twelve pieces that match the typeface of 'Greifswald' contain brief fragments of words that look like the names of ships, displacement in tons, number of guns, and so on.'

'This protocol — it would be a secret document?'

'It is, *monsieur*. It contains not merely descriptions of all the vessels in the Imperial Marine, but the naval codes, and their periodic changes, as they will be used up to the year 1900. The Greifswald volume is one only of a series of eight books which together comprise *The Hansa Protocol*. The others, named after the other Hanseatic towns, deal with army dispositions, military signals, the location of the secret munition dumps, and many other facts of vital importance to the Imperial German war machine.'

Box surveyed the neatly docketed items in their chalked rings, and felt a sudden glow of pride in what he and PC Kenwright had achieved together. He would have to tell Superintendent Mackharness, of course, and he would use the occasion to bring up the question of Kenwright's rank.

He looked at the tall, thin man in blue-tinted glasses, and suddenly saw behind the lugubrious man in black to the encyclopaedic expert on German naval and military practice. This oddly named man with the French title and German name was one of Colonel Kershaw's secret servants.

'Monsieur Veidt,' asked Box, 'I was wondering whether you're a German yourself. There seem to be a lot of Germans mixed up in this business — '

'I come from Alsace, Monsieur Box. You will have heard of it, no doubt. My family once lived in Strasbourg, but we were driven out of there in 1871, by the people who are currently passing themselves off as the true Germans — the Prussians, and their growing empire.'

Monsieur Veidt pulled on a pair of woollen gloves, and turned towards the passage leading out of the drill hall. Then he stopped for a moment, and looked at Box. His eyes were hidden behind his tinted glasses, and there was something rather inscrutable about him.

'We people of Alsace, Monsieur Box,' he said, 'have never really known who or what we are. Sometimes we're Germans, other times we're French. Such are the accidents of history. I have a German name, and my native language is a form of German. But, *monsieur*, I am in my heart a Frenchman, exiled from his native land.'

*   *   *

Sir Charles Napier stared sombrely from the window of his room in the Foreign Office at the gaunt leafless trees on Duck Island, the bird sanctuary beside the lake in St James's Park. He hated the winter. Its chill grip transformed the most enchanting prospect to a bleak wasteland.

'There'll be heavy snow by weekend, Kershaw,' he said.

Colonel Kershaw made a sound of assent. Napier turned away from the window, and sat down at his vast mahogany desk. It was late afternoon, and it had been necessary to have the lamps lit. A banked-up coal fire blazed in the grate.

Napier surveyed his visitor for a moment. Colonel Kershaw had carefully selected a chair some distance from the Under-Secretary's desk, as though to emphasize his status as a mere visitor to one of the great centres of governance. He had also declined to remove his smart, double-breasted over-coat, and had placed his silk hat and ebony walking-stick on the floor beside him. Napier wryly assumed that he was expected to collude in the fiction that Colonel Kershaw had just dropped in for a chat, and that he wouldn't stay, thank you.

'What did Her Majesty think of the business at Chelsea?' asked Kershaw.

Napier ran his hand through his hair. Dash it all, why should he feel as nervous as a junior clerk whenever Kershaw turned up? The fellow only ever darkened the Foreign Office doorstep when something, somewhere, had gone wrong.

'Her Majesty was not pleased,' said Napier. 'She sent for me at some ungodly hour of the night, and I stood for half an hour while she

180

poured scorn on the Foreign Office, its heads of department, and its servants. It was not a pleasant half-hour, Kershaw. She was very cool, and very distant. When she's in that mood, she frightens me to death.'

Kershaw felt a pang of commiseration for Napier. Queen Victoria in censorious mood could be devastating. Perhaps it would be his turn, next.

'Did you tell her about Seligmann's memorandum?' he asked. 'Young Fenlake almost literally snatched the thing out of the jaws of death and delivered it to you unscathed.'

Sir Charles Napier smiled rather cynically. Fenlake and Kershaw were both officers in the Royal Artillery, that vast body of 13,000 gunners constituting a single enormous regiment of Her Majesty's Army. A number of Kershaw's agents — 'secret servants' as they were called — had been recruited from the Artillery. Perhaps Kershaw would try to poach young Fenlake from the Foreign Office?

'I managed to stammer out my excuses, Kershaw, and then told Her Majesty about Fenlake's success, and that, when the right moment came, the memorandum would be sent speeding across Europe to the Chancellery in Berlin. She was — well, she was not impressed. She said ... she said terrible things.'

'What kind of things?'

'She said that it was really not a matter for congratulation that a trained courier should succeed in delivering a letter from one part of Chelsea to another. As for speeding across Europe, she said she'd deliver the memorandum herself, if that would help me. I can recall her exact words, Kershaw. I'm not likely ever to forget them! 'I dare say, Under-Secretary', she said, 'that with a certain measure of luck I might survive a private visit to Berlin without the butchers of the Wilhelmstrasse impeding my progress. But if all else fails, you might care to deliver the memorandum by means of the general post!''

Sir Charles Napier expected Kershaw to conceal a smile behind his hand. Instead, the colonel sat in thought for what seemed like a whole minute. Then he spoke.

'Why not let my crowd deliver it? Seligmann's memorandum, I mean.'

Sir Charles sprang up angrily from his desk. He had been waiting for this moment. It was not welcome, even though he had secretly determined to accept any offer of help that Kershaw cared to make.

'Is that why you've come here today?' he

182

demanded. 'What's your game, man? Do you think my couriers are incapable of doing the thing properly?'

'What did the Queen think?' asked Colonel Kershaw softly. Napier blushed.

'The Queen — '

'The Queen, Napier, has more experience of secret diplomacy than the two of us put together. She's been the confidant of prime ministers and foreign secretaries for over fifty years. I'm not disparaging your men, but I'm suggesting that your methods lend themselves to dangerous manipulation. Fenlake's a good fellow, but he's the type of man who sticks to the rule-book. That's why I've never attempted to steal him from you. You know what I mean by the rule-book. Your couriers follow the folio code of the day — '

'Precisely! So the Foreign Secretary, and anyone else in high authority, can find out where my couriers are at any single minute of any single day. That is the strength of the folio code assignments. They've been in use since Palmerston's time. I know all about your so-called 'crowd', Kershaw, your secret servants, and your amorphous band of 'nobodies', as you like to call them — '

'You're wrong, Napier! You *don't* know about them! That's the whole point. All my crowd operate by word of mouth only.

Nothing is written down. One of my very best people, for instance, has just booked in to the hotel where I'm staying. He knows I'm there. I know he's there. We don't need to pass each other pieces of paper.'

'My couriers — '

'Your couriers, Napier, because of the folio codes, can be located, followed, and spied upon, by anyone who has access to the folios of the day. The system is fraught with terrible dangers. Look what happened to Stefan Oliver. Did Her Majesty mention *him* when she was being scornful at your expense?'

Sir Charles Napier jumped as though he had been shot. 'You know about him?'

'Well, of course I do! And so did somebody else — somebody lethal, Napier. Young Fenlake escaped with his life by sheer good fortune, I've no doubt. Our enemies are determined that Baron von Dessau shall not receive that memorandum from poor Seligmann. They want him unimpeded by prudence for their great rabble-rousing meeting in Berlin on Friday the thirteenth. Nine days hence, Napier! So let my crowd deliver the memorandum. My crowd don't write things down, you know. We all follow the old army adage: 'No names, no pack-drill'. They will succeed, you see, because nobody knows who my crowd are.'

Sir Charles sat down again at his desk. It was no good getting hot under the collar with Kershaw. He'd known him since boyhood. He was a man of sterling worth, and a supremely clear thinker. He spoke bluntly at times, but he never did so for personal advantage. He was wrong about the folio code system, of course. There must be another reason for this sudden unexpected interference.

'You're up to something, aren't you? You're plotting something devious, Kershaw. Why should I give you Seligmann's memorandum? Surely you're not contemplating dragging yourself across Europe in this confounded winter weather — '

Colonel Kershaw laughed, and held up a hand to stem the Under-Secretary's flow of words.

'My dear Napier! If you will give me the memorandum, I will undertake to see it delivered safely into the hands of Baron von Dessau at his residence in Berlin-Charlottenburg well in time to dim his ardour for war. The man who just booked in to Bagot's Hotel is the man who will make the delivery. He is one of the most experienced of my secret servants.'

'All right, Kershaw. You shall have it your own way. To be quite honest with you, I was prepared to go along with you, anyway. We're not running rival services. But I insist on being present when you hand over Seligmann's memorandum to this nameless prodigy who is going to deliver it.'

'Of course. And the 'nameless prodigy' will be Major Lankester, a man who is not unknown to you.'

Napier sat back in his chair, and gave a sigh of satisfaction.

'At last, something that we can agree upon! I know Lankester's reputation stands high. But I still think you're up to something, Kershaw!'

Colonel Kershaw laughed. He could see that Sir Charles Napier was pleased and relieved at the outcome of the meeting. He picked up his hat, hauled himself up off his chair, and quietly left the room.

When Kershaw had gone, Sir Charles Napier sat in thought. The wily fox! He was up to something, all right. Some subtle procedure was unfolding itself in Kershaw's Byzantine mind, and he hadn't told him one half of it. Still, sending Major Lankester as courier would mean that young Fenlake could be rested for a while, which was a good thing. It might be a sensible move to return him to his regiment. Well, there was other work to do.

Sir Charles Napier dismissed the business of the memorandum from his mind, and turned his attention to some papers touching upon the stability of Peru. Immersed in the details of a knotty problem, he lost track of the time. Towards five o'clock a telegraph machine in an office on the ground floor began its busy, menacing chatter. Outside, the sky darkened further, and the gas lamps glowed more brightly. It continued very cold.

9

Miss Whittaker Takes a Hand

Louise Whittaker walked along the lane leading to Lavender Walk, and recalled the last time that she had ventured as far out as Chelsea. It had been just after the Christmas of '91, when the weather had been unusually warm. Louise had called on the old German scholar, examined his page of ancient manuscript, and satisfied her curiosity about the Belvedere. Now Dr Seligmann was dead. 'It was a political assassination, Miss Whittaker,' Arnold Box had declared.

And Ottilie . . . She had liked her immediately when they were introduced at a dinner party in Jena. A petite, slender girl, she had spoken excellent English with a vivacious, animated air of someone eager for knowledge of the world and its ways. She had sensed that Ottilie Seligmann was not an intellectual girl, and that her interests lay almost entirely in the possibilities of making a good marriage. Even now she could recall her bright blue eyes, and her blonde hair arranged with seeming artlessness as a frame for her small face.

Louise emerged from the lane into Lavender Walk, and pulled the bell at the side of the front door of Dr Seligmann's ancient Tudor house. She felt unaccountably nervous. Should she have written first? Somehow, it seemed better to call personally in this way to convey her condolences. Ottilie, she felt sure, would be pleased to see her again.

The door was opened to her by the same butler who had admitted her to the house on the occasion of her last visit. He smiled in recognition, and stood aside for her to enter the old, panelled front hall.

'Miss Whittaker, is it not? I am Lodge, the butler. It's nice to see you again, miss.'

'Fancy you remembering me, Lodge! Since those days, I hear, Miss Ottilie Seligmann has come to live here. I met her once, in Jena, but I had no idea that she was living in England.'

'Yes, indeed, miss. She's been with us for over six months, now. Let me show you into the morning-room.'

As the butler preceded her into a room on the left side of the hall Louise saw a fair-haired young woman descending the stairs. She held firmly to the banister rail, as she seemed intent on reading some entries in what looked like a household account book.

Louise followed Lodge into a quiet little room with a single narrow window, from which she could just glimpse the blackened and ruined shell of the Belvedere.

'As a matter of fact, Lodge,' said Louise, 'I've called to offer my condolences on the frightful death of poor Dr Seligmann. Is Miss Ottilie at home this morning?' Lodge smiled.

'Well, miss, I fancy you've just seen Miss Ottilie descending the stairs! Had she not been so absorbed in her book, she would have seen you. I will tell her that you are here.'

Louise Whittaker made a motion with her hand as though to restrain him. The blood was pounding in her ears. What did this mean? The woman on the stairs was blonde and petite, and her eyes were blue; but she was emphatically not Ottilie Seligmann.

Suddenly the old house seemed to exude a stifling menace.

'On second thoughts, Lodge,' she heard herself saying, 'I will write formally. I see that I was wrong to come unannounced. I'd be obliged now if you would not mention my visit to . . . to Miss Ottilie.'

'As you please, miss. Perhaps we'll see you later in the week.'

So, Arnold Box, thought Louise, here's something important that you didn't know about! You were joking when you made me the sole member of your female posse, but the joke has rather turned against you . . .

That woman was an impostor, and the police must be told. When Louise gained the main road, she hailed a passing cab, and told the driver to take her to King James's Rents, Whitehall Place.

★　★　★

Lieutenant Fenlake and Vanessa Drake waited for a cab to make its rather leisurely way along Whitehall, and then crossed the carriageway. The soot-stained pile of the Admiralty rose behind its screening colonnade of stone. They stood for a moment at the gas lamp in front of the arched entrance, as though uncertain what to say or do next.

'You'll be all right by yourself?' asked Fenlake. She could see that he was concealing his impatience, his wish to hurry through that arch and into the warren of offices constituting the old Admiralty buildings.

'I'll be fine, Arthur. I'll walk back to Trafalgar Square, and get an omnibus home from there. The National Gallery's a wonderful place, and it was a fascinating exhibition. It would have been nice to have stayed a bit longer.'

Her eyes strayed across the road, where she

could see the dingy entrance to Great Scotland Yard. Somewhere in that warren of poky streets Louise Whittaker's friend, Inspector Box, would be working away in his office. No dull routine for him! Mr Box had discovered that Arthur was not, after all, being led into dangerous paths at the gaming-table. She wondered for a moment how he had found that out. How fascinating it must be to work as a detective!

She would always feel kindly towards Arthur Fenlake, but it had become more and more obvious that this handsome, rather unimaginative young man was married to his work. A wife, at this stage in his career, would become a resented inconvenience. Well, she had begun to realize that herself. She would contrive ways of letting him know that she would always be there as a friend, and leave it at that.

'I might have to go to the Continent,' he said. 'Any day, now.'

She looked at him, as he stood near the lamp standard, so smart and unconsciously elegant, longing to get through that arch and into the fray. He had the appearance of a wealthy young man about town, but he was not that.

'You're not just a soldier, are you?' she suddenly asked him. 'Ordinary soldiers don't have urgent business so often at the headquarters of the Navy.'

He shied away from her like a frightened colt.

'What? Of course I'm a soldier, Vanessa. What an odd thing to say. I'm just . . . I'm just a soldier. I *must* dash. I simply must! You'll be all right?'

Vanessa Drake smiled, and laid a hand lightly on his.

'Yes, Arthur,' she said, 'I'll be all right.'

★ ★ ★

Louise stood uncertainly for a moment on the cobbles, and looked up at 2 King James's Rents. The general impression was one of grimy windows in a soot-stained façade. A number of weathered iron Maltese crosses showed where tie-beams ended. Arnold Box always referred to this place as 'The Rents', and she could see that there were other ancient, dilapidated buildings attached to it at various odd angles. She mounted the steps and found herself in a dim vestibule that smelt of stale gas and mildew. An elderly police sergeant in uniform stepped out from a narrow front office, and looked at her enquiringly over a pair of wire spectacles. He was a heavily bearded man, who walked with a limp.

'Inspector Box, ma'am? He's in the streets at the moment, but he should be back soon. You can wait on the bench there by the entrance, or you can step into the office here, if you like.'

Miss Whittaker accepted the hospitality of the office. It was a gloomy place, smelling of stale ink and wet serge. The ceiling was stained and cracked, and the room was lit by an unadorned fishtail burner. 'In the streets'? Whatever could that mean? Whatever his errand, he'd forget all about it when he had heard what she had to tell him.

The sergeant busied himself at a tall desk, writing in a ledger. From time to time other men came in, some uniformed, some in civilian clothing, to address various cryptic remarks to the old sergeant. They all glanced briefly at the lady visitor, and then ignored her presence entirely.

Presently, Louise Whittaker heard the sound of raised voices somewhere on the floor above. Two men were evidently indulging in a noisy argument. To her alarm the violent altercation increased. A high-pitched but powerful tenor voice launched itself into some kind of vehement denunciation, only to be drowned out by a positively frightening stentorian bellow. There was silence for a while, and then the whole process was repeated. This time, there was the sound of a chair crashing over.

The elderly sergeant sighed, and produced a substantial set of handcuffs from the desk. He smiled at Miss Whittaker, and limped out of the room, swinging the handcuffs as he went.

In a few moments the frightful row upstairs abruptly ceased, and the stentorian voice relieved itself of some kind of admonitory speech.

Miss Whittaker glanced out into the hall, and saw the bearded sergeant walking with measured tread down the stairs. The handcuffs were now tucked in his belt. He was followed by a wiry little man in merchant navy uniform. His ginger beard bristled with indignation, but there was a certain cowed look about him. His face was red, not with anger but with blushing. He looked neither to right nor left, and bustled indignantly out into the street.

'In Heaven's name, Sergeant, what was that dreadful altercation? I feared that violence was about to be done.'

The sergeant smiled and shook his head.

'Oh, no, ma'am, there was no fear of that. It was just a gentleman connected with one of our cases having a difference of opinion with

Superintendent Mackharness upstairs. In cases like that, I usually go up and wave the handcuffs about. It always does the trick. That was the gentleman, him what just went out now. Naval sort of man, he was.'

'Is Superintendent Mackharness a pleasant man? He sounds quite stern through the ceiling.'

The sergeant seemed struck by Louise's question. Evidently it was a matter he'd not considered before. He put his pen down on the desk, and stroked his beard thoughtfully.

'Pleasant. No, miss, since you ask: he's not pleasant. Not in the least. But he's the senior officer here, and people must speak respectful when they go up to see him. Respectful.'

The sergeant returned to his labour of writing in the ledger. It had begun to rain, and it was getting quite dark in the little office. The sergeant turned up the gas, and threw a scuttleful of coal on to the fire. Somehow, the action only emphasized the chilliness of the gloomy place.

Louise Whittaker began to long for her neat and well-ordered house in Finchley. Was it really possible, she wondered, for a woman ever to be a detective in a place like this? Why did it have to be so wretchedly drab?

A jaunty young man in plain clothes popped his head through the door and said,

'Digger Davies has just turned up, floating in the Regent's Canal. Head stove in by a brick. Thought you'd like to know, Pat.'

The jaunty man caught sight of Louise Whittaker.

'Beg pardon, miss,' he said, 'I didn't see you there.'

'So your name's Pat, is it?' Louise faltered. She was cold and apprehensive, and felt impelled to speak to her saturnine companion rather than just sit still, a useless piece of decoration in a rough and threatening world. She had imagined Inspector Box in a small, book-lined office, receiving her with his usual confused gallantry, and then listening with dawning appreciation to her revelations. It was not going to be like that.

'Yes, miss. Sergeant Driscoll, known as 'Pat'. Ah! I think this will be Mr Box, now.' They both heard the sound of iron tyres grating to a stop on the cobbles of King James's Rents. 'Yes, here he is. He'll be with you presently.'

'Thank you, Sergeant Driscoll. I'll just — '

A frightful crash of doors flying open drove her words from the air. From the safety of the office she saw a mass of struggling men fall into the entrance hall. One of them was Inspector Box, whose hat rolled away across the floor as a brawny arm circled his throat.

There were three uniformed policemen in the grunting, struggling heap. One of them prised the arm from Box's throat in time for him to shout, 'Get the darbies on him, for God's sake, Wilson! Stamp on his hand, Jack, or he'll have your guts out with that blade!'

Without warning the whole seething heap rose a few feet into the air and a hideous soprano voice began to shriek out threats and obscenities. Louise Whittaker caught sight of a convulsed face, black with grime, a loose red mouth apparently filled with broken teeth, and rolling bloodshot eyes.

There was a clatter of boots from some unseen corridor and several more men appeared. In a few moments, the hideous prisoner was subdued and turned on to his stomach. One of the reinforcements forced his squirming wrists into a pair of handcuffs. The knot of detectives stood up. One big, heavy young man with a badly scarred face held a handkerchief to a knife slash below the jaw line. Inspector Box roughly turned the captive on to his back and stared into his contorted grimy face.

Louise felt sick. This was horrible. They were all brutes . . .

'You're going downstairs, Baby-Boy,' Box panted. His face was convulsed with anger. 'You're going in the bear-pit to cool off, and then I'll be down to ask you a few questions.'

The loathsome soprano voice burst out again into a string of obscenities. Box's voice rose to a dangerous shriek.

'Shut it, do you hear! You're done for, Baby, so keep a civil tongue in your head. If you start your cursing again, we'll gag you. You wouldn't like that.'

Inspector Box retrieved his hat and stood up, while the group of policemen dragged the now subdued prisoner away towards the basement steps. The whole violent episode had lasted no more than five minutes. To Louise Whittaker it seemed an age.

Box and the scarred man pushed open some glazed doors and were about to enter a room that she could not see when an elderly man in a frock coat appeared at the head of the stairs. He stooped a little, and sported fine, white, mutton-chop whiskers. The man seemed to have been totally unaware of the affray that had just taken place.

'Box,' the elderly man called down, 'up here, if you please. Half an hour hence.'

Box made some reply that Louise Whittaker could not hear, and then disappeared through the glazed doors with his companion. The bearded Sergeant Driscoll got up from his desk.

'Mr Box will be able to see you now, miss,'

he said. He, too, seemed not to have noticed the frightening struggle that had taken place within feet of where he sat. She followed him from the gloomy front office and crossed the bare floorboards of the entrance hall. The sergeant pushed open one of the glass doors and said, 'Miss Whittaker, sir.'

Box glanced in her direction, but his flushed, angry face seemed not to see her.

'I don't want him up tomorrow on the police-court sheet,' Box said. 'I want him on a Surrey Magistrates' Warrant. He's been round my neck for three years. I'll swing for him one day, Sergeant Knollys. I'll do time for him. I want him down for good.'

Why had she imagined for one moment that she could belong to Arnold Box's violent world? She had no right to be here, interfering. These men laboured night and day to hold back the tide of chaos and anarchy that constantly threatened society. Box's world did not consist exclusively of the affair of Dr Otto Seligmann. Why had she come?

Box suddenly caught sight of her, and the anger melted from his face as though by a miracle. He hurried across from where he had been standing by a large table, covered with a jumbled sprawl of papers and books.

'Miss Whittaker! Come in. How nice to see

200

you. This is my office. I'm sorry it's not very shipshape at the moment ... This is my colleague, Sergeant Knollys.'

'Pleased to meet you, miss,' said Sergeant Knollys.

The big, scar-faced man had been standing by a large fly-blown mirror, holding a blood-soaked handkerchief to his jaw. He turned round as he spoke, and smiled, and she was startled to see in his smile a knowledge that she and Box were acquainted. Surely he didn't talk about her? Surely ...

'Sit down in this chair near the fire, Miss Whittaker,' said Box. 'Sergeant Knollys, if you're going to bleed all over the place you'd better go. You need stitches in that gash. Go and find Dr Cropper, and tell him to sew you up. Then go down to Beak Street and see Mr Shale. Or if you're too bloody to go, send Wilson or Roberts. Mr Shale will get us a Surrey docket before tonight.'

When the glazed doors had swung closed behind Knollys, Inspector Box seemed to Louise to undergo a subtle change. The determined brutality that had animated him receded, and she saw once again the diffident, confiding friend who came out to Finchley in an omnibus to talk and have his tea with her. The large, grimy room began to take on a more intimate atmosphere. She saw the fireplace, the mirror with its notes, the round-faced railway clock high on the wall. Somehow, the office now seemed smaller and more intimate than when she had first crossed its threshold.

Box sat down opposite her, and looked keenly into her eyes. 'What's the matter?' he asked.

'Mr Box, I have discovered some information of vital importance, and I have come straight to you here at King James's Rents to impart it to you.'

'What's the matter?' Box repeated his question. 'You look different . . . intimidated, if that's the right word. What is it?'

Louise Whittaker felt herself blushing. It was like him, she thought, to let concern for her feelings override his professional curiosity.

'I thought it would be so simple, Mr Box. I would come here and give you the benefit of my wisdom, and go away smirking with self-satisfaction. Instead of which, I stumbled into a rough, crude world of violence . . . There was a frightful row upstairs between that superintendent and some kind of sea-captain — '

'Was there, now? Well, he'll tell me about that in half-an-hour's time. I wonder who won that particular row?'

'The superintendent did. He bellowed like a bull. I thought the ceiling would fall.'

Inspector Box laughed, and leaned back in his chair.

'And then, while I was sitting in the front office with Sergeant Driscoll, you burst in with those others, and went rolling around on the floor, all spitting and cursing. That horrible man with the squeaky voice! He was like an animal. And here was I, with my clever little discovery, all ready to amaze and stun you. I should never have come.'

'I see. So having accepted my offer to join my special posse, you want to back out? You've decided that it's just a job for brutes?'

She could hear the hint of mocking challenge beneath the words, and began to form a reply, but Box continued.

'Any other day of the week, Miss Whittaker, this place would have been as quiet as the tomb. You just happened to choose this day of all days, when Superintendent Mackharness decided to erupt like a volcano, and I had to bring in Baby-Boy Contarini, one of the most desperate villains in London. We chained him to the window frame in the growler, but he nearly had us over on the bridge. He's as strong as an ox, is Baby.'

'What has he done?'

'You've heard about the Islington Pawn-brokers? Well, Baby-Boy is the one who slit their throats. He did that, and burned them up in their shops to cover his tracks. But he wasn't quite clever enough. It's a long story — another story. So you want to back out?'

It was her turn to laugh. He was so obviously glad to see her, and so clearly determined to make her stay the course. And so she would.

'No, Mr Box. I don't want to 'back out', as you so inelegantly put it. In future, I'll choose a quieter day, when you're deep in contemplation. You and Sergeant — Knollys, did you say?'

'That's it, miss. Jack Knollys. Now, you'd better tell me what you've discovered. In a quarter-of-an-hour's time I'm due upstairs to hear the latest words of wisdom from my lord and master.'

★ ★ ★

Lieutenant Fenlake watched Vanessa Drake for a moment as she walked off towards Trafalgar Square. She'd be all right. There were plenty of people about. Anyway, she was a Londoner born. It wasn't as though she was a visitor, or anything like that.

He hurried under the archway, and through one of several dark doorways in the block of buildings to the right of the front court. His journey took him along a matted corridor and three sets of swing doors, which brought him to a long, dim room, where a dozen soberly dressed clerks were writing away busily at their desks. One of the clerks, an elderly puckish man with a smooth round face, looked up, and put his quill pen down on the desk.

'Mr Fenlake, sir! I'm afraid there's to be no rest for you today. There's a new assignment waiting for you!'

The clerk took a small buff envelope from a pigeon-hole, and handed it to Fenlake.

'There you are, sir. You're folio 8 of the 6th January, unsealed at 4.24 p.m. It's a return assignment, Mr Fenlake, so you'll need to come back here to the cipher-office to close and seal when you've done.'

Lieutenant Fenlake tore open the envelope and extracted a slip of white paper. He read it through, and then thrust it without comment into his pocket. It was a routine task, an initial meeting with another courier, a new man who needed to be shown the ropes.

'Thank you, Anson. I'll be on my way. But tell me, aren't you usually over there, at that desk by the staircase?'

'Usually, sir, yes. But one of the cipher-clerks didn't sign in today, so we're doubling up, if you see what I mean.'

One of the clerks . . . Fenlake stared at the desk, with its blotter, pen rack, and set of pigeon-holes, all made in dark mahogany. It was Anson who dealt with his assigniments, but he could recall the man who usually sat at this desk near the door, a young man, neatly dressed, self-effacing. He'd once caught his eye, and received a neutral glance from the man.

That face . . . He saw it again in his mind's eye, enlivened by exertion, soot-stained, eyeing him with a strangely intense and cynically amused expression. A Scotsman — the man with the plank at Chelsea.

'This clerk? What is his name?'

'His name's Colin McColl, sir. He's been with us on a part-time basis nigh on a year, now.'

Fenlake said nothing. It was time for him to leave the Admiralty by a rear door that gave on to St James's Park. Should he walk up to the Foreign Office now, and alert Sir Charles Napier to what he had just discovered? It was only a step away. But then, if Colin McColl was one of their own people, how could he have been an assassin? Was Sir Charles wrong about that?

Well, the matter would have to wait until the morning. Duty called, and he would make his way to 3 Thomas Lane Mews, near Grosvenor Square. He had been there on a number of occasions before. It would be prudent to walk over to Carlton House Terrace, and take a cab from the rank at the corner of Waterloo Place. As he skirted the vast, sombre expanse of the park, some part of his tidy mind hoped that Vanessa Drake would be all right.

* * *

Inspector Box felt tired. The desperate struggle with Baby-Boy Contarini had fatigued him more than he'd cared to admit. What a day for Miss Whittaker to pay a surprise call! Still, her information confirmed what he and Knollys had suspected all along. The young woman called Ottilie Seligmann was an impostor. Well, they were all being discreetly watched — Ottilie, Count Czerny, the housekeeper, and the secretary. They could wait.

He sat down in his accustomed chair near the fire, and lit a thin cigar. It was just after five, and quite dark outside. The old gas mantle flickered and spluttered. Box could hear the faint movements of other people in distant rooms. A coal settled in the grate.

His mind turned to Dr Seligmann. He must have acquired a complete set of *The Hansa Protocol* and hidden it away behind those dummy books in the Belvedere. Then someone had found out . . . Perhaps the false Ottilie had done some snooping. Seligmann was a German, a subject of the Kaiser. Didn't that make him a traitor? To some people, like those angry men in St Swithin's Hall, he would be a traitor. But to others — well, to hold the keys of the German military machine meant some guarantee of peace.

He glanced at the paper calendar hanging beside the fireplace. Friday, 6 January, it said, the Feast of the Epiphany. There was just one week to go before the Pan-German rally in Berlin. Box wondered when the memorandum was to start on its journey.

The old sergeant from the front office came in through the swing doors, carrying a slim ledger, which he placed in front of Box on the desk. The incident book.

'How late does this go, Sergeant Driscoll?' asked Box.

'To five o'clock, sir. The duty officer at Whitehall Place will compile the night book from six onwards. Is it all right for me to go off now, sir?'

Box removed the slim cigar from his mouth. 'That's quite all right, Sergeant. PC Kenwright will be back soon.'

Sergeant Driscoll saluted, and left the room. Without leaning forward in his chair, Box dragged the incident book towards him across the cluttered table, and opened it where a piece of blotting paper marked a place.

The teeming millions . . . There was never any relief from the constant wave of crime surging through the vast metropolis. His eyes scanned the carefully written entries — Parker, Emmanuel, jeweller, stabbed at such-and-such an address; O'Hanlon, Patrick, taken up on suspicion of murder; Fenlake, Arthur, shot dead at such-and-such an address —

Box sat up straight in his chair. All trace of tiredness had left him.

'Fenlake, Arthur, shot dead in premises at 3 Thomas Lane Mews, Grosvenor Square.'

Within a minute Box was in a cab, rattling through the bitter cold streets towards Grosvenor Square.

★ ★ ★

Box could hear the murmur of the crowd before he turned the corner from the square into Thomas Lane Mews. The narrow lane was thronged with the usual parcel of loiterers, tradesmen and know-alls, who gazed at the grimy brick front and dirty windows of number three as though they could read its secrets.

The door of the house opened to admit him, and was immediately closed after him. He stood in a dusty hall, where a stout, whimsical looking inspector had come out to greet him. He spoke with a kind of suppressed chuckle, which indicated the kind of man he was. He wore a smart but comfortable uniform, and carried his round pillbox hat in his hand.

'I saw you striding along the pavement just now, Mr Box,' he remarked, 'which made me ask myself, 'What does *he* want?' And then I thought to myself, 'Why not ask him?' You'd better come through to the back room.'

'How are you, Mr Graham?' asked Box. 'I know you'll not mind me coming. It's just that there's a little link here with something I'm engaged on.'

Inspector Graham motioned with his hand to a plain wooden desk, which, with two upright chairs, completed the furnishing of the room.

'There he is, Mr Box, on the floor behind the desk. Shot at point-blank range in the back. Revolver, I'd say, though we can't be sure till later. Dr Cheshunt's coming. Poor young man. I don't think he could've been thirty, by the look of him.'

'Why was he found? The house looks empty to me.'

'Someone heard the shot. Someone who knew the house was empty. They sent for us. I've examined the body. There were some letters and papers in his pocket, which tell us who he is. Arthur Fenlake, his name was. A lieutenant in the Royal Artillery. Are you going to associate yourself with this?'

Inspector Box looked down at the young man's body. This dead man was Vanessa Drake's young man. The manner of his death had the deadly hallmark of Colin McColl. Stefan Oliver, too, had been shot in the back. It was an economical way to murder a man, because there was no possibility of a struggle. You took your victim by surprise.

Arthur Fenlake had spun round with the force of the shot, and was lying on his back in a pool of dark blood. His arms were outstretched, the left hand contracted into a tight fist. The face, and open eyes, expressed not fear, but surprise. Box had to use both hands to prise open Fenlake's fingers. He removed a slip of paper from his hand and quickly read it. He drew in his breath sharply.

'Associate myself? No, Mr Graham, I'll not do that. I've seen all I need to see. I don't think you'll find out who did this for a long time. It's a Foreign Office affair — you know the kind of thing I mean.'

He handed the slip of paper to Graham, who read it out aloud.

'Go to SH3. New courier reception. Canning.'

Inspector Graham handed the document back to Inspector Box. He shook his head, and smiled ruefully.

'I'm getting too old for this kind of work, Mr Box. I'm getting careless. I should have seen that paper in his hand. Not that it makes any sense to me.'

'Fenlake was still clutching that note when he was shot, which means that he'd only just entered this place when the killer struck. This is Secure House Number 3, Mr Graham, a kind of secret trysting-place for Foreign Office couriers. Was there any sign of forced entry?'

'No. I think both killer and victim used door keys to get into this place.'

'Very likely. There's treachery here, Mr Graham. That name, 'Canning', is used by the Foreign Secretary and his deputies as a code-name.'

'An enemy within the gates?'

'Exactly. But what I don't understand, is why that enemy should want to make away with this poor young man.'

'Maybe he doesn't like Foreign Office couriers.'

'Maybe not, Mr Graham. And you're not getting too old, or careless. You're getting too fat! Try running round the block every day, or take a course in the dumb-bells. You suggest that our killer doesn't like couriers. You're a cynical devil, Mr Graham, but I think that, in this case, you might have hit on the sober truth.'

10

The Mistress and her Servants

Colonel Kershaw stood in front of an ornate carved desk in a very chilly, high-ceilinged chamber, which seemed at first glance to be part library and part armoury; but the bound volumes on the shelves looked undisturbed by enquiring hands, and the collection of fierce swords and daggers reposed harmlessly in glass cases. The fanciful mock-Gothic fireplace contained nothing warmer than a confection of yellow and brown dried grasses.

Into this room presently came a little woman of seventy-four, dumpy and homely, yet bringing with her immeasurable dignity. Queen Victoria had reigned as Queen of Great Britain and Ireland for fifty-six years. For seventeen years she had been Empress of India. Sovereign of the most powerful nation on earth, she held sway over one-fifth of the world's population. She sat down on a damask-covered chair behind the desk, while unseen hands silently closed the door through which she had entered.

Etiquette forbade any conversation before

the Queen had spoken. Kershaw stood rigidly before her for what seemed to him at least ten minutes, measured by the relentless ticking of a number of clocks. He noted the sheen of her black silk widow's weeds, and the exquisite fineness of her white lace veil. She had donned small, round, gold-framed spectacles before entering the room, and gave her attention wholly to a collection of documents that had been laid ready for her on the blotter.

Finally, Queen Victoria carefully removed her glasses, folded them, and placed them on the desk. When she spoke, Kershaw was conscious of the contrast between her involuntarily forbidding presence and the bell-like sweetness of her voice.

'Good afternoon, Colonel Kershaw. We say that as a matter of courtesy, though of course there is nothing good about it at all. Nothing. We are conscious of failings, of complacency, of a falling away of the effectiveness of the organs of governance. When we think back over the last half-century, we are reminded that home and foreign affairs were at one time managed with greater success.'

The Queen dropped her eyes for a moment to the documents on the desk. Colonel Kershaw wondered whether all the other rooms in Windsor Castle were as relentlessly freezing as this discreet little chamber at the entrance to the Private Apartments.

'Last Saturday, Colonel Kershaw,' the Queen continued, 'a Foreign Office courier, Stefan Oliver, was murdered, and thrown by his murderer from a boat into the Thames. Did you know that?'

'Yes, Ma'am.'

'Last Tuesday, one of Britain's staunchest friends, Dr Otto Seligmann, was blown to pieces in Chelsea by means of an Infernal Machine. Did you know *that*?'

'Yes, Ma'am.'

'How could such things occur in our capital? We summoned Sir Charles Napier here, and told him that this kind of thing had to stop. And now . . . What are we to say about this slaughter, only yesterday afternoon, of a staunch and loyal young officer in a so-called 'secure house' belonging to the Foreign Office? Lieutenant Arthur Fenlake was instrumental in delivering to Sir Charles Napier a memorandum written by Dr Seligmann — '

Colonel Kershaw began to frame a reply, but the Sovereign held up her hand to enjoin silence. She had grown very pale, a change emphasized by the deep black of her customary mourning dress.

'Lieutenant Fenlake was thirty-one. What a

waste of a young life! What contempt for the Queen's Peace! Oliver, Seligmann, Fenlake — these are blows against us! These murderous assassinations, Colonel Kershaw, are symptomatic of a greater and more serious disease in the body politic. The country is riddled with traitors. They are everywhere — in the houses of the great, in the military encampments, and in the very seats of government — '

'Ma'am — '

'We have not yet finished speaking! These traitors, and their sympathizers, are gaining ground. They are mesmerized by the rhetoric of my grandson William, and his agents. William — the Kaiser — is a man who likes to appear strong. But he is weak — weak in body and spirit, and we fear that one day he will bring the whole of Europe to ruin. Meanwhile, we must do our utmost to prevent that. And so, once again — once again, Colonel Kershaw, I have sent for you.'

The Queen had abruptly abandoned the royal plural, and with it some measure of the anger that she had felt as Sovereign. The change of pronoun let Kershaw know that the scolding was at an end, and that he was to be treated now as a confidant. The Queen permitted a little smile to play about her mouth.

'You appear to be shivering, Colonel Kershaw. Are you cold? If so, I will tell them to light the fire.'

'No, Ma'am, I am not at all cold. Perhaps just a little un-warm.'

The smile lingered for a brief moment on the Queen's face, and then her mood became grave once more.

'Sir Charles Napier, the Under-Secretary, is a very capable man. A brilliant man. In his way . . . I should very much like to induce him to retire to that estate of his in Wiltshire. A peerage, perhaps? Well, I'll speak to Mr Gladstone about that. And, of course, to dear Lord Salisbury.'

The Queen seemed to have lost sight of Kershaw for a moment. He stood quite still, waiting for her next words.

'That memorandum of Seligmann's — my government is anxious to convey it safely to certain parties in Germany. But you already know about that.'

'Yes, Ma'am. I have, in fact, already interested myself in it.'

'Ah!' It was a little sigh of satisfaction. 'I wondered, you know, whether you had already moved in the matter. Whenever I see you, Colonel Kershaw, I think of Francis Walsingham and Robert Cecil, who ran the secret services in olden times. Have you seen

218

the picture of Queen Elizabeth at Hatfield? The Queen's cloak is covered with embroidered eyes and ears, which I believe represent her secret servants: unseen, they saw all, unheard, they heard all. Whenever I see that picture, and what it may signify, I think of myself, and of Walsingham and Cecil. And then I think of you.'

The Queen stopped speaking, and simply looked at the slight, sandy-haired man standing stiffly in front of her. He knew what he had to say.

'Your Majesty, I have the honour to head your Department of Special Services. I have long considered the rot setting in throughout your realm, and believe that now is the time for me to act. But I cannot act effectively unless Your Majesty grants me full powers to over-ride and to commandeer.'

'We give you those powers, Colonel Kershaw. I have already told Mr Gladstone that I would do so, if the need arose. Do what you will, and use whatever means you deem necessary. Cleanse our realm of treachery! Our people shall not be delivered into the hands of alien oppressors.'

Queen Victoria stood up. Colonel Kershaw bowed deeply. He kept his head inclined until he knew that Her Majesty had left the room. A liveried footman appeared, and conducted him from the private apartments. He emerged from the chill audience room into the cold winter afternoon.

'Well done, old girl,' he muttered to himself. 'I'll not fail you!'

★ ★ ★

Vanessa Drake stood a little apart from the other mourners, who formed a kind of tableau of dignified grief where they had assembled on one of the snow-pocked paths between the graves at Highgate Cemetery. The carriages had been halted at the beginning of the long avenue, and they had all walked its entire length until they reached the great cedar of Lebanon at the centre of the circular road. An unrelenting wind soughed through the tall, swaying trees, and blew dried snow from the draped urns, marble crosses and granite columns of the countless grand, gaunt tombs.

Arthur had been an orphan, like herself, and both his parents lay here, in the grave newly opened for him. The black-coated, black-gloved mourners on the path, the women veiled to the ankles, the men with long mourning bands trailing from their silk hats, were his uncles, their wives, and his cousins. They had travelled down from

Hereford, and would return there later that day.

Nearer to the grave, where the snow had been trampled into slush, a group of military officers had taken up their position, their blue and scarlet uniforms making a dash of colour among the general dreariness. Although it was bitterly cold, they wore no cloaks. There were other soldiers standing in disciplined formations on the paths.

The military chaplain's white surplice billowed out behind him, and his voice, though high and clear, was carried away by the gusting wind. The coffin was committed to the earth, and Vanessa saw the chaplain close his book, and step back from the grave. Surely, that was the end of it? What was happening now?

A detail of soldiers appeared, six young men wearing dark-blue uniforms, and carrying rifles. In response to a series of brief orders barked out by someone unseen, they took up positions around the grave, swiftly raised their rifles, and fired a single deafening fusillade into the air. The sound echoed and re-echoed from the turrets and tombs, and a flock of shrieking crows rose up, protesting, from the trees, to the bleak sky. At the same time, the knot of officers drew their swords, and executed the complex sword-play of the 'present arms'.

Vanessa suddenly experienced a surge of pride which for a moment swamped her grief and anger. For she had been angry and resentful at the waste of her friend's life in the pursuit of some secret government exploit that wasn't allowed to reveal itself to the light of day. The pride of that moment, when the rifles fired as one, seemed to banish her smouldering resentment.

The mourners moved slowly towards the avenue, that would take them back to the carriages. The gravediggers hovered discreetly with their spades. The soldiers and their officers began to disperse. One officer, though, began to walk towards Vanessa, clearly intent on greeting her. She wondered who he was, and hoped that he would not detain her long. She wanted to go back quietly in a cab to her lodgings near Westminster Abbey, and to think about Arthur there.

She looked at the man who was approaching her, picking his way cautiously among the snow-covered graves. He was a slightly built, sandy-haired man with a pleasant but rather weary expression. He looked about fifty years of age. It was difficult not to be impressed by his appearance. He wore a blue jacket, with rows of gold braid and a scarlet collar, and blue trousers with a red stripe. He carried a black busby, with a red badge and a white plume, in the crook of his right arm, while his left hand steadied the scabbard of his dress sword. As he stepped on to the path, he greeted her with a gentle, confiding smile.

'Miss Drake? Please accept my condolences. I am Lieutenant-Colonel Adrian Kershaw, of the Royal Artillery.' She could see now the grenade badges on his collar. Poor Arthur, on the rare occasions that he had worn uniform, had sported the same grenade badges. He offered her his arm, and they walked slowly together down the path.

'Will you be joining the others, Miss Drake? I believe there's to be a reception at the Highgate Tavern.'

'No, Colonel Kershaw. I shall go straight home. Were — were you Arthur's superior officer? He wasn't an ordinary soldier, was he?'

'The answer to both your questions is no, Miss Drake. No, I was not Arthur Fenlake's superior officer. And no, he was not an ordinary soldier. Fenlake was a special courier, seconded from his army unit to the Foreign Office. I'm not allowed to tell you why he was killed — murdered. But I *can* tell you that he died on active service. That is why the Queen decreed a military funeral for him today.'

'The Queen?'

'Yes. It was Her Majesty's express wish.'

They had reached a small, single-storey lodge set back from the avenue, and partly cloaked by trees. The front door opened, and an elderly man in a gardener's smock came out on to the doorstep. Vanessa could see into the room beyond, where a fire was cheerfully burning.

'Will you drink a cup of tea with me, Miss Drake? You have only to step inside the lodge. It will restore your spirits after this melancholy business, and help to drive away some of this biting cold.'

Vanessa looked searchingly at him for a moment, and then at the elderly man, who had walked away purposefully into the cemetery. She glanced up at the sky. The fitful daylight had a greenish hue, and black clouds scudded across Highgate village. There would be torrential hail, perhaps, or the final victory of the skirmishing snow. She nodded her head, and together they entered the lodge.

★ ★ ★

'No, Miss Drake,' said Kershaw, putting his cup down on the saucer, 'I was not Arthur's

224

superior officer, though you'll appreciate that we belonged to the same regiment. Arthur had been seconded to the Foreign Office, where he worked for the Under-Secretary, Sir Charles Napier, as one of his most valued couriers. I have charge of a different crowd of people entirely. They are folk who keep constant watch, and carry out assignments that help to guarantee the safety and stability of our country. Do you want to hear more?'

'Yes.'

'I have two kinds of people working for me. First, there are professionally trained men and women, drawn from all ranks in society. They are required to take great risks. You will find them in the nobility, in the professions, in the working population. These people are known as secret servants, and they receive an annual purse from the Treasury.'

Colonel Kershaw sipped his tea for a while, and Vanessa gazed at the flickering flames in the rusty grate of the little room. They were both sitting on upright Windsor chairs, placed on either side of a spindly tea-table.

'And then,' Kershaw continued, 'there are the others — the 'nobodies'. They carry out small tasks that are part of a greater project. Rather like a piece of embroidery, you know, where you can work very closely on a particular detail — a panel of an altar frontal, say — and not feel bothered about losing sight of the whole design.'

Colonel Kershaw glanced at her briefly as he said this, and she realized that he knew how she earned her living.

'The nobodies are unpaid, but know that they will never be in want, never be without friends in time of need. They are people like the cemetery gardener, whose assignment it was to make this tea for us, and to ensure that we are left alone in this lodge. Yes, the nobodies are people like him. People who will receive a verbal summons to do a certain thing at a certain place, and will do it without demur. They are people like *you*.'

'Like me?'

'Yes. In fact, you met one of my nobodies quite recently. Mrs Prout, she's called.'

'Oh! It was in my friend's club. I was moaning about how dull life was, and this Mrs Prout told me all about her adventures in China — '

'Yes, and she did that, Miss Drake, because I wanted to know what kind of young woman you were. Lieutenant Fenlake was still alive, then, and you were his friend. In addition to that, I knew that you possessed a certain skill that could prove very useful to me.'

'A skill of mine?'

'Yes. In three days' time, Miss Drake, on

Friday the 13th, an event will take place in Berlin that could set Europe ablaze, and plunge Britain into war. But you — with your special skill — could take part in an enterprise that would prevent that catastrophe.'

'But my employer — '

'There will never be any difficulty about that, Miss Drake. Or about reimbursements for lost earnings. So will you join my crowd? Will you help me to bring Arthur Fenlake's work to fruition? There may be danger, but you will never be more than a breath away from help.'

Vanessa Drake suddenly smiled. She looked at the cheerful fire in the lodge grate, and at the man in dress uniform sitting opposite her. That black crepe band on his sleeve was for Arthur. By accepting Colonel Kershaw's offer, she would be uniting herself with Arthur's unquestioning devotion to his country. She thought of his last words to her, as they parted outside the Admiralty. 'You'll be all right, won't you?' Yes; she would be all right.

'Colonel Kershaw,' said Vanessa Drake, 'tell me what I have to do.'

★ ★ ★

Louise Whittaker paused in her meal to sip a glass of seltzer, and glanced across the quietly sumptuous dining room of Bagot's Hotel. The large room was heavily panelled in polished mahogany, but was prevented from being gloomy by an elaborately carved and coffered plaster ceiling. The room was skilfully lighted by shaded oil lamps, and a vast fire blazed away in a wide grate. There were a good many military and naval types taking dinner, but also a sprinkling of civilian guests and their wives. It was very comfortable, and the service was excellent.

On the way down to dinner from her room, Louise had glanced out through a window on the landing, and had seen the vast blanket of white snow lying over Archbishop's Park. Down in Carlisle Place, though, the snow had been churned to brown slush by the passing traffic on its way to the bridge.

Louise put down her glass, and looked at Vanessa Drake, who was sitting opposite her. She saw the excitement in her young friend's eyes, the animated sparkle that had been there when she had first confided this adventure to her. But she saw, too, the slight tremor in the girl's temple, and the paleness of her face.

'What's the matter, Vanessa?' she asked softly.

'I think it's nerves,' the girl replied in a low voice. 'Do you realize that poor Arthur's funeral was only yesterday? I had to give an immediate answer to Colonel Kershaw, and agree to take a room here last night. It's the eleventh today. The mission starts tomorrow, and the memorandum that poor Arthur delivered to Sir Charles Napier will start its journey to Berlin.'

Vanessa suddenly realized that she was being indiscreet. She lowered her voice. 'It's not like an ordinary hotel, Louise. There's always room for people connected to the colonel. And then he said it would be better if I had a woman companion — being alone might draw the wrong kind of attention to me. I told him about you. It was good of you to come, Louise.'

'Not good of me at all! I have a lost reputation with Arnold Box to redeem! But come now, Vanessa, what's the matter with you?'

'I told you. It's nerves. I enjoyed the first assignment just before dinner — Colonel Kershaw was there in the room, watching me work, and encouraging me. There was another gentleman there, too, who seemed very grand, but very reassuring. But it's the second assignment — I'm sure I'll tremble so much that I'll make some frightful mistake — '

Two waiters appeared, removed their plates, and brushed down the cloth with napkins. Would they take coffee at the table, or in the sitting-room? They would take it at the table.

'Vanessa,' said Louise Whittaker, 'you are talking like a heroine in a cheap novel, the kind of female who trembles like an aspen in the presence of the menfolk, and is for ever casting her eyes down! But there, I mustn't scold you — I found out the other day that not everything in the male garden is rosy. Not by any means.'

She recalled briefly the dirty and distorted face of Baby-Boy Contarini, and his frightful profanities, shrieked out in a grotesque soprano voice. No; there was no room for tremblers in Mr Box's female posse.

'Would it help if I came into the room with you?'

'Oh, Louise, would you? I'm going to need a steady hand, and I'm afraid of ending up like your aspen, trembling and quivering, and ruining everything. I know that Mr Box will be there, too — '

'Yes, Mr Box will be there, but it would complete the trick if I were there as well. The three musketeers. After all, we've worked well as a team before — first as theatre critics at the Savoy, and then as trenchermen at

Simpson's in the Strand.'

She was pleased to see Vanessa smile, and by the time that the coffee had arrived, the girl was her own vital self again.

★ ★ ★

'Devilish handsome gals over there, Lankester,' observed Surgeon Lieutenant Goldsmith, glancing across the dining-room. 'I wonder who they are? The little blonde one booked in last night. Her stunning friend arrived in a cab at noon today.'

'I don't know who they are, Goldsmith. Friends of Mother Prout's, I gather. And you're far too old to have frivolous thoughts about young ladies, so you'd better give your full attention to finishing that plum pudding.'

The old retired naval officer chuckled, and did as he was told.

Major Lankester would have preferred to dine in his own room, but Kershaw had advised against it. He'd been glad to share a table with old Goldsmith, a red-faced man with spiky white hair and quizzical white eyebrows, who had a fund of good naval stories to tell, and a fondness for the gaming-tables second only to his own. It was very rare, these days, to see Horatio

Goldsmith at Bagot's.

Lankester glanced across at the two young women who were sharing a table near the fireplace. The elder one was a real beauty, raven-haired, and with an assured presence. The fair girl was no more than twenty, and very pretty. She was listening intently to something that her companion was saying. There were other ladies present in the dining-room, some with their husbands. They were probably couples up from the country for a few days of business and shopping in the capital.

'So what's brought you up to Town, Goldsmith? Last time I saw you, you swore that you'd never leave that place of yours at Brighton again. Rheumatism, or something. You said your travelling days were done.'

Surgeon Lieutenant Goldsmith carefully garnered the remaining custard from his plate, and consigned it to his mouth. He darted an uncomfortably shrewd glance at his companion, and said, 'Duty called me, Lankester. Something someone at the Admiralty wanted to know about. So I'm holed up here for a day or so. And what about you?'

'Oh, just passing through, you know. It's Wednesday today. I'm off to the Continent tomorrow, and hope to be back in London

232

again late on Saturday. I expect you know the kind of thing I'm doing — ah, here's the coffee.'

Lankester glanced at the large clock above the fireplace. It was just after nine. Two hours earlier, in one of the rooms of Bagot's Hotel not available for guests, he had reported to Colonel Kershaw. Sir Charles Napier, the Under-Secretary, had been with him. Napier had brought the memorandum with him from the Foreign Office, and the three men had formally examined it, noting the wax seals, and the special ciphers that identified it. At Kershaw's behest, Lankester had brought with him the jacket of the suit that he intended to wear for his journey to Berlin the next day.

'I will return this coat to you personally, Lankester,' Colonel Kershaw had said, 'when you retire this evening. You will find that the memorandum will have been sewn into the lining in such a way that no prying eyes would ever suspect that there was a hidden pocket there. Sir Charles Napier will stay here with me, and watch the seamstress complete the task. I wish you God speed.'

There had been a subtle uneasiness in Kershaw's manner, as though his usual assurance had temporarily deserted him. Sir Charles Napier, too, seemed to regard the matter with distaste — or was it contempt? Lankester had suddenly felt compelled to speak. He was still shocked and profoundly upset by the sudden violent death of his young friend Lieutenant Fenlake. Kershaw had told him all about the murderous Colin McColl, and his smouldering resentment caused him to speak more boldly than military custom allowed. Why did Fenlake's assassin remain a free man?

'Sir,' he had said, 'our fellow-officer, Lieutenant Arthur Fenlake, was found shot dead by this fellow McColl in one of the so-called 'secure houses' belonging to Sir Charles Napier there — '

'You are speaking out of turn, Major,' said Kershaw sharply. 'Fenlake is not the issue here.'

'With respect, sir, I *will* speak! I intend no disrespect to Sir Charles Napier, but Fenlake must have been lured to his death by one of Sir Charles's own Foreign Office people. Or there's somebody in Whitehall who talks too much off duty. Too many people know too much. I'm an old hand at courier work, sir, as you know, but I shall be exceedingly nervous this time round.'

To his surprise, Colonel Kershaw had shown no anger at his untypical insubordination. Instead, he had sighed, and glanced at

Sir Charles Napier, who shook his head, but said nothing.

'Well, Lankester,' Kershaw had said, 'your caution does you credit, and perhaps we deserve to stand rebuked. But you mustn't think that, in choosing you to deliver this memorandum at the eleventh hour to Baron von Dessau in Berlin, I am throwing you to the lions. You will be shadowed at all times, from the moment the Dover train leaves Victoria at ten-thirty tomorrow, until the time that you conclude the business, and leave Berlin. It is the element of surprise, we are convinced, that will so unnerve the baron that he will call his curs swiftly to heel. So you have only a single day to cross Europe. Sir Charles and I will make quite sure that nothing and nobody is allowed to stand in your way.'

Somehow, the words were unnerving rather than reassuring. Lankester had already drawn himself briefly to attention, and turned towards the door, when Colonel Kershaw had treated him to a few parting words.

'You have hinted at the presence of an enemy within the gates, Lankester. Well, let me assure you that there are no rotten apples in my barrel. They can't get in, and if any turn rotten when they are in — well, they can't get out.'

By eleven o'clock that evening, the air in the deserted card-room at the rear of the hotel was thick with cigar smoke and the reek of brandy, and Surgeon Lieutenant Goldsmith's face had grown as red as a lobster. Lankester reckoned that the old boy was already half seas under, but his old, pale-blue eyes were still sharp and shrewd, for all that. Goldsmith and Lankester were two of a kind: no amount of alcohol could dim their senses. The old naval officer had talked with great animation of the casino at Monte Carlo, and the gaming-houses of Cannes. When he ran out of stories, he surged to his feet, and disappeared from the room for a few minutes, returning with two generous glasses of brandy. He put them down rather uncertainly on the table, and produced two packs of cards from a drawer in one of the green baize-topped tables.

'Here you are, Lankester,' he said, with a throaty chuckle, 'a little nightcap, with my compliments. Best Highland malt whisky. There's nothing like it for banishing the fumes of lesser spirits. Now, let us have a couple of hands of bezique. I'll show you one or two tricks you may not have come across in that place of Gordon's you go to.'

Half an hour later, the two men parted. Surgeon Lieutenant Goldsmith remained sitting at the table, looking rather rueful. Major Lankester smiled, pocketed the three sovereigns that he had won quite effortlessly, and made his way upstairs. As he neared his room, Colonel Kershaw appeared from a turn in the corridor, handed him his jacket, and bade him goodnight.

★ ★ ★

Downstairs in the card-room, Surgeon Lieutenant Goldsmith started from a slight doze to see Colonel Kershaw standing near the door. He made a perfunctory effort to tidy up the cards spread out across the green baize table among the glasses and tall brass ashtrays. Damn it, Kershaw always had that effect on him!

'How did it go?' asked Kershaw.

'It was all as you might have expected, Kershaw. The fish rose to the bait. Are you sure you're right about this business, though? Really sure, I mean?'

'Really sure, Horatio, alas! Thank you, as always. It's after midnight, and time for you to make yourself scarce. I'll get Mrs Prout to find you a cab.'

Once in his room, Major Lankester turned the door key in its lock. He divested himself of his evening clothes, and dressed himself for the next day's journey. He examined the jacket, and saw how a skilful seamstress had sewn the memorandum into the lining so subtly that there was nothing to be seen. Nevertheless, it was reassuring to feel the bulk of the sealed document lying securely in its concealed pocket.

Lankester put the jacket on, and buttoned it up. Then he extinguished his bedside candle, and lay down, fully clothed, on the bed. He intended to stay awake until morning. He had laid his plans well, but there was always danger. Poor young Fenlake! If ever he came face to face with this skulking assassin, Colin McColl, he would call him to account for young Fenlake's death.

Stay awake . . . He felt desperately tired. Bagot's was safe enough. Its corridors, he knew, were patrolled constantly during the night by porters who looked suspiciously like trained soldiers, fitted awkwardly by the management into civilian clothes. Bagot's was that kind of hotel. Stay awake . . . Major Lankester's eyelids began to flicker, and soon they closed. Within a few minutes, he was in the inexorable grip of a profound sleep.

* * *

Somewhere in the darkened hotel a clock struck three. Floorboards creaked on the landing. Presently the key of Major Lankester's door turned, apparently of its own volition, in the lock, and the door was opened. Three figures silently entered the room. There was the rasp of a match and a sudden flare, and the candle on the bedside table was lit. The major did not stir.

One of the intruders stood on guard at the door. A second unfastened the major's jacket and held it open, while the nimble fingers of the third carefully unstitched the lining. The memorandum was deftly removed, and a seemingly identical packet substituted. Once again the skilled hands worked with needle and thread, sewing up the lining. The second intruder rebuttoned the jacket and extinguished the candle. The night visitors quietly left the room, and once again the key turned in the lock as though moved by a hidden hand. Not a word had been spoken. Major Lankester continued to be held in the grip of a profound sleep.

11

Evening at High Cedars

Major Lankester's eyes slowly opened and focused on the bright white of the ceiling. For a moment he wondered where he was, but then was reassured to see that he was in his familiar snug room in Bagot's Hotel. He felt stiff and cold, part of the penalty of sleeping in his clothes.

Memories of the previous evening returned with a rush of images, and he jerked upright with a surge of fear. What time was it? How long had he been asleep?

He pulled open his jacket, saw the neat stitching in the lining, and felt the reassuring bulk of the packet behind it. But he felt no sense of relief. Something had happened, something that threatened danger. But what was it? Why did he feel so heavy and leaden? Surely it couldn't have been those few brandies last night with old Goldsmith?

Major Lankester's spirits revived when he came down into the dining-room. It was only eight o'clock, but there were quite a few people taking breakfast. Cups and saucers

240

tinkled, waiters flitted across the room, bearing trays. One of the porters came across from the lodge with his copy of *The Times*. It looked as though all was well.

★ ★ ★

Colonel Kershaw stood in a small, cramped, glass-sided booth, which clung like a limpet to one of the walls high above the platforms of Victoria Station. He looked down intently for a few moments through a pair of field-glasses, and then turned to look at Vanessa Drake, who was standing rather disconsolately near a table covered with railway guides and timetables. She had proved to be a brave girl, but she was very young, and in need of encouragement.

'Come on, missy,' he said, gently. 'You're to be in on this.'

'I don't like to,' Vanessa whispered. 'He was so kind to poor Arthur — '

'I know. But people are very complex, Miss Drake, and they can do good things one day, and bad things the next. You did your task superbly last night, so Mr Box tells me. You, and Miss Whittaker there, who bullied me into letting her go with you into Lankester's room. So come and stand here beside me, missy, and do as you're told. The Dover train

241

will be here in less than a minute.'

Vanessa crossed the small room, and stood beside Kershaw. He smiled at her, and for a moment she fancied that he had given her a very slight wink. Then he addressed her friend Louise.

'You'd better come here, too, Miss Whittaker,' he said. 'You're not one of my crowd, like missy here, but you were in at the start of this venture, so it's only fitting that you should be in at the end.'

Louise crossed the wooden floor of the little room and joined Kershaw at the long glazed window. Far below she could see the thronging platforms of the great terminus, and smell the sulphurous smoke rising from the many locomotives standing with steam up at the buffers. Arnold Box was down there. Perhaps he'd bring that great bear of a man with him. What was his name? Knollys. Sergeant Knollys.

From where they stood they could see one of the great clock-faces, and just as the large hands signalled ten o'clock, the train from Dover came smoothly to a stop at the platform below them, and proceeded to emit a devastating shriek of steam.

The platform staff leapt into life, opening doors, trundling trolleys, and sliding open the doors of the luggage van. What appeared to be hundreds of passengers alighted from the train to join the mêlée of confusion on the platform.

In the glass booth, Colonel Kershaw trained his field-glasses on the crowd.

'There he is,' said Kershaw softly. 'He's walking along towards the first-class carriages. He's carrying a small valise, and a folded newspaper. Dear me! How very unoriginal!'

Louise and Vanessa could both see the smartly dressed figure of Major Lankester weaving purposefully through the crowd towards the first-class coach, which was immediately behind the engine and its tender.

Kershaw trailed the glasses slowly along the platform towards a magazine stall, where a rather portly middle-aged man with gold spectacles and a deerstalker hat was leafing through a periodical.

'Do you see that man in the deerstalker? The man by the stall? That's Ephraim Stolberg, a trader in State documents. I thought he'd be here. Either Stolberg, or Klaus Müller, who's another trafficker in secrets. Now — watch!'

They saw Major Lankester pause for a moment by the stall, and pass his folded newspaper to the man called Stolberg, who immediately disappeared into the press of people on the platform.

★ ★ ★

Major Lankester kept his eyes on the magazine stall near the end of the platform. Was he there? Yes! Mr Stolberg was seemingly dipping into a magazine, as though wondering whether to buy it or not. Lankester smiled, and grasped his copy of *The Times* firmly in his right hand.

His thoughts turned almost involuntarily to Mr Gordon. Mr Gordon had been very civilized about Lankester's unpaid account. That, of course, was how it should have been. Lankester was no shrinking amateur at the tables, and Gordon had been accommodating like this before. But there were limits to credit — limits on both sides. He sometimes made fun of Gordon's foppish attempts to look like an English gentleman, but he respected him, nonetheless. It was not right that the man should have to drop discreet hints about payment by making polite enquiries after his health at Bagot's Hotel. He now owed Gordon just over one thousand pounds. With luck, he would repay that debt by the weekend.

As he passed the stall, Lankester paused briefly, and thrust the newspaper into

Stolberg's waiting hand. At the same time, he felt an envelope being put into the pocket of his overcoat. Neither man had so much as glanced at the other. He now had £1,500 in negotiable bonds in his pocket. Wrapped up in the newspaper that he had given to Ephraim Stolberg was the late Dr Seligmann's memorandum to Baron von Dessau.

Part of the throng and press on the platform seemed to realign itself, and become an alarming circle of hostile men. Lankester felt the colour drain from his face, and heard the blood pounding in his ears. There were other noises — the hiss of steam, the babble of voices, the rumbling of trolleys, and then a single voice asking him the most deadly question of all.

'You are William George Lankester?'

He lunged desperately at the little Cockney policeman in the bowler hat, but in a second he had been pinioned by a huge, scar-faced brute of a man. The little Cockney tugged open Lankester's overcoat and jacket, to reveal the torn lining which he had hastily ripped open in the cloakroom at Bagot's before leaving for Victoria.

'William George Lankester, I arrest you on the charge that you did, at London, on the twelfth of January of the current year . . . '

The man who had pinioned him now

clapped him in handcuffs like a felon. Two other men, who looked liked soldiers out of uniform, began to frog-march him away from the Dover train while the policeman was still speaking. Where were they taking him? He was conscious of mute, staring faces in the crowd, and heard whispered questions from startled passengers. 'What's he done?' 'Pickpocket, most likely.' And then, from somewhere near the ticket barrier, he heard someone say, 'Good God, it's Lankester! Look at his face! He's handcuffed . . . What's he done? He's a major in our regiment. Artillery . . . '

They left the safety of the platforms, and a stolid railwayman guided them across the maze of snow-pocked tracks until they came to a grimy engine coupled to a single carriage, standing at a service bay. The posse of silent men hauled Lankester up into a cold compartment, where they joined him. The Cockney policeman handed what was evidently an arrest warrant to one of the men, and then slammed the door. The railwayman locked it from the outside with a brass-handled key. In moments, the dark, unscheduled train was moving out of Victoria Station.

Inspector Box's boots crunched on the ballast as he made his way back along the line

246

to the public platforms, secure and dry under the great arched span of the station roof. He walked slowly up the incline towards the buffers, and saw that Colonel Kershaw was waiting for him.

'Well done, Box,' he said. 'I'm more pleased than I can say. Lankester was one of my best men, but in the last year quite simple missions in which he was involved managed to fail. And then, his private means were quite modest, but he never lacked for money. He was an inveterate gambler — well, you know that, of course. Perhaps I kept him in my service longer than I should have done.'

Arnold Box smiled to himself. Did Kershaw think he was an utter chump?

'Colonel,' he said, 'what you've just told me about Lankester is very touching. But I rather suspect that there was more to this morning's little exercise than merely catching a dubious character who could have been picked off more privately, and certainly more cheaply, than in full public view at a railway terminus. I think you were on the look-out in case Colin McColl turned up, and that you were very pleased when he didn't. Turn up, I mean.'

They walked in silence along the platform for a while. The Dover train had departed, and there were now few people about. Colonel Kershaw looked approvingly at his companion.

'So you saw that, did you? Well done, Mr Box. Yes, I was hoping that McColl wouldn't turn up, because his absence confirms in my mind that — well, I think you know what's in my mind.'

'What will you do now, sir?'

'Do? I'll think, Box, and wait. That man Stolberg has gone off in great glee with a sealed packet containing blank paper. The real memorandum, so expertly extracted from Lankester's jacket last night by Miss Drake, is at this very moment speeding on its way to Berlin.'

'You put a man on the Dover train?'

'Oh, no, Box. The man I sent is a quite unimportant fellow who works as a traveller for a wine merchant. He left on a train for Harwich at five o'clock this morning. He'll pass into Germany by way of the Hook of Holland.'

They had reached the station concourse when Kershaw seemed to make up his mind about something.

'Box,' he said, 'have you heard of High Cedars, Lord Mount Vernon's place in Warwickshire? Well, there's going to be what the papers call a 'glittering reception' there this weekend, and most of the guests have already arrived. I'm going there tonight, and so is Sir Charles Napier. Will you come down there, too? I can easily square things with the commissioner, if that's necessary. There are things I need to tell you, Mr Box, which are best not blurted out in public.'

'Won't Lord Mount Vernon object to someone of my class turning up at his country seat? I don't have evening togs, and all that kind of thing, Colonel Kershaw.'

'Don't worry, Box. We'll keep you well out of sight, so as not to scandalize the company! And Lord Mount Vernon won't object in the least. He's one of my secret servants.'

★ ★ ★

Arnold Box took his seat beside Colonel Kershaw in the closed carriage that had been sent to meet them at Upper Henkley Halt, a deserted railway platform set among the encroaching fir plantations of Lord Mount Vernon's country estate in Warwickshire. They had been the only passengers in the little train that had toiled there from Warwick. The driver and fireman were already preparing the locomotive to reverse out of the trees, and back on to the main line.

Colonel Kershaw pointed out of the

carriage window to his left.

'Do you see that little spur of line passing through the trees over there, Box? That's a rather special way of reaching High Cedars, but it's not available to the public at large. That's the grim road Lankester travelled when the special train took him away from Victoria this morning. There's a secret government facility at High Cedars, Box, and my traitor is lodged in a cell there for the duration. He's not the first to be brought here to Warwickshire, and I don't suppose he'll be the last.'

The carriage driver turned the horse's head away from the railway line, and they plunged through a dense wood of conifers. After a drive of nearly half an hour, the trees quite suddenly fell away, and Box saw an enormous rectangular sandstone mansion rising dramatically from a hillside.

'High Cedars,' Kershaw volunteered. 'Apparently, it was built in the 1830s — a true product of the Railway Age. Lord Mount Vernon told me that it was designed by Cubitt for a newly ennobled corn-chandler. It was meant to overawe by its sheer size, and as you can see, it has a quite bewildering number of square windows. It has a few other useful features, as well — but that's between you and me. Cubitt claimed that it was built in the Grecian style. Maybe it was, I don't know. All these trees pre-date the house. They're firs of some kind, certainly, but whether they're actually cedars is a moot point. Cubitt said that they were cedars.'

'And what happened to the ennobled corn-chandler, sir?'

'Well, he went bankrupt in 1840. The house was in the ghostly care of an aged caretaker for a few years, and then it was bought by the eighth Lord Mount Vernon, a gentleman who had an eye for a bargain. It's his son, the ninth Lord Mount Vernon, who lives there now. He was once renowned as a crack shot, a cricketer, and a big-game hunter. As I told you this morning, he's one of my crowd.'

The carriage came to a halt under a massive *porte-cochère*, and a liveried footman appeared at the front entrance of the mansion. Box made to alight, but Kershaw placed a retaining hand on his sleeve.

'Box,' he said, 'you and I will of necessity part company here for a while. You'll be taken up to the top floor, where you'll find some very decent accommodation waiting for you. I have business of a social and professional nature to attend to for most of this evening, but I will see you up there without fail before midnight.'

Colonel Kershaw alighted from the carriage, and Box followed him.

'Incidentally,' said Kershaw, 'although most of this house belongs to my friend Lord Mount Vernon, the top floor, and the cellarage, have been permanently commandeered by me.'

* * *

A talented string orchestra played cheerful but soothing music as a fitting background to the many conversations taking place in the Grand Salon of High Cedars. A vast hall, rising through three storeys to a coffered ceiling, it was renowned for its grand staircase and the galleries leading from it. There would be dancing later in the evening, and at midnight a display of fireworks on the rear terrace.

Throughout the Grand Salon, and in the galleries, many small tables had been set, and there were buffets near at hand, attended by liveried footmen. Wines of choice vintage had appeared from the cellars, and conversation was animated.

At one of the tables laid out in an upper gallery, Colonel Kershaw sipped dry champagne, and glanced from time to time over the balustrade at the brilliant assembly in the hall below. At the same table with him sat a very heavy, healthy man in evening dress, a man whose florid face broke from time to time into an attractive smile.

'You know, Kershaw,' he said, 'I can't think why you persuaded Mount Vernon to invite me to this do. Dashed odd, the whole thing. Far too many foreigners gabbling away. They'll be the ruin of this country.'

'You're becoming too bluff and insular, Hamish,' said Kershaw. 'That's what comes of living up there in the barren wastes of Caithness. It'll do you good to mingle with a few exotic foreigners here at High Cedars.'

Kershaw's companion laughed good-humouredly, and glanced up as a man in faultless evening dress approached their table. Kershaw turned round, and stiffened with something approaching excitement. Thalberg! He'd no idea that he'd be at High Cedars.

'Now here's a chap after my own heart, Kershaw,' said the man called Hamish. 'I like this fellow. I met him in London at one of Salisbury's receptions for diplomats. I can understand him when he speaks. Damned if I can remember his name, though.'

'I like him too, Hamish. I also like the things he tells me. He's rather in the same line of business as I am, you know.'

'Oh! Do you want me to go, then?'

Hamish half rose from his chair, but Kershaw pushed him back with a laugh. 'Oh, stay where you are! Try to imagine that you're still at school: just listen, and shut up.'

The new man bowed in the German fashion, and Kershaw introduced him. 'Sir Hamish Bull of Caithness. Hamish, this is Count von und zu Thalberg.'

The count, who was clutching a glass of champagne, sat down in a vacant chair.

'Well, gentlemen,' he said in perfect English, 'this is very nice. One can pretend here for a brief weekend that the world is civilized. Everybody seems to be here, as far as I can make out. Mrs Pole-James, novelist and reformer, is here, and has kept me in a state of desperate politeness for the last half-hour. Lady Mary Horton-Stuart, the darling of the salons, is as fascinating as ever. She confided to me that she is actually thirty-five! 'Impossible', I said. I happen to know that she's forty-two!'

His two companions laughed, and Sir Hamish Bull visibly relaxed. Then the count caught Kershaw's eye with a special glance that Kershaw recognized. Thalberg was a high-ranking officer in Prussian Military Intelligence. He was also a fervent Anglophile.

Kershaw knew that he was about to be told

some things of interest, probably served up in a roundabout way. The business of Lady Mary's age had been the signal.

'Lady Mary, you know, reminds me a little of Adelheid von Braun. Did you ever meet her? She left Germany about four years ago, and I thought she'd come to England. But it may have been Paris. A very charming young lady, but not perhaps as young as she seems. Like Lady Mary, you know. It must have been Paris, otherwise she'd have been here tonight, I'm sure.'

The Prussian aristocrat turned to Sir Hamish Bull, who was sitting well back in his chair, enjoying the convivial atmosphere of High Cedars.

'Sir Hamish, I remember seeing you once at Lord Salisbury's levee for the Diplomatic Corps. I'm sure you would have liked Adelheid von Braun. A lovely, blonde girl, she was. Her father, Colonel-General von Braun, was a very devoted and fanatical Prussian, with vast estates in Eastern Prussia. How admirable! The true Junker! He was more royalist than the Kaiser himself, so the Kaiser said to me on one occasion.'

Colonel Kershaw looked thoughtfully at Thalberg. Adelheid von Braun . . . At least, it was a name, if not as pretty a name as Ottilie Seligmann.

'Well,' Thalberg concluded, 'it must have been Paris she went to. Somebody told me she'd made a secret marriage to a Hungarian fellow, which may be true or false.'

'Hamish here,' said Kershaw, 'is rather nervous of foreigners, Count. He's a Scotsman, you see. They're just about getting used to the English.' Sir Hamish grinned, but said nothing.

'A Scotsman, hey?' said Thalberg. 'Well, I knew a Scotsman once. A very dangerous, devilish kind of Scotsman. A lone wolf, as they say, and not very fond of the English. He wanted to sell something to a man in St Petersburg — '

'What?'

'Oh, didn't you know that, Kershaw? Yes, my Scotsman is a very German type of Scotsman at the moment, too German for comfort. But he's not averse from doing deals with Russians when the mood takes him. He was in Petersburg last month.'

Kershaw relapsed into silence. Sir Hamish looked doubtfully at Count von und zu Thalberg.

'Look here, Count Thalberg,' he said, in rather injured tones, 'you spoke about your German Scotsman being too German for comfort. What do you mean by that? You're a German yourself, aren't you?'

'Yes, indeed, Sir Hamish. But there are Germans and Germans.'

Sir Hamish beckoned a passing waiter and took another glass of champagne from a tray. He took an appreciative gulp.

'I can't get the measure of some of you foreigners. I'm a Scotsman, you know. I don't wear a kilt, or toss the caber, and so on, but I'm Scots through and through. I've never heard of a Scots German. Not until now, anyway. There's a woman turned up in my part of the world who's apparently a Polish Bohemian. Why can't foreigners just be French, or German, or whatever they are?'

Colonel Kershaw leaned over the table and took the glass of champagne out of Sir Hamish's hand. He looked at him steadily and coaxingly. His voice was soothing and quiet.

'Hamish, think, and then speak. What does your Polish Bohemian lady call herself?'

'Call herself? Mrs Feissen. She's a Pole. But a fellow I know who speaks Polish says she isn't a Pole. He says she's a Bohemian. Not one of those gipsy violinists, but a woman from Bohemia. Oh, dash it all, a Check. That's the word this fellow used. A Check. Damned odd, I should have thought.'

Colonel Kershaw returned the glass of champagne to Sir Hamish, and leaned back in his chair. He glanced knowingly at the count, who smiled.

'Sometimes, Count von und zu Thalberg,' said Kershaw, 'I think that Providence speaks directly through the oddest mediums. It must be a gift from the gods to be told that. About this Mrs Feissen, you know. There was a certain Polish lady living in Chelsea who suddenly left, saying that she was going to Warsaw. Evidently, she was making that voyage via Glasgow — that's where we lost her. My crowd, you know. Yes, I think it was Providence who decreed that I should angle an invitation to High Cedars for old Hamish there.'

★ ★ ★

At midnight, a brilliant display of fireworks on the terrace of High Cedars lit up the black winter sky above the encroaching woods. It was seen as a signal that the evening's celebrations had ended, and the many guests assembled to be lighted up to bed.

Colonel Kershaw had slipped away from the company, and made his way up a set of obscure back stairs to a landing on the top floor. He took a key from his pocket, and unlocked a stout door, which gave him access to a series of hidden rooms. There was a sparsely furnished business room, containing, among other things, an electric telegraph, and beyond this, a sort of council chamber, where Inspector Box sat in one of a number of chairs drawn round a blazing fire.

'How are you, Mr Box? Have they treated you well?'

'They have, sir. Food and drink aplenty, and a firework display. I couldn't have asked for more.'

Colonel Kershaw smiled, sat down in one of the chairs, and withdrew his cigar case from the inside pocket of his dress coat.

'Will you smoke a cigar with me, Mr Box?'

'I will, sir.'

Kershaw played a match over the end of his cigar until it was glowing to his satisfaction, and then flicked the match into the fire.

'This evening, Mr Box,' he said, 'a friend of mine, Sir Hamish Bull of Caithness, told me — in a rather roundabout way — that Mrs Poniatowski, the housekeeper at Chelsea, is living in his part of the world, under the name of Mrs Feissen. One of my crowd shadowed her from Chelsea when she left, but he lost her in Glasgow. Sir Hamish Bull also told me that she isn't a Pole, but a Czech — a Bohemian, you know.'

'A Bohemian? And her name is Feissen? But that's — Yes! That's the name of the concern that made the explosive used to blow up Dr Seligmann! 'Feissen Werke'.'

'Yes. So now you can see a new complexion on things, can't you? Right in the heart of Dr Seligmann's household was — well, I'll tell you who she was. My people in Germany have sent me reports about her. Maria Theresa Feissen is the widow of the great Bohemian armaments manufacturer, Wilhelm Feissen. She is now the working principal of that concern. Both Feissens were fanatical pan-Germanists — '

'Pause there, if you will sir — hold on . . . This Mrs Feissen must have known Colin McColl. She must have supplied the explosive. She must have arranged for that crate to be delivered from Germany'

'Exactly, Box. And as you very cleverly discovered, the object was to destroy the Belvedere, and with it Seligmann's copy of *The Hansa Protocol*. And now she's in Scotland, in the wilds of Caithness. Why, Box? What is she planning now?'

Box drew on his cigar, and looked at the cheerful fire. He let a string of images pass through his mind. The unseemly rows between Miss Ottilie and her sour-faced housekeeper. Her raging dislike of Count Czerny . . . 'He will go. And that Polish woman. She, too, will go.'

'Sir, have your people found out anything interesting about Miss Ottilie Seligmann? From the start of this business I've had men shadowing the various people in that house. Miss Ottilie never seems to go anywhere, or do anything much. She seems to spend most of her time writing letters. The butler posts them regularly in the pillar box at the end of Lavender Walk.'

Colonel Kershaw smiled, and threw the butt of his cigar into the fire.

'Miss Ottilie's letters are quite harmless. They're purely chatty things to English friends, or letters to fashionable shops. Some are private affairs, and one or two are written in German to people abroad. But they seem to be quite ordinary.'

'How do you know that, sir?'

'I've read them. I'm not going to tell you how we intercept them, Box, but it's very ingenious. Something to do with the stamps. Of much greater interest is something else that I was told tonight, this time by a German diplomat called Thalberg. Our friend Miss Whittaker was right. The young woman at Chelsea is not Ottilie Seligman: she is yet another fanatic, and her name is Adelheid von Braun.'

'I wondered all along about her, sir. So did my sergeant, Jack Knollys. Ottilie Seligmann didn't ring true — '

Suddenly, almost with a sense of shock, the pieces of the puzzle rushed together. Box had been hovering for a week on the edge of discovery, and now the obscurities had cleared away. He began to speak, urgently and persuasively.

'Colonel Kershaw, what we have witnessed at the house in Chelsea has been the dispersal of a gang of assassins after the successful completion of a mission. It has all been disguised as a series of rows and antipathies, and we've watched from the sidelines as the gang dispersed. Like all gangs, I expect it will regroup when the time is ripe. Once the mission was accomplished, they could disperse. So Miss Ottilie staged those rows, first with Mrs P. and then with Count Czerny, so that they could flee — if that's the right word here — without anyone suspecting that they were the killers. All the neighbours saw was the spectacle of a few excitable foreigners squabbling with each other. The only innocent party in that house is Schneider, the German secretary.'

'I believe you're right, Box. We have witnessed the dispersal of a gang. Which means, of course, that the gang must have assembled at Chelsea in the first place. The false Ottilie, and the malevolent Mrs

Poniatowski, were successful in becoming part of the household of their deadly ideological enemy, Dr Seligmann.'

'Their object, as we know,' said Box, 'was to destroy *The Hansa Protocol*, and neutralize Seligmann's bargaining power with the German war party. But they must have found it very difficult to keep the truth from Count Czerny.'

Kershaw gave Box a half-amused smile.

'Are you going to disappoint me at this late hour, Mr Box? It was brilliant of Count Czerny to pose as a champion of peace, and to spout rhetorical nothings that told the sober truth. He is a bold man, a man who took the chance of revealing to you the existence of the *Eidgenossenschaft*, and then linking Colin McColl directly to it. Count Czerny, I have no doubt, was so convincing, that he managed to convince you of his own innocence. When Czerny left the house in Chelsea, he crossed the Channel with all his effects, and Europe swallowed him up.'

'Sir — '

'Mr Box, it is late, and we have both had a long and tiring day. Let us talk again tomorrow, after that telegraph machine in the other room has sprung to life, and brought us an account of tomorrow's Pan-German Rally in Berlin.'

12

Baron von Dessau Smiles

Inspector Box stood at one of the windows in the sparsely furnished business room on the top floor of High Cedars, and looked out at the fir trees, which were bathed in the weak sun of the winter morning. A bank of dark cloud was beginning to show itself above the woods, and patches of green had appeared on the narrow lawn beyond the rear terrace. The relentless grip of the recent icy weather was beginning to relax in preparation for a thaw.

The door of the room opened, and Colonel Kershaw came in. He was followed by Sir Charles Napier, and a tall, bronzed man of forty or so, dressed informally in tweeds. He had jet-black hair and side whiskers, and looked out on the world from shrewd grey eyes.

'Gentlemen,' said Kershaw without preamble, 'this is Detective Inspector Box, of Scotland Yard. He is intimately bound up in this business of Seligmann and Lankester, and I beg you both to accept without demur that he is my colleague and associate. Box, you have seen Sir Charles Napier here before. This other gentleman is our host, Lord Mount Vernon.'

As he was speaking, a young man in a sober black suit came into the room, and at a nod from Kershaw, he began to busy himself with the technicalities of bringing the telegraph machine to life. Mount Vernon and Napier joined the operator, and Colonel Kershaw drew Box aside.

'Mr Box,' he said, 'I thought I'd tell you that I've borrowed your sergeant, Mr Knollys, and sent him back to London on a little commission. I hope you can spare him.'

'I can, sir, provided that you hand him back to me in good condition! Is it in order for me to ask whether or not the memorandum got safely to Berlin?'

'Yes, Box, it arrived there late yesterday afternoon. I've already informed Sir Charles there of what happened. My wine merchant's traveller delivered the memorandum to a man at the British Embassy, who immediately took it out to Baron von Dessau's residence in Charlottenburg. Apparently, the baron opened it, read it, smiled, and said nothing.'

A faint humming sound told them that the young man had activated the electric telegraph. When the time was ripe, the machine would stutter into life, bringing the morning's news from Berlin.

'I wonder what made the baron smile?' asked Box. Napier heard him, and nodded in agreement.

'I wonder, too,' said Napier. 'I thought the idea was that he should quake and tremble at what poor Seligmann had written?'

'Well, yes, Sir Charles,' said Kershaw, 'but that was before Colin McColl — and the *Eidgenossenschaft* — had blown the Belvedere to smithereens, and with it, Seligmann's copy of *The Hansa Protocol*. That memorandum said, in effect: 'If you don't restrain the dogs of war in Berlin, I shall reveal all the secret naval and military codes of the German Empire to the British Government.' It was meant to be a containing exercise, a means of guaranteeing the peace of Europe by a careful adjustment in the balance of power.'

Sir Charles Napier nodded vigorously in agreement.

'Quite right, Kershaw. At last, you're talking the kind of language that I can understand. And yet — '

'And yet the baron smiled! He did that, presumably, because Seligmann's threat was now worthless. Once von Dessau has addressed his devoted mob in half-an-hour's time, we'll be able to judge the full reasoning behind that smile.'

Lord Mount Vernon stirred in his chair.

'You know, gentlemen,' he said, 'I've been wondering about that memorandum of Seligmann's. Are you quite sure, Kershaw, that it said — well, what you said it did? About the dogs of war, and the secret codes, and all that?'

'Oh, yes. I read it, you see — '

'What!'

Sir Charles Napier sprang to his feet. He looked beside himself with rage.

'You damned scoundrel, Kershaw! I might have known you'd do something outrageous, something that flies in the face of all diplomatic practice — '

'Hold your fire, Charles,' said Kershaw. 'You'll do yourself an injury with these virtuous outbursts. Apoplexy, you know. Of course I read it! One of my people opened it as soon as I received it at Bagot's Hotel, and then resealed it afterwards. It said exactly what I said, only it was in German, which, fortunately, I can read.'

'You shouldn't do these things, Kershaw,' said Sir Charles Napier. 'You'll trip yourself up one of these days. Some damned traitor will be looking over your shoulder while you're steaming the stamps off envelopes, or whatever other nefarious things you do.'

'Talking of traitors,' said Colonel Kershaw, 'I went down to the cellarage very early this morning, and confronted Lankester.'

'And what did the fellow have to say for himself?' asked Napier, his face flushing with anger.

'He confessed his guilt immediately. He had conducted several similar pieces of business with Ephraim Stolberg during the past twelve months or so, mainly to cover heavy gambling debts. On this occasion, a faked assault on Lankester had been arranged to take place on the train to Dover. He was to have been found, bruised and dazed, with the lining of his jacket ripped open and the memorandum gone. Stolberg had already paid him the fruits of his treachery.'

'And who was to be the recipient, Kershaw? Who's going to open that packet of blank paper that you substituted? It can't be anyone in Germany — '

'It's on its way to St Petersburg. They'll buy anything there, you know. It's all grist to their Slavonic mill. I knew it would end up there. Or in Constantinople. Lankester was very obliging in his confession. He belonged to a little group of freelance spies who sell their secrets for money rather than political conviction. Ephraim Stolberg and his wife Rita, Klaus Miller . . . They're dangerous, of

268

course, but ultimately containable.'

There was silence for a moment, and then Kershaw asked a question.

'What do you want me to do with Lankester? He's held here on Mr Box's warrant. We can't keep him here indefinitely.'

'Tell him to go,' said Napier, his voice choking with anger. 'Tell him to resign from the service, resign from his regiment, and hide himself away from the sight of men. Tell him to resign from his clubs. Either he can do all that, or wait for me to initiate a Process of High Crimes, which will send him to Dartmoor for life. I think I know what choice he'll make. I don't want things disturbed, Kershaw. Let all these traitors continue falsely secure, so that we can pick them off, one by one.'

'You're absolutely right, Napier,' said Kershaw, 'and it's very decent of you not to throw my criticisms of *your* service in my face. What you suggest is what I myself would have advised. Perhaps you will care to leave Lankester to me? I will tell him what our judgement has been.'

'Thank you. I'm grateful that you are to spare me the prospect of facing that man without striking him to my foot — but listen! There's the telegraph beginning its chatter. It's time to hear the report from Berlin.'

269

★ ★ ★

Half an hour later, the four men left the business room, and reassembled in the adjacent council chamber. Arnold Box watched his companions, and wondered what they had made of the pages of narrative which the young operator had rapidly scribbled on a pad of standard yellow telegraph forms. Sir Charles Napier and Colonel Kershaw sat with stacks of the papers on their knees. Both men's faces were inscrutable. Lord Mount Vernon caught Box's eye, and pulled a wryly comic face. Finally, Colonel Kershaw spoke.

'I'm beginning to wonder, gentlemen,' he said, in his quiet, rather world-weary voice, 'whether I am rapidly getting out of my depth in this business. Baron von Dessau was free to whip up his followers to fever-pitch this morning. He could have urged an immediate expansion of the German Reich beyond its borders, and certain units of the German Army would have taken that as a signal for action. Am I right about that, or is there something I've missed?'

'No, you're right, Kershaw,' said Sir Charles Napier. 'Thousands of hotheads had assembled to hear their hero in the squares and gardens around the Imperial Palace. He was greeted by prolonged cheering, and the singing of various rabble-rousing songs. It was a smouldering of resentment against moderation, Kershaw, and von Dessau could have fanned the flames. I happen to know, too, that France would have immediately sought a compromise. This was to be the dreaded Friday, the thirteenth, the day of doom. Instead of which — we have *this*!'

Napier struck the pile of sheets on his knee with the back of his hand.

'Listen to what he said: 'Germans, loyal subjects of the Kaiser, you look to see the Empire burst its narrow borders, and expand to east and west. But, friends, believe me, the time is not yet! A little while more, and we will give you a victory beyond your wildest dreams!' And so on, and so forth. In other words, he told them all to back off. And apparently they did. They sang the National Anthem, and dispersed. The raging fires of conflict proved to be a damp squib. Why?'

'I don't know,' Kershaw replied.

'I think *I* do,' said Box.

The eyes of Kershaw, Napier, and Lord Mount Vernon turned to look at him. They all seemed startled at the sudden interruption, as though Inspector Box was little more than an afterthought. Kershaw smiled a little.

'Pray elaborate, Mr Box,' he said.

'Gentlemen,' said Box, 'on the evening of

Tuesday, 3 January, a murderous assassin called Colin McColl succeeded in destroying Dr Otto Seligmann's copy of *The Hansa Protocol*, blowing Dr Seligmann to smithereens in the process. Some minutes later, McColl met and talked to Lieutenant Arthur Fenlake in Dr Seligmann's garden. McColl knew that Fenlake had just visited Seligmann. In fact, Mr Fenlake was at that very moment carrying the precious memorandum in his pocket.'

Sir Charles shook his head impatiently.

'That's all very interesting, Inspector Box, a well-ordered epitome of what happened. But the point is, that poor Fenlake delivered the memorandum to me, unscathed.'

'Why, sir?' asked Box. 'Why was he unscathed? Why didn't McColl follow him from Lavender Walk, and get the memorandum from him? He'd killed Stefan Oliver when he thought the memorandum had begun its travels. When he found that he'd merely stumbled into your rehearsal, he threw the blank paper, and its courier, down at your feet. So why didn't he kill Fenlake, and take the memorandum?'

'I don't quite see — ' Kershaw began.

'Please, sir, let me finish. Here's another thought to ponder. Had the bomb gone off five minutes earlier, the memorandum would

272

have been destroyed! But you see, by then, it wouldn't have mattered. McColl wasn't interested in your precious memorandum. The threat contained in Seligmann's memorandum, gentlemen, was always an irrelevance, because Baron von Dessau intended all along to make the Berlin mob back off, in return for a promise. He promised them something, and they believed his promise. It would be prudent if *we* believed his promise, too.'

Colonel Kershaw's face had become animated with a mixture of excitement and satisfaction.

'Go on, Box,' he said.

'The promise that Baron von Dessau made, gentlemen, was this: 'We will give you a victory beyond your wildest dreams!' He stayed his hand this morning in Berlin, because he knew that something tremendous was going to happen without the need for mob oratory. Colin McColl knew that, too, which is why he acted in the way he did. A victory beyond their wildest dreams. If it's beyond their wildest dreams, then it's probably beyond ours, too.'

'But what *is* it, Box?' Napier demanded impatiently.

'I'm convinced that it's something to do with Scotland, sir. A woman who called herself Mrs Poniatowski, and who posed as Dr Seligmann's housekeeper, turns out to be Maria Feissen, the head of the Feissen arms concern in Bohemia. She is now living in Scotland, near the estate of Sir Hamish Bull in Caithness — '

'What!' cried Sir Charles, springing to his feet in his excitement. 'Come, now, Inspector Box, what do you know about this business? How do these things leak out? It's a fast and closed State secret — '

'Beg pardon, sir,' Box interrupted, 'I don't know what you're talking about, but evidently I've said the right thing. Mrs Feissen was part of a gang who had infiltrated the household of Dr Seligmann. The others were Count Czerny and the so-called niece, Ottilie Seligmann. They engineered a clever way of dispersing after they'd murdered the unfortunate doctor, and destroyed his copy of The Hansa Protocol. And working hand in glove with them is another Scotsman, this murderous Colin McColl. Together, they're going to deliver the German war party 'a victory beyond their wildest dreams'.'

Box suddenly stopped speaking. What would these high-class gentlemen think? He'd been haranguing them as though they were naughty boys caught pilfering from a sweet-stall. But he saw the look of respect in their faces.

'Napier,' said Kershaw, quietly, 'what is this 'fast State secret' concerning Scotland? If I don't know about it, then it must be fast indeed. Scotland . . . There have been certain movements of shipping during the past few months. Could it be that?'

'For goodness' sake, Kershaw, don't blurt these things out in that cavalier fashion! I don't know anything about it. The Foreign Secretary was sent a note by Admiral Holland, head of Naval Intelligence, to ask for certain Scottish infantry units to be assigned secret duties in the area of Caithness, under the aegis of the Admiralty. The Foreign Secretary showed me the note, and it was my duty to acknowledge it.'

Colonel Kershaw got to his feet. He seemed to be making a heroic effort to control his anger. His face had gone very pale, and he clutched the sheaf of yellow telegraph forms as though he would crush them to pieces.

'Box, I knew I'd done the right thing in luring you into this business. Well done! Scotland! There have been sightings of ships of the line moving through the Irish Sea since late December . . . Manoeuvres, that's what they said, when one of my folk made a polite enquiry. Napier, this is some damned secret Admiralty business, I'll be bound. You know what Holland's like! He's no time for my crowd, of course, that goes without saying. And he's jealous of *your* people. It's some damned smug trick of Holland's. I'm going back to London at once. Box, you'd better come with me. I thought we'd seen the end of this business this morning. Now I fear that it's only just beginning.'

★ ★ ★

Fritz Schneider sat at a little desk in his upstairs room at the house in Chelsea, and savoured the unaccustomed calm that seemed to have descended on the old Tudor dwelling. Since Mrs Poniatowski's departure Miss Ottilie had become less abrasive, and more willing to give her full attention to winding up her late uncle's affairs in England.

On the tenth of the month, His Excellency Count Czerny had departed for Germany, after enduring some very tiresome and rather scandalous tirades from Miss Ottilie. He'd given as good as he got, but on the doorstep of the house Miss Ottilie had seemed to relent a little. She had suddenly hugged the Count briefly, much to His Excellency's surprise and embarrassment! Miss Ottilie was in her sitting-room across the passage, writing letters. She had told him that she would leave quietly for Berlin within the next few days.

Schneider had come upstairs to clear out this little desk, and to bundle up what letters and papers he wished to take back with him to Leipzig. Here was his old letter-case, which had been given to him by his former employer, a renowned professor of music at the Leipzig Conservatoire. All these letters were part of his personal history.

But what was this? An unopened envelope, addressed to a Miss Whittaker, at Maybury College, Gower Street. Miss Whittaker . . . He remembered her, now. A beautiful young lady scholar, who had called the year before last, when Dr Seligmann had procured a page from an ancient manuscript, and had invited her to look at it. The *herr Doktor* must have come up to this room, and hidden this letter where he knew that it would be found. A strange, sinister proceeding . . . What should he do? What was the etiquette? Miss Ottilie was now head of the household. It was not for him to act in anything without her knowledge.

He looked up from his desk, and saw Miss Ottilie standing in the doorway, watching him. He sprang to his feet, clicked his heels, and bowed his head in the Saxon fashion.

'You look pale, Fritz. What has happened? You will tell me, yes?'

'It is nothing of moment, Miss Ottilie. I have found a letter from the late *herr Doktor*, addressed to Miss Whittaker, at an address in Gower Street — '

'Whittaker?' Miss Ottilie's voice held an uncharacteristic sharpness. 'I recall the name, but cannot remember — ah! Yes! She called the other day, so Lodge told me, but would not stay. Another of Uncle Otto's dreary scholar friends. You had better give me the letter. I can then decide if it is still of any relevance. You understand me, yes?'

Fritz Schneider blushed, and avoided Ottilie's eye. What on earth was he to do?

'Miss Ottilie, I beg that you will not ask me to give you this letter. After all, it can be of no importance. It will be some matter of scholarly detail, no doubt. The *herr Doktor* would wish me to deliver it, as the last service that I can render him — '

'Very well, Fritz. We must not upset your Saxon rectitude. Go. This college — it will be one of those dreary institutions near Euston Station. You had better take a cab. And when you have rendered this last service to the *herr Doktor*, I urge you to start your arrangements to return to Saxony. If you do not, you will find yourself here alone, with only the mice for company! Go!'

Ottilie Seligmann waited until Fritz Schneider had left the house, and then she hurriedly dressed herself for a foray into town. Within minutes, she was hailing a cab from the rank at the end of Lavender Walk.

'Where to, miss?' asked the cabbie, touching the rim of his hat. He'd often taken this German lady into town. Very fetching she was, too, though she looked a mite pale today. Well, that was understandable. She'd had a lot of trouble, poor young soul.

'Do you know Morwell Gardens, near Bedford Square? Take me there, if you please.'

Ottilie settled down in the cab, and thought of Fritz Schneider. He had been an excellent secretary to Dr Seligmann, a man who understood the nature of duty, and one of the best kind of German. She had urged him more than once to return to Leipzig. So had Mrs Poniatowski. But Fritz liked to take his time. And now, his Saxon honour had constrained him to refuse her sight of the letter to this woman Whittaker.

'Some matter of scholarly detail', he'd said. Did he really think that? Fool! What fools some decent people were!

* * *

Vanessa Drake put down the square of golden damask that she had been hemming, and gave her full attention to her friend Louise Whittaker, who had burst unceremoniously into her lodgings near Dean's Yard, Westminster. It was a tall, gaunt building, that had once been the convent of an Anglican sisterhood. A steep staircase led up from the street to a landing, from which two corridors branched, each containing what at one time had been the nuns' cells. They had been adapted very sympathetically to create a number of sets of rooms for single women.

'A letter? From Dr Seligmann?' Vanessa exclaimed. 'Oh, Louise! How exciting! Have you opened it? What does it say?'

'I haven't opened it yet. What on earth can it be? It was brought to our college in Gower Street by poor Dr Seligmann's secretary, Herr Schneider. Apparently, he'd found it slipped into his writing-case. This is Dr Seligmann's handwriting. He knew my address at the college, you see.'

'Oh, *do* open it, Louise! It may have something to do with our adventure — something that Colonel Kershaw should know about!'

Louise Whittaker tore open the envelope, and removed a single sheet of paper, which she spread out on Vanessa's round table. The printed letter heading showed that it came from the house in Lavender Walk. It was dated Monday, 2 January, 1893 — two days before Dr Seligmann's death:

My dear Miss Whittaker

I have conceived this subterfuge of writing a letter to you, because you are an outsider, and someone whom I can trust. I well remember our meeting together, and your interest in the old panelling of my library.

I will not burden you with an account of my fears — my conviction that somewhere in my household there lurks a potential assassin. I have lost trust in those closest to me, except for my faithful secretary, Herr Fritz Schneider. He is a man of regular habits and method, and when he finds this, he will faithfully deliver it to you.

I fear that I am being watched as I write this. The Belvedere is a secluded place, but its walls seem now to have eyes!

I remember that when you visited me, you mentioned a friend at Scotland Yard. Call upon that friend, and tell him that there will be a great calamity on the 25th of this month. I have heard it spoken of — whispered about the house, but I do not know for certain what it is.

How pathetic is this communication! You will think it the ravings of a foolish old man. But I beg you, dear Miss Whittaker, do as I ask, and tell your friend at Scotland Yard. The 25th of this month of January will bring a great calamity to England. Let the authorities be alert to the threat of danger. Would to God that I could tell you what it is!

In the nature of things, I will be dead when you receive this letter. And so, I salute you from beyond the grave.

Otto Seligmann

Louise Whittaker sat in thought for a minute, pondering Seligmann's letter. Vanessa had picked up the square of damask again, and had begun to size some brilliants, which she intended to attach by silver thread to the gorgeous fabric. Louise saw the tears standing in the girl's eyes.

'How very sad,' said Vanessa. Louise sighed, and picked the letter up again.

'Yes. But a bit flowery, don't you think? Poor Dr Seligmann talked like that. Talked the way he wrote, I mean. But that doesn't mean that there's no substance in this letter. I'll do as he said, and take it to Mr Box. Have you a sheet of paper, and a pencil?'

'You're not going to post it to him, are you?'

'Of course not! I intend to brave whatever horrors are waiting for me this time at King James's Rents, and deliver this letter personally. No, I simply want to follow good scholarly practice, and make a copy of the letter. After all, it was written to me. I always make copies of important documents.'

Vanessa supplied the necessary paper and pencil, and then sat watching her friend as she wrote. Louise often spoke as though she resented men, and their dominant role in life. But 'Mr Box' was forever on her lips. He was her swain in waiting — but he'd be waiting forever if Louise didn't make some kind of move. Her academic attainments had been hard won, and people of influence were beginning to listen to women of Louise's calibre. But academic qualifications weren't everything.

'There you are!'

Louise Whittaker folded the copy that she had made, and put it carefully into one of the pockets of the rather mannish grey jacket that she was wearing. It was part of a stylish costume suit, worn with a crisp white shirt-blouse. One of its advantages was its two capacious pockets! She picked up Dr

Seligmann's letter from the table, and put it carefully back in its envelope.

'And now, I suppose I'd better take another cab, this time to King James's Rents, though I could walk it from here, I expect. I wonder — '

Neither girl had noticed that the door of the room had been almost silently opened. It was the sudden draught from the staircase that made Vanessa look up in alarm. A man stood on the threshold, a man of thirty or so, clean-shaven and fresh-looking, with what seemed to be the beginnings of a tense, unpleasant smile insinuating itself across his even features. He was well if rather primly dressed in a dark-grey suit, covered by a tightly buttoned black overcoat.

'Can I help you?' Vanessa's voice faltered, as she looked into the visitor's hard blue eyes. She added, bravely, 'It is customary to knock before entering a lady's room.'

The visitor slowly closed the door behind him, and stood with his back to it. He seemed to dominate the room, as though he had commandeered it, and they now occupied it merely on sufferance. When the man spoke, it was with the quiet and pleasant accent of the educated Scotsman. He ignored Vanessa completely, and addressed himself to Louise.

'You are Miss Whittaker? You are holding a

letter. Is that the letter from Dr Otto Seligmann, which Fritz Schneider gave to you? I see by your expression that it is. Give it to me.'

Louise quickly slipped her arms behind her back. She was terrified of this quiet, respectable young man, but she was not going to let herself be bullied.

'I will do no such thing! How dare you burst in here — '

With a spring like that of a panther the young man bounded from the door, and swung Louise round by the shoulders. He snatched Dr Seligmann's letter from her hand, and thrust it deep into his overcoat pocket. Louise stumbled as she tried to steady herself, and fell to the floor.

Vanessa Drake began to scream. Even as she did so, she marvelled at the terrifying noise that she emitted. The young man turned towards her with a snarl of rage, and at that moment the door of the room seemed to fly off its hinges as an enormous scar-faced giant of a man hurled himself with an oath at their unwelcome visitor.

Louise Whittaker quickly got to her feet, and joined her young friend, who was cowering in a corner of the room. 'It's Jack Knollys, Mr Box's sergeant!' she whispered to Vanessa. The two men seemed to be locked together in a kind of wrestling-hold. They flung each other around the small room, knocking furniture over, and panting with their deadly efforts to subdue each other.

The sinister Scotsman suddenly pulled himself clear, threw open the door, and dashed across the landing. In a second Jack Knollys had sprung after him, and both men went crashing down the narrow staircase. Despite a warning cry from Louise, Vanessa immediately followed them. Blood was welling up on Knollys' right cheek. She saw the lithe Scotsman's hands close round Sergeant Knollys' throat, and started to run down the stairs.

Knollys suddenly brought his legs up under his opponent's body, and flung him against the wall of the stairwell. At the same time, he sent a massive fist crashing into the Scotsman's temple. Vanessa saw the blood start from a gash above the man's right eye.

Colin McColl clutched his head, and blundered out into the narrow street. Knollys heaved himself to his feet and ran out after him. Vanessa stood halfway down the stairs, looking at the rectangle of dull light beyond the open door. It had been a terrifying episode, but it had left her with a feeling of exhilaration. In some strange way, she felt that she had become Arthur Fenlake's heir.

***

Sergeant Knollys sat gingerly on an upright chair while Vanessa Drake bathed the wound on his cheek. She had brought a small enamel bowl half full of cold water, to which she had added a generous amount of iodine. Louise Whittaker watched her young friend with a certain wry amusement, and wondered . . .

Vanessa had regularly fallen for a succession of quiet young men since she was sixteen, and had eventually tired of them all. There had been Dennis, a clerk in the Prudential Assurance Office, who had eventually married a young lady clerk in the same concern. Jonathan had been a pupil teacher, a devoted swain, who could talk about nothing but Froebel's Principles. He had married another teacher as soon as he had reached the sober age of nineteen.

Edwin, Stephen, Albert — all earnest, basically conformist young fellows, they had ultimately bored Vanessa, and she had sent them on their respective ways with her relieved blessing. Arthur Fenlake had been no different. True, he had brought with him the glamour of commissioned military rank, and they both knew, now, that he had worked as a secret courier for the Foreign Office. But Arthur Fenlake had really been no different from Dennis, and Jonathan, and Edwin, and the rest. He and they had been worthy fellows. All had been unsuitable for a girl who craved some kind of excitement.

Vanessa continued to clean the blood away from Jack Knollys' cheek. The great giant winced occasionally as the iodine bit into what was, in fact, a scrape rather than a cut.

' 'Staunching', said Knollys, 'that's what they call it in novels. 'She staunched the blood from his manly brow'. Have you done, yet? This is nothing, you know. I've had far worse scrapes than this in rugby matches.'

Vanessa laughed, and stood back to look at her handiwork. What a mess he was! That huge scar, and those black stitches under his jaw! If she hadn't known who he was, she'd be frightened to death. But he was a handsome fellow, for all that, when you looked beyond the scars.

'You were coming down those stairs to rescue me, weren't you, Cornflower?' said Knollys. 'Don't you ever do that again, do you hear? That man — well, you know who he is, don't you? Your guvnor's told you all about him, I expect. Colonel Kershaw, I mean. He's the man who murdered Dr Otto Seligmann.'

'Why did you let him escape, Sergeant Knollys?' asked Louise.

288

'Well, Miss Whittaker, I didn't actually 'let him escape'. He was too quick for me, and I lost him at the turning into Broad Sanctuary. If I'd subdued him just now, then Kershaw or no Kershaw, I'd have hauled him off to the nearest police cells. He's a killer, Miss Whittaker, and by rights he should be behind bars until he goes to the gallows.'

Knollys caressed a large gold signet ring on the middle finger of his right hand, and added, 'I've left my mark on him, Miss Whittaker. We'll know him again when we see him.'

'Where is Mr Box now?' asked Louise. 'And how was it that you arrived here so providentially today? I can scarcely believe that all this has happened!'

'Mr Box is out in the sticks at present, miss, taking counsel with the great ones of this land. I expect he'll be back in London soon enough. And I didn't actually arrive here. I was here already! Colonel Kershaw borrowed me from Mr Box, and told me to guard Miss Drake here night and day. I'm holed up in a room at the end of that other corridor. When Miss Drake screamed, I charged through the door.'

Vanessa remembered some words that Kershaw had spoken to her after Arthur's funeral. 'There may be danger, but you will

289

never be more than a breath away from help.'
He had proved to be true to his word.

Louise took her copy of Dr Seligmann's
letter from her pocket, and handed it to
Sergeant Knollys.

'The original of this letter, Mr Knollys, was
brought to me at Gower Street by Mr
Schneider, the late Dr Seligmann's secretary.
Evidently, that man followed him here, with
the intention of taking the letter from me. He
was successful, but he did not know that I'd
already made a copy of it.'

Knollys put the copy of the letter in his
pocket without opening it. Evidently, his
mind was elsewhere. He picked up Vanessa's
piece of embroidered damask, and examined
it curiously.

'What's this?' he asked. 'All this silver wire,
and these little gemstones — '

'It's a morse. The fastening of a cope. It's
for one of the Abbey canons.'

Knollys put the piece of embroidery down
on the table, and stood up. Louise noted the
subtle change in his manner as he did so. He
had suddenly put aside his friendly intimacy.

'Miss Whittaker, and you, Miss Drake, I
don't want you to be at further risk from that
man McColl, or from any of his associates. I
want you both to put some things together,
and move into Bagot's Hotel. You'll be safe

there, and it's all expenses paid, according to Colonel Kershaw. Will you both do that?'

Louise glanced briefly at her young friend, and saw the eager light in her eyes. It was an eagerness tinged with relief.

'Of course we'll go, Mr Knollys,' said Louise. 'It's the sensible thing to do.'

'Then I'll go at once and summon a cab for you, Miss Whittaker. You'll want to go out first to your house in Finchley. I'll send a plain-clothes man to accompany you there.'

'And the copy of Dr Seligmann's letter?'

'Rest assured, Miss Whittaker. I'll place it in Mr Box's hands as soon as I see him again.'

Jack Knollys looked thoughtfully at the slim girl with the blonde hair and the lively blue eyes. Vanessa caught his glance, and blushed.

'A morse, hey, Cornflower?' said Jack Knollys. 'Well, well, you learn something new every day.' In a moment he had left the room, closing the door quietly behind him.

Vanessa Drake sat at the table, holding the basin of water, but making no attempt to get her things together. She gazed at the closed door with something approaching rapture.

'Oh, Louise!' she said, after a while. 'Isn't he just . . . just — oh, Louise!'

Louise Whittaker laughed. Somehow, the

fear that McColl had engendered had completely disappeared. Vanessa's youthful spirits helped both of them to triumph over fear.

'Never mind all that, Miss Drake,' she said sternly. 'Get your hold-all from the cupboard, and pack your things. 'Oh, Louise' indeed! Come, girl. Duty calls!'

13

A Sip of Prussic Acid

Fritz Schneider emerged from the premises of the Apollo Café in Frederick Street, near Gray's Inn Road, his mind still full of intricate chess moves. It was good to escape from the forlorn atmosphere of the house in Chelsea, from the sense of desolation and lack of purpose, and pass an idle hour or so in the company of other European émigrés. The Apollo Café, run by a Belgian and his German wife, catered for such people.

What could have been in that letter from Dr Seligmann that he'd delivered yesterday to Miss Whittaker? It was no business of his, of course, but it had been a peculiar affair. It had not been in the *herr Doktor*'s nature to be secretive. Still, Miss Ottilie had forgiven him his stubbornness over the matter. Very soon, now, she would return to Berlin, and he would settle quietly again with his spinster sister in his native city of Leipzig. The days of glory had passed away.

Still musing over the cunning of his recent chess opponent, Herr Schneider hurried along the crowded street to where a crossing had been swept through the melting banks of snow, and stepped off the pavement.

At that moment, what appeared to be a runaway horse and cart came careering straight at him. He had just time to notice the bareheaded driver, and to register some surprise that the man shouted no warning, before he was thrown violently beneath the threshing hoofs, and one of the iron-tyred wheels ran over his right leg. The cart and its driver thundered past, and they were soon lost to view in the press of horse-traffic.

A crowd gathered, and a man threw his overcoat across the dazed and bleeding figure. Before he lost consciousness, Fritz Schneider listened to the drone of voices from the throng of men and women surrounding him.

'I tell you, it was done deliberate!'

'He didn't stand a chance, poor thing!'

'Here's a bobby!'

The realization came to him with a sense of shock. That voice had been right. It had been a deliberate attempt to run him down. His eyes closed. A doctor, accompanied by a stretcher party, arrived on the scene from the nearby Royal Free Hospital, and the crowd parted to let them through.

★ ★ ★

At 2 King James's Rents, the fire in Box's office grate was still well banked-up, but the bitter cold of the earlier part of January had all but dissipated, and a rapid thaw was developing. The sky above Whitehall was very dark with rain-clouds, and the gutters were beginning to sound with the running of melted snow.

Inspector Box had donned the little round spectacles that he wore for reading. Sergeant Knollys sat quietly opposite him, waiting for his chief to finish leafing through his report on Colin McColl's invasion of Vanessa Drake's rooms in Westminster. Presently, the inspector looked up, and smiled.

'Tickled your fancy, did she?' he asked, and had the satisfaction of seeing his hulking great sergeant blush. They were the very words that Knollys had used against Box when he had been initially smitten by Miss Ottilie Seligmann. Still, he'd soon got that young woman's measure. She was an impostor, an accessory, almost certainly, to the murder of Dr Seligmann, and perhaps she was other things, too . . . It was a bad, sad world.

'I can tell by the style of this report,' Box continued. 'It's hardly the sober prose of the average sergeant's notebook. 'The young lady showed great courage . . . Miss Drake gave her account of the incident clearly and fearlessly' . . . '

Inspector Box removed his glasses, and threw them down on the table. He shook his head in mock disgust.

'I can't leave you alone for a few hours, Sergeant Knollys, without you involving yourself, first, in vulgar fisticuffs, and then in a romantic attachment. Had I known this was going to happen, I wouldn't have let Colonel Kershaw poach you from me. So Miss Drake tickled your fancy, did she?'

Sergeant Knollys suddenly laughed.

'Yes, sir. Since you ask me, she *did* tickle my fancy. And I rather think that I tickled hers! So I'll take it from there, if that's all right with you. As for McColl — well, I don't think he actually wanted a fight, because he had further business elsewhere. He wasn't armed, either. McColl's up to something, and as I see it, sir, we should go all out after him, whatever Colonel Kershaw thinks.'

'I'm inclined to agree with you, Sergeant. And whatever it is he's up to, it's going to happen in Scotland. According to that letter from Seligmann to Miss Whittaker, it'll be on the twenty-fifth of this month — '

Arnold Box suddenly recalled his interview with Herr Schneider, the fussy, punctilious secretary at Chelsea. He had shown him the altered calendar — altered to show the date Wednesday, 25 January.

'That calendar, Sergeant Knollys. The calendar at Chelsea. Dr Seligmann was trying to leave a warning. It was he who altered that wooden calendar! The twenty-fifth . . . What's so special about that?'

Sergeant Knollys did not seem to hear what Box had said. He had risen from his chair, and was standing with one arm leaning on the mantelpiece. He seemed suddenly dejected, as though grappling with some kind of unwelcome thought. When he finally spoke, Box realized what had been on his mind.

'Why did McColl murder Lieutenant Fenlake? I've been thinking about that ever since I met Miss Drake. Fenlake was her beau. Maybe I'm feeling guilty about taking his place — '

'Pardon my interrupting, Sergeant,' said Box, 'but you're talking nonsense. Piffle. You'd be entitled to feel guilty if you'd murdered poor Lieutenant Fenlake yourself, in order to pay court to Vanessa Drake. But you didn't. Fenlake was murdered by Colin McColl for reasons of his own. He lured young Fenlake to that so-called secure house in Thomas Lane Mews by means of a genuine coded slip, and then shot him in the back.'

'But why, sir? Why did he shoot Lieutenant Fenlake? What harm had he ever done him?'

'He shot him, Sergeant, because . . . because he'd recognized him. Yes, that's it. Fenlake had recognized this McColl when he pulled him away from the blaze in the Belvedere. That's what I think, anyway. He probably didn't know where he'd seen him at the time, but McColl knew that Fenlake would remember. So McColl lured him to the secure house, and shot him dead. It's a bad, sad world, Sergeant.'

A heavy chair scraped across the floor-boards in the room above, and the ponderous stumping tread of Superintendent Mackharness began its progress towards the upstairs landing. As always, the gas mantle rocked in sympathy, its tin shades rattling. The trick was to get out into the lobby before he reached the door. Box was waiting obediently when the stooping figure in a frock coat appeared at the head of the stairs.

'Box,' said Superintendent Mackharness, 'up here, if you please. I'll not keep you more than a few minutes.'

★　★　★

The smell of mildew in Mackharness's gloomy office was overpowering, but the superintendent didn't seem to notice it. Box could smell eucalyptus mingling with the resident aromas of gas and decay, and realized that Mr Mackharness had developed one of his colds.

'You wanted to see me, sir?'

'Well, yes, otherwise I would not have called down to you. Close the door tight shut, will you, Box? That catch tends to spring out of its socket, so give it a good push. That's it. Now sit there in that chair, will you, and listen to what I have to say.'

Mackharness produced a large brown handkerchief, and blew his nose violently. What was this new scent? Ah! Snuff. The superintendent rummaged around for a while among a pile of documents on his desk.

'I know you've been out of town for a few days, Box,' said Mackharness at length, 'and I'll not bother you for an account of your doings. Not yet, at least. But I've had a communication — here it is — from the commissioner, who informs me that you have been seconded for an indefinite period of time as an aide to one of Her Majesty's Special Officers of State.'

Mackharness cleared his throat, and looked very solemn.

'I want you to understand, Box, that this kind of thing is an unusual honour. A signal honour. This special officer is a gentleman called Colonel Kershaw. You're to meet him at a venue given in this sealed note.'

The superintendent handed Box a small white envelope. It was slightly damp, and smelt of oil of peppermint. It was abundantly clear to Box that his superior officer had no idea that he had been working closely with Colonel Kershaw ever since their encounter in the foggy garden of Dr Seligmann's house at Chelsea. Box decided not to enlighten him.

'A great honour, then, sir.'

'Yes, indeed. The commissioner says that I should release you from normal duties 'as, and when, Colonel Kershaw requires'. I shall be happy to do so. A few little points, Box, and then I'll let you go. This Colonel Kershaw will be a very clever man, I expect. Don't try to outsmart him, as you try to outsmart me. Be civil, listen, and act on his commands.'

'Yes, sir.'

Mackharness eyed his subordinate critically, and sniffed. Box concluded that the sniff was connected with the cold, and was not meant as an adverse criticism.

'You've always been a smart man, Box, well turned out and dapper. Well done! So for your meeting with Colonel Kershaw, I'd suggest just a little bit more — er — polish.

Buff up your boots a bit. Give your coat a good brush down. And wear a dark tie. I think that's all. Good morning.'

'Good morning, sir. I'll bear what you say in mind. Try a handful of menthol crystals in a basin of hot water, sir. Put a towel over your head, and inhale — '

'Get out of here, Box! Do you hear? Go!'

As Box closed the door of the superintendent's room, he winced as his superior officer was racked by a bout of exuberant coughing.

★ ★ ★

'Inspector, will you accept a suspicious death? It's a request from 'C'.'

Arnold Box had stopped half way down the staircase to listen to a uniformed constable who was standing in the vestibule, rain dripping from his gleaming cape on to the wet floorboards. Box still held Kershaw's sealed note in his hand. He pulled a wry face.

'I'm not sure that I can, Constable,' he said. 'See if you can find Inspector Wilson. He's in the building somewhere.'

'Sir,' said the constable, 'it's a suspicious death at the Royal Free Hospital — '

Box steadied himself on the banister rail, and tried to banish the sudden pounding of blood that had come into his ears. The Royal

Free — surely it wasn't Pa?

'An accident case, sir, brought in from the street, yesterday. Died in the night, but they think it's not a natural death.'

Box's world swung back into place.

'All right, Constable. I'll go right away. Who asked for me?'

'Inspector Wright, sir, of 'C'. And the dead man's name was Schneider. A German, he was. Fritz Schneider. Knocked down yesterday in the street.'

★ ★ ★

Arnold Box listened patiently while the impressive woman in the starched uniform of a matron told him her story. She had begun to speak as soon as Inspector Wright of 'C' Division had left the chilly visitors' room on the ground floor of the Royal Free Hospital, to pursue his enquiries elsewhere. Matron was obviously very upset, but had so far succeeded in maintaining strict control of her emotions. She was a big woman, with a very healthy-looking pink and white face. Her bright grey eyes regarded Box with a frankness born of years of exercising authority.

'Detective Inspector Box? We have not met before, even though your father is one of our

302

patients. I am Elizabeth Barton, the matron here. This hospital exists to treat the sick poor, and is staffed almost entirely by females. Nevertheless, there are male doctors in attendance, as you know. Last night a man purporting to be such a doctor approached one of our patients, Mr Fritz Schneider, and gave him what the poor man may have thought to be a sleeping-draught. The intruder was not a doctor, and the substance that he gave to Mr Schneider was a noxious poison.'

Matron Barton suddenly abandoned her self-control, burst into tears, and hid her face in her hands. When she spoke, Box heard the voice of the compassionate woman hidden behind the mask of the professional administrator.

'Oh, dear! What am I to do? Such a thing has never happened here in all my years of service. That poor man was brought in here yesterday, because he was knocked down by a runaway horse and cart in Frederick Street. It's just on the corner from here, which is why we received him.'

Box recalled something that Inspector Wright had told him before the matron had appeared on the scene. Witnesses to the incident in Frederick Street had sworn that Schneider had been deliberately run down. A failed attempt at murder? Perhaps.

'Can you tell me what kind of injury Mr Schneider had sustained? I knew him, Matron, you see, and I'm very sorry and angry about this. He was a prim and prickly kind of man, but I couldn't help liking him.'

'I know, Mr Box. He was in great pain, but all he would do was apologize to us for all the trouble he was causing! Poor man . . . His right leg was badly fractured, and there were open wounds that could have festered if not treated quickly. Mr Howard Paul saw him almost immediately, and was going to attempt to reset the limb later today. But now . . . '

By a monumental effort of will, Matron Barton composed herself.

'But come, Mr Box, I will take you upstairs to the surgical ward. Your father, I know, is very anxious to talk to you.'

'How is he, Matron? I've not been able to call in as often as I'd like.'

'He's doing very well, Mr Box. He's been rather feverish for the last two days, but that's only to be expected. His leg is making great strides — Oh, dear! I hope that doesn't sound too frivolous! Come, I'll conduct you up to the ward.'

★ ★ ★

304

'How are you, Pa?'

Old Mr Box was sitting half upright, supported by a mound of pillows. His face was flushed, but his eyes shone not with the light of fever, but the excitement of the chase.

'I'm fine, Arnold, I'm fine. Now pull up that little stool and sit down, while I tell you what happened up here last night. That poor German man, Mr Schneider, was brought in here yesterday. He was supposed to have been run over by a cart. They put him in that bed over there, the fourth one along from the door. He was looked after, and fussed over, and seemed to settle down to sleep — '

'What time was he brought in, Pa?'

'Well, I'm telling you, aren't I? Don't interrupt. He was brought in just after three o'clock. Nothing untoward happened until just after midnight. I've had a bit of a fever, and couldn't sleep very well. The night lamps were lit on the big table there, and we all settled down as well as we could.

'At a quarter past twelve, a man came into the ward. He was wearing the kind of long, white coat that the doctors wear, and was carrying a medicine bottle and a glass — one of those little frosted tumblers. I had my eyes half closed, but I was watching him, because he didn't ring true.'

'What do you mean by that, Pa?'

'He didn't behave like a hospital doctor. Usually, when they come on to the ward, they glance at every patient as they go along — they're interested, you see, even if you're not one of their particular patients. This man looked neither to right nor left. He made straight for Mr Schneider, and — I'd better tell you what he looked like, first. He was of slim but wiry build, five feet ten inches high, fresh complexion, with a half-healed scar on his forehead.'

Arnold Box thought to himself: Colin McColl couldn't shoot poor Schneider in the back. Not in a quiet hospital ward. He had used more subtle, but equally deadly means of silencing a potential nuisance.

'You're marvellous, Pa! Still on duty! This ward's your new beat . . . What happened next?'

'Mr Schneider woke up, and he and the so-called doctor talked for a minute or so. Then Mr Schneider said, 'I fancy I've seen you somewhere before, Doctor.' And this man replied, 'Very likely, Mr Schneider. Where three and a half million people are cooped up together in one city, their paths may cross and re-cross.' And then the man uncorked the bottle, and poured some liquid into the little frosted glass.'

Old Toby Box seized his son by the wrist,

and looked at him with a sudden shade of horror in his eyes. His voice dropped to a whisper.

'Arnold, you could smell the peaches ... There was nothing I could do: I'm helpless here. He held the glass to poor Mr Schneider's lips, and he drank it. Prussic acid. He would have been dead before that man had reached the ward door.'

★ ★ ★

Inspector Box stood in the deep porch of the Royal Free Hospital, and looked out at the gleaming wet cobbles of Gray's Inn Road. It was raining steadily, but there was a freshness in the accompanying breeze that helped to banish the memory of the intense cold and persistent snow of the earlier part of the month.

He took Colonel Kershaw's envelope from his pocket, tore it open, and read the note inside. It told him to come to the rear entrance of the Admiralty building, in St James's Park, at five o'clock. It was already after four. A solitary cab came slowly along the street. Box hailed it, and told the cabbie to take him to Horse Guards Road.

★ ★ ★

307

Colonel Kershaw was waiting for him under a kind of Doric pillared veranda at the back of the Admiralty building. Box joined him, and together they stood looking out across the park. Kershaw seemed disinclined to move from the sheltered spot.

'Mr Box,' he said, 'perhaps your superintendent has spoken to you? Good. I thought that he was owed some kind of explanation for your mysterious absence from your usual hunting-grounds. There's no need, by the way, to tell me about the unfortunate Schneider. I already know about that. Some day soon, Box, we'll avenge these deaths. Oh, yes . . . But now, very quickly, here are a few points. Seligmann's letter to Miss Whittaker was very interesting, particularly its reference to something happening on the 25th of the month — '

'I recall, sir, that Dr Seligmann's wooden calendar had been altered to show that date: Wednesday, 25th January. I think he did it himself. It must mean something.'

'Yes, Box, it must. All I know about it is that it's the feast of the Conversion of St Paul. It seems to have no other significance. What we must do now, Box, is beard Admiral Holland here, in his lair. He's the head of Naval Intelligence, and he's hugging some damned smug secret close to his bosom, something to do with Scotland.'

Colonel Kershaw turned abruptly, and pushed open the tall glazed door, flanked by two great stone anchors, that would take them both into the hushed corridors of the Admiralty. As they entered the rear vestibule, Kershaw paused for a moment. There was something else he wanted to say.

'Our friend Mrs Poniatowski, Box, has installed herself in Caithness, on Hamish Bull's doorstep. Why? What possible naval presence could there be in Scotland, apart from the odd patrol-boat? The British Home Fleet is Channel-based. It always has been. Only Admiral Holland can answer our question.'

* * *

Rear Admiral Holland, Box judged, was not far off the retirement age of sixty, but his manner betrayed the energy and resolve of a much younger man. He looked well in uniform, which he wore without self-consciousness but with perhaps just a touch of complacency.

The admiral ushered Kershaw and Box into his darkly panelled office with its maps and globes, and its chart-covered desk. He sat in a high-backed chair in front of an enormous painting of iron-clad warships at anchor in a spacious harbour. Parchment-shaded lamps added an aura of quiet opulence to the room.

'Well, now, Colonel Kershaw, whatever brings you into the offices of the Queen's Navy? I got your note, and made a little space and time for you. How good to see you! Sit down. And you, Mr — er — '

'This is Detective Inspector Box of Scotland Yard. I am about to talk of Intelligence matters, Admiral Holland, but I must insist that this officer shares our confidences. You will have heard of the assassination of Dr Otto Seligmann. Inspector Box here has discovered that Seligmann was holding a copy of *The Hansa Protocol* and its attendant volumes as a means of neutralizing the German war party.'

'So I have heard, Kershaw. Sir Charles Napier was good enough to inform me of that interesting fact.'

'Therefore you will also know that agents of the German war party have succeeded in destroying those volumes. Box and I have identified a gang of fanatical Pan-Germanists who, we are both convinced, are about to commit some kind of outrage connected with our naval defences.'

The admiral settled himself further back

in his chair. He permitted himself a little smile.

'This is all club talk, Kershaw. Those who shout the loudest are not always the doers of deeds. The British Home Fleet is more than capable of looking after itself.'

Colonel Kershaw reined in his temper with considerable difficulty.

'I have a direct commission from the Queen, Admiral Holland, to prevent any such outrage from taking place. Will you now tell me what measures have been taken to protect the Channel Fleet, or must I bring you a penned order from the Queen herself?'

Admiral Holland regarded the earnest secret service chief with an almost indulgent amusement.

'There's no need to bother the Queen, Kershaw. You — and your celebrated crowd — are a number of years too late with your fears for the Channel Fleet. I suspect that your little gang of German anarchists are also very much out of date.'

Box saw Holland glance rather doubtfully at him for a moment before continuing. Here's a man who liked to keep Navy business strictly within the confines of the Navy and its own intelligence services. Well, Box could understand that. The admiral was getting on Kershaw's nerves, but he had all the appearance of a man to be valued and respected.

'Naval policy, Kershaw,' Holland continued, 'is moving with the times, largely as a result of an alliance between senior officers such as myself and a gaggle of younger men who are still walking the decks. The British Mediterranean Fleet, as you will know, is commanded by my old friend Admiral Sir George Tryon. With him at the helm, no foreign power would dare to upset the balance of naval power in the Mediterranean, which means that people like me can safely concentrate on home affairs.

'Let me tell you, Kershaw, about the thinking of our informal alliance, which, I may say, has been successful in making its views official naval policy. For too long our warships of the Home Fleet have been concentrated on the Channel area, as though we were still threatened navally by France. That, I may say, has not been a remote possibility for the past sixty years. But plans are going forward to swing the concentration of fleets up from the Channel towards the German Ocean — the North Sea, as some people are now calling it.'

'The German Ocean? You mean — '

'The tactical and strategic reasons for that move may not be immediately obvious to you, Kershaw. The only threat to our Navies in that area, as you are fully aware, must come from the growing ambitions of the German Empire. It is therefore our wish to organize and equip a British Grand Fleet, and ultimately, when it is up to full strength, exercise it openly for the benefit of anyone who cares to contemplate its might. With Tryon in the Mediterranean, and the projected Grand Fleet in the German Ocean, any potential aggressor, Kershaw, will be effectively hemmed in, and rendered powerless.'

Admiral Holland warmed to his subject, and Box found himself enthralled by the man's knowledge, and his enthusiasm for expounding it. He saw that Colonel Kershaw had decided to remain silent until the admiral had finished his exposition.

'Speed is always of the essence,' Holland continued, 'and new engines are being developed, new types of cruiser, new, awesomely armed battleships! All these will move in concert under commanders who will be free of antiquated approaches to naval warfare. Of course, there are diehards who want us to doze on complacently, thinking that command of the seas is a divine imperative assigned to Britannia, and that we need to do nothing. Younger minds, for once, know better.'

'They often do,' Kershaw murmured. Holland seemed not to hear him.

'Now, in the long term, Colonel, we aim at establishing massive, impenetrable harbours for this Grand Fleet at Rosyth, and possibly at Scapa Flow, in the Orkneys. But since 1890 we have begun an intensely secret rehearsal of our intentions, first in certain remote creeks and harbours in the Pentland Firth, lying off the north of Caithness — I beg your pardon?'

Kershaw had allowed a gasp of realization to burst from his lips.

'There it is, Box, do you hear?' he cried. 'Caithness! The mist is clearing, at last. Mrs Poniatowski, our explosive Bohemian, is living openly near Hamish Bull's estates at Caithness — I'm sorry, Holland. You don't know what I'm talking about — '

'No, I don't! So let me continue. Most of these places are lying off the north of Caithness. Later, we envisage a much larger concentration of anchorages in the northern lochs of Ross and Cromarty, from Loch Broom to Cape Wrath. These vast areas of anchorage can be sealed off from public access at any time, and it has been shown that the entire Home Fleet could be stationed in these areas until such time as the Rosyth and Scapa Flow harbours are built.'

314

'My people have observed fleet movements in the Irish Sea.'

'Yes, Kershaw, it's all part of the same business. These are dangerous times, as you well know. If the German Admiralty were to get wind of our plans, there would be a very ugly incident, and it would give the German war party ample fuel to stoke its incendiary fires. That's why we've carried out these manoeuvres with great subtlety and caution. So set your mind at rest about the Channel, Kershaw, because the fleets aren't there.'

Box listened to Holland's complacent, almost patronizing voice as he expounded Naval policy for the benefit of his visitors. Didn't the man appreciate the irony of the situation? With every word the admiral spoke, another fragment of the puzzle fitted into place. Holland's words unwittingly made clear what the German conspirators intended to do. The Home Fleet had moved to Scotland. So had Mrs Feissen. So, no doubt, had Colin McColl.

Box glanced at Colonel Kershaw, and mouthed the words 'Conversion of St Paul'. Kershaw, who had been sitting in absorbed silence, suddenly found his voice.

'If I were to say January 25th, Admiral Holland, would it have any significance for you?'

A frown of annoyance creased the admiral's brow.

'Really, Colonel Kershaw, this is too bad! No one should know about the 25th. Not even the people here know about it. Just Her Majesty and His Royal Highness. Very well, you may as well be told. On that day, the whole of the Home Fleet will have completed a secret rehearsal — no less than its arrival in concentration in the provisional harbours. Indeed, all but a few of the capital ships are already there. HMS *Fearnought* arrived from Portsmouth last Thursday, the 12th. It's one of the greatest exercises that the Royal Navy has ever undertaken.'

Colonel Kershaw took a few moments to frame his answer. When he did speak, it was with his usual dry, rather world-weary tone, but there was a tremor of anger underlying it.

'When you speak of His Royal Highness, am I to understand that you are referring to the Prince of Wales?'

'I am. On the 25th of this month, as a seal of the royal approval of the new strategy, the Prince of Wales will step on board HMS *Leicester*, which will then pass through the fleets arrayed overall. The *Leicester* came up from Portsmouth at the same time as HMS *Fearnought*. The whole brilliant exercise has been overseen by a very able man called

Commodore Cartwright, acting in concert with his captains. I assume that one of your untiring minions picked up that date, the 25th, from one of my careless people here.'

A hideous vision suddenly arose, unbidden and unwelcome, before Box's eyes: HMS *Leicester*, torn apart by a massive explosion, plunged to the bottom of the sea, taking with it the Prince of Wales. The Empire would respond with ungovernable rage, thirsting for retribution. The German war party thirsted for conflict. Well, if that vision were to become reality, they would have their desire, with a vengeance . . .

Box was recalled to the present by Kershaw, who had swallowed his anger enough to respond to Holland's complacent words.

'I am, as you know, Admiral Holland,' said Kershaw, 'usually *au fait* with the activities of Naval Intelligence, because you, or others here at the Admiralty, have the courtesy to send me the occasional note. On the matter of the 25th January, apparently, it was thought that I was not to be trusted — '

'My dear Kershaw, you know that isn't true! I simply judged that the fewer who knew about the 25th, the better.'

'Very well. And I want you to know that my knowledge of that crucial date, Admiral, came not from some talkative junior here at the Admiralty, not from what you're pleased to call my 'untiring minions', but from that police inspector there, and his colleagues, who have trudged and tramped through snow and slush for a week or more turning up clues and following up leads. It was Inspector Box there, and his sergeant, who brought that date, the 25th, to light.'

Box saw the look of haughty distaste on Admiral Holland's face. This man was jealous of his rival in a way that Sir Charles Napier, the professional diplomat, was not.

'Well, then, Kershaw, your police friends have brought it to light. I congratulate you, and them. But I fail to see why the matter should throw you into a panic.'

'Well, then, Admiral Holland,' Kershaw replied, 'here is a small piece of information that might interest you. At this very moment, living in Caithness, is a woman called Maria Theresa Feissen. She is an explosives expert, the person ultimately responsible for the destruction of The Belvedere at Chelsea. She is in Scotland, Admiral, because she had found out about the twenty-fifth long ago.'

'How could this foreign woman have found that out?'

'How? Somewhere on the other side of this wall is the Admiralty Cipher Office. No doubt

318

you could lead me to it, if I were to ask you. And in that office worked a man called Colin McColl. While working under the same roof as you, he murdered two Foreign Office couriers. Yesterday, he poisoned Otto Seligmann's secretary. And he it was — have no doubt of this, Admiral — who found out the secret of the 25th, and delivered that secret into the hands of our enemies.'

Holland had gone very pale. He seemed to be struggling for words. Kershaw held up a hand, as though to stop the admiral from speaking.

'Make no comment now, Admiral,' said Kershaw. 'This is not the moment to look for rats in the ship. It is, rather, the moment to prevent the ship from sinking.'

It was odd, thought Box, that he felt no satisfaction at seeing an admiral turn pale with fright. He had too much imagination, perhaps, to react in that way. This man in the well-fitting uniform was about to face a daunting challenge to all his lofty assumptions of superiority. Would he prove able to meet that challenge? Box hoped so, for all their sakes.

Colonel Kershaw glanced at the massive painting of warships at anchor in the sunlight of some utopian haven. He permitted himself a rare unpleasant smile.

'In the Royal Artillery, Admiral, they speak of a target that is not aware of its presence in the gun-sights as a 'sitting duck'.'

'What do you mean?' the Admiral quavered.

'I mean, Holland, that you have successfully penned in the entire British Home Fleet where the people who blew up The Belvedere in Chelsea can give even greater exercise to their explosive talents. It's the 18th today: the 25th is in precisely one week's time. Unless something is done soon, that day will go down in history not only as the greatest disaster that the Royal Navy and this country has ever endured, but as the day when the heir to Britain's Throne and Empire was blown to pieces, and Europe plunged into war.'

14

'Something Terrible is Contemplated'

When Kershaw and Box emerged from the rear entrance of the Admiralty building, the colonel seemed disinclined yet again to leave the shelter of the Doric pillars. He stood in silence, pulling on his gloves, and fastening them at the wrist. Something in Kershaw's manner prepared Box for what he was going to say.

'Well, Mr Box,' said Kershaw at last, 'I think we've put Admiral Holland on his mettle. He's a good man, you know, despite the harsh things I felt compelled to say to him just now. He and I will manage this business well enough between us.'

It was a clear dismissal, the kind of abrupt quietus that you had to expect if ever you became entangled with Colonel Kershaw's affairs. When he said 'go', you went. It was ironic, though! As far as Old Growler knew, he'd just been taken on by Kershaw that very morning. Now, on the very same day, he was being shown the door.

'What will you do now, sir?'

'Well, I think this is going to be a joint naval and military exercise. When I heard at High Cedars that Mrs Poniatowski was holed up in Caithness, I had a quiet word in Sir Hamish Bull's ear. I wanted his house, you see, as a headquarters. He very sensibly agreed to spend a week or two at his London house in Eaton Square. It would help him to while away the winter agreeably enough.'

Arnold Box laughed, and a certain tension that he had detected in Kershaw was immediately dissipated. Perhaps the colonel had expected him to throw a tantrum . . .

'That weekend at High Cedars, Box, whetted Sir Hamish's appetite for the luxurious life. It was the dry champagne, I think that did it!'

Kershaw still seemed unwilling to move. Evidently he had something more to say.

'Look here, Box, you don't feel slighted about this, do you?'

'Not at all, sir. I know all about the difficulties of exercising authority. It's not as easy as some folk think. I've been caught between two stools in this case. Left to myself, I'd have arrested the whole lot of them on suspicion by now! I'd have already put them where they could do no further harm. But I can see that mine's a blinkered view, and that your people have to look at a broader canvas. No, sir, I'm not in the least slighted.'

'Good man! It's a seductive and persuasive notion of yours, to have arrested the whole lot of them and locked them up for questioning, and so forth. Why didn't you do so? I suspect the answer to that question is that you've joined my crowd in spite of yourself!'

'I think you may be right, sir.'

'Well, if I'm right, you'll see how I've got to juggle with the Prime Minister, the Foreign Secretary, Her Majesty's Government, and Her Majesty's Loyal Opposition. I've got to think of the Kaiser in Berlin, and the President in Paris, and the Czar in St Petersburg. Above all, I have to use the means at my disposal to root out the real traitors in our midst, and prevent a hideous war with Germany. So let's see how things develop in Scotland.'

Although it was not as cold as it had been earlier in the month, the diagonal sheets of rain falling across the park formed a dismal prospect. Box was getting tired of the Doric pillars, and Kershaw, he felt, had said all that he wanted to say. It was time for them both to move.

'Are you going to defy this rain, sir, and make tracks for wherever you're going?'

'Yes, come on, Box. Let's make a dash for

Whitehall. We'll get our death of cold, standing here.'

The two men hurried across Horse Guards, holding their heads down to escape the driving rain. When they reached Whitehall, Kershaw stopped at the entrance to the War Office. He looked speculatively at Box for a moment.

'Thank you for all you've done this last week, Mr Box,' he said. 'I knew you'd turn up trumps! I've no doubt that there will be interesting developments up there in Scotland, and I had already intended to keep you informed by telegraph. I'll send sporadic reports to a man called Baldwin, one of the operators at Charing Cross Telegraph Office. They'll be in the usual police code. Baldwin's one of my nobodies. He'll bring any messages directly to you at King James's Rents.'

'That's very good of you, sir.'

'Not at all, Box. I made a few arrangements, you see, before ever you and I darkened Admiral Holland's doorstep. It's as well to be prepared, don't you think? Anything you care to send me should be directed to the Naval Quay Telegraph Station, Caithness. I arranged that, too, before-hand.'

'Well, sir,' said Box, 'I wish you success in Scotland. I take it that you'll allow me to pursue any enquiries of my own here in London? Without prejudice, as they say.'

'Well, of course, Mr Box,' Kershaw replied. 'Do I ever interfere with the even tenor of your daily round?'

Colonel Kershaw smiled, raised his hat to Box in salute, and passed out of sight through the imposing portals of the War Office.

* * *

Box picked up a report on the problem of traffic congestion in the metropolitan area, flicked through its pages, then threw it down on the table. Sergeant Knollys looked up from his notebook.

'What's the matter, sir? Are you vexed that we've both been dumped by Colonel Kershaw? Perhaps 'shelved' would be a better word.'

For once, Box made no attempt to respond in kind to his sergeant's banter. Knollys had told him how he had settled Louise and Vanessa into Bagot's Hotel, where he had received a politely dismissive note from Kershaw, thanking him for his trouble. Well, 'shelved' was not the right word, either. There was more to it than that.

'Where's Count Czerny?' he said, more to himself than to Knollys. 'I borrowed Tracker

Thompson from 'B' Division to keep a special eye on the noble count. He followed him to Calais, where he was met by a group of harmless-looking German gentlemen, and conveyed away somewhere by coach. Maybe he really is back in Germany, pulling the strings of those murderous puppets of his — Baron von Dessau, and the rest of them.'

'Maybe he's somewhere else, sir,' Knollys countered. 'Maybe he's quietly slipped back into England. I've made a few enquiries about Count Czerny. He belongs to some of the best clubs, and is supposed to be a crack shot. He's a very wealthy man, with several residences on the Continent. He's also got a steam-yacht, called the — I've got it written down here, somewhere — yes, the *Princess Berthe Louise.*'

'A steam-yacht? There are possibilities there, Sergeant. And here's another question for you: where's Miss Ottilie Seligmann? She's gone, too. Gave our man the slip by walking into Peter Robinson's in Oxford Street, and disappearing via a few twists and turns through the back way into Regent Street.'

Box sprang up from the table. The office seemed stifling, a monument to inertia. He was tired of standing about in the rain, and sitting idly by the fire in King James's Rents.

'And what about Colin McColl — '

'There's a lead there, sir. Miss Ottilie wasn't as careful as she should have been, and one of our people saw her make an interesting foray from Chelsea to Euston, a few days before she made herself scarce.'

'Euston!'

'Yes, sir. Poor Mr Schneider took that letter of Seligmann's out to your Miss Whittaker, at Maybury College, in Gower Street. Soon after he'd left the house in Chelsea, Miss Ottilie took a cab to Morwell Gardens, near Bedford Square. That's only a stone's throw from Gower Street. I think she was alerting an accomplice.'

Box had been struggling into his overcoat while Knollys was talking. A fresh light of battle had been kindled in his eyes.

'And maybe that accomplice was our friend Colin McColl,' he said. 'Come on, Sergeant, let's get out to Morwell Gardens!'

Morwell Gardens proved to be a quiet enclave of lodging-houses near Bedford Square. A few enquiries brought them to the house they wanted. Yes, a Scotch gentleman had taken rooms here for a while. Very quiet and respectable person. Yes, that was right: his name was Mr McColl. No, the rooms hadn't been re-let. Of course they could look around, but they were furnished rooms, and the gentleman had left nothing worth taking behind.

The landlady at 23 Morwell Gardens led Box and Knollys to a spacious room on the second floor of the four-storey house, and left them alone. They opened cupboards and pulled out drawers, felt under the mattress in the small adjoining bedroom, and examined the washstand. There was nothing of Colin McColl left on the premises.

'Nothing, Sergeant Knollys,' said Box, 'with the possible exception of these!'

He removed a tight wad of creased and folded newspapers from a waste-paper basket in the sitting-room. He and Knollys spread them out on a table. They bore the marks of boot blacking, and were slightly yellowed at the edges.

'These papers have been discarded from an attache case,' said Box. 'Perhaps McColl decided to use fresh paper to wrap a pair of boots for his next journey. *The Portsmouth Daily News*. There are three of them: Monday, 9 January, 1893. This one's the Tuesday, and this one, Wednesday . . . .'

'So Colin McColl was in Portsmouth last week, sir. He was there for at least three days. That was the week when we were very much preoccupied with the treacherous Major Lankester, Bagot's Hotel, and the rest of it.'

328

'Yes, Sergeant. Portsmouth . . . And by the Friday, he was back in London, being pulverized by you at Miss Drake's place in Westminster. What was he doing in Portsmouth? He worked for part of the time at the Admiralty Cipher Office. There seems to be a special naval flavour about McColl.'

Box recalled the dramatic interview with Admiral Holland. Portsmouth had been mentioned. Something to do with HMS *Fearnought*, and another warship. What was it? The *Leicester*. Portsmouth . . .

'Sergeant Knollys,' said Box, 'there's a picture coming into focus, a picture that I don't like very much. Let's get back to Scotland Yard. I'm going to send a telegraph to an old comrade-in-arms, Bert Fielding, who moved to Portsmouth in '89. Inspector Fielding. We'll send it from Whitehall Place. Bert might come up with a few answers.'

★ ★ ★

It was just over half an hour later, after Box had sent his message, that the telegraph machine at the office in Whitehall Place began to spell out a reply. The constable on duty expertly converted the coded message into plain speech, and handed his note pad to Box.

Portsmouth. 18 January 93. Reply Number 1. HMS *Fearnought* and HMS *Leicester* tied up at the South Railway Jetty Portsea Monday 9 January. Both ships received complement of shells for magazines. Both set sail Tuesday 10 January for restricted destination. Reply Number 2. Your description fits a well-known general naval engineer called Angus Macmillan. He worked on both ships. Expert in bunkering work and general mechanisms. Assisted at the loading of shells into both ships on Monday 9 January. A. Fielding. Port Police.

'Angus Macmillan. A name to conjure with, Sergeant,' said Box. 'I'll keep this information to myself until Friday, and then I'll send it up to Colonel Kershaw in Scotland. He'll be there by then. He may have shelved us, Sergeant Knollys, but never let it be said that we shelved *him*. By Friday, he'll be settled in Sir Hamish Bull's house in Caithness. What did he say it was called? Craigarvon Tower. Sounds a bit bleak to me. I wonder what Colonel Kershaw will think of it?'

★　★　★

Craigarvon Tower, a four-square building of weathered granite, rose gaunt and grey through the mist of rain that enveloped the rugged demesne of Sir Hamish Bull, Baronet. The tower had stood for 700 years or more, relentlessly battered by the winds coming in from the Pentland Firth and the North Sea. There was scarcely any shelter along all the seventy miles of bold, rugged coast that girded Caithness. Once part of the kingdom of Norway, Caithness held many remains of the ancient Norsemen. Barrows and ruined stone huts were scattered widely through the area.

The two or three other titled landowners in the area had long ago sought more comfortable estates further south. The Bulls had chosen to remain in their ancient Highland home, within sight of the land's end and the plummeting cliffs, and the great sheltered bay called Dunnock Sound.

Admiral Holland and Colonel Kershaw, well muffled against the wet cold, emerged from the castellated front entrance of Craigarvon Tower, and began a laboured walk through an ill-defined estate of undulating land, where sheep and cattle grazed, and sparse, stunted crops showed that this corner of Scotland suffered from severe winters, and late wet springs.

Holland was profoundly uneasy. He and Kershaw had made the journey to Scotland by scheduled trains rather than by 'special', in an attempt to preserve their anonymity, and it had been a tedious journey in the extreme. Could they hope to have arrived in Scotland unobserved?

'Kershaw,' said Holland, as they emerged on to a steep, stony path, 'you know that I was called upon by a deputation of officers from the Home Fleet this morning. They included Commodore Cartwright, the commander of the flagship. I mentioned him to you when you visited me with Box at the Admiralty.'

Holland smiled rather sardonically, and glanced at Kershaw.

'I alerted them to the dangers of the current situation. They all expressed concern, and gave me assurances that everyone would be on extra alert. When they considered that they'd extended all the correct courtesies due to my rank, they took their leave, and returned to Dunnock Sound.'

'So they didn't believe you.'

'No, they didn't. I could see that Cartwright thought I'd become a chair-bound theorist, who could be fobbed off with soothing words and well-turned compliments. Cartwright's a friend of the Prince of Wales, you know. Keeping such exalted company may have gone to his head. Well, Kershaw, they may think what they like! You have the Queen's mandate to override and to commandeer, so you and I must act in concert, with whatever help we can muster.'

They reached the end of the path, which had brought them to the summit of the cliff. There they stopped, and looked down into the vast protected haven of Dunnock Sound. It was an awesome sight that met their eyes.

Stretching away far to the western shore of the Sound a mighty fleet lay at anchor. It seemed impossible that so many great ships could have been built, let alone brought together in such a colossal show of strength. Grey and menacing, the superstructures of the vessels towered upwards through the blur of cold rain. Line after line of great battleships could be seen, and around them a whole navy of cruisers, lightly armoured and with smaller guns, the scouts of the fleet.

Admiral Holland pointed down towards a magnificent ship in the centre of the flotilla, a ship to which all the others appeared to be doing homage. It rose awesomely above the forest of masts, turrets and smoke-stacks, the jewel in the Royal Navy's crown.

'HMS *Fearnought*,' said Holland 'Twenty thousand tons displacement, a speed of twenty knots, ten twelve-inch guns in those five turrets. No ship of any navy on earth could withstand a salvo from her.'

Kershaw looked down at the fleet. He could see innumerable sailors at work on the decks, dwarfed by the size of the vessels and the height of the cliff where they stood. Clouds of seagulls swooped and cried around the forest of masts.

'What ship is that lying near her to the right, Holland?'

'The ship off her starboard bow? That's the cruiser HMS *Leicester*, in which His Royal Highness will sail through the fleet'

Admiral Holland let his gaze drift across the lines of ships as far as the western shore and its huddles of buildings, almost lost to view in the dullness of the fine rain. Years in a warm Admiralty office had not diminished his immunity to bad weather, and he stood quite unmoved by the wet and cold of the cliff.

'I don't see what these hot-heads can do,' he said. 'The whole shoreline is guarded by soldiers of the Scottish regiments. The entire area is virtually sealed off until the thirtieth, when they lift anchors.'

Colonel Kershaw did not reply. He stood wrapped in his cloak, looking fixedly out and away from the fleet towards the dull, fermenting waters of the North Sea. He was very still. Holland stole a glance at him. What was he thinking about? There was nothing of interest there, though far out to sea the winking lights of some kind of vessel could be seen, either at anchor, or proceeding very slowly north.

Admiral Holland stirred restlessly. He was chafing at Kershaw's absorbed silence.

'What are you looking at?' he asked testily. 'There's nothing to see.'

'Heligoland.'

'Heligoland? Well, you can't see that from here. It's an island about forty miles off the German coast. There's no one there but a few herders and fisherfolk. But I appreciate your mentioning it. We ceded it to Germany in '90, as you know, and it's obvious that they'll establish a naval base there. Really, you'd have thought the Great Powers — but there, the Germans have done nothing in Heligoland yet.'

'No, they've done nothing there yet, Holland. But they will.'

Kershaw stopped for a moment, and looked down the path towards the grim, rain-soaked tower below them. There seemed to be no life about the place, just rain, and a quiet breeze. It was too quiet! He recalled the previous day's interminable railway journey from London. A man had got on the train with them in London, changed whenever they changed, and was with them when they had transferred from the main line on to the Highland Railway.

It wouldn't do, at this juncture, to mention that man to Holland. He had almost certainly not seen the man, as he had been careful to keep out of their sight as much as was possible. He'd been a soldier once, but the proud mien had deserted him. It had been replaced by a seedy, furtive ugliness . . .

They reached the rough track that ran in front of Craigarvon Tower.

'Come, Kershaw' said Admiral Holland, 'it's time for us to think and re-think, and that can best be done in the shelter of the Tower. Things are too quiet here. Suspiciously quiet. Nothing's happening, so there's nothing we can do. What on earth can these madmen be contemplating?'

'Whatever it is,' said Kershaw, 'it will be to do with explosives. Something terrible is contemplated — 'a victory beyond your wildest dreams', as Baron von Dessau told his dangerous rabble in Berlin. Why hedge the matter about with ifs and buts? That victory can only be an act of destruction by explosives associated with the great fleet down there in Dunnock Sound.'

He thought for a moment of the telegraph

message that he had received earlier that day from Inspector Box in London. It had suggested very sinister possibilities. Well, he had the secret means of making investigations of his own. Holland could be told whatever was necessary when the time was ripe.

Holland made no effort to refute what Kershaw had said. The two men walked soberly across the wet grass to the ancient tower of Craigarvon. The single narrow door was opened to them by a uniformed marine with a fixed bayonet on his rifle. They passed inside, and the door was firmly slammed and bolted. Craigarvon Tower had become what it had often been in the past, an impregnable fortress.

★ ★ ★

'Inspector Box! My pleasure, I'm sure! We don't often see you over here. Come in, and see if you can find a chair somewhere. And you, Sergeant Knollys.'

Mr Mack's spacious domain at the Home Office looked to Box rather like a roofed scrapyard. As they stepped over the threshold from a tall, narrow corridor, the two detectives almost collided with the burnt and detached door of a free-standing safe, which had clearly been blown off its hinges in some kind of explosion. It was twisted out of shape, and its green paint had been scorched by fire. There were similar pieces of wreckage arrayed around the room, and leaning against the walls.

Box and Knollys picked their way across the bare boards between piles of yellowing documents and manuals, and sat down in two Windsor chairs drawn up in front of Mr Mack's massive desk. There was not an inch of space visible. Most of the desk was covered in small boxes and pieces of iron pipe. Everything seemed to have a brown-paper label attached. The air was thick with pipe smoke, and the ceiling stained yellow with the tobacco-smoke of decades.

'What can I do for you, Inspector Box?' asked Mr Mack. He seemed genuinely delighted to see them, and his old face managed a wintry smile. He was wearing his usual rusty black suit, to which he had added a blue woollen muffler.

'I'd like a little chat with you about shells,' said Box. 'Just a little introduction, if you see what I mean. I expect you know all there is to know about shells.'

Mr Mack joined his fingers together, and looked critically at his visitors.

'Well, Mr Box, it's very kind of you to say so. But I'd like to get clear in my mind what you mean by shells. I take it you don't mean seashells? No, well I thought you didn't. Just my little joke. But there are shells and shells, Mr Box. First, there's your common-or-garden shells. Then there's your armour-piercing shells. And your high explosive shells — beautiful, they are. Then there's your shrapnel shell, your thin-walled, your artillery shell, your naval shell — '

'Pause there, Mr Mack, I beg of you,' said Box, holding up his hand to stem the flow of words. 'The naval shell, I think, is what I'd like a little chat about. A few informal words, if I may put it that way.'

Mr Mack rummaged around among the detritus on his desk until he found a short clay pipe, which he proceeded to light. There followed a period of snuffling, interspersed with a number of throaty coughs. Mr Mack's mild, pale eyes began to water.

'The naval shell, Mr Box, and you, Mr Knollys, comes in two kinds, the armour-piercing and the high-explosive. They have a sharp point at the front, and a fuse in the base. The point sometimes has a soft steel cap, which absorbs the shock of first impact, so that the shell can penetrate the armour before it bursts. They burst, you know. That's the theory, anyway.'

'It's amazing, Mr Mack, the things you

know. And these naval shells — they go into the ship's guns — '

'They go into the ship's *magazines*, Mr Box. You've heard of a magazine, haven't you? You've got to be careful about sparks and naked lights in magazines. More often than not they'll have a copper floor. Tread carefully, if ever you find yourself in a warship's magazine.'

'They're in racks — ' Box ventured.

Mr Mack hauled himself up with a sigh, and pulled open one or two drawers in a tallboy. With a little bleat of triumph he pulled out a backless book, which he flopped down on his desk. For a few moments he began worrying at the pages until he had found what he wanted.

'There you are. There's a diagram of a battleship. It'll save you making wild guesses about racks, and so on. That's HMS *Hazard*. A lovely ship, that, of eighteen thousand tons. There's your magazine, you see.'

Mr Mack pointed to part of the diagram with a heavy index finger pitted with tiny blue points of embedded gunpowder, one of the minor disadvantages of spending his life with dangerous explosives.

'Moving away from the stern, we pass over four compartments of the ship, and then, below where you see that twelve-inch gun in

340

its barbette — its turret, you know — you'll see the magazine.'

Mr Mack, warming to his subject, seized a magnifying glass from his desk, polished it quickly on his muffler, and handed it to Box.

'See? Notice that it's below the water-line, for safety's sake. And below the magazine, there's a separate shell room, and the revolving hoist, that takes the shells up to the barbette.'

Inspector Box ran the magnifying glass across the diagram, noting the vast engine rooms, the coal bunkers, and the boiler rooms. He silently marvelled at the sheer size of the great warship.

'There are four more magazines here,' he said, 'sited beyond the boiler-rooms towards the prow.'

'That's right,' said Mr Mack, sitting down again in his chair, and puffing away at his clay pipe. 'They're to service the two forward gun turrets. So now you see where all the shells are kept on a big warship. Is there anything else you'd like me to tell you?' He added, very shrewdly, 'I suppose all this is the other end of The Belvedere business?' Box nodded his assent.

Sergeant Knollys had said nothing since he and Box had entered Mr Mack's smoky Home Office kingdom. But he had been eyeing the old explosives expert speculatively while Box had been examining the diagram. There was a hint of mischief in his eyes when he asked a question.

'I was wondering, Mr Mack, why you have these plans of warships here in your office. Is there a purpose in that, or do you just like warships?'

'Sergeant!'

Box's tone held mild reproof, but Mr Mack only chuckled.

'Seen through me, haven't you, Sergeant Knollys? Well, everyone to his trade. That goes for me, as well as you. I have these plans of warships so that I can contrive ways of blowing them up! Devise tricks and traps to send these great vessels to the bottom of the ocean! It's all part of the business of knowing your enemies. Try to think what they'd do, and see if it's possible. Forewarned, as they say, is forearmed.'

Arnold Box thought once more of the over-confident admiral, and his pride in the great battleship HMS *Fearnought*, which had apparently arrived in Caithness on the previous Thursday, after its journey up from Portsmouth.

'If ever you felt like turning your skills in the direction of HMS *Fearnought*, sir,' asked Box, 'what particular explosives would you use to send her to the bottom of the ocean?'

Mr Mack did not reply for a moment. He glanced shrewdly at Box, and then once again hauled himself to his feet.

'Explosives? I'd use whatever came to hand, Mr Box. Trinitrophenol, nitrocellulose — to put it more simply, I'd use the contents of the magazine themselves as my fiendish device! There's no point in taking a bomb into a warship when it's carrying enough high explosives in its magazines to lift the decks!'

Mr Mack beckoned them into an adjoining room, which proved to be a very untidy workshop. There was a metal-topped bench, a lathe, a small furnace, and a jumbled collection of pieces of broken machinery. A grimy slit of a window looked out on to the rain-soaked expanse of St James's Park.

'This is what I'd use, gentlemen,' said Mr Mack, dragging a kind of oil-covered drum from beneath the bench. He made a half-hearted attempt to wipe it clean with a grimy cloth.

'This is what you'd call a detonator. Ridgeway's Limpet Igniter. A nifty piece of work, just eight inches in diameter. See those magnets? And the timing mechanism? This one's broken, but you can see the idea. The magnets clamp the device to the fuse in the base of a shell. You set the clock, and when

343

the time that you've set comes round, that steel rod in the centre there activates the fuse plate, and the shell explodes.'

Mr Mack turned some exposed clockwork mechanism with his hand, and the steel rod shot out with an alarming thud of metal. He threw the device back into the gloomy recess under the bench, and wiped his hands on the grimy rag.

'And then, of course, Mr Box, the other shells in the magazine explode in sympathy. What we call the 'brisant' effect. And the magazine's a confined space, with armoured steel walls, so the force of the magazine going up blows the ship to pieces. And that sympathy . . . that 'brisant' effect, can spread to neighbouring ships, and then — well, then, Mr Box, you could lose the whole fleet.'

15

The Watcher in the Fields

Angus Macmillan lived on the shores of Dunnock Sound in a village that was rapidly being turned from a poor rural street of cottages subsisting on stone-cutting, to a poor rural street covered in coal dust. For over a year, colliers had come round Duneansby Head from England, and dumped their cargoes into the old stone-yards along the waterside. Now, Angus Macmillan, pulling a handcart that wet Saturday through the mud towards the Naval Quay, could breathe in the fine black coal dust as well as the yellow dust from the stone quarries.

A group of neighbours watched Angus as he passed them. He waved a hand in greeting, but they knew that his time was precious, and he didn't stop to chat. He'd been a wanderer, had Angus, and was not often at home there, in Thirlstane village. When he was, he'd drop into the alehouse, and tell them tales of another Scotland, a land of bagpipes, and grouse moors and distilleries, and a host of other fine things. Here, on the shores of the

Sound, there was only hard work, poverty and dust.

The nice thing about Angus Macmillan was that he always fitted in immediately when he returned from his journeying. He would open his rambling and ruinous flint cottage in the trees above the road, one or other of them would bring him up some kindling, and there he would be. This time he'd brought a little wife and her taciturn mother to live with him. The little wife was flighty, you could see it in her eyes. Angus had better watch out. And the little wife too. For Angus Macmillan was known to have a foul, unforgiving temper, though with those he liked he could be pleasant enough.

Angus Macmillan spoke the Gaelic, though not well. His family had come from those parts, and his father had been a Thirlstane man, though he'd gone abroad long years ago, and married a foreign woman. Angus had always been a wanderer. He'd been to Clydeside and worked in the bowels of ships, readying and priming the coal bunkers. Then he'd gone to England. Now, it seemed, the new fleet depot had brought him back to Thirlstane. With his skills, he could make seven shillings a day down at the coaling basin.

★ ★ ★

As Macmillan dragged his handcart on to the
setts of the Naval Quay he was challenged
rather half-heartedly by two armed marines.
He grinned at them as he began to undo the
ropes holding a tarpaulin over the cart.

'Och, away with your guns, lads. You know
quite well who I am.'

'Aye, we ken that fine,' one of the two
marines replied, 'we've seen your ugly mug
off and on since last autumn. But you're a
real will-o'-the-wisp, aren't you, Angus?
Flitting round, here and there . . . You're like
a conjurer with his tricks: now you see it, now
you don't!'

Angus Macmillan laughed.

'I'm a ship man, Soldier, and ships are
always on the move. A ship man follows the
ships! Where would they all be, with their fine
vessels and their tall funnels, if it weren't for
the likes of me? It's very fine for you fellows,
too, strutting around here on the quay with
those rifles, but there's no glamour down
there, among the boilers.'

He had brought his cart right to the edge
of a wooden landing-stage where a trim
steam-cutter lay anchored. It contrasted
sharply with the grimy bunkering vessels
anchored further along the quay. One of the

marines put down his rifle and helped Macmillan to drag a polished wooden box down from the cart.

'There's not much glamour up here, either, is there, Jimmy?' said the other marine. 'Just standing still in the cold, challenging the likes of poor Angus there.'

'Och, stop your whining. Let's get the man out to the *Fearnought*.'

It was 21 January. The following Monday the coaling-up of the fleet was to take place in readiness for the 25th. For a whole frantic day the air would be dark with the dust of thousands of tons of coal emptied by unending lines of men through the deck-ports into the bunkers of the warships. It was essential that the chutes and the door-mechanisms functioned without faults. Angus Macmillan was skilled in that particular aspect of heavy coaling operations.

Within minutes, Macmillan and his box of tools were on board the steam-cutter which began its journey, weaving skilfully through the cruisers towards HMS *Fearnought*. The two marines on the quay resumed their watchful guard.

'There's that skulking spy again,' said the man called Jimmy, motioning with his head in the direction of a well-dressed but seedy man of about forty leaning against the wall of a

348

small brick office. 'He was there yesterday, too. Hey, you! Clear off out of it!'

The man rolled himself upright off the wall with a kind of studied insolence that made the marine flush with anger, and strolled off into the rain-soaked stony village behind the quay gates.

★ ★ ★

Later in the day, Angus Macmillan was brought back to the pier in the cutter. His box was hauled up on to his handcart, and he began his slow uphill journey home. He reached his cottage, and his mother-in-law came out to help him lift the heavy box down prior to dragging it into the house.

The cottage lay half hidden in a clump of stunted oaks. It was in a state of semi-dereliction, but at one time must have been home to a large family. There were four large rooms on the ground floor, and a number of disused store-rooms facing into the trees on the hillside that rose above the Thirlstane road.

Once across the threshold, Colin McColl shed the strong Scots accent that he had employed as Angus Macmillan. He looked at the woman who was supposed to be his mother-in-law, and read the signs of something amiss in her furrowed brow.

'All has gone well, Frau Feissen,' he said, 'but you look vexed. What has happened?'

Frau Feissen shrugged her shoulders. She motioned McColl to follow her into one of the sparsely furnished rooms of the dwelling, where a fire burned fitfully on an open stone hearth.

'It is Miss Ottilie,' said Frau Feissen. 'You'd better do what you can to placate her. She's still seething about what was done to Fritz Schneider. She vented her rage on me this morning — with no result, as you may imagine! I think that, tonight, it will be your turn.'

Frau Feissen turned as Ottilie entered the room. The older woman pulled a wry face at McColl, and slipped away, leaving the murderous Scotsman and Ottilie Seligmann alone together in the firelit room.

'What is the matter with you, madam?'

There was a dangerous ring to McColl's voice that would have silenced most women. It served only to kindle Ottilie's pent up wrath, which exploded in a barrage of words.

'The matter?' she cried. 'What is the matter? Fritz Schneider's death is the matter! I have held my peace for Germany's sake, but now I will speak out. How dare you exceed your orders! Poor Fritz! What harm had he ever done?'

Ottilie Seligmann's eyes flashed with a dangerous fire born from the arrogance of her Junker ancestry. The fire was almost immediately quenched by a flood of tears.

Colin McColl's lip curled in something like contempt.

'Your onset of tenderness does you no credit, Countess Czerny,' he said. 'Schneider was dangerous to our cause, because he was a fool. A dangerously naïve fool. He had become the unwitting go-between for our enemies — '

'You murdered him! When your hired thug failed to kill him with his vile horse and cart, you crept into that hospital, and poisoned him! *Feigling*!'

Colin McColl made as though to lunge at the enraged Ottilie. His face was drained of all colour.

'Silence, you frantic woman! You fling that word 'coward' in my face. But it was I who risked life and limb to destroy the traitor Otto Seligmann, and with him the copy of *The Hansa Protocol* that he had stolen for the use of Germany's enemies. True, it was you who discovered it, hidden in the Belvedere, but it was I who triggered the mechanism, at great personal risk. I do always what is needful to usher in the New Age. As for Schneider, I had no personal feelings about him one way or the other. I had no personal feelings about Oliver, or Fenlake, or a dozen others whom I have sent to perdition.'

Ottilie, he could see, had made a monumental effort to regain control of herself. It would not do to antagonize her further.

'We must be careful, Countess Czerny,' he said, in milder tones, 'not to fly at each other's throats. You know what is at stake. Very soon now, the great victory will be ours. One of the marines down at the quay today said that I was like a conjurer. He spoke more of the truth than he could possibly imagine.'

'Ah, yes,' said Ottilie softly, 'the trick — the sleight of hand. If you fall into their hands before the 25th, confessing to that trick will serve you well. But think! *There are only four days left!* When I think of that, my anger dies!'

'I am glad,' said McColl. 'In one way, this whole glorious project owes its origin to you! You befriended that girl, Ottilie Seligmann, when she was dying of consumption at Jena. Everyone, so I was told, commented on your uncanny resemblance to her, despite a certain difference in age — '

'It is true! She and I were like sisters. She

was a good German, unlike her uncle, the traitor. The Herr Doktor Otto Seligmann accepted me as his niece. He had not seen her since she was a child. Maria Feissen was already established as housekeeper, and so matters took their course . . . '

Ottilie moved restlessly. She glanced around the dim room with distaste, mingled, so McColl thought, with fear.

'Four days!' she cried. 'They cannot pass quickly enough for me! Soon it will be done, and my husband will spirit us away from this benighted land. How I hate this place! This loathsome hovel, and the so-called village beyond the road. His Excellency my husband would not deign to stall his cattle in a place as wretched as that! This house is dark, and alive with sounds. I hear noises, footsteps — '

'There is no one here but us three, Countess. I am tired of searching the place every time you fancy that someone is walking about.'

'You are right. It is nerves. So you must forgive me, and my severe language. You will forgive me, no? Ah! Here is the good Maria. All is in order, Frau Feissen.'

The door had opened quietly, and the woman who had called herself Mrs Poniatowski came into the room. She looked as grim and forbidding as ever, but her eyes shone with a purposeful fanaticism.

'I heard your voices raised,' she said. 'I hope that you are not falling out with each other? The tension up here in this cursed wilderness is getting on your nerves, no doubt. But think of the prize that is so nearly in our grasp! Calm yourself, Mr McColl. You have done excellent work. Countess, your role in this business has been vital all along. We are a dedicated group, are we not? We each have a role to play. So let us do our work for the Fatherland cheerfully, and without complaint. Dear Countess Czerny, do not let personal animosities or anxieties put our victory at risk. As for poor Fritz — well, I, too, was fond of him, and warned him many times that it would be wise to return to Saxony. He did not heed my warnings, and so he had to pay the price . . . '

Ottilie seemed to be subdued by the older woman's words, and Colin McColl visibly relaxed. Mrs Poniatowski's voice assumed a coaxing and conciliatory tone.

'Do not spoil things at this late stage, dear friends, by quarrelling. Soon, it will all be over. His Excellency is holding himself in readiness. Play your parts! Be true to your destiny! Remember the rallying cry of the *Eidgenossenschaft*: for Kaiser and Fatherland!'

In one of the ruinous chambers at the rear of the cottage, the well-dressed seedy man who had been warned off from the Naval Quay waited for the voices of the Queen's enemies to recede as they left the room. With a deftness born of experience, he crept quietly from the dim store-room where he had been crouched in hiding, and slipped noiselessly away into the trees.

★ ★ ★

Colonel Kershaw walked round the stony bulk of Craigarvon Tower, which was bordered by a flint-strewn path. His course lay downward from the gaunt pile, and across a bleakly exposed ploughed field, at the far end of which there was a ruined bothy, little more than a dry-stone shed, with the tattered remains of a thatched roof. Kershaw pulled the skirts of his long military overcoat around him, stooped low, and passed under the lintel of the gaping doorway.

There was scarcely any shelter inside, but it was a convenient place for a meeting. Waiting for him was the well-dressed but seedy man whom the guards had driven away from the Naval Quay. He wore a well-cut black overcoat, and had the look of someone who had once been a gentleman, but who had fallen on evil times. He sat on a pile of fallen stones. Kershaw gingerly sat down near him, but did not look at him.

'Well?' said Kershaw abruptly. The other man replied in low tones.

'They're all there, holed up in a cottage at Thirlstane village. Colin McColl, Ottilie Seligmann, and Mrs Poniatowski. I have seen them.'

'How did you contrive to do that?'

'I gained entrance to the cottage. It's a rambling, ruinous kind of place, and it was easy enough to hide away from their sight. I saw them, and I heard what they said to each other. Let me tell you what they said.'

When the man had finished his account, he added, after a brief pause, 'I will now do whatever you ask me to do.'

Kershaw sat silent for a moment. He kicked a loose stone, which rattled across the ruined floor. He sighed, and rested his chin on his hand. Then he spoke.

'You do realize, don't you, Lankester, that I can do nothing to save you?'

'Yes,' said the other man, in the low voice of a man without hope. 'Yes, I know that. Nevertheless, I will do whatever you ask me to do.'

'Very well,' said Kershaw. 'Listen carefully to what I have to say. Somewhere in that cottage near Thirlstane village, McColl will have hidden a letter. The letter was written by the late Dr Seligmann to a young woman called Miss Whittaker. A copy of that letter is fortunately in our hands, but McColl has the original. Do you know what I'm talking about, or must I go over it all?'

'No. Naturally, I know all about it.'

'The contents of that letter are harmless enough, but it could be used by the German war party to its great advantage. McColl will make the contents of that letter public in Germany. 'The peace party is the party of traitors!' he'd say, and the ordinary German man in the street would believe him. Find that letter, and bring it to me.'

The forlorn Lankester inclined his head, but made no reply. Kershaw looked at him, and sensed that the man was holding something back.

'There are other things that you know,' he said, sharply. 'Why do you not speak?'

'I am ashamed to speak too much in your presence, for fear of hearing your contempt for me in your voice when you reply.'

'Whatever you hear will be what you have deserved. It is part of your sentence. Speak!'

'McColl is known up here in Caithness as Angus Macmillan. He migrates here for certain periods of the year. He was in

357

England for most of last week, but appeared up here on Thursday, the twelfth.'

'Who told you all this?'

'A broken-down old gossip I met in an alehouse, a kind of halfwit, with decades of stone-dust in his lungs. I plied him with ale, and asked him a few harmless questions. It's amazing what that type of man sees and hears. Angus Macmillan comes down to the Naval Quay with his cart, which contains his box of tools. He's been on HMS *Fearnought*, and also on HMS *Leicester*. I don't suppose he's been down there among the boilers and the bunkers for the benefit of his health.'

Colonel Kershaw recalled the telegraph message that Inspector Box had sent him from London. He had mentioned the name Angus Macmillan, and had suggested that he and Colin McColl were the same man. Now, this wretched, shivering renegade had confirmed the truth of what Box had discovered.

'I believe you're right. McColl's been up to no good in the bowels of those two ships. Perhaps the time's come for us to take a look. On Monday, the coaling of the fleet takes place. By then, I expect, he'll be up and away. Angus Macmillan . . . Well, well. Colin McColl's father was a Scot, but his mother was a German. Something tragic happened to her. So far, I've been unable to find out what it was.'

'I can tell you that. I assumed you knew. Colin McColl's mother was murdered by a French mob in Alsace, in 1871. Her crime, apparently, was being German.'

'I didn't know that.'

Colonel Kershaw stood up, and looked at the rain-soaked, unshaven man sitting patiently and hopelessly on the broken stones.

'You fool, Lankester!' he said. 'Look what you have found out in a single day! You homed in on that old man in the alehouse like a pigeon coming back to its loft. Think now what talent you have thrown away, what public and private esteem you have lost for ever!'

The wretched man made no reply, but he seemed to shrink back further into the shadows. Kershaw turned on his heel and left the ruin. He set out across the ploughed field that would bring him to the warmth and shelter of Craigarvon Tower. The thin rain was still falling, and the meagre fields looked barren and blighted. Kershaw suddenly paused, and turned round. Lankester had emerged from the bothy, and was beginning to drag himself away towards the road beyond the field. Kershaw called his name, and he obediently stopped in his tracks, waiting until the colonel had reached him.

'I can get you a position with a trading company in the Malay Straits,' said Kershaw. 'If you want it, you know how you can contact me.'

Lankester looked Kershaw in the eyes for the first time.

'Thanks. But first, I will do what you have ordered.'

Colonel Kershaw made no reply. He retraced his steps across the fields towards Craigarvon Tower.

★　★　★

That Saturday evening, a blazing fire in a vast stone grate threw its orange glow on the trophies of arms and mounted spoils of the hunt adorning the walls of Craigarvon Tower's great hall. Other light came from fitfully burning oil lamps, and whatever daylight managed to penetrate through the glazed slits of windows.

Both Kershaw and Holland had received a batch of telegraph messages, which were spread out in front of them on the table. Kershaw was relaxed and thoughtful. Holland was unusually agitated, containing some special anger only with the greatest difficulty.

Kershaw said nothing. When the right time came, Admiral Holland would unburden himself.

'I'm pleased to hear,' said Kershaw, glancing at a telegraph form, 'that Sir Charles Napier has already begun a ruthless purge at the Foreign Office. I expect your people will be doing something similar, Holland. They could make a start in your Cipher Office! The Press, thank goodness, have not got wind of the matter, or they'd have manufactured a national panic of it by now.'

'With very good reason,' said Admiral Holland, hotly. 'I'm glad Napier's thought to tell you what he's doing. One slight advantage of being an admiral is that I was able to order that self-satisfied bunch down at the Naval Quay to give us an open telegraph line to London.'

'Napier says here that there's more to come. He's ordered a visitation of our embassies, particularly in central Europe. You know, I think the Queen might revise her ideas about Napier. The last time I spoke to her she seemed to think that he was ready for the scrapyard.'

Holland smiled, and shook his head. It was not every day that someone whom he knew spoke nonchalantly about the last time that he'd spoken to Queen Victoria. He picked up another sheaf of telegraph forms from the table.

'I've got a message here, Kershaw, from an equerry to the Prince of Wales. It's apparently been sent to me as a matter of courtesy — presumably as a kind of placebo, to keep me quiet. His Royal Highness will arrive in Caithness on Tuesday morning, the 24th, at eight. He'll be travelling overnight in the royal train, but will change to a special carriage when he transfers to the Highland Railway.'

'He's not coming here straight away, is he?'

'Oh, no. He's staying at Firth Lodge, Lord Westerdale's place, some miles south of here. He'll come to the fleet with as much informality as possible, at noon on Wednesday, the 25th.'

'Has the Prince any inkling of this business, do you think?'

'I think so, Kershaw, though I can't be sure. This other message here suggests that someone in London may have alerted him to the fact that something unusual is going on up here.'

Holland passed the second message to Kershaw.

Once in Scotland, I will regard myself as being under orders. Whatever you advise, I will do. Albert Edward P.

Admiral Holland stirred restlessly. He threw the telegraph messages down on the table, and blushed with indignation.

'What's the matter, Holland?' asked Kershaw gently. 'What is it?'

It came as a relief to Admiral Holland to give vent to his pent-up anger.

'I went down there this afternoon, Kershaw, to the Naval Station on the shore of the sound. I was received by Commodore Cartwright. I told him about our fears that explosive devices may have been hidden in the bunkers of the *Fearnought* and the *Leicester*. He listened. I told him all about you, and about the special powers that you have from the Queen — '

'And I suppose he took no notice of you? They never do, you know.'

'He said that he would have the boiler-rooms and bunkers of both ships thoroughly searched — after he had received permission to do so from Admiral of the Fleet the Lord Leyster and Stayne. I'm not much loved by that particular nobleman, Kershaw. Once my name's coupled in his mind with obstruction and inconvenience, he'll make sure that I'm not able to make any more attempts to rock the boat!'

'And do you mind?'

'Damn it all, Kershaw, no! I don't mind.

I'm with you all the way. And if you have ways of circumventing these complacent idiots, then pursue them.'

'I will, Holland, have no doubt of that. In any case, there's a glimmer of light in the offing. I've not been idle, you know. Although I may be sitting here inert, I rather think that one of my crowd is very active down at Thirlstane village. For a little while longer — just a little while — we must watch and wait.'

★ ★ ★

On Sunday morning, Admiral Holland declared his intention of taking a walk up to the cliff top with his binoculars. He admitted to Kershaw that he felt much better for having 'let off steam' the previous evening, and that his temper would be further improved by a walk in the morning air.

'Anything's better than just sitting here, doing nothing, Kershaw,' he declared.

Once he had reached the summit of the cliff, Holland flinched at the winter rain, which was being blown inland in drifts by the wind. The grey sea moved and churned uneasily to the horizon. Well muffled in his long naval greatcoat Admiral Holland planted himself defiantly in the face of the elements and looked through his binoculars. Not more than a mile out he could see a vessel, either moving very slowly north or at anchor. He focused upon it with his powerful binoculars. Black hull, white superstructure, metal masts, a raked buff painted funnel . . . A steam-yacht.

★ ★ ★

'A steam-yacht,' said Captain Neville Dawson, commander of the patrol-boat HMS *Fortune*. He closed his telescope. 'We'd best go out and take a look.' HMS *Fortune* had rounded the point of Dunnock Raise some minutes earlier, and the watch had immediately alerted him to the presence of an unknown vessel in what was technically a restricted area.

Within twenty minutes, HMS *Fortune* was within hailing distance of the yacht. The two vessels rose and fell beside each other on the choppy North Sea waters. Captain Dawson took a megaphone handed to him by a sailor, and called out:

'What ship are you?'

There was no response at first, but then a fine figure of a man appeared on the bridge of the yacht, a semi-circular structure immediately in front of the funnel. Well over six feet tall, with blond hair escaping from beneath his yachting cap, it was possible to see his bright blue eyes shining even in the dim light of the Northern Scottish day.

'This is the steam-yacht *Mary Tudor*, out of Hull, bound for Norway. I see from the ensign that you're a Royal Navy vessel. Do you wish to board us?'

The blond man's voice was so powerful that he could be heard without the aid of a megaphone. He had a pleasant, well-modulated voice. As he spoke, one or two members of his crew came on deck and stared curiously at the patrol-boat.

'Who are you?' Captain Dawson demanded. 'You are sailing in restricted waters.'

'My name's Chesterfield. Sir Mark Chesterfield. I'm skippering this yacht myself. Sorry about being in the way. I've heard nothing about this sea-lane being restricted. What's your name, anyway?'

'Dawson. Captain Neville Dawson. Please up anchor at once and proceed. There's no call for us to board you.'

'Thank you, Captain. Good luck!'

The giant yachtsman waved an arm in a desultory salute, and disappeared from the bridge. In less than a minute Dawson could hear the yacht's anchor being hauled in. He gave the necessary commands and HMS

Fortune turned across its own wake and sped back towards Dunnock Point. The steam-yacht also altered course, and proceeded quickly north.

★ ★ ★

Towards mid-afternoon a visitor called at the Tower. The stone-flagged entrance chamber of the building had been transformed into a guard room, and the two men could hear the challenging voice of the soldier on duty. In a moment, the soldier appeared in the great hall. He was a smart man of thirty or so, wearing the dark-blue uniform and red-piped forage cap of the Caithness Highlanders.

'There's a Captain Dawson to see you, sir,' he said to Admiral Holland.

'Dawson? I don't recall the name, Corporal. You'd better show him in here.'

In a moment Captain Neville Dawson, commander of the patrol-boat HMS *Fortune*, had been ushered into the hall. At Holland's invitation, he took a seat by the fire, but did not remove his uniform overcoat.

'Captain Dawson,' said Holland, 'let me introduce my colleague, Lieutenant-Colonel Kershaw, of the Royal Artillery.'

'Gentlemen,' Dawson began, 'a certain incident took place today as my boat rounded the point of Dunnock Raise. I think you should hear about it.' Dawson gave the two men an account of his afternoon's adventure.

'Well done, Dawson,' said Admiral Holland when the commander had finished speaking. 'You did right to report the incident to me. I saw that steam-yacht myself, and wondered what it was doing out there.'

'The man who came up on the bridge said that he was Sir Mark Chesterfield — '

'Chesterfield, hey?' said Holland. 'I don't think I've heard of him. But he was quite right, of course. There are no actual restrictions on sea-traffic in the area. Only if someone got too close would we want to question them about who they were. Which, indeed, is what you did this afternoon. Chesterfield . . . No. Do you know the name, Kershaw?'

For reply, Colonel Kershaw took a wallet from his pocket and extracted a photograph. It showed a very tall, fair-haired man in an exotic, heavily-braided uniform. 'Was this your yachtsman, Captain Dawson?'

He passed the photograph to their visitor.

'Why, yes,' said Dawson. 'So you know him, sir. Who is he?'

He handed the photograph back to Kershaw, who successfully stifled a smile. The captain's transparent naïvety amused him.

'That, Captain,' said Kershaw, 'is a man called Count Czerny. He is an Austro-Hungarian nobleman, and head of a group of most dangerous and fanatical enemies of this country. He has a very useful gift: he tells truths as if they were lies.'

'But — Why, the man was English! I spoke to him!'

Captain Dawson was very English himself. He seemed personally affronted that Kershaw should regard Sir Mark Chesterfield as anything other than a True Blue Englishman.

'Count Czerny,' said Kershaw firmly, 'is an Austrian. He had the good fortune to be brought up in England. He went to school there, and speaks English perfectly. But I have it on very good authority that he is a consummate liar of the most dangerous type.'

Dawson's forehead had creased in hopeless puzzlement. What was this damned colonel talking about?

'So there you have it, Captain Dawson. Czerny is a dangerously persuasive man. Some normally very astute people have fallen under the spell of Count Czerny's rhetoric. Obviously he was successful in making you yet another victim of his persuasive charms.'

It was time, thought Holland, to come to the rescue of a fellow sailor. Why leave him to the tender mercies of this sinister army colonel?

'It was good of you to come up here and tell us this, Dawson,' said Admiral Holland. 'Let me walk back with you part of the way. I'll try to give you a clearer picture of what we're talking about.'

The two sailors passed through the guard room, and presently the great entrance door was slammed shut and bolted.

16

The Coaling of the Fleet

By Sunday evening it became evident that the coaling of the fleet on the following day was going to be a very wet and hard exercise. Rain began to pound the headland by dusk, and during the early evening it rolled inland, saturating and chillingly cold.

Dinner was served in the hall at seven, and was eaten in a brooding silence. The inactivity and sense of helplessness was beginning to take its toll.

At half-past eight, the corporal came into the hall and whispered to Kershaw, who excused himself and left the room. The corporal led him to a small stone chamber containing shelves full of oil-lamps and drums of lamp-oil. There was a wood stove here, so it was possible to sit comfortably while the torrential rain thundered against the thick glass of the narrow window-slit.

Lankester crouched before the stove, clutching a glass of whisky, which someone — the corporal, perhaps? — had given him. Steam rose from his wet clothes. He did not look up as Kershaw closed the door and sat down on a wooden bench. As in the ruined bothy, so now in the lamp-room, Kershaw asked the single question, 'Well?'

Lankester delved into an inside pocket and drew out an envelope.

'It was in a tin biscuit-box under a pile of rags. There were other documents there, but I left them. I have read it. McColl and Czerny could have made great capital from that document. So, of course, can we.'

As Lankester said the word *we* his voice trailed away into a tone of hopeless melancholy. Kershaw affected not to notice.

'Is there anything else of moment you need to tell me?'

'Yes. McColl and his 'family' are packing up. His work is done, and he will not be involved in the coaling operations tomorrow. But I believe he may have seen me hanging round the Naval Quay. When he misses that letter, he may well come after me. If so, I shall be ready for him.'

Colonel Kershaw gazed at the glowing stove. Lankester sipped his whisky thoughtfully. Kershaw got to his feet.

'You must stay in the castle tonight. It is both foolhardy and dangerous to our plans if you venture out again in this storm. Leave as soon as it's light. I will tell the corporal to prepare you a warm place somewhere.'

'You will trust me in the castle unsupervised?'

'Yes.'

Colonel Kershaw left the room, closing the door behind him.

Lankester finished his whisky. After several nights shivering in a subterranean Norse dwelling on the edge of a bog, the warmth of the lamp-room was luxury indeed. It reminded him forcibly of the comfort of Bagot's Hotel, and he smiled wryly to himself. Bagot's! Another world, another era, it seemed now. Major Lankester got to his feet as he heard the corporal approaching. At last, he was to have a good night's sleep under a proper roof. Tomorrow could take care of itself.

★ ★ ★

When the sun rose on Monday morning, Lankester was ready to greet it. He felt refreshed after a good sleep in dry quarters, and after a rough breakfast of bread and tea he was let out of Craigarvon Tower through a rear wicket-gate, which was immediately closed and barred behind him. He set off down the stony track that would ultimately take him to Thirlstane.

Colonel Kershaw, too, had been an early riser. He stood at a window embrasure on the stone stair of the Tower, and watched Lankester as he picked his way through the stones of the steeply descending track. He was about to turn away when he saw Lankester stop abruptly and look about him. Then he left the path and began to walk swiftly in the opposite direction towards the cliff. Had he seen Colin McColl?

Kershaw hurried down the stair and went to the guard-room in the castle porch. The corporal in the uniform of the Caithness Highlanders came to attention as he entered.

'At ease, Corporal,' said Kershaw. 'Do you recollect the man who came to see me last night?'

'Yes, sir. I let him in through the rear postern. I've only just let him out again.'

'Well, I want you to go out now, and trail him. He's approaching the cliff from the south side of Craigarvon Tower at this moment. Try to keep out of sight if you can, but your prime duty will be to protect him. Go armed, and shoot without hesitation if he seems to be seriously threatened.'

'Yes, sir.'

The corporal selected a rifle from the rack on the far wall, and loaded it. He slung the weapon over his shoulder, came to attention

374

in a salute, then opened the door. A squall of cold rain dashed into the porch. Kershaw closed the door, and went to sit thoughtfully at the fire. He had done what he could.

★ ★ ★

Major Lankester had gone only a few hundred yards when he realized that he was being stalked. A trained and experienced courier, he was used to situations of this nature. He stopped abruptly, and concentrated all his faculties in an intense effort to sense from what direction the danger came. Then he turned off the path and made his way purposefully towards the cliff.

As he walked through the cold rain he thought of the quietly spoken Scotsman in the cottage at Thirlstane, who had boasted to his fellow-conspirators of his success as a murderer. He had a score to settle there. Poor young Fenlake's blood still cried out for vengeance.

He stopped again, and listened. He had detected a slight fall of stone to his right. He fell to the ground and began to slither silently through the muddy grass towards a large boulder. Colin McColl, he knew, would be behind it, waiting for him. Colin McColl would have found out about the letter, and he was not a man to forgive being thwarted so seriously.

Major Lankester moved like a snake through the grass and stones towards the boulder. Gradually, almost imperceptibly, he came in sight of McColl, who was crouching down, as though ready to spring, his gaze fixed on the path rising upward from the castle to the cliff Nearer . . . nearer . . .

With a leap and a cry of triumph Major Lankester threw himself on Colin McColl, and bore him to the ground. He had the satisfaction of seeing the venomous rage and disbelief on the face of his enemy.

Lankester's sudden attack had proved too much even for the lithe and strong Colin McColl. He found himself pinned to the ground by the weight of Lankester's broad frame. The soldier's brawny forearm lay across the other man's throat, inexorably squeezing the breath out of him. He held the Scotsman in a vice-like leg-hold as they struggled round the protecting boulder and came perilously near the edge of the cliff. Lankester unclenched his teeth to spit out a question. 'Why did you shoot young Fenlake?'

'Because he saw me at the house in Chelsea. We exchanged some pleasantries in the garden there. Nobody on your side gets a good look at me and lives.'

The words were gasped out with a venomous intensity, despite the continuing throttling pressure of Lankester's arm.

'I was going to avenge Fenlake's death. I was going to choke the life out of you. There's only one way to save yourself. I know that you've planted infernal machines down there in the fleet. Tell me where they are hidden. Tell me! Tell me!'

The strong arm pressed inexorably and skilfully across the Scotsman's throat. McColl's senses began to swim, and the pounding in his ears seemed now to blot out the noise of the implacable weather. He found that he could gasp out a few words.

'There is a time-bomb placed in the bunker of the *Fearnought*. There is a second, identical bomb in the bunker of HMS *Leicester*. Curse you! How did you find out?'

During this brief exchange McColl had stealthily slipped his right hand into an inner pocket, where his fingers closed round the butt of a heavy Mauser pistol.

'You are wise to tell me,' said Lankester, 'otherwise I should have killed you. Now I will merely render you unconscious. It will be for the law to deal with you as it wishes. But I can subject you to a little more discomfort if you do not tell me how to disarm the devices. Where is the key to turn off the time-clocks?'

The reply was a horrible, half-strangled giggle. Lankester suddenly increased the pressure on the other's jugular vein.

'Tell me!'

The giggling ceased, and the damaged voice took on an air of gloating triumph.

'You have thwarted us by finding the traitor Seligmann's letter, but in this matter of the devices, you can do nothing. Today the fleet will be coaled up, and the devices will be hidden from sight by tons of coal. But even if they were found, you could not defuse them. They do not work by keys. They work by a combination lock. Solve that, and you can open the plate covering the control switch. But you will not solve it, and I will not tell you what it is.'

With a sudden convulsive movement of his whole body the Scotsman lurched to his feet, and Lankester followed, still firmly clutching his enemy. They were now within a few feet of the cliff edge, and its 400 feet drop to the rocks below.

Colin McColl fired the hidden pistol at point blank range. There was a hideous report which sent the gulls screaming up into the sky.

Major Lankester died immediately. His

body was flung backwards and landed on its back in the rain-sodden grass.

The force of the shot flung the already weakened McColl backwards, and he teetered on the edge of the cliff before righting himself. The signal-flags . . . the flags that he'd hidden among those stones on the cliff edge. Ah! They were still there! He must signal to Count Czerny now. There, anchored out to sea, was the steam-yacht *Mary Tudor*, waiting.

As he stood up with a flag in each hand and turned towards the sea, a single rifle shot rang out from the sheltering rocks.

McColl made no sound, but a grotesque look of surprise came to his face. He reeled drunkenly, and then plunged headlong over the cliff to the rocks 400 feet below.

★ ★ ★

In the gleaming oak-panelled stateroom of HMS *Fearnought*, Commodore Cartwright put down his china cup on to its china saucer, and said, 'It's dashed inconvenient, Captain Webster, but that's what Lord Leyster and Steyne has decreed. It's not at all what I'd expected. It's that fellow Kershaw's doing, I'll be bound.'

Commodore Cartwright tossed a telegraph

form across the table to the Captain of HMS *Leicester*.

Search bunkers of Fearnought and Leicester for explosive devices. Insist Admiral Holland be present. Prevention in this case better than cure.

Captain Webster handed the telegraph form back to Cartwright, and pulled a wry face.

'Hardly a convenient time for conducting a search, sir,' he said. 'It's just after nine o'clock now. The coaling of the fleet is scheduled for eleven o'clock precisely.'

'Well, we'll just have to exercise patience, Captain. I don't blame Admiral Holland for this nonsense. After all, he was one of the architects of our modern naval policy. But when I heard that he was holed up on the cliffs there with Colonel Kershaw, I tried to keep a polite distance. Army personnel should keep their noses out of naval business. Especially that one. He's a dark horse.'

'Hear, hear! So what will you do now, sir? There's less than two hours to go.'

'I've asked Captain Dawson to go up there to Craigarvon. He's already met Holland and Kershaw. I've told him to invite both of them down here to witness the search, and stay on

380

for the coaling, if it takes their fancy! We've three hundred tons of coal left in our bunkers here on the *Fearnought*. I expect you've something similar?'

'Yes, sir. We've something like two hundred tons. It'll be a confounded nuisance, and the civilian men will grumble, but it shouldn't take us too long to sift through that kind of tonnage.'

Captain Webster stood up, and saluted.

'Thank you very much for giving me breakfast, sir,' he said. 'With your permission, I'll get back to the *Leicester*, and set things in motion there.'

'Permission granted, Captain. And now I'll prepare myself for an interview with our chief stoker!'

★ ★ ★

'Sir! I must speak to you at once!'

The corporal had flung down his rifle when Colin McColl had plummeted from the cliff top, and had bent down over Lankester's inert body. It had taken him only a moment to ascertain that he was dead. He had looked up when Colonel Kershaw and Admiral Holland had come running from Craigarvon Tower in response to the bark of the rifle.

'The fellow I shot, sir — the enemy — he

told your man that he'd planted a device in the *Fearnought*, and another in the *Leicester*. He said that he'd put them in the bunkers. I was crouching behind that rock over there. I heard everything he said — '

'Well done, Corporal. I'll see you're commended for this action. What's your name?'

'Menzies, sir. The enemy said something else. He said that the two devices had combination locks on them, so they couldn't be turned off. He laughed, sir.'

'Laughed?'

'Yes, sir. He said that the devices would soon be hidden from sight by tons of coal. Very pleased with himself, he was, even though your man was choking the truth out of him.'

After Menzies had finished speaking, the three men stood in silence, ignoring the fine rain, and looking down on Major Lankester's body. One by one, other members of the small garrison came out of the Tower, to be followed by the civilian servants. By common consent they gathered mutely at the fatal spot.

Colonel Kershaw looked round the circle of watchers. He was pleased as well as surprised to see them.

'Men,' he said, 'the body lying dead at your

382

feet is that of Major William Lankester, of the 107th Field Battery of the Royal Artillery. He was an agent of the Secret Intelligence Service, and has died here on active duty at the hand of one of the Queen's enemies.'

Kershaw had spoken from the heart, but his words had also been designed to restore the wretched Lankester's reputation. Word would soon get down to London that, far from being a traitor, Lankester had been engaged on a dangerous secret mission that had cost him his life. It wasn't true, of course; but Lankester had earned his posthumous reward.

There was an angry murmur from Kershaw's audience. It was an informal gathering, not a parade, and one of the soldiers took off his greatcoat, stepped forward, and draped it over the inert form. Colonel Kershaw turned to Corporal Menzies.

'Corporal,' he said, 'I want you to arrange a burial-detail. You, and four others from this company. Dig a temporary grave here, at the cliff top . . . Have we a Union Jack on the premises?'

'Yes, sir.'

'Very well. Wrap Major Lankester's body in the Flag, and bury him where he fell. Let the men fire a volley.'

Just at that moment, a figure in naval uniform appeared on the path leading up from Craigarvon Tower. Holland, peering through the fine rain, saw that it was Captain Dawson. The captain looked with some bewilderment at the scene, as though he had stumbled unwittingly on the rehearsal of a dramatic sketch.

'Gentlemen,' he said, saluting, 'Commodore Cartwright sends his compliments, and would you care to step down to the Naval Quay. We are about to search the bunkers of HMS *Fearnought* and HMS *Leicester*.'

★ ★ ★

It was just before eleven o'clock that Admiral Holland, who seemed to be just one of a dozen grimy labourers with shovels working in the vast coal-bunkers of HMS *Fearnought*, spotted the end of a green metal cylinder. It had been secured with wooden battens behind the two or three hundred tons of coal still lying in the bunker, a leftover from the long haul up from Portsmouth.

Holland had arrived at the Naval Quay at ten o'clock. He had been formally piped aboard HMS *Fearnought*, had duly saluted the quarter-deck, and then demanded to be taken below. He had descended the steep companionways and iron ladders that took him down to the dim region of the coal bunkers. He had briefly introduced himself to the startled chief stoker, had asked to be provided with a set of overalls, and had immediately joined in the punishing work of moving a mountain of coal away from the bulkheads. It was many years since he had experienced such a sense of exhilaration.

Holland turned to the chief stoker, a burly, muscular man who had crawled after him through the narrow tunnel into that particular chamber of the bunker.

'Do you see that?' the admiral whispered. 'Open your lantern, and shine it over here.'

The Chief Stoker did as he was bid, and looked at what the admiral had found. A device in the form of a blunt-ended cylinder, with a green-painted metal case. There seemed to be a small dial, perhaps a clock face, and beside it a set of knurled wheels — a combination lock. Beside the dial and the lock was a small recessed hatch, fitting tightly, and with no handle or other means of opening.

'Looks like a shell to me, sir.'

He spoke quietly, but his words reverberated down the tunnel, and were repeated by other voices back in the gloom. A shell!

'It's not a shell, chief stoker,' Holland

replied, 'but it's something very like one. It's quite safe at the moment, but we've got to get it out of here, and up on to the quay. After that — and if we're still in one piece — I'll make them give us both a glass of grog!'

The man grinned. For some time he had forgotten that this hard-working, friendly man was a rear-admiral.

'I'll hold you to that, sir!' he said. In a moment he had begun to drag the device out of its wooden moorings. It clanged menacingly on the gritty steel floor of the bunker.

'We'll push it back down the tunnel sir, in front of us,' said the chief stoker. 'It's heavy, but not as heavy as all that! Come on, sir, let's get it to blazes out of here!'

★　★　★

'So, Holland' said Colonel Kershaw, 'that's that! It very much looks as though we've beaten them.'

'It does,' said Admiral Holland. 'One device lodged in the *Fearnought*, and another in HMS *Leicester*. And little thanks to these polite colleagues of mine in the ward room! I think, Kershaw, that I'm going to teach Commodore Cartwright and his colleagues a few stern lessons. They all forgot their place, and my rank. Today's success has been due to quite a different kind of sailor — '

Holland, who had resumed his dark-blue service uniform, turned round and beckoned to a grimy, thickset man in the uniform of a petty officer. The man came forward, and saluted.

'Colonel Kershaw,' said Holland, 'I want you to meet Chief Stoker Reynolds, of Her Majesty's Ship *Fearnought*. It was he and I together who saved the fleet today.'

'Well done, Chief Stoker,' said Kershaw, returning the man's salute. 'I don't suppose you know who I am, but through me your Queen and country thank you.'

The man flushed with pleasure, stammered a few words, and retired. Kershaw could see the profound respect for Holland reflected in the chief stoker's eyes.

Holland looked with distaste at the two identical devices that the soldiers were busy lashing to the carts. They gleamed a malevolent bright green in the dull morning light.

'While Reynolds and I had a glass of rum together, we examined those sinister devices. We could see from the dials on the time-clocks that they've been set to explode at noon on Wednesday. Presumably they'll be safe enough till then. I'm going back on to the *Fearnought*, Kershaw. There are certain things I wish to say. What will you do?'

'I'll haul these things back up to Craigarvon. There's a remote field at the edge of the estate where they can be corralled in isolation until Wednesday. But first, I'm going to send a long telegraph message to Inspector Box in London, and another one to Mr Mack, at Home Office Explosions. I want them both to get up here, Holland, with all the speed they can muster.'

Admiral Holland glanced briefly once more at the two green cylinders strapped to the carts.

'I thought you'd agreed that we'd defeated them?'

'I think we have, but I want the expert's opinion. Better safe than sorry.'

★   ★   ★

Oblivious to the driving rain and poor light, the swarming gangs of civilian labourers worked like automata at the coaling of the fleet. The noise of thousands of tons of coal thundering down the chutes from the decks of the battleships and cruisers was indescribable. It was as though all the demons of hell were shouting in triumph.

The air was palpably thick with coal dust, which rapidly turned to black moisture in the rain, covering the decks of the ships and the faces of the men.

HMS *Fearnought*, as the pride of the fleet, was coaled first. Within half an hour its bunkers were filled to the brim with hundreds of tons of finest furnace-coal. When, towards late afternoon, the light failed, the great fleet was ready to receive His Royal Highness the Prince of Wales on the coming Wednesday. A week later, the fleet would up anchors, and set its triumphant course for Portsmouth.

★   ★   ★

In a wet, bleak field high above Craigarvon, Arnold Box watched Mr Mack, who was stooping down to peer at the two menacing green canisters that had been placed on trestles and surrounded with a wire mesh fence. Box, who was holding the elderly expert's battered Gladstone bag, saw him clear the mist of rain away from one of the dials, and read the time set for detonation. Twelve o'clock. It was already nine o'clock on the morning of the 25 January.

Box looked at the elderly man with open admiration. The journey up from London had been a frantic nightmare, achieved by the engagement of a cold and cheerless special train, which had twice been held up by signals, despite assurances that all lines would be clear. Had that been an example of railway muddle? Perhaps. Or maybe it had been something else. They had arrived, exhausted, at Craigarvon only half an hour earlier. In three hours' time the Prince of Wales and his retinue would arrive to review the fleet.

Mr Mack straightened up, and beckoned to Colonel Kershaw, who stood some way off. Box could see the anxiety in the elderly expert's eyes as he launched into speech.

'These cylinders, Colonel Kershaw, are what we call Sprengel's Canisters. They've got two chambers inside, one containing nitric acid, and the other certain special chemicals. Neither the acid, nor the chemicals are explosive until they're mixed. This little clockwork device here at the end can be set at any interval from fifteen minutes to a hundred and twenty hours. Like a clock dial, you see. And when you've set the clock, you fix it with the combination lock — those three little knurled wheels with numbers on them.'

'And these Sprengel's Canisters can lift the decks of a warship?' asked Kershaw incredulously.

Old Mr Mack shook his head violently.

'Of course they can't, Colonel! They're used for blasting purposes, in mines and quarries. If they went off in a ship's bunker, they'd certainly make a mess, but they wouldn't raise the decks, let alone sink the ship. You can see where all this is leading, can't you?'

'I can, Mr Mack. These things were deliberately designed to deceive — no wonder that Colin McColl laughed when he revealed their whereabouts to poor Lankester! And if these things are merely decoys, then there must still be devilish devices hidden in the *Fearnought* and the *Leicester*. Mr Mack, we're in your hands for the moment. What shall we do?'

'The first thing to do, Colonel, is to render these canisters harmless.'

Mr Mack opened his Gladstone bag, and produced a large clawhammer, with which he smashed the glass pane covering each of the time-clocks. Kershaw and Box instinctively flinched. Mack had retrieved a tattered code-book from the bag, and was rapidly flicking over its pages in the rain. He suddenly gave a little cry of satisfaction, rapidly twirled the knurled combination rings, and slid open the recessed hatches, revealing a small brass ring, which he pulled. They saw him start in surprise.

'They're empty! There's nothing inside the casings — no acid, no chemicals . . . Colonel, I must inspect the magazines and shell stores in the *Fearnought* and the *Leicester* straight away. Box — will you come down with me below-decks? You know what I'm expecting to find, don't you?'

'Yes, sir. One of Ridgeway's Limpet Igniters, attached to one of the shells. I'll come down with you.'

'Thank you, Mr Box. You're a — a shining ornament, if I may say so. We'll start in the *Leicester* first, Colonel Kershaw. It has just the one magazine, which doubles as a shell store. Mr Box and I studied some blueprints on the way up here. Now, it's going to be a race against time, so I don't want any obstruction, or jealous rivalries putting us all in danger of annihilation — '

'There'll be no obstruction, Mr Mack. I can guarantee that. And so can Admiral Holland. He's down there now, at the Naval Quay, awaiting your instructions.'

★ ★ ★

At ten o'clock, a small brass band assembled on the Naval Quay, ready to play suitable music when His Royal Highness appeared. Black clouds lay so low over the sea that it was impossible to see the horizon, or indeed across the sound. Someone had suggested that the band be protected by an awning, but this idea was negated, as not playing fair. A red carpet was rolled up in readiness. To have laid it out before the arrival of the Prince would have invited disaster.

The Prince's visit to the fleet was to be quite informal. Its purpose was simply to set his cachet upon the new naval policy, which, by unspoken assumption, would lay the foundation of Britain's sea strategy in his own coming reign as King. Because of the informal nature of the visit, therefore, he would be accompanied only by a small suite of seventeen persons, and would arrive in a procession of four closed carriages with outriders found by the Gordon Highlanders.

The band essayed a few mournful bars, and then entertained the incurious seagulls to a rather mournful waltz.

In the dim interior of HMS *Leicester*'s magazine, Mr Mack, clad in a loose suit of linen overalls, slid on his back beneath the eighth shell rack. Box, crouching some feet behind him, heard his sudden sigh of satisfaction. He edged nearer to the elderly expert, pushing the Gladstone bag ahead of him. Above him, the copper ceiling of the chamber seemed to threaten him with the weight of the ship above. The magazine was only four feet six inches high at this point. Box thought briefly of the firelit office at King

James's Rents. He'd never grumble about its dilapidations again, ever . . .

'Mr Box, this is the one, this shell in number four cradle — can you see?'

Mr Mack repositioned an electric lantern which was attached to a thick rubber cable leading to the ship's generator, and the wicked limpet-like device sprang into Box's view. Small, but deadly, it proclaimed its origin in prim white letters arranged in a semi-circle: *Thomas Ridgeway & Co., Birmingham.* In the confined space of the magazine, Box could hear the quiet but regular ticking of the clock mechanism. He vividly recalled the remarks that Mr Mack had made when he and Knollys had visited him at the Home Office.

'When the time that you've set comes round, that steel rod in the centre there activates the fuse plate, and the shell explodes . . . And the magazine's a confined space, with armoured steel walls, so the force of the magazine going up blows the ship to pieces.'

'Mr Box, will you hand me that little toffee hammer, and the half-inch chisel with the green handle? I'm going to defuse this thing. It's just the one, thank goodness. Then you and I can go over to the *Fearnought*.'

Two sharp taps of the hammer, a delicate

manoeuvring with the chisel, and the purposeful ticking of the clock abruptly stopped. Mr Mack sighed with relief, and wrenched the magnetic igniter away from the shell.

17

Loyalties

In the wardroom of HMS *Fearnought*, Commodore Cartwright addressed his assembled officers. If he was nervous, he contrived not to let it show in his voice. Nevertheless, he knew that Admiral Holland was still somewhere on board his ship, and that the Home Office explosives expert was already descending by means of the hydraulic hoists to the magazines.

'His Royal Highness, gentlemen,' he said, 'will be accompanied by Her Majesty's Lord Lieutenant of Caithness, the Lord Strathspey. Also present in the suite will be the Lord Treasurer of Scotland, Sir Wheeler Tuke, Baronet. The band-master has been instructed to strike up 'God Bless the Prince of Wales' as the Prince steps down from his carriage — '

'Is all well on HMS *Leicester*, sir? Sorry to interrupt, and all that.'

The speaker was a senior captain, more used to the authority of his own bridge than listening to lectures on protocol. His words echoed what all the others were thinking. 'What? Yes, all's well there. And all will be well here, I've no doubt. So just shut up, will you, Bob? I want this reception to go off without a hitch.'

Commodore Cartwright cleared his throat, and continued.

'His Royal Highness will be conducted immediately to luncheon here, on the flagship, after which he will be taken by launch to HMS *Leicester* for his progress through the fleet. Every vessel in the fleet, gentlemen, will have steam up, and will be arrayed overall. It's going to be a great 'sea-ballet', if I may put it like that, to show His Royal Highness something of the manoeuvrability of the new capital ships.'

The assembled officers listened. Perhaps all would indeed be well, as the Commodore asserted. Certainly, by some miracle of human endeavour all trace of the grimy squalor of Monday's coaling had disappeared, and everything shone bright and clean.

HMS *Fearnought* boasted four magazines. Mr Mack and Inspector Box clung to the rails of the hydraulic hoist that was taking them, and Chief Stoker Reynolds, down into the bowels of the great battleship. They could hear the throbbing of the engines, the hissing of many pipes, and what was for Box the unfamiliar whine of electric generators. There was a smell of fresh oil in the hot air.

Mr Mack spoke quietly, as though nothing particular was in train.

'It's half past ten. We have one and a half hours to search these four magazines', he said, 'and make all safe. Chief Stoker Reynolds, I want you to go into the two aft magazines now, with some of your own men, and search through the cradles for any sign of the devices that I've described. You'll do it more quickly than I can. I'll wait here, by the hoist. If you find any, then shout for me immediately. When we've done here, we'll go forrard.'

Chief Stoker Reynolds and his men took just over a quarter of an hour to search the two aft magazines. Four separate summons took Mr Mack and Box into the copper vaults where the shells lay in their cradles. Four limpet igniters, each bearing the now-familiar inscription: '*Thomas Ridgeway & Co., Birmingham*', had come to light. Three of them yielded successfully to Mr Mack's toffee hammer and half-inch chisel.

The fourth proved a tougher proposition, as the glass window had been replaced by a solid steel cap, secured by a bolted flange. Mr Mack worked away slowly and methodically, using a small hack-saw to cut through the bolt. The air was hot and close, and sickly with the smell of oil.

★ ★ ★

At eleven o'clock the red carpet was unrolled along the quay, and the petty officer in charge glanced anxiously at the sky. The band, still denied an awning for form's sake, endured the cold rain and the wind blowing off the German Ocean, and essayed a few tentative bars of 'God Bless the Prince of Wales'.

On the far side of the Sound, hidden from the fleet by the banks of low cloud, a little steam-launch moved away into the mist. On board were a pretty young woman, and an older woman of vinegary aspect. The launch set a firm course away from the anchored fleet and out to the open sea. After a quarter of an hour, the two women could just discern the rising bulk of a yacht, with lights dowsed but steam up, straining at its anchor. Soon, they would be safe in Heligoland, from whence they would be conducted by their jubilant friends to the glittering splendours of Berlin, the heart of the Reich.

It had taken Mr Mack a quarter of an hour to neutralize the fourth igniter, and it was nearly a quarter past eleven when he and his companions arrived in the area of the forward magazines. Number 2 magazine, they found, contained only one of Ridgeway's Igniters. It was one of the original glass-windowed models, quickly and easily made safe. Mr Mack consulted his watch.

'We've exactly forty minutes left,' he said, 'and just Number 1 magazine to search. With a bit of luck, we'll be done here in fifteen minutes or so. Then we can make ourselves scarce.'

At first sight, it seemed that Colin McColl had not reached this particular chamber. The shells lay in their cradles, their regulation fuses visible in the light cast by the electric lantern. It was as they neared the port bulkhead that Mr Mack saw the device. Painted a sullen grey, it was attached by two thick steel bands to the shell that it had been designed to detonate. There was no sign of a clock mechanism, though Box, who had crawled after Mr Mack to the far side of the copper-roofed chamber, could hear the sinister ticking.

Mr Mack's fingers hovered around the

device, examining and probing. Box noticed that the elderly expert was holding his breath. This device was not from Ridgeway's of Birmingham. Box could see clearly the white lettering: *Feissen Werke*.

'Can you make it safe?' Box whispered.

'No.'

As Mr Mack uttered the fatal word, Admiral Holland appeared at the entrance to the magazine.

★ ★ ★

Constrained lines of steam rose from the funnels of the fleet. The rumour began to spread through the ranks of ratings drawn up on the deck of HMS *Fearnought* that the Prince's carriages had been glimpsed from the crow's-nest. It was coming slowly down from the slight hill a mile or two to the south of Craigarvon. Commodore Cartwright, in full ceremonial uniform, took up his position at the head of the companionway with his second-in-command, and the senior commanders of the fleet.

Suddenly, Admiral Holland erupted on to the deck from one of the hatches, and the powerful whine of the hydraulic lifts could be heard. Holland was followed by a determined group of men in overalls.

'What on earth — '

Commodore Cartwright turned red with rage. What was this new eccentricity? Had the fellow gone mad?

'Commodore,' cried Holland, 'I am assuming command of this ship for the next hour. Then it is yours again. Men, stand fast! There is a dangerous shell being brought up from Number 1 magazine. You can serve yourselves best by remaining where you are until further orders are given.'

There was a murmur from the assembled sailors, but they made no attempt to break ranks. They had all heard about this Admiral Holland from Chief Stoker Reynolds.

'Sir,' said Commodore Cartwright, suddenly subdued, 'what do you want me to do?'

As he spoke, a silent team of men appeared, trundling a heavy shell on an ammuntion cradle along the deck. They were followed by Mr Mack and Inspector Box, two incongruous civilians in bowler hats.

'We've about twenty-five minutes, Cartwright,' Holland whispered, 'to prevent this ship being blown sky high. A boat — I need a boat . . . What's that little steam-launch down there?'

'It belongs to the fleet commissariat — '

'And, thank God, it's got steam up. Men, get that devilish thing down over the side, and on to the deck of that launch. Use the steam-derrick. Strap the shell to the deck, or wedge it tight where it can't roll off Careful! Careful!'

The whole company watched fascinated as the deadly shell was lowered down from the deck of the battleship in the cradle attached to the deck windlass. There was a subdued cheer when it gently touched the deck of the steam-launch, where the men accompanying it lashed it firmly to the rails. A rowing boat appeared, and the men, together with the two-man crew of the steam-launch, were rowed to safety.

'You there, Leading Seaman,' shouted Holland, to one of the men drawn up on the decks, 'break ranks, and go down on to the deck of that launch. Tie the wheel, do you hear? Then open steam and send her out away from the fleet and into the open sea. Once on the move, dive for your life. If you do it well, I will personally see to your immediate promotion.'

'Aye aye, sir!'

As the leading seaman sprang into action, Holland murmured to Cartwright, 'Ten minutes.'

It seemed an age before they heard a defiant whistle as the leading seaman opened steam, and the launch moved rapidly with its deadly cargo away from HMS *Fearnought*. Holland watched it through binoculars, and saw it pass HMS *Leicester*. He saw the leading seaman emerge on to the deck beside the fatal shell, and immediately dive from the port bow. He swam strongly to the safety of the *Leicester*. The launch disappeared into the mist which lay beneath the bank of full black rain clouds hanging over the sea.

It was ten to twelve. The hoofs of the horses could be heard as the Royal procession of four closed coaches with their military outriders appeared at the far end of the Naval Quay. The band immediately struck up 'God Bless the Prince of Wales'.

Commodore Sir Frederick Cartwright walked slowly down the gangway on to the quay. He was conscious of the magnificent sight that he presented in his blue and gold full dress uniform, with sashes and medals, and a commodore's blue and gold hat. His long naval sword drooped down to the setts on the quay.

The coaches stopped, the doors were opened, and a collection of men in plumed hats or silk toppers emerged into the rain. There was a sudden unfurling of black umbrellas. Commodore Cartwright allowed his glance to stray beyond such lesser persons as Lord Strathspey and Sir Wheeler Tuke. Yes! Here he was — burly, bearded, and in his own way rather terrifying: His Royal Highness the Prince of Wales.

★   ★   ★

Far out beyond Dunnock Sound, Count Czerny trained his telescope on the little steam vessel fast approaching his yacht, the *Princess Berthe-Louise*, which was moving discreetly out into the safety of the German Ocean. Not so very long ago, he mused, he had told a thick-headed captain called Dawson that it was the *Mary Tudor*, and he had believed him.

What was the purpose of this odd little launch? He could see its name now, painted on the prow: *Avenger*. He smiled. There was nothing that such a puny vessel could do to avenge the mighty cataclysm approaching the British Fleet. Within days there would be war, and Britain's mastery of the oceans would be shattered for all time.

Then Count Czerny saw the deadly cargo on the little boat. Even through the sea mist he could read the words embossed on the grey detonator: *Feissen Werke*.

★   ★   ★

The Prince of Wales loathed being unpunctual, and he nodded in satisfaction when an equerry murmured that it was just two minutes to twelve. He stepped on to the squelching red carpet, and received the formal salute of his friend Commodore Sir Frederick Cartwright. Cartwright was holding some kind of scroll, which meant that he was going to make a speech. It was damned cold, and damned wet. The speech could wait.

'Your Royal Highness, on this day of national jubilation — '

'Yes, yes, Freddy, quite so. I'm very cold, and very hungry. So where are the eats?'

It was as the Prince uttered these words, that the *Avenger* and the *Mary Tudor* met. For years after the event, people talked of the ball of fire in the sky off the coast of Caithness. Two ships, one a large steam-yacht, had literally risen in the air, begun to fall apart, and had then been engulfed in a massive, pulsating cocoon of flame. The rain had been evaporated out of the clouds, and it was minutes before the further explosions ripped the disintegrating vessels to pieces with a vile roar. Massive pieces of ship rained down upon the sea, there was a turbulence of the waters, and then the clouds closed in and re-formed. For several hours afterwards a pall of black smoke, half a mile high, hung over the ruin.

'Yes, Freddy,' said His Royal Highness, as the visitors passed up the gangway of the *Fearnought*, 'very impressive. A remarkable welcome to the fleet, if I may say so. Over luncheon, you must explain to us all what it was supposed to represent.'

* * *

Sir Charles Napier stood at one of the tall windows of his office overlooking St James's Park. It was 8 February, and although there were no real signs of spring, the day had proved to be very sunny, and warm enough for people to take their time as they strolled on the margins of the lake.

Napier gave his attention to one of the obituary notices in *The Morning Post*. It was not his customary reading at that time of the day, but he had been alerted to this particular notice, which he had been waiting rather impatiently to appear.

ENGELBERT, COUNT CZERNY

The tragic demise of Count Czerny will be a matter of profound regret to his many friends and admirers in England. A seasoned yachtsman, and an established figure at Cowes, he enjoyed wide popularity for his manifest enjoyment of English life and society. He was educated at Stowe School and Cambridge, and it came as a surprise to many on first meeting him to discover that he was not an Englishman born.

The fatal explosion on board his steam-yacht, the *Berthe-Louise*, is thought to have been due to a collision with some unidentified vessel adrift in the North Sea. The Admiralty, at the instigation of the First Sea Lord, is carrying out a full investigation.

Engelbert, Count Czerny, was a nobleman of the Roman-German Empire, an Austrian subject, and a man with a vision of unity for all the nations of Europe . . .

Sir Charles Napier closed the paper, but continued to stand at the window, looking down at the park. Thank goodness, he had prevailed over more imprudent counsels in the Cabinet meeting to which he had been summoned. There had been calls for a public exposé of Czerny and his dangerous gang, but that would have led to a shattering of the delicate balance of uncertainties that was steadying foreign policy at that moment. So England could mourn for one of its favourite foreigners, and speak fondly of his prowess at sport, his loyalty to the late striver for peace Dr Otto Seligmann — and so on, and so forth. That was much the best way.

Surely that was Kershaw now, walking gravely across the lawns towards the suspension bridge? Yes, it was the wily old fox himself, in his long black coat with the astrakhan collar, and the tall silk hat, which he wore at a slightly jaunty angle. And who was that with him? It was that perky Cockney police officer — Box. Well, he'd leave them to it. The business of poor Otto Seligmann and the *Eidgenossenschaft* was closed. And sealed. There would be time, now, to look more closely at that business of the compromised senators in Ecuador . . .

★ ★ ★

Inspector Box and Colonel Kershaw crossed the suspension bridge that would take them over the five-acre park lake and out into the Mall. Apparently, Kershaw had an appointment with someone in St James's Palace in half an hour.

'This is the only occasion I have had, Box, to talk to you since our return from Scotland.

I wouldn't write to you. I never write to anybody. But as you're free of King James's Rents for the morning, you may as well come for a stroll with me. One can be fairly indiscreet in a park, but walls, as you know, have ears.'

Kershaw said nothing more until they had crossed the bridge, and were on the skirts of the park. He then judged the time right to speak.

'On Monday last, Box, just ten days after we concluded that business up in Scotland, Count Czerny's body was washed up on the shore at Langaton Point, on the Isle of Stroma. One of my people went there to identify him. There was no doubt whatever that it was he.'

'And what about the ladies, sir? Miss Ottilie and Mrs Poniatowski.'

Colonel Kershaw smiled, and looked fondly at Box. How formal he was, for such a young man! 'The ladies', indeed! They were harpies, feeding their fanaticism on human lives.

'So far, Mr Box,' he said, 'there has been no trace of your ladies. Perhaps the next storm will deliver them back to these shores as dead and executed prisoners of the people whom they sought to destroy.'

Box said nothing. He waited for Kershaw

to precede him through the park gates into the crowded Mall. He could see the great gatehouse of St James's Palace rising above the trees. It was good to be back in London again.

'Or perhaps, Mr Box,' Kershaw continued, 'those ladies of yours had decided on some other destination than Count Czerny's yacht. We don't know for certain that they ever boarded the *Mary Rose* — or the *Berthe-Louise*, to give it its true name. So maybe this summer, Mr Box, one of my people may glimpse an elegant young lady taking the waters at Baden-Baden, and another may spy a sour-faced but prosperous lady of a certain age, sipping a seltzer at Carlsbad. I've known stranger things than that happen in my time.'

Colonel Kershaw glanced thoughtfully at Box. It would be a very long time, no doubt, before he worked again with this perky young inspector. He had proved to be an invaluable ally. He was discreet, too. There were other things that he had a certain moral right to know.

'The Kaiser was furious when our ambassador to Berlin called on him, and told him what had been happening. He actually apologized, which, of course, he was not expected to do. The accepted diplomatic fiction, of course, was that the Kaiser hadn't the slightest inkling of what the *Eidgenossen-schaft* was up to.'

'Apologize, did he? That was very nice of him, sir.'

'Yes, wasn't it? I met Count von und zu Thalberg in Paris last week. He told me that the Kaiser raged so furiously when the ambassador had gone, that his courtiers feared for his sanity. He's not ready for war yet, you see, and he's too canny a bird to be pushed in that direction before his time. Anyway, Mr Box, the upshot of it all was that Baron von Dessau, the warmonger-orator, was found shot dead at his villa in Charlottenburg.'

'Suicide, then?'

'Possibly. Or maybe one of his own side blamed him for failure, and made away with him. Or perhaps an agent of a foreign power seized the opportunity of his disgrace to — er, well, even things up a little, you know.'

'Strewth!' said Box softly, almost to himself. It wouldn't do to dwell too much on what the colonel had just hinted.

Colonel Kershaw stopped at the entrance to the palace. He offered his hand to Box, who shook it, and bowed.

'Goodbye, sir,' he said. 'Perhaps we'll work together again sometime.'

412

'I hope so, Box. Goodbye. I expect you know that Admiral Holland had been knighted? It's in this morning's *Times*. Goodbye.'

★ ★ ★

Inspector Box settled down in a seat on the top of an omnibus that would take him to Baker Street, and opened the copy of *The Times* that he had bought from a newspaper stall near Spencer House. Struggling against a sudden breeze that sprang up as the omnibus turned into Piccadilly, he opened the paper at the Court Circular.

Yes, there it was: *Her Majesty has been pleased to invest Admiral James Holland RN with the dignity of the degree of Knight Bachelor.* A well deserved honour, too! Holland had performed prodigies of inventiveness and bravery up in Caithness. He'd come back to London a changed man, and the changes had all been for the best.

Box was about to discard the newspaper when his eye caught another line in the Court Circular. He whistled in surprise.

'*Her Majesty has been pleased to confer upon Lieutenant-Colonel Adrian Kershaw, RA, Extra Equerry to Her Majesty, the*

413

degree of Knight of the Most Honour-able Order of the Bath, in the Military Division.'

'Well done, sir!' said Box to himself. 'And well done for not even bothering to mention it to me!'

When the omnibus reached Baker Street, Box changed to the familiar Light Green Atlas conveyance, that would take him out to Finchley.

★ ★ ★

'Today, Mr Box,' said Louise Whittaker, 'I declare a holiday from adventure. Perhaps we'll allude to recent events a little later. But let us get our priorities right. I want to know how your father is progressing. So when you've drunk that cup of tea, and consumed that slice of fruit loaf, you had better tell me.'

Box relaxed in his armchair, and allowed himself to glance around the room. There was the big table in the window bay, covered with open books and sheets of paper. There were the glazed bookcases, and the mantelpiece with its neat array of ornaments. And there was the mistress of the house, as calm, amused, and beautiful as ever.

'Pa is making wonderful progress, Miss

Whittaker. Yesterday, he was placed in a wheeled chair for the first time. He seems to have taken on a new lease of life ... He suffered terrible pain for years with that leg, you know. Terrible, it was. And very soon now he's to go down to a rest-home at Esher. The Police Benevolent Fund arranged that, on account of him having been a policeman for so many years.'

'I'm so very glad,' said Louise. 'Esher's a very pleasant, quiet place. Perhaps we could visit your father there, once he's settled.'

'We?'

'Well, yes. You don't mind, do you? Your papa and I could gossip about you while you walked in the grounds. Then I'd find out what you're really like!'

They both laughed, and then Louise, who was sitting opposite Box at the fireside, set her cup and saucer down on the hearth.

'Mr Box,' she said, 'it was a great adventure, but now, if you don't mind, I should like to resign my position as sole member of your female posse.'

She held up a hand to fend off Box's protest, and gently shook her head.

'No, please listen to what I want to say. One day, perhaps, there really will be lady police officers, but I know now that I could never be one of them. I enjoyed staying at

Bagot's Hotel, and all that, but that was because I was looking after Vanessa. I was guarding her, if you like. But when I think of Colin McColl seizing that letter from me, and those fights — you, with that monstrosity at Scotland Yard, and Mr Knollys struggling with McColl — well, I feel sick with fear. I can't bear it, I'm afraid. So, please accept my resignation!'

Yes; he'd wondered whether Miss Whittaker had the right temperament for police work. Miss Drake certainly had the kind of careless courage necessary for the rough-and-tumble of daily policing, but he'd always had doubts about his beautiful academic friend and ally. No harm had been done by putting her to the test.

They passed a pleasant hour together, recalling some of the events of the Amelia Garbutt case of the previous year, and considering the likelihood of something interesting developing between Jack Knollys and Vanessa Drake. When the time came for Box to return to King James's Rents, Box reverted to the matter of Louise's resignation from the 'posse of one'.

'With respect to your resignation, Miss Whittaker,' he said, 'am I to lose your professional services entirely?'

Louise Whittaker regarded him with the

special amused expression that always made him feel an utter fool.

'Well, no, Mr Box,' she said. 'That would never do. I want to be here for you when you need to get away from King James's Rents, and think aloud about a case. I want to be your advisor, someone who can give you a female slant on things. And I want to be your friend. I'm working at it, you know.'

'Working at it?'

'Yes. I'm hoping that one day my attempts at charming you will be sufficiently successful for you to stop calling me Miss Whittaker, and try Louise for a change.'

'Louise?'

'Yes. It's the female form of Louis. There's nothing to be afraid of.'

'But Miss Whittaker, if I was to call you Louise, you might then feel obliged to call me Arnold — '

'Well, so I would, Arnold. There, I've done it!'

'Oh, Louise — '

'But you'd best go now. You've been here for hours, and you'll miss the omnibus. Besides, the neighbours will start to talk if you don't go.'

Arnold Box laughed, and picked up his hat and gloves from the table. 'Goodbye, then, Miss Whittaker,' he said. 'I'll let myself out.'

'Goodbye, Mr Box,' Louise replied, sitting down at her great table in the window bay. 'Solve your crimes, and keep us safe!'

★ ★ ★

Vanessa Drake put down the golden silk stole that she had been hemming, and settled back in the upright chair at the round table of her sitting-room in Westminster. Had it all been a dream? Had she really unstitched the lining of a dangerous man's pocket in the deep of the night? Had she really watched as Jack Knollys struggled desperately with a ruthless killer?

She glanced at a framed photograph of Arthur Fenlake, which occupied a place of honour on the mantelpiece. How very young he looked! She would always remember him with pride and affection. He was one of England's many heroes. He had taken her to exhibitions at the National Gallery, and once to a picture-hanging at the Royal Academy. She wondered whether poor Arthur would have approved of Jack Knollys.

Jack had taken her to see Hetty Miller at the Alhambra in Leicester Square. The square had sparkled with hundreds of bright gaslights, and although it was raining, the rain hadn't seemed to matter. After the show, they had eaten supper in a plush and gilded café in Regent Street. There was nothing mean about Jack . . .

There came a knock on the door, and Colonel Kershaw walked in. He must have seen the leap of excitement in her eyes, because he smiled kindly at her, and said, 'It's not a call to business, Miss Drake. I just happened to be passing. How are you?'

'I'm very well, thank you, sir.'

'Good. I expect you know, don't you, that Major Lankester died a hero's death in the end? I know you were sorry for him, because he'd been a good friend and mentor to Lieutenant Fenlake.'

He glanced briefly at Fenlake's photograph, and then looked thoughtfully at Vanessa for a moment.

'There's nothing much going forward at the moment, missy,' he said, 'but if you were to receive a call to arms from me again, would you still respond?'

'Oh, yes, sir!' Vanessa's bright blue eyes sparkled with excitement.

'Good, good. I'm glad. I knew you had it in you to be one of my crowd. I'll go, now. Meanwhile — I've brought you a little something from the lady who owns Bagot's Hotel. Not Mrs Prout, you know.'

Colonel Kershaw took a small package

from his pocket, and placed it on the table. Before Vanessa could ask any further questions, he had gone. The package contained a small leather case. She opened it, and gasped in delighted surprise.

Nestling in a bed of crimson velvet was a solid silver plaque, about two inches tall, and an inch across. It had no clasp or chain, and was evidently not designed to be worn, but kept as a special treasure. The royal monogram, VR, had been inset in gold, surrounded by a circlet of tiny diamonds. Deeply engraved in firm Roman lettering below the monogram were the two words: LOYALTY'S KEEPSAKE.

★ ★ ★

Sergeant Kenwright, standing alone in the empty drill hall, squared his shoulders, and prepared to walk through the low passage into the front office. He could hear the faint murmur of voices drifting through the tunnel-like entrance, telling him that both Mr Box and Sergeant Knollys were there.

Kenwright was not a vain man, despite his great stature and his flowing spade beard, but he wished just then that there was a bit of mirror pinned up somewhere in the drill hall. He stretched out his arms in front of him, and looked at the three brand-new stripes sewn on each sleeve. Sergeant! He could hardly believe it! Well, it was time to face whatever ribbing may be coming his way. He stooped down, and walked through the low passage into Inspector Box's office.

'Congratulations, Sergeant Kenwright!'

Box waited for Kenwright to salute him, and then he and Knollys rose from the table to shake hands.

'I can hardly believe it, sir,' said Kenwright. 'All I did was sort through a lot of fragments, and arrange them into some kind of decent order — '

'Your work showed us what the German conspirators were up to, Sergeant. You've carved out your own niche here at King James's Rents. They're already asking about you over at Whitehall Place. I shouldn't be surprised if they don't try a bit of poaching, soon.'

'I hope not, sir. I wouldn't fancy working anywhere else. It's lovely at the Rents.'

Sergeant Knollys had opened a cupboard beside the fireplace, and removed three bottles of India Pale Ale, together with three chipped enamel mugs.

'Time for a celebration, Sergeant Kenwright,' said Knollys. 'Did you know that yours is the only rank in the police to bear military insignia? The three stripes of a sergeant. Clerk Sergeant, in your case. But don't forget: we're all civilians! So here's a health to the Queen, and confusion to all her enemies!'

The three men sipped their ale from the chipped mugs. The fire burned smokily in the old grate. The gas mantle shuddered and spluttered in the ceiling. Box remembered the chilling dangers of Caithness, and thought: he's right. It's lovely at the Rents.

'So, sir,' said Kenwright, setting his mug down on the table, 'I've been rewarded far beyond my dreams. And I believe those high-up gentlemen who worked with us have been given knighthoods. I don't suppose — '

'No, Sergeant,' Box interrupted. 'No rewards for me. Or Jack, there. Or for poor old Mr Mack. No fear. But in my case, I can truly say, virtue is its own reward.'

'And modesty likewise,' Knollys added. 'Talking of which — '

Knollys stopped abruptly and scrambled to his feet. Superintendent Mackharness was standing half in and half out of the room, holding one of the swing doors open with a large hand. Box attempted to stand at attention. Sergeant Kenwright maintained a frozen salute, as though he was part of a wax tableau. Mackharness treated Box to a brilliant smile.

'I'll not trespass too much on your time, Box,' he said. 'I just thought I'd look in personally, and say thank you. Well done! Perhaps I don't commend you as generously as I should, but in this matter, I felt it only right to come down here and thank you in person.'

Strewth! What was the matter with Old Growler? Was he going soft?

'You're too kind, sir,' said Box.

'Not at all, Box. I got the menthol crystals from Curtis & Company, the chemist's in Baker Street, and did just what you advised, with the hot water, and the towel, and so on. It worked like a miracle. The whole wretched trouble had dissipated by next morning. So, thank you. I think that's all. Good day, Sergeant Knollys. At ease, Sergeant Kenwright.'

Superintendent Mackharness began to close the door, but then thought better of it. 'Incidentally, Box,' he said, 'there's an extraordinarily sinister business developing out at Hoxton. Perhaps you'd care to come upstairs, now, so that I can give you the gist of the matter. I shan't detain you for more than a few minutes.'

This, thought Box, is more like it! Fresh

villainy among the teeming millions. It would always be like that. Inspector Box took a hasty leave of his two sergeants, and hurried up the stairs that would take him to the mildewed office of Superintendent Mackharness on the upper floor of 2 King James's Rents.